SPECIAL MESSAGE TO READERS

This book is published by

THE ULVERSCROFT FOUNDATION,

a registered charity in the U.K., No. 264873

The Foundation was established in 1974 to provide funds to help towards research, diagnosis and treatment of eye diseases. Below are a few examples of contributions made by THE ULVERSCROFT FOUNDATION:

★ A new Children's Assessment Unit at Moorfield's Hospital, London.

★ Twin operating theatres at the Western Ophthalmic Hospital, London.

★ The Frederick Thorpe Ulverscroft Chair of Ophthalmology at the University of Leicester.

★ Eye Laser equipment to various eye hospitals.

If you would like to help further the work of the Foundation by making a donation or leaving a legacy, every contribution, no matter how small, is received with gratitude. Please write for details to:

THE ULVERSCROFT FOUNDATION,
The Green, Bradgate Road, Anstey,
Leicestershire, LE7 7FU. England.
Telephone: (0533) 364325

I've travelled the world twice over,
Met the famous: saints and sinners,
Poets and artists, kings and queens,
Old stars and hopeful beginners,
I've been where no-one's been before,
Learned secrets from writers and cooks
All with one library ticket
To the wonderful world of books.

THE CHARMED CIRCLE—PART ONE

The story of three sisters told against a wide canvas sweeping from London to the Scottish Highlands to the seamy side of Hollywood. Their story is mainly the story of Julia, the youngest, as it takes her through the Battle of Britain to the beginning of a stage and film career. Julia's sisters, Constance and Alex, live through their own stories: Connie's of steadfast love: Alex of love renewed as she moves into the world of Washington journalism. Finally the trio is drawn once again into a tight union as they face a murder trial headlined across the world.

Books by Catherine Gaskin
in the Charnwood Library Series:

BLAKE'S REACH
I KNOW MY LOVE
SARA DANE
A FALCON FOR A QUEEN
PROMISES
CORPORATION WIFE
THE LYNMARA LEGACY
FAMILY AFFAIRS
THE SUMMER OF THE SPANISH WOMAN
DAUGHTER OF THE HOUSE
THE TILSIT INHERITANCE
THE CHARMED CIRCLE—PART I
THE CHARMED CIRCLE—PART II

CATHERINE GASKIN

THE CHARMED CIRCLE:

PART I

Complete and Unabridged

CHARNWOOD
Leicester

First published in Great Britain in 1988 by
Wm. Collins Sons & Co. Ltd.,
London

First Charnwood Edition
published September 1989
by arrangement with
Wm. Collins Sons & Co. Ltd.,
London

Reprinted 1990

British Library CIP Data

Gaskin, Catherine, *1929–*
The charmed circle: part one.—Large print ed.—
Charnwood library series
I. Title
823′.914[F]

ISBN 0-7089-8523-8 v.1

Published by
F. A. Thorpe (Publishing) Ltd.
Anstey, Leicestershire

Set by Rowland Phototypesetting Ltd.
Bury St. Edmunds, Suffolk
Printed and bound in Great Britain by
T. J. Press (Padstow) Ltd., Padstow, Cornwall

For Sol
yesterday, today, tomorrow
with love

August 1940

1

IT was a balmy, sunny afternoon over the south-east corner of England. Julia tried to learn her lines, with one ear cocked to the long oasthouse where her mother practised—over and over again one small phrase from the Mozart sonata—was it K310? Julia could never remember the Köchel listings. She sighed as she listened. It was difficult enough to live up to a father who was a famous actor, twice as difficult to have a mother who was regarded by many as among the finest pianists of her time.

Her mother was leaving on tour soon, not just a tour of the provinces, but of the United States, a tour arranged by the Ministry of Information. Officially it was to raise funds for refugees—which refugees? Julia had asked, since the world seemed to her full of them. Unofficially it was to bring Britain and its need to the notice of every American newspaper, every magazine, every radio station which could be persuaded to photograph or interview Ginette Maslova. It should not be a difficult task, as the memory of Ginette Maslova's famous father, the Russian conductor who had scaled the heights of the American musical scene, was still fresh. Her mother was to play in benefit concerts, and she was a very persuasive woman. She might be regarded as a great pianist; she was also, even in her forties, a very beautiful woman. Her marvellously slender, tall figure, clad in one of the shimmering concert gowns which Julia thought of as miracles of colour and brilliance, her little speech at the end of the concert, slightly accented by her native French, appealing for help for refugees, would be, in fact, one of the best propaganda machines Britain could send to the USA whose help was needed so desperately.

The "Phony War" had ended at last. The declaration of war last September had sent children, and many of their mothers, fleeing from the cities. Those who could manage it had gone overseas. They had left the cities, and nothing had happened, no air raids, no bombing. Many had returned, bored by "the country", which they didn't understand or like or feel comfortable in. But now Dunkirk was over and done with, the British Expeditionary Force had returned, almost intact, but without arms or the means of defending their country, much less waging war. And Goering had at last decided to send his Luftwaffe to bring Britain to surrender, as France had surrendered. The Battle of Britain was now raging in the skies over south-east England. The people were leaving the cities again, fearful. And Julia's mother worried over the polishing of one tiny phrase of Mozart.

Julia went back to the lines she was trying to memorize. Cordelia was an impossible role—far better to have been Regan or Goneril. But Cordelia had been assigned to her, so she must play it for her teachers at the Royal Academy of Dramatic Art, well aware that she would be judged more harshly because her father was who he was.

Her mother, perhaps in frustration because she could not achieve the perfection she desired, had abandoned the Mozart sonata. That would be for cities in the USA not large enough to have symphony orchestras, in which she would give recitals. She now launched into the first, slowly building chords of the Rachmaninov second concerto, a work which always brought audiences to their feet, the irresistible concerto, the big tear-jerker. That she would play, along with the Tchaikovsky first, the two Brahms, the Beethoven fourth wherever a symphony orchestra existed. She would endure battered, ill-tuned pianos, inadequate orchestras, mediocre conductors to raise money and sympathy. She would also play with the greatest, and be worthy of them. Her mother, that seemingly delicate figure, was renowned for playing the huge works usually requiring the strength of a man. Julia tried to pull her attention back to what she was memorizing "*. . . in the most terrible and nimble stroke . . .*" She stopped.

The noises overhead forced themselves upon her. They were at it again. The Germans had come over to bomb the airfields in this corner of England to dust, the fighters had come to escort them, and to destroy the terrier-dog defiance of the Spitfires and Hurricanes of the Eleventh Group of the Royal Air Force Fighter Command, who fought with maniacal determination to defend their fields. On everyone's mind was the knowledge that with Fighter Command defeated, the cities would lie open to the bombers. So the Squadrons scrambled to their planes, on a telephone order, many times a day, fought day after day. The pilots were more valuable than the planes, which, with difficulty, could be replaced. The trained men could not. Only last week a fighter pilot had come down in Anscombe Wood, there, darkly gathered at the ridge of the low hill within Julia's gaze. Watching the parachute and the man descend, farmers had gathered with shot guns, and where they didn't have shot guns, with pitch forks. They had waited for the enemy, and had found a British pilot. He was unhurt, except for his pride. He had lost his plane, but he had seen his opponent in the aerial battle turn into a deep spiral, trailing smoke and flames. The farmers had given him food and beer, and driven him back to his airfield. He had thanked them, and said he would be flying again tomorrow. They never even asked his name, just what soccer team he supported. He had replied, with a distinct Welsh accent, that he played rugger. That was the acid test to distinguish friend from foe, who might be landing in an RAF uniform.

Julia heard the *crump crump* sounds of bombs landing behind Anscombe wood. The Germans must have been trying for Biggin Hill again, and now, on their return run to France, were letting their bombs fall at random. Nearer there was the shriek and whine of fighter planes engaged in deadly combat. She never thought of going to the Anderson shelter constructed in the vegetable garden. No one ever used it. But the sound, the noise, made the study of her lines impossible.

She went to the long French windows cut into the fabric of the fourteenth-century manor house, and her eyes searched the skies above. She could see nothing. She opened one of the doors, its glass criss-crossed with strips of paper, and stepped out onto the lawn. Across a neat green stretch, in the oasthouse which had been converted long ago, when her mother had first come to England, into a music room and a library, her mother's playing had not paused. They were all so used to it now. She had reached the big crashing chords at the end of the third movement; Julia doubted that when her mother played she heard anything else at all. Then, as she listened to both sounds, the first, tightening premonition reached her, the first clutch of fear. Something still out of sight, but close by, was happening. The whine of an engine became shriller, like the death cry of an animal. It came hurtling into sight at last, a flame-engulfed machine, spinning, weaving, wildly out of control. The noise now was thunderous, blocking out whatever her mother played—if she played at all. Even she must have stopped. There was an actual sensation of heat as the fireball descended. Involuntarily Julia stepped backwards. But the glass doors offered no shelter or protection, any more than the ancient wood and wattle building did. The aircraft skimmed the trees of the orchard, coming from the direction of Anscombe Wood. It seemed to bounce off the trees once, and lift, and then it ploughed on. She saw it hit the oasthouse. The world was all flame and heat, and the smell of instantly burning old dry wood — heat and dust. The shock from the impact threw her backwards. She hit her head on the edge of a footstool.

When she raised herself again the oasthouse was engulfed in flame, like some gigantic pyre. It was barely possible to distinguish even the shape of the aircraft in the twisting, burning wreck. The building and the plane were melded into one. The engine of the plane, living a demonic life of its own, ploughed through the end of the oasthouse, and into the tall beech hedge. Julia started to run, and the heat and the shock waves pushed her back. She tried to cover her face, but could not. For an instant she thought she saw a figure writhe within the inferno. But it was only for a second or two. She stood there, and saw her mother, the piano, the books, the long beams, everything, consumed. In the last moment she was aware of consciousness, she saw, as some kind of cruel fantasy, that the fuselage of the plane, which had endured for some minutes, bore the well-known three rings of the Royal Air Force.

It had been one of their own which had killed her mother.

Her father, Sir Michael Seymour, reached Anscombe only hours after Julia telephoned the theatre. He was in rehearsal for *The School for Scandal.* He had stood with Julia as firemen combed the wreckage, at times laying his bare hands on the still-smouldering beams as the search for his wife's body continued. When he saw the pitiful thing they finally brought out, he was forced to turn away, staggering, clasping a hand over his face. His arm went about Julia's shoulders blindly, seeking her support. "Oh my God! . . . my darling . . . my beloved . . ." What was laid on a stretcher was light and of no substance, covered quickly with a blanket. They found no other body there. The French doors to the drawing-room still stood open, their glass smashed, despite the tape, the frames hanging askew. The furniture and carpet were soaked with the water the firemen had poured on the small manor house of Anscombe, a jewel set in the sweet beauty of the Kentish countryside, when its wooden shake roof had been threatened by sparks from the inferno of the oasthouse. Overhead the German bombers from France, with their fighter escort, had begun another run towards the airfields of England.

She took her father into the dining-room, away from the sight of the oasthouse. Stella, who had passed from the role of nanny to the family, to housekeeper and general dogsbody, brought sandwiches and tea. Apart from Cook, she was the only domestic staff they had left. Stella sniffed, her eyes puffy from weeping. "Eat!" she commanded Sir Michael. He didn't seem to hear her. Julia went and brought a bottle of brandy. The bottle rattled against the glass as he poured, and then drank the draft in one swallow, and poured again. He sat and consumed the next more slowly, staring unseeingly at the uprooted rose garden which had been sown with vegetables.

"It's been on the six o'clock news," Stella announced. "As if she was—like the Queen, or something . . ."

"She was!" Michael shouted. "But she was like nobody else!" He drained the glass. The telephone rang.

"It's started," Stella said. "Shall I answer. . . ?" She looked at Julia.

"No—I will."

The calls kept coming all evening. Julia was aware that an extra operator had volunteered at the little local exchange to help handle the many calls. "I'm so sorry, Miss Seymour," the two operators had each said. One added: "Such a lovely lady. We'll do our best, but there are so many calls . . ." And amid the log jam, Julia was aware, there would be the despairing calls from her two sisters.

Just after eleven o'clock, an official RAF car arrived. No less a figure than a Wing Commander alighted. He was led by Stella to the dining-room. As Michael Seymour rose to greet the officer, he staggered. He had refused all food that evening, but had sat solidly drinking.

"I had to come, Sir Michael. Simmon's the name. I'm stationed at Hawkinge." Hawkinge was one of the bases on the very front line of the battle, one from which the airmen had to scramble many times a day to try to intercept the German fighters and bombers as they crossed the perilously short strip of the English Channel. He remained standing, even though Michael had waved him to a chair.

"It was one of our chaps whose plane hit here. I'm his CO. He's one of our very best. Won a DFC when his squadron was in France. Great pilot. Bit of an ace, really. He's brought down a lot of German planes. He was badly shot up today, but he managed to bail out. Got smashed up as he landed, too. Hands badly burned. They've patched him up after a fashion. The latest report was that they think he'll live—but he's got a lot more to go through before he flies—if ever he flies—again."

Michael shook his head. "Look—very decent of you to come. I appreciate your effort—the time. With all that's going on. But I really don't want to know. I wish him the very best of luck, but I don't want to know anything about him. All I know is that those boys are fighting—and dying—every day. Had one of them come down just over the hill the other day. They're all brave young men—and if we survive, we'll probably owe it to them. They're fighting a front-line battle in the air, and we happen to be underneath. Not his fault. The fortunes of war . . ."

In a gingerly fashion the Wing Commander had responded to Michael's increasingly impatient gestures for him to be seated. "I thought, Sir

Michael, that was what you might think. I really didn't want to intrude. But when this chap came out of the anaesthetic, some idiot let it drop that it was all on the wireless—about your wife—about Lady Seymour—er, Madame Maslova. He made one of the nurses swear that she'd ring Hawkinge. Someone, he insisted, was to come to see you to say . . . well, what can one say? How can he possibly say he's sorry? I have come to represent him. We all regret civilian casualties, but to have killed *her* . . ."

"Might have felt worse if his 'plane had ploughed into Canterbury Cathedral. My wife was mortal—as we all are. None of us are monuments. She can't have felt anything for more than a few seconds. She was at the piano. She would probably have described it as the perfect way for a musician to go. Ah, but—oh, for God's sake, man, have a brandy. Simpson, is it? Have a good stiff one. It helps . . ." Julia realized her father was terribly drunk.

"Not a monument no . . . Wouldn't have wanted to be. A real woman. The young man, whoever he is, shouldn't feel that it was an uncommon death. Tell him that. A plane dropping on the Cathedral would have been a loss of our heritage. Diving into a row of houses could have killed a dozen women . . . a score of women . . ." The marvellously controlled voice, controlled even in grief and drunkenness, went on. The Wing Commander moved uneasily on the edge of his chair, taking swift sips of the brandy Julia had poured, listening, as people had always listened, to her father. The famous, handsome face, lean, dark-eyed, the chiselled chin-line bowed towards the glass, had already taken on deep lines Julia had never seen before, as if a knife had carved them downwards. Lines she had been rehearsing that afternoon came back . . . *"in the most terrible and nimble stroke . . ."*

He spoke of her mother with love, and that was the truth. It seemed unimportant now that he had had several affairs with other women. In time, as had her mother, as had her sisters, Julia had come to see that the affairs were just that—affairs. Her father loved women. He admired and desired them. The long periods when he, or Ginette, had been on tour, and he alone, had been the reason for those affairs. Other women were the objects of desire or admiration. His wife was both of these, and much more; the woman he truly loved. All of that was in his voice now—self-reproach, anger, near-despair. "I loved her, you see," he repeated to the Wing Commander. The black-out curtains were drawn, and the room lit by a single lamp. Michael Seymour's expression was utter desolation. Now his eyes, as well as his voice, wept.

In the hall, the telephone rang yet again. Julia went to answer it, and the Wing Commander took the opportunity to leave. He shook Michael's hand. "I'll tell our young man . . ."

"Yes, tell him. Say . . . say 'a necessary loss'. We all make sacrifices. Must do . . . thanks for coming . . ."

It was, finally, Alex on the phone. "It's taken hours to get through." Julia's eldest sister's voice was firm, unwavering. "They said at the theatre that Father had left long ago. They've been very decent here—laid on a car for me. I'll be there before morning." That would be a car from *The Record*, the newspaper for which her sister worked. "How is Father taking it?

Yes . . . as I imagined." Alex's tone dropped to a low pitch. "Did you . . . did you see it happen, Julia? God!—like that! You could have gone too! I had to wait here until we'd gone to press. I haven't an idea where Greg is, but I expect he'll turn up. I never know what he's covering. We're getting reports of a lot of enemy action. It's front page news, you know. About Mother. I saw our story for the morning edition. It didn't seem real. There's a picture of her. I had to accept it when I saw that. My favourite picture of her. I wish they hadn't used it. She didn't seem to belong so much to me as to everyone else."

"She did belong to everyone," Julia said softly. She guessed from the silence that tears had started for Alex, tears postponed and swallowed back all evening while she finished whatever she had been working on for the paper. It was typical that she would have seen the paper go to press before accepting the gesture of the press baron, Lord Wolverton, who owned *The Record*, of the offer of a car to take her home.

Other women would have broken down and wept, would have left their desk. Not Alex. It was these qualities in her, rather than her striking good looks, which resembled their father's, which had captivated the man, Greg Mathieson, who was one of the Wolverton's syndicates best known and respected correspondents. He was divorced, with one child, and fourteen years her senior. Like most journalists, he seemed perpetually broke. It did not seem the sort of marriage someone like Alex Seymour might have been expected to make. Her parents had counselled waiting, offering neither approval nor disapproval. Alex had waited a year, and then, when Greg Mathieson had finally returned from his assignment with the British troops in France, where he had waited with them on the beaches of Dunkirk until almost the last moment, sending dispatches when he could, enduring the strafing and the exposed position, wading into the sea to climb aboard almost the last of the armada of little ships which had come to take them home, Alex had waited no longer. She had married him in June, with no word to her parents, and two friends from *The Record* as witnesses. Michael and Ginette had made the best of it. Alex was twenty-six, and had waited long enough.

The Seymour London flat was too small for the occasion, so Michael had hired the River Room at the Savoy and invited all their friends to celebrate—all their friends, and, it seemed to Julia, half the staff of *The Record*, as well as Lord Wolverton, who was a long-time friend. The worlds of theatre and music and journalism had gathered, and Michael and Ginette had smiled, as if the marriage had been their idea all along. "It can't last," Julia had heard someone say as she sipped black market champagne among the throng. "A bloody waste of a girl like that . . ."

Julia did not agree. She liked Greg Mathieson. She liked him even better as she began to read his pieces. He had the rare combination of a man who could analyze the battle action he observed, whether it was the German sweep into Belgium, the Dunkirk evacuation, or the simple, small triumphs and tragedies of war. This morning his report in *The Record* came from an undisclosed airfield somewhere on the south east coast. Daily he watched the scramble to the hastily refuelled aircraft, waited for the often depleted squadrons to return.

Today, instead of commenting on the count of

numbers of British and German aircraft shot down, he had chosen to write a story about the non-return of a pilot whose dog had waited in vain, had refused to eat or rest, had howled, and greeted the landing of each aircraft with hope, and then had slunk off in growing despair. The dog's name was Tuff. On the third day the Squadron Leader, newly promoted because of the death of a friend, could stand the howling no more. He had risked an hour off-duty, and taken the terrier to a small cottage some miles from the airfield, near the village pub where the squadron all went when there was time. The cottage housed eight children, six belonging to the family, and two evacuees. He had hoped for distraction for the dog. Greg had gone with him. On its front page *The Record* had carried a picture of Tuff, perched on a rocking chair, surrounded by eight adoring faces, being fed a biscuit. It was on such things the country's spirit, at this moment, also fed, and Greg Mathieson knew it. And it was in such a way that they would report the death of Ginette Maslova, depicted as a heroine, and the grimmer details would be omitted.

Later, when Julia felt she could not possibly take any more phone calls, when her father had fallen into a drunken, but not peaceful sleep in the big bedroom he had shared with Ginette, clutching the worn grey rabbit which had been his wife's good luck mascot and which had accompanied her to every concert, waiting in the dressing room—later, when even Stella had gone to bed, the phone rang again. From the kitchen Julia had gone to answer it. She was in her dressing-gown, waiting for Alex, waiting to warm the milk and stir in the cocoa. She knew that this time the call would be from Constance—Connie. The familiar, loved voice was strained, but in control. She was at Bentley Priory, Stanmore, the headquarters of Dowding's Fighter Command. She worked there as a plotter in the Operations Room. "I've just come off duty. It was pretty fierce. They didn't tell me until then. They've got a car going to Hawkinge, and they'll drop me off at Anscombe. I have seventy-two hours compassionate leave. I'll be with you soon."

Connie—she would bring warmth and order to everything; her calm presence might even help make some sense of the carnage, soothe the futile anger Julia felt at the taking of a precious life, might even drive away, for a time, the stench of charred old wood. She was mid-way in age between Alex and Julia; she had always seemed the fulcrum on which the other two had teeter-tottered in their relationship, sturdy, immovable. In the dazzling array of talent and temperament in which she had grown up, Connie had seemed like a fixed lode star—while aspiring to no stardom. Constance. How well she had been named, Julia thought, and it was not for the first time. How she ached for Connie's presence when she knew it would be all right to give way, to let the tears flow. Their father would pass into her care. The affairs of the house would flow through her hands. They would lean on her, as unconsciously they had been doing ever since she had emerged from childhood into sturdy adolescence.

Julia heard the sound of wheels on the gravel. Alex would have directed the driver past the front door and round to the back of the house. The painted-out headlamps, which gave only slits of light, would have shown little of the wreckage of the oasthouse. But it was a night of a bomber's moon. All night the skies above had been heavy with the sound of their motors, the drone of the bombers, the sharper whine of the fighters. The moon would have shown too clearly, hurtfully, the twisted mass of the beams of the oast-house which had fallen in upon themselves, fallen on their mother. Julia switched off the kitchen light before pulling back the blackout curtain from the door. In silence the two sisters put their arms about each other. It seemed for minutes they stayed that way. No tears came, but Julia sensed the heartbeat that was as swift as her own, the choked words that would not immediately come.

Julia remembered the other presence. "Would . . . would your driver like something? There's cocoa . . . Perhaps a whisky?"

"Thank you, but I'd better be on my way." He wouldn't want to intrude, Julia thought. He might be hungry, or longing for a drink, but he would have seen the outline of the oasthouse as plainly as Alex had. No more than the Wing Commander, would he want to stay.

They sat for a long time close together at the corner of the big kitchen table, almost huddling as if trying to gather comfort and strength from each other. In fragments Julia told the story in the random words she could find. The sound of the bombers and the fighters began to taper off. A bird had started to utter its first cry of the day in the beech hedge where the engine of the plane had come to rest. Perhaps it had lost fledglings in the fire. Perhaps it merely called to its mate.

"She was practising," Julia said. "She kept playing one little phrase of Mozart over and over—you know how she was. Then she seemed to get angry with it. She played the Rachmaninov—straight through—not stopping to go back on anything. The sounds of the planes almost seemed like an orchestra—accompanying her. Perhaps she felt that way too. I don't think she ever stopped playing until the plane hit. I couldn't hear. It was too close."

Alex's hand went tentatively to Julia's face. She traced the line of both eyebrows. "You were pretty close to the fire. Did you know your eyebrows are singed? And your hands . . ." In a most uncharacteristic gesture, she raised Julia's hands to the light, and close to her own lips. She touched the bandages Stella had wrapped about both palms. "Does it hurt, love?"

Julia shook her head. She had hardly noticed this small pain beside the greater one. "The doctor came. He gave me something for the pain. And he gave Father something too—it's sort of knocked him out. That, and more than half a bottle of brandy. It really hasn't begun to hurt—not yet. I keep thinking of her—"

"Don't!" Alex said curtly. "It can't have been more than a few seconds." She went back on what Julia had told her their father had said about it not being as bad as Canterbury Cathedral taking a direct hit. "He can't have meant it."

"He would have. A histrionic gesture, I suppose—but he can't help being what he is. You must tell Greg that. It might be her finest memorial. He *did* love her so. He's like a child now, clutching her rabbit . . ."

The early dawn had come. Above them, the skies were silent, radiant. It seemed that the weary warriors who battled for supremacy in that sky had, for a time, withdrawn—but only to regroup again. Except for the birds, now in full chorus, the world seemed hushed. A sweet, soft English morning, in the waning of an English summer. It should have smelled of roses and dew. But the smell of ancient charred wood hung over it, and the achingly cold touch of death.

The sound came at last, momentarily stilling the bird calls. The gravel spluttered against the old walls of the house as the car roared up. There was no hushed reverence in the sound. It was immediate and urgent.

Connie stepped out of the passenger seat of a rather beaten-up military car. She paused to say something to the occupant of the back seat—perhaps offering hospitality, as Alex had. Then her hand went up in a trim salute. The back seat passenger would be an officer on the way to Hawkinge. They had had, from Bentley Priory, to cross London in the blackout, and make their way to Kent. They had managed it in remarkably quick time.

The light from the kitchen streamed out, the blackout no longer needed. The Seymour sisters were known in the world of the press and the theatre for their good looks. From their parents they had inherited fine bones, long necks and jawlines which could never photograph badly. They all moved with a kind of liquid, lightning grace which was their mother's gift at the keyboard, their father's gloriously smooth presence on the stage. "The sensational Seymours" they had been called, even young Julia, who had barely passed out of adolescence. Only Connie did not seem to be aware of how she struck others, unaware of her own beauty. But she had inherited the best of both her mother and her father.

She was the middle child, and the best of all the family had.

She pushed her cap back off her unpowdered face, her blue uniform baggy and wrinkled after the long night on duty, the long ride. One thick, unflattering stocking had begun to slip over the sensible military shoes. Her weary anguished face was still as beautiful as the English morning.

She held out her arms to them, and they came running. "Darlings . . ." Worldly-wise, Fleet-Street hardened Alex, and young Julia, still groping for her way in the world, came running. Connie's arms encompassed them both. Their heads bowed together, and at last they wept.

Above, as the light grew, the first RAF scramble of the day went up, to repel the invaders. The brief peace of the morning was gone.

Two days later Ginette Maslova was buried in the churchyard of the square-towered church of Anscombe which dated from Norman times, and was recorded in the Doomsday Book. Greg Mathieson had joined his wife and her family. It was he who was mainly responsible for getting what remained of the oasthouse demolished. At first Michael had objected. "It should be her memorial . . ." But his farm manager, Harry Whitehand had interjected with the sureness of someone who knew Michael as a friend. "Don't be a fool, man! It's a danger to anyone who goes near it. You want some kids to get killed when that last wall comes crashing down? Look—we'll do something. Later. Plant it up with something pretty. When there's time . . ."

Michael had given in, and retreated once again to

the dining-room, and the ever present bottle of brandy. Harry Whitehand had brought two farm-hands and a tractor. Greg Mathieson had helped rig the ropes, and the whole household had flinched as they heard the crash of the falling rubble, and the dust had once again clouded the air, and choked them. The windows of the drawing-room were boarded up until they could find a glazier and glass to fix them. And overhead the battle had still raged.

When it was time to bury Ginette Maslova, they had all walked the mile along the dusty country lane to the church where her coffin lay. The petrol for cars could not be spared. It was as beautiful a day as the one on which she had died. Michael, holding Connie's hand, walking with Julia at his side, Alex and Greg, Stella, Cook, Harry Whitehand and all the farm workers and their wives following, had audibly gasped as they had approached the village green, the cricket pitch, the church shaded by its oaks. All around the green, horse-drawn vehicles, tractors, and whatever other form of transport people had been able to manage, were gathered. A quiet crowd of villagers and what were still thought of as "the gentry" of the neighbouring estates stood waiting. Flowers, gathered from cottage gardens and the few picking borders not already ploughed under for vegetables, lay piled against the coffin.

"Who would have imagined . . ." Michael murmured. "I thought they hardly knew her."

"They knew her," Alex whispered, almost fiercely. "They knew her since the last war. They loved her because Grandfather did. And then they loved her for herself. We were all born here. They don't forget that."

People had come from London, either by car, using precious petrol, or by the unreliable train service, which must have taken many hours. Some great names of the world of music stood there, the world of the theatre, from Fleet Street, humbly silent as the family passed among them. Hands were out-stretched in sympathy, the rough hands of farm workers, the smooth hands of those who earned their living in softer, but not easier, ways. Julia saw several large, important-looking cars parked about the green. She looked around for the face of D.D.—David Davidoff—the producer, impresario, probably the family's closest friend who had been part of all their lives. He stood with tears pouring down his jowly mid-European features, just inside the lych gate. With him stood Lord Wolverton, Alex's boss—"Old Woolfie" as they had called him from childhood. His English reserve would not permit him the luxury of tears, but his features were hauntingly sad.

The story of Ginette Maslova must have been in the minds of many as the service was conducted, as they had sung the old, familiar, comforting hymns. The organist of St. Paul's, Christopher Lloyd, had managed to make his way down from London, and he struggled valiantly with the old, gasping organ. They sang hymns which bound them together in this moment of their country's greatest peril, and another wave of German bombers with their fighter escort crossed the English coastline. As they moved out of the church, Christopher Lloyd played *"My country, thee I vow . . ."*

Many of the congregation, Julia realized, could remember when Ginette Maslova had come to Anscombe at the beginning of the First World War, the bride of young Michael Seymour, whom she had met, and married, some said in such reckless haste, in France, lingered with him for a brief honeymoon, and then, in the face of the German advance, and at Michael's order, had departed with her parents for England, and to Anscombe. She was already pregnant with their first child. They had all been received with gracious bewilderment by Michael's father, Guy Seymour, whose family had farmed Anscombe's nearly eight hundred acres for so many generations they had almost lost count.

It had been disappointing and painful for Guy Seymour to realize that his only child, Michael, would not follow him into running the farm, but had, while at Oxford, chosen, instead, to become an actor. There was no history of such a thing in the family. But his son was already beginning to make a small name for himself on the London stage and in the provinces, when the war had broken out. Michael had at once joined the Army and gone to France. No one quite knew how he had had time or opportunity to woo and win his young bride. That the marriage had not had her father's approval was evident.

Igor Maslov's name was beginning to be known well beyond the Continent—a controversial, but increasingly popular conductor. He had left Russia with his wife, Svetlana, and their ten-year-old daughter, after the 1905 Revolution, because he had fallen out of favour with the Imperial Court, and because he considered the Czarist rule too repressive. In France, they began to call their daughter Ginette.

He had been encouraged by his friend, Diaghilev, and often conducted the unfamiliar scores of the Ballet Russes—scores by Stravinsky, Ravel, de Falla.

To make a living he had conducted what audiences had expected to hear, though the Germans thought their native composers, Brahms, Beethoven, Schubert came out sounding too much like Tchaikovsky. He had been on the podium when his daughter, Ginette, had made her debut at age twelve, in the Mozart twenty-first piano concerto. He and his daughter had been invited to America, and had notable triumphs, though Maslov dismissed the American audiences as "provincial", and was too well aware that the appeal of his beautiful child had outweighed his own.

Then he had sternly returned her to her teachers at the Paris Conservatoire, telling her she still played like a child, and must now grow up in music. By seventeen she was again playing for audiences, assured, authoritative beyond her years. Maslov had been jealous when one Paris critic had written: *. . . a rare talent which can only flower to greater beauty.* He had been furious when she had secretly married this unknown and virtually penniless young British officer, who aspired to be an actor. He had declared that Ginette was still a child at heart, and did not know that heart. But as the German armies had swept towards Paris he had heeded the pleading of his son-in-law, and crossed the Channel to England. He and his wife had spent an uneasy two weeks at Anscombe, taking for granted the ready hospitality Ginette's new father-in-law, a widower, had offered. They could stay as long as they liked, he said. As long as it took to win the war, and free the country to which they wanted to return. No one any longer talked of it being over soon.

But the Maslovs had no taste for the country. It was a place to visit, not to live. They longed for their musical and literary friends. Igor was offered a guest conductorship in London, and they had gone eagerly. There was talk of another American tour. They kissed their daughter a fond farewell, and talked of being there when the baby was born.

That left a quiet, homesick, almost inarticulate Ginette alone with her father-in-law. Where she had expected him to be stiff and correctly English, she found him gentle and concerned for her, in a way he never made too obvious. If he was disappointed in the profession his son had chosen, or the wife he had chosen, if he grieved that there was not a younger son to carry on at the manor of Anscombe, he never said so. With the growing knowledge of the slaughter in Flanders, there was serious doubt that his only child would survive at all. He did not hope for the miracle that Michael would suddenly turn to farming, to caring for the small, beautiful estate; he just prayed that he would return alive. He did not even express the hope that the child Ginette carried would be a son.

In those months of waiting for the baby's birth, Ginette's father gave concerts in London. He and Svetlana paid another visit to Anscombe, and tearfully told her that he must take up the offer of an American tour before the baby was born. It was, after all, necessary to earn one's living. With typical Russian impulsiveness Igor had given Ginette all the money they had managed to save from his London fees, saying she must not be a burden on this too-kind Guy Seymour, whom he privately thought stultifyingly dull. He had bade her take great care of their grandchild, to practise her music, and to sing to her child so that it would be born with music in its soul. He was tactful enough not to mention that there was no piano at Anscombe. Ginette had never felt more alone in her life as she saw them off at the station, they obviously relieved that a duty was done, and that only music lay ahead of them in America. They were facing a perilous and uncomfortable journey across the Atlantic, and seemed quite light-hearted about it. "Are all Russians so . . . so careless of danger?" Guy had asked Ginette.

"Fatalistic—and melancholy. So they laugh and get drunk to shut it all out," she replied.

Guy Seymour realized her aloneness, her solitude. Unknowledgeable in music himself, he had realized that she starved for it. When her parents had gone, he had apologized. "My dear, how could I have been so blind? Of course you need music. I will see what I can do . . ."

Even in those days of the 1914–18 war time scarcity he had found the materials, and somehow found the men to put into repair the oasthouse, where the hops had once been dried. It had been used as a playroom by Guy and his brother, and had been let go back to spiders and dust when they had grown up. He refurbished it as best he could, and begged the loan from a friend of a baby grand piano. He had the chimney swept, and lit a fire there every morning to dry the place out. He had spent three days in London in the unaccustomed pursuit, for him, of music manuscripts. He was amazed at the stacks of music Ginette required. "After the baby," she said, "a teacher . . ."

"But surely . . . well, I thought you already *knew* all this music stuff."

"I am only beginning," she said. She was touched and warmed by his kindness, by his concern for her.

She began to hope her child would be a son, who would not turn out to be an actor or a musician, but would farm the fields of Anscombe as the Seymours had done for so many hundreds of years.

While her body grew rounded and bigger with her child, she had gone back to the scales and arpeggios; shyly Guy asked her why she didn't play any *music*—music as he understood it. "I have been away from it for a long time. I am afraid of the way I would sound. Warming up, first, Father." That he understood. "Is it terrible for you—all this music?" Ginette asked. "You would rather something you used to dance to . . ."

"Not at all," he said, and meant it. "I'm learning there's far more than that."

On a day close to the birth, he had brought her a glass of sherry in the oasthouse before lunch. He had carefully watched her diet, as he did her health. She had raised her glass to him. "Now, a little Mozart, I think. If you can forgive the fumbling, the wrong notes. I hope the baby does not hear too well." She had played a Mozart sonata for him, a seemingly simple thing, which he guessed was not simple at all. She had been amazed to see tears in his eyes. "I have disturbed you?"

"No—you have made me very happy." This beautiful girl, born in Russia, as foreign a being as he could have imagined, was suddenly the daughter he had never had, the sister he had never seen, the mother he had loved, the wife who had died too young, after she had given him only one child.

She gazed at him across the piano. "You have given me so much. Such calm here. Peace in which to let my child grow. He will be a very strong child. He will grow up here, and be the one you wanted Michael to be. He will be here when he is grown up—when his foolish parents have gone on making music and play-acting, and he will farm Anscombe as you have, and walk the fields. He will be Russian in his love of the land, and he will be English in the way he cares for it. He will be christened in the church of Anscombe, and he will be called Guy Michael . . . and tucked at the end, so his other grandfather will not be hurt, we will put Igor. But he will be English . . ."

But the telegram which went to Michael in France read:

A BEAUTIFUL DAUGHTER, ALEXANDRA, HAS BEEN BORN. GINETTE AND BABY WELL.

LOVE, FATHER.

"I'm sorry, Father. Next time a boy. As soon as Michael comes home, we will make another baby. And it will be a boy. For you."

"It couldn't matter less," he had replied, looking adoringly at his grand-daughter. He had stayed near Ginette during her labour, and had been terrified that she might die, as so many of his family had. "Get strong, and play your music to your baby. We will want you both well when Michael comes home."

An ancient wooden cradle had been placed near the fire in the oasthouse. For two years Ginette had played her scales, had played Bach and Beethoven and Mozart, and had watched her daughter begin to crawl, and then to walk. Once a week she had gone to London for a piano lesson, feeling guilty because she did no useful work. "Your time will come," Guy had said. "It is your duty to preserve your talent—even to preserve your hands. The world has as much need of your kind of woman as those good souls who hoe their vegetable patches and roll bandages."

Anscombe was too small, too medieval in its layout to be requisitioned as a convalescent hospital, so Ginette finally prevailed on Guy to let her offer voluntary help at the home of one of his neighbours whose house was being used as a hospital. She began humbly, washing dishes and scrubbing floors. Guy fussed over her hands, and somehow found lanolin, which he himself, without the slightest self-consciousness, rubbed into them. Gradually, as news of Igor Maslov's success in the United States began to cross the Atlantic, the hospital authorities pressed Ginette into service to do a little Sunday afternoon entertainment for those they nursed.

At first she had simply played at a badly tuned piano in the hall of the mansion, the popular songs they requested—*Keep the Home Fires Burning; Tipperary; Rose of No Man's Land.* She had sung the lines, and the French-accented voice had enchanted them. Then someone had realized that she was a musician in her own right, and more as a compliment to her, than to please the men, had suggested she play something of her own choosing. So she played, at times, a little Mozart, Chopin, Schubert. One day, when there had been no one available at Anscombe to take care of her child, she had brought Alex, as she was called, with her to the hospital. At the end of a long day being cared for, and spoiled, by the kitchen staff, the tired child had slumped on the floor against the piano, sucking her thumb. Then Ginette had sung, in Russian, a lullaby.

There was no applause at the end; the child had fallen asleep, but tears welled in the eyes of the men. The golden-haired mother had picked up her very dark-haired child, and bowed her goodbye. Hands had reached out to touch her as she passed. "Looked like a painted picture, she did, with the kid, an' all," one of the men had said. "A madonna" the Medical Commandant, who had been passing and stopped a moment to listen, had commented. Some of the women, who had also served at that hospital, had carried that memory to Ginette Maslova's funeral during the Second World War. Country people have long memories.

They had had a telegram from a hospital in Reading that Michael had been sent there after being wounded in France. Guy had held Ginette's hand in the train as they had journeyed to see him. "It can't be so bad," he said, to comfort her. "The bad cases die in France." He didn't mention that the bad cases who survived, got sent home to England.

It was a shrapnel wound to his leg. They had waited through anxious days because the doctors feared gangrene would develop, and the leg have to be removed. Michael joked feebly through the pain. "Well, at least it wasn't my face. I would have spent the rest of my life playing Richard the Third." After long weeks, with the danger past, he had been sent to the hospital close to Anscombe, where Ginette worked, and had seen his daughter for the first time. He had sat with the other men and officers for the little Sunday afternoon tea time concert Ginette gave, holding his daughter like a precious charge, and gazing with adoration at his wife. Then he had been allowed back to Anscombe to convalesce. He had sat each day on the lawn, or inside the oasthouse, and listened to his wife practise, walking at times to keep his leg exercised, and to keep Alex from disturbing her mother.

"My darling—I don't know how I had the temerity to marry you. You belong on a world stage, like your father, not a housewife buried in the country."

She had shrugged. "All in good time, Michael. In good time. I am young. An artist needs to grow. I grow here in this peace, the beautiful place your father gives to me. I grow with Alex. I am not a bad mother, am I, Michael? Not a bad wife to you?"

Their love-making was both tender and passionate, and they were both more mature than the lovers who had come together so briefly in France. But when the convalescence was over, and Michael was ordered back to France, Ginette had wept for more than his going. "I am not with child," she had sobbed to Guy. By now she felt that her most intimate thoughts could be shared with him. "I had so hoped . . . I am afraid, Father. He goes back again . . . so few return." She had increased her work at the hospital, now being trusted with more than menial chores. She resumed her once-a-week piano lessons with her London teacher, who had scolded her for some rustiness in the playing, but complimented her on the changes in her approach to it. "At last you play like a woman, not like a precocious child," he had said. "I begin to think you will match what your father predicted for you."

Alex was growing, and learning to ride a very old pony at Anscombe. Her grandfather taught her, and she wept stormy tears when she was not allowed to accompany him on his tour of the estate. "Later, my pet, when you are older. And poor old Pony is too tired to carry you all the way . . ."

The war ended, not in a blaze of glory and victory, but in a terrible exhaustion of great armies who had fought each other to a standstill. Michael returned with the rank of Major, and a DSO. He also joined the ranks of those looking for work as an actor—no longer so young, but with his good looks refined and rendered like steel. "We have all been case-hardened," he said. "I don't think now I could ever play Romeo." But he played numerous minor Shakespearian roles, and won some individual praise for them. He did his stint in playing in repertory companies through the provinces, enduring the discomforts, the separation from his family with good humour. Ginette prepared for her first London recital, and told him she was going to have a child. Unlike Michael's modest successes, her recital was a triumph, and critics and impresarios realized that Igor Maslov's daughter had not burned out as a prodigy, and must now be regarded as a serious talent.

Constance was born at the end of 1919. Her grandfather Maslov had returned, with Svetlana, for a series of concerts in England. He listened to Ginette play with grave composure. "You have become better than I would have hoped." He shrugged and held his palms upwards. "Though how you have managed to do it in that bourgeois backwater I will never know. Though I do admit Peter Danilovitch is not an unworthy teacher."

Peter Danilovitch had been known as the St Petersburg Conservatoire's best piano teacher. He had moved on to Paris two years before Maslov himself, and then had established himself in London. Ginette had instinctively sought him out as her teacher. "But now you need others—other influences."

"I have a child—and a young baby. There is a limit—"

He shrugged. "So? Women are always having babies. Did that stop Clara Schumann? She had eight, and was the greatest pianist of her time, after Liszt. As soon as the baby is old enough to travel, and I have finished this tour, you will come to us in New York. I will select your teachers—"

"I have a husband, Father."

He shrugged again. "So? Let him find a job in New York for a year. Let him stay at home and take care of the babies. Who cares? This marriage was a mistake from the beginning. Though the old man—" he referred to Guy Seymour who was the same age as he, "has not done badly by you."

"He has been the world to me."

"So you no longer love your own father—"

The tug-of-war started, and did not end. Ginette appeared at Queen's Hall as soloist in the Beethoven Fifth Piano Concerto with her father conducting. It was a charity concert for war veterans. She was immediately offered a contract to do the full Beethoven cycle by HMV with her father. But the recording would have to be in New York. "Not yet!" her father decreed. "She needs more training. When my daughter records, it will be the best. She must come to New York to study for a year. For two years." Igor Maslov was very dissatisfied with the current recording techniques, and did not wish to commit Ginette or himself.

Michael packed her off on a ship with her parents and the two children and a young Nanny, Stella, whom Guy Seymour paid for. "I'll be with you soon," Michael promised her. He had a tentative promise of a part on Broadway.

It was nearly six months before he came. He was the alternate lead in a group which would perform Shakespeare on Broadway and then go on tour throughout the States. He stayed at Ginette's parents' large apartment on Central Park West, a strange Gothic-like building called The Dakota, and had silently witnessed the world of music flow in and out. Only a few of his own group were admitted. "They don't understand actors," he said simply, to Ginette. And it was true. He suffered the silent disapproval of his father-in-law for the months he was in New York, nearly choked on his hospitality.

"Keep your money, my boy," Maslov had said grandly, "actors always need money. And I can easily take care of expenses here."

"I heard Mozart died a pauper. And I can take care of my own children." But it was true that Maslov was enjoying a great success as a conductor. He travelled regularly to Boston and Philadelphia and Chicago. What irked him was that he had not been offered the permanent conductorship of any orchestra. Reluctantly he recorded the cycle of Beethoven symphonies, still not happy with the sound he heard —but they brought money, and added to his audience.

Michael chafed under Maslov's patronage, and was glad to set off on tour. He hardly knew his own children, and they didn't understand his role as father. Ginette worked ceaselessly for her coming Carnegie Hall debut. Alex constantly cried for Anscombe, and "Grandfather". They all knew she meant Guy, and that did not please Maslov. On Michael's opening night in Chicago as *Hamlet*—the first time he had ventured on the role, Ginette telephoned to wish him luck, and to shout down the crackling line that she was pregnant. "Soon, my darling—soon. I will make this debut here. I will do the concerts with him in Boston and Philadelphia. And then, when your tour is finished we will go home. Our baby will be born at home, with Father."

"Home?" he echoed, with some bitterness. "Where is home? —and who is Father?"

"Home is Anscombe. Father is Guy. And you are the father of our son. This time it will be a boy."

The schedule was completed as she predicted. Michael had scored something of a triumph during his tour, and he had been able to hone his parts without being under the eagle eyes of the English critics. He radiated a new confidence, and a presence on the stage that made him outstanding. He had even dared to make himself into Caesar in *Caesar and Cleopatra* in a special, short run arranged in New York, and he had brought it off. It was the first time he had played Shaw, and the reviews were excellent. Ginette was heavily pregnant when they arrived in Southampton. She fell into Guy Seymour's arms. "Home again, Father." Maslov, still angry at her departure, had gone to San Francisco to conduct the newly opened Opera, and then journeyed to Los Angeles to the novelty of conducting at the Hollywood Bowl. He was becoming a conductor known to the masses, and that made him suspect in musical circles.

Ginette's child, born at Anscombe in 1921 was a girl. They named her Julia Svetlana, after Guy

Seymour's mother, and Ginette's mother. Ginette gave concerts in London and Manchester three months after Julia's birth. Her father came over to conduct her in the five Beethoven concertos at a series of concerts at the Royal Albert Hall. Michael had an unprecedented four month run in *Hamlet*, and the critics, some grudgingly, were beginning to write of him as being, perhaps, in the long tradition of the great Shakespearian actors. Ginette added the two Brahms concertos to her repertoire, and broke away from her father's yoke to play them as she wanted to, under other conductors. She toured France and Scandinavia, having added Grieg and Liszt and Rachmaninov to what some people were beginning to call a "flashy" repertoire. But in Paris she had given a recital of Ravel only, and the critics had claimed her as one of their own, recalling her debut, at twelve, in that city.

She had come back, exhausted, thankful, happily to Anscombe, to find that Michael had contracted to open on Broadway in *Outward Bound.* It was a run of the play contract, and so would be of indefinite length. Ginette rested, and then went to Berlin, much against the wishes of Michael, who still had mixed feelings about all Germans, to play in two concerts with Furtwangler. That engagement finished, she followed Michael to New York, and this time they had their own apartment. Stella was still with them, and Alex had been left at home with "Grandfather". She was eight years old, and had a governess. She had been adamant that she did not want to go to New York. "I like it here better . . ."

Maslov had been furious at the independence of his daughter and son-in-law, declaring the Dakota apartment had plenty of room for them all, including the babies. But he could not keep himself away from his grand-daughters, and showered them with gifts they did not comprehend. He was plainly jealous of Michael. They were barely civil to each other. Ginette had been engaged to do a series of concertos with her father as conductor, and a new sense of struggle began to be heard when they performed together, Ginette imposing some of her own interpretations and tempi on her father. They collaborated in one of the first radio transmissions of a symphony concert; the public had grown fascinated by the tales of the clashes of temperament between father and daughter. "It's that Furtwangler," Maslov roared. "He has ruined her."

Michael had heard himself say, "I think he's made her."

"And what would you—an Englishman—know about music?" Maslov had found his niche with the public, but he remained faithful to his Russian heritage and to his friends, trying, whenever managers would permit it, to slip the music of Stravinsky into his programmes, to play the music of the Diaghilev-inspired ballets "Firebird", "Petrushka" even the outrageous "Rite of Spring". He conducted Ravel's "Daphnis and Chloe", de Falla's "Three Cornered Hat". He remained, as most Russians did, eternally homesick for his native land. He played Russian music in a way no other conductor seemed able to match, and in the Tchaikovsky piano concertos, he and his daughter were a perfect match of soul and fire.

Away from Maslov, Ginette and Michael enjoyed New York as only those who had tasted its success could. Michael hired a white Rolls-Royce to drive

Ginette about the city; he bought jewellery he could not afford for her—trusting that the money would show up somehow. He demanded that each new concert gown should be a masterpiece. "You want the dress to be more than the music?" Maslov had stormed. Between them, Ginette and Michael spent every penny they earned. They partied and dined and danced, after the theatre, in the spirit that only the new jazz age would know, but were wise enough, and professional enough, never to let such energetic romps sap their strength for their tasks.

"You bring serious music into disrepute," was Maslov's verdict on his daughter's behaviour. He disapproved of the late suppers at Sardi's, where Michael always had a prominent table. He disapproved of most of the American attitudes Ginette adopted, and Ginette shrugged off his disapproval. Ginette and Michael quarrelled and loved, and lived life with the full enjoyment of the young who knew they were both exceptional people. After two concerts in San Francisco at which her father did not conduct, Ginette came back to New York and Alex's grubby, ill-spelled note. *Grandfather is sik.* Ginette cancelled several concert engagements and booked herself and the children on the first available ship, after receiving an evasive reply to the cable she sent to Guy Seymour. Michael could not leave the play, and tended to be dismissive of the idea of his father being seriously ill. "You can't go on the notion of a child, Ginette. She could have meant he had had a cold."

But she did go, and was rapturously welcomed at Southampton by Guy and Alex. "My dear, but it's nothing," he had protested. "Perhaps I've been overdoing it a bit. That farm . . . always something to be done, and precious little money to do it with. Doctors don't know what they're talking about half the time. A few little chest pains. Everyone my age has them." But she thought he looked strained, and he seemed to breathe heavily after any small exertion. "You shouldn't have cancelled those concerts. You shouldn't have left Michael."

"I *should* have left my father," she retorted. "We were on the verge of coming to blows. Perhaps I shouldn't have left Michael. But we were living too much . . . what is it . . . the good life. Drinking, staying up late . . . bad for both of us. I don't think he'll stop because I am not there. But as for me, I have used you as an excuse to come home. I need rest and quiet."

She returned to Peter Danilovitch for some lessons, some consultations about her deepening ideas on interpretation. She practised daily for long hours in the oasthouse, which was beginning to be transformed into a room of rare beauty. Books lined one whole long wall, French windows gave more light, there were two pale silken Persian rugs on a newly laid parquet floor. One concert in San Francisco had bought her a Bosendorfer piano. She had set aside enough money from hers and Michael's spending sprees to install central heating in the manor house, and she extended it to the oasthouse. She played with her children and watched them grow. She got to know Alex again. She was happy, but impatient for Michael's return. The run of *Outward Bound* had been extended. *I miss you terribly*, he wrote. *I'm being good, but life's boring without you—Sardi's after the theatre, and then early to bed*. That couldn't be earlier than two am, Ginette knew. *I want to get back to you, my love, and my babies. Kiss them for me. I long to be in your arms again.*

Guy Seymour appeared well enough to Ginette. His vigour seemed restored. He was cheerful, and clearly delighted to have her and the children at Anscombe with him. The governess was an extravagance, Ginette thought, but without her they would have had to think about a boarding school for Alex, and that Ginette could not bear. Between the governess and Stella, all the children's needs were taken care of; she and Guy supplied an overabundance of love. She decided to accept an offer to appear in two concerts with Sir Henry Wood during the Promenade season, to play the two Brahms piano concertos. Guy Seymour proudly escorted her to both, and sat in the dressing-room, clutching the worn grey rabbit she had carried with her since her first appearance on stage with her father in Paris. Michael sent extravagant baskets of flowers on each night. *Home soon*, he cabled. *Handing over my part to someone else*.

But he did not come soon enough. He was in the last week of his appearance in *Outward Bound* when Guy, dining quietly with Ginette after the children were in bed, suddenly slumped forward at the table, sending china and silver clattering to the floor. He slid from his chair, and lay among the pieces. They made him as comfortable as they could, with a blanket over him, and a pillow under his head. Ginette forbade the brandy which the cook thought was the remedy he needed. The doctor arrived half an hour later, but by that time Guy no longer responded to Ginette's urgent voice. "I'm sorry, Mrs. Seymour. He's gone. I'm so glad you were here with him. He was very fond of you, you know. And he wouldn't let me tell you how serious I considered his condition to be. Just said: 'I refuse to be an old nuisance'."

By the time Michael reached Anscombe his father was buried, and Ginette bereft. He comforted her as best he could, and cursed himself for delaying so long. "I was never much of a son to him. Never did any of the things that might have made his life happier or easier . . . except to marry you."

"Hush," she replied. "you did what you had to do. No one can make a farmer out of a man who wants to act, or the other way around. *I* cannot be the daughter my father would like me to be. He would like me unmarried, without husband or children. With only him in my life. He wants me as his puppet doll, playing just how and what he directs. *Your* father gave me a home, love, and the freedom to be and do what I wanted. It is a debt I can never repay."

Michael stayed with her quietly at Anscombe for a few weeks. Then she saw his restlessness begin to emerge. "I have to earn a living for us, darling. Can't live off you. Perhaps we should sell Anscombe—have a big house in London for all of us."

"You cannot sell Anscombe! I would never permit it. I promised your father one day there would be a son . . ."

He had looked at her incredulously. "You can't seriously think we must hang on to Anscombe just for that! There may never be a son. And I can't farm the place and work in the theatre as well. We'd have to employ a steward . . . we'd have to—This place *eats* money. My father spent his whole life trying to repair the neglect and mistakes *his* father made. To pay off his debts. We're barely breaking even now.

We could sell it, and live so comfortably . . ." He stopped as he saw her obdurate expression. "Well . . . at least let's have a flat in London. Staying in digs and hotels isn't right. A place for the children . . ." His features softened and he bent and kissed her. "For a son, if he comes . . ."

There had been no son, or any other child, much to Ginette's disappointment. They had lived the peripatetic lives of an actor and a working musician, Ginette more often touring than Michael, as he had settled into longer runs on the London stage, often declining Broadway because it meant being away from home too long. The London flat was convenient, but Anscombe was, for Ginette at least, home and refreshment. Her fame grew, as Michael's did. She played a few times a year with her father, their differences never entirely resolved. But a wary respect had grown between them. They made their peace, and her marriage to Michael, now that he was successful, received Maslov's reluctant blessing. The debts on Anscombe were finally cleared, and improvements were made. Ginette gratefully walked the fields with Harry Whitehand, the steward. "There must be a lot of peasant in me," she once said to him. "I have a feeling for the land . . ."

In the mid-twenties had come what sounded to Maslov's ears the miracle of electric recording. He enthusiastically engaged Ginette to make the Beethoven piano concerto cycle with him. It was an enormous success with the public which had before this lain beyond their reach. He was furious when she then accepted Toscanini's invitation to do the two Brahms concertos. Toscanini then recorded the Rachmaninov and Tchaikovsky concertos with her. The dislike and jealousy Maslov displayed towards Toscanini was well known. Toscanini, aware of the near idolatry in which he was held in the United States, behaved as if Maslov did not exist. But he had lavish praise for Ginette Maslova, and they made other recordings together, while Maslov fumed. She then angered both men by making recordings with Furtwangler, Toscanini's great rival. The fury and the storm delighted Ginette, and amused Michael. "Few people would dare be so independent," he said. "You've offended three great conductors . . ."

She shrugged. "If I'm any good, they will want me again."

The frenetic Twenties passed into the far more sombre Thirties. The children grew, and mostly they remained one another's friends. Ginette saw to it that they were separated as little as possible, especially when she was away on tour. They all eventually attended the same school. Ginette kept on Stella, who could take care of the small crises which arose when Ginette had to be away from them. All their holidays were spent at Anscombe. They grew used to their father being only a Sunday visitor there. They grew used to the sophisticated, bohemian world their parents inhabited. They hardly realized it was an unusual childhood.

They all went to see their father act—he was at his best in Shakespeare, but could turn a nice show of comedy and satire in George Bernard Shaw. The playwright himself came several times to Anscombe. They attended their mother's London concerts. They were permitted to be present at some of the parties their parents gave, in which the worlds of music and theatre mixed. They became used to the famous and the fashionable. Alex finished school, and went to Girton College, Cambridge. Ginette sighed. "She is almost a woman . . ." Ginette was happy with her life, overlooking Michael's occasional flirtations with other women. For her there had only ever been one man. She intended to keep him.

Her father came regularly to conduct in London, and always when he did, Ginette would appear in concerts with him. She gave an annual concert tour in the States. The battle of temperaments went on between her and Maslov, more muted now. He still bitterly resented his daughter's seeming disloyalty in accepting engagements to play with Toscanini. He never attended any concert at which she did so.

Ginette was grateful for the rock of security she and Michael had built in their marriage when the cable came that Igor Maslov had been killed, and Svetlana severely injured in a train crash on their way from New York to Chicago. She and Michael and Alex were on the first ship leaving Southampton. Ginette received the news of her mother's death during the Atlantic crossing. The double funeral in New York was an event which the whole musical world turned out for, and because of Michael, the theatre world also paid its respects. Toscanini appeared, and no one could guess from his demeanour that any question of a rivalry between him and Maslov had ever existed.

"Maslov was a great show-biz man," Alex heard as she trailed, and somehow lost sight of her parents, in their procession up the aisle of the church. "He could play an audience like a violin."

Sadly, Ginette closed her parents' New York apartment, sending most of their treasures, the signed portraits of the famous, the collection of her father's recordings, the beautiful antique pieces her mother had indulged in as her husband's success grew, the jewelled Russian icons, the three Fabergé pieces, to Anscombe. Michael and Alex had had to return almost at once. Ginette could linger a little, supervising the packing, gazing from the windows of the half-stripped apartment as the dusk fell over Central Park. Had she ever told her father she loved him? That their quarrels had been the difference of temperament, not dislike? Had he been aware of the joys and jealousies of her marriage to Michael, the shared love of their children? If he hadn't known, it was now too late. She wrote loving letters to Michael, and each of the three girls. They, if no one else, must know how much she loved them.

Michael was seduced into going to Hollywood, mostly by the money offered, but also the thought of gaining a much wider audience, to make two films. He had come rushing back to Ginette when the news of his affair with a co-star had become the source of too much gossip. This time he really feared that even Ginette's fierce loyalty would not stand the strain. "My darling, forgive me. I don't believe that, until I thought I might lose you, I ever realized how much I love you. You are my soul . . . Without you I don't believe I would—could—exist."

That next year he had played his first *Lear*. Ginette had watched him prepare for this supreme test, and recognized a new maturity in him, as if his world had truly been shaken, and he had been afraid. He was an enormous success. The critics spoke of "A new Seymour—one whose depth we have not seen before!" In the New Year Honour's list he received his knighthood. Ginette was both Madame Maslova, and Lady Seymour. She and Alex accompanied him to Buckingham Palace where he knelt before the King, and was dubbed by the sword on both shoulders. He was considered young to have been so recognized in the theatrical world, but there appeared to be few commentators who begrudged him his honour. The party they gave on the evening of his investiture was enthusiastically attended, and Ginette believed that most of the congratulations were genuine. There was laughter and champagne and toasts to Michael.

But in the background, in the corners where people stood and talked seriously, there was the *frisson* which lay over that whole year of 1939. Most of them feared war. They all hoped it would not come.

It had come in September, but it was nearly a year later that the line of battle was drawn in the skies over the south-east of England. Two weeks after Ginette Maslova was killed, Goering turned his bombers aside from the airfields, and directed them against London and other big cities. Afterwards, the historians would say that the Battle of Britain was then won, but the Blitz had just begun. This no one knew the day that Michael and his daughters, his son-in-law, with all the attending farm families, had walked from Anscombe to the church, and had seen the green ringed with vehicles. Then they still anticipated invasion. The famous there mixed with the unknown and the humble in that sea of faces. Michael moved through them in a daze, shaking hands, unable to speak a word, his great, beautiful voice stilled.

It seemed to Julia that a horde of people followed them on the walk back to the house—those who had come from London, friends from around Anscombe. A tea was waiting for them at the house, preparations Michael had not been consulted about. He had thought only of Ginette in those days since her death; that others besides himself and his family would want to stand by her grave, would take enormous trouble to do so, had not occurred to him. His own grief was enough, he had implied. She must know, that fragile bundle of bones, that only he in the world loved her with such passion, such reverence. Even her daughters, his beautiful children, had loved her in a different way. He didn't need the rest of the world to be there with them. He was silently resentful of their presence, knowing it to be kindly meant, but unwanted.

At the house he went at once to bring up bottles of whisky from the cellars, poured drinks lavishly, downing his own first one in a gulp, and quickly pouring a second. It was the only way he knew that the pain of the presence of others, while he wanted to be alone with Ginette, could be endured.

"There must be a memorial service in London," D.D. said. "This is just a handful of the people who would have liked to be here. She was a wonderful woman, Michael," he had protested, as he saw the headshake of refusal. "You owe her this. Owe it to your friends. Look, let me take care of things . . . I'll start the arrangements going."

"I don't want . . ."

"Life goes on, Michael, and mourning one's friends is part of it . . . life *will* go on . . ."

Six weeks later, with London suffering the nightly hammering of the Blitz, St. Margaret's Westminster, was packed with those who had come to listen to words spoken about Ginette and Michael, their talents, their laughter, their marriage, their love. It was impossible to speak of one without the other. The music was sumptuous; D.D. had had no difficulty in bringing together a sizeable orchestra, because almost every musician in London had wanted to be part of the service to honour Ginette Maslova. A famous contralto sang:

> When I am laid in earth . . . Remember
> me!,
> but ah, forget my fate.

At the conclusion of the service Michael had walked with an expression of stone down the aisle, Alex beside him, Connie and Julia following. He did not wait to shake the hands of any who had gathered; it was evident he only wanted to be away from the throng.

D.D. had provided his Rolls and enough petrol to bring them to the service, and return them to Anscombe. The last words of D.D. as he had stood beside the car had been; "As soon as you're ready, dear friend, I will fix up a little something for you in London. Cannot have you off the stage for too long . . ." Nothing was said about *The School for Scandal* which Michael had been rehearsing, and had abandoned. Michael did not reply.

Connie had been given two days' leave, and Alex was returning to Anscombe with them. Michael sat in the passenger seat beside D.D.'s driver, who was too old for the forces, but did his stint as a fire watcher. When at last they cleared the suburbs of London, leaving behind the devastation of the bombing, the gaping holes where buildings had stood, the cratered roads blocked off, Michael had turned piteously to the three women seated in the back.

"What will I do now? What in God's name will I do now?"

Alex spoke, bluntly, her words as swift and sure as the knife of a surgeon who must cut away a diseased part. "You will do what you have always done. You will go on stage and play your part. It is your duty, Father. It is the only thing left to do."

2

MICHAEL did not return to the stage, as Alex had urged. He returned to nothing but an indulgence of his grief. The London Blitz had virtually closed the theatres. At first they had been closed by Government order, then reopened by public demand. But the night-after-night hammering that London took did not encourage audiences to attend, and when they did, they were mostly servicemen on leave, and others looking for a good time. Comedies and music-hall were what they demanded. "I won't be missed," Michael had said.

"You're simply using it as an excuse," Alex had said. "There must be something you could do."

But he had fallen into a lethargy from which none of them could rouse him. Alex was living with Greg Mathieson in their London flat. They seldom bothered to go to air raid shelters, preferring to take their chances. Greg was often gone for days at a time, on assignments to various parts of the country. Occasional pieces by Alex now carried her by-line. She was encouraged by Lord Wolverton to write the kind of up-beat pieces which would raise morale, stories of courage and heroism, stories of simple acts of endurance.

"It's all the 'Britain can take it stuff'," she had once said, with some bitterness, to Julia. "I could almost be writing the scripts for Movietone News—all for export to America. What I don't write is that people are often cowardly, and dead scared. They fight each other like dogs in the shelters for the better places. They don't share their food or their pillows. Sometimes, they're downright cruel. I've even seen people looting the bombed-out buildings—if there's anything left worth taking. Of course there *are* heroes—plenty of them. The firemen, the ambulance men and women, those incredibly wonderful women who just rush out and keep them supplied with tea and sandwiches. The Air Raid Wardens. The other night I saw—well, I saw a fireman just sort of swept into a kind of firestorm. Buildings on both sides of the street burning like mad, and the suction just—just well, swept him in."

"And what were you doing so close to it that you saw this?" her father had demanded. "You take stupid risks, Alex. There's enough to write about without going into the battle itself."

"How can I know the battle, if I don't see it?"

Michael had turned back to his whisky and did not reply. The days had shortened into winter, and he sat by the fire in the dining-room—the one room, apart from the kitchen where the Aga stove was kept going, which they kept heated. He sat there, an open book on his lap, which he rarely attempted to read, a glass of whisky by his hand. Julia began to wish that the cellars had not been so well stocked before the war. She and Stella and Cook ran the house; Julia did not return to the Royal Academy. She sensed it would be a near-fatal act to leave her father alone in these months. Instead she worked every hour of daylight about the farm, mucked out the stables which housed the farm-horses they had been obliged to return to for pulling the plough and the farm carts, boiled up the swill and cared for the pigs, fed the poultry, reared rabbits which she could not bear to see slaughtered. She began to learn to drive a tractor—they had only two. She made friends with two Land Army girls who had arrived, and who lived with the wife and children of their former gardener, who had joined up. But her true job, she knew, was to keep her father alive through these first terrible months when his will to live had seemed to desert him.

Christmas provoked no feeling of festivity. Julia's twentieth birthday in early 1941 passed almost unnoticed. She sat with her father and Stella at night, and tried to make conversation, but there was little to talk about, except the bombing of their cities, and the shipping losses in the Atlantic, which were only briefly mentioned in the papers, so that the morale of the civilian population would not be further undermined. Much, though, was made of the British offensive in the Middle East, and the taking of Tobruk; then they began to hear about a German general called Rommel. Back in September, when their heads had been sunk in grief, Germany, Italy and Japan had signed a Tripartite Pact. The omens for the future they only grasped at the times when Greg visited, and talked of the reality of what might happen.

In this winter of darkness, Michael went back to reading Ibsen, Strindberg and Chekhov, relearning the parts, and he asked Julia to cue him on his lines. She listened and discovered again why her father was held to be a great actor; sometimes she would learn a part to play opposite him, however inadequately. "Someday, Pet, when you're older, you could make a great *Hedda Gabler*. And Nora in *The Doll's House*."

But Stella, who sat and listened, would shiver and remain silent. "It's all so depressing," she once complained to Julia. And more often than before, she retreated to the kitchen to listen to the popular radio programmes with Cook.

Julia tried to get as many of Michael's friends as possible from the theatre to come to Anscombe. Their company brightened him. D.D. came whenever he could, and Lord and Lady Wolverton. Julia helped Cook and Stella to try to turn the simple meals they served into something festive, always knowing that what they did was propped up by the excellence of the wines the cellar afforded. There were brief resurgences of spirit in Michael during these times. Occasionally someone could make him laugh. But no one could seriously urge him to return to the theatre when there was scarcely a theatre to return to. The Ministry of Information was becoming interested in the thoughts of producers who wanted to make what were virtually propaganda films but there had been no victories for the British to boast about, and therefore no likely subjects. Someone had suggested historical subjects, which would remind people of the victories of the past. Scripts based on Wellington and Nelson and Drake lay about the house, unread by Michael.

Only one thing seemed to interest him during those months. Piece by piece, using a horse and cart, sometimes just a wheel-barrow, he had cleared the debris of the oasthouse. The bricks which had not crumbled were neatly stacked in one of the barns, a few of the beams not completely consumed by the fire lay beside them. No one asked him what he intended to do with them. When the ground was completely clear, he requested a hand rotavator from Harry Whitehand, and he hauled hundreds of barrowfuls of well-rotted manure from the piles around the cow byres. When the earth where Ginette Maslova had died was completely prepared he began to make the rounds of his neighbours to beg cuttings from their roses, even uprooting whole rosebushes where they still remained. Most rose gardens, as the one at Anscombe, had been dug up and replanted as vegetable gardens.

Michael brought out the old charred beams and with Harry Whitehand's help, had built a trellis for the climbing roses. "Later—after the war, we'll use the old bricks to put a wall behind it, for shelter." Some people thought it morbid. Alex had urged him to reseed the plot with grass.

"Oh, do leave him be," Connie had said. "It's what he *wants*. A grave in the churchyard doesn't mean anything to him." He read everything he could about roses, a subject which had never interested him before. He asked for advice. In February he saw the first tender buds begin to swell, delighted with those bushes which gave life, mourning over those which had failed the transplanting.

"I can't believe Father is reduced to this," Alex said. "Tending a rose garden, and fondling a whisky bottle."

"Time," Connie counselled. "For God's sake, Alex, give him time. We all grieve in our own ways. He must be allowed to grieve."

"Perhaps you're right," Alex replied, rather grudgingly. "But I'd like to see him out there doing something for living people, not burying himself with the dead. And *you*, Julia—when are you going to shake yourself out of this? When are you going to *do* something."

Julia looked down at her broken nails, her calloused hands. "I don't feel exactly unoccupied."

Greg Mathieson's even tones broke in. It was one of the few times that they were all together at Anscombe, one of the times when Connie was able to get leave to coincide with a visit from Alex and Greg. "Listen—all of you! Don't *you* start quarrelling. That's the last thing your father needs. Connie's right." He looked directly at his sister-in-law. "I suppose I should add, 'as usual'. But that isn't the way I mean it. There is a time for grieving, and everyone does it in their own time, and in their own way." He turned to his wife. "If I got killed—"

"You'd better not get killed," she retorted sharply, "or I'll murder you. If you got killed, I'd probably work myself to death to try to forget it. So that'd be two of us."

How fiercely beautiful she looked, Julia thought, as her face had coloured with emotion at the very possibility of her husband's death. She was so dark, like their father, with his eyes and brows and hair. Connie seated beside her, looked tired after coming off a straight month's night duty at Bentley Priory. She was wearing an old sweater and corduroys, but in her their mother's classic beauty was undimmed. She had been the only one to inherit her blue eyes, she had the exact shade of her corn-coloured hair, that sweep of long neck and jaw. Everyone regarded her as the best-looking of the three sisters, and she seemed unaware of it. Julia didn't know what to think of her own looks. She felt that her features were still unformed—mixed up. She had her father's dark eyes and a darker blonde hair than Connie's, straight dark brows in an oval face. They weren't the sort of looks that would readily get her ingenue parts in the theatre. Perhaps, she thought, she'd be one of those actresses who played bit parts until they were old enough to play character parts, whose careers amounted to nothing much. She reflected on the nightly pounding of the cities by the Luftwaffe, and even dared to let the treacherous thought creep in that there might not, after all, be any career. Perhaps this truly was the end for Britain.

The wind gusted and howled about the house. Would this be the winter of their defeat? It was heresy even to think of such a thing, but she guessed that many secretly thought it.

She began to collect the cocoa mugs from the kitchen table and take them to the sink. Their father had gone upstairs an hour ago, nursing a glass and a bottle. She knew he craved sleep, and got little of it. Many nights she had heard him moving through the house, making his way by the light of a torch which shone through the gap between the bedroom door and the old, sloping floor. It was as if he sought her mother, and yet knew the search was useless. Sometimes she got up and brought him to the kitchen, to sit before the Aga, while she made cocoa, thankful that, because they lived on a farm, they were never short of milk. Sometimes he sat in silence, sometimes he talked of the early days of his marriage, the times when Alex had been the only child, and he mired in the trenches of Flanders. Sometimes he talked of the years when she and Connie had been born. He talked of her grandfather, Maslov, and was able to laugh at the battles they had fought for possession of Ginette.

"What a stupendous old tyrant he was!" he had said in unwilling admiration. "I never knew if he was really as good a conductor as he and some of his hangers-on made out. He had a good press—and quite a few critics. But he was flamboyant enough to stay on centre stage. His music was like that. He certainly knew how to conduct a row, and I mostly came off the worst . . . whenever I've had a row scene on the stage, I've modelled myself on Maslov. Ah, those were the days, Julia. Your mother and I—loving and quarrelling. But we knew the quarrelling wasn't important. The love was . . . I hope you have a love like that some day, Pet. Something that sweeps you off your feet, and you can't say 'no' to. I hope it isn't disastrous. I hope it's something great and glorious. I wish you what I had."

He would stare at her. "I see so much of her in you. An expression . . . the way you move. More than the others." His face often looked haggard under the rumpled dark hair. He wore a baggy old dressing gown, something over a sweater, added for warmth. There was little of the famous actor about him at those times. He looked a care-worn man, more than his almost fifty years, who thought his life had ended in the holocaust which had consumed his wife.

Now Julia looked at her two sisters, but particularly at Greg, the only man among them. He too wore old, comfortable clothes, and she thought she saw lines and some grey hairs which had not been there when he and Alex had married. Smartened up, in his war correspondent's uniform, he looked younger, nearer to Alex's age. He rarely talked about the assignments he was sent on. What he wrote appeared in the news-papers—as much as the censors would allow. Some things he wrote were for overseas consumption—mainly aimed at the United States. She guessed that he was briefed on more secret things, things which the Ministry of Defence deliberately revealed to a chosen few in the hope that knowledge, not ignorance, would ensure that they did not pry any further, ask no more questions. He had been with General Wavell, and then, more importantly, with his field commander, Lieutenant-General O'Connor, in North Africa as they had defeated the Italian forces, and had been there at Beda Fomm when the Italian army had surrendered. The road to Tripoli was open, but the Allied troops were held back. Perhaps Greg knew why, but his dispatches did not hint at his knowledge. The British were then engaged only in the air and at sea. Greg had been recalled to London by Wolverton. There must be some other place for him to go. There, inevitably, would be other partings for him and Alex. Julia thought she saw the knowledge of it sometimes in the small, quick, intense looks that passed between them.

The next afternoon, a Sunday, as they had sat in the unexpectedly warm March sunshine, and had tea on the lawn, while Michael had wandered away to look again at the swelling buds on the roses, Greg had told them that he would be making a journey to Washington. "This Lend-Lease Bill the senate has just passed is vitally important to us. Wolverton wants some interviews with those senators who backed it most strongly—the reasons why. If I'm lucky, there just might be an interview with Roosevelt. Wolverton is quite a chum of Elliot Forster. His papers have given Roosevelt his biggest backing—and God knows how many hundreds of them he owns, as well as his string of radio stations, not to mention *Insight*. He's not a 'hands-off' proprietor—his editors think as he does, or they go. Through him we might just swing that interview . . ."

His thoughts were far away on the possibilities of such a meeting, Julia didn't doubt that he had already begun framing his questions. He didn't say how he would get to Washington—the long, uncomfortable journey by military aircraft, or the slower, infinitely more perilous journey by ship, ziz-zagging in convoy, all portholes blacked out, constantly wearing a life-jacket, and with the ever-present sense that any second could bring the swift wake through the water that meant the passage of a torpedo. Alex's face assumed a look of blankness, as if she feared to envisage that journey. She certainly would not speak of its dangers. She would not betray now, or ever, any sign of the fear that might clutch at her heart.

A chill little wind blew over the garden, reminding them that it was still March. Alex shivered, and got to her feet, extending her hand to Greg to pull him up. "Too cold out here." Michael came towards them, finishing his inspection of the rose garden; his walk was shambling. From that distance he seemed almost an old man. Connie started to put the tea things together on the tray. "But it will soon be spring," she said. "How long will you be in Washington, Greg? Long enough to see the cherry blossoms?" She rose, holding the tray. "I'm sorry. I ought to know better than to ask questions like that."

He grinned at her. "You're darned right. I'll be there as long as it's fruitful for me and the powers-that-be to keep me there. No dates in this business, Connie. No promises, either. If I do a good enough job . . . well, who knows how these things go." He put his arm around his wife's shoulders, and as they walked across the lawn he bent and kissed her cheek; it was almost a gesture of comfort.

"He's trying to prepare her for the fact that he could stay a long time," Connie murmured to Julia.

"She already knows," Julia answered quickly.

Behind them Michael said, "Someone told me soapy water was good for roses. Keeps off the green fly. You'll save the soapy water, won't you, Julia."

"Yes, Father. Of course." Connie had an instant's vision of Julia hauling the sparse bathwater down to the rose garden, along with all her other chores. She and Alex, with their specified jobs, didn't, she thought, have much idea of what Julia actually did at Anscombe; she suspected that it was much more than she was given credit for. Julia had once, vaguely, hinted at joining one of the forces, but it had been no more than a hint. They all knew that she would stay at Anscombe until their father broke out of the web of grief which bound and made him almost helpless.

He was, Connie thought, a rather indulged man. She thought of the thousands who had suffered a similiar loss, or worse. Some who had returned to find not only their houses gone, but whole families. She thought of the grey-faced men and women she saw on the train on her infrequent journeys to Anscombe, her few trips to central London, people who walked through the rubble of the bombed buildings to their offices, weary from a night without sleep, but expected to go on with their jobs, some of whom would arrive to find their offices bombed or blasted, and they would begin the process of relocating in cramped and sometimes almost intolerable conditions. Some started again from nothing, and were expected to do so. Her father and his rose garden seemed a million miles removed from the grim endurance of the populations of the big cities.

In a bleak mood she followed the others into the house. Early tomorrow morning she would return to Bentley Priory, and the job of tracking the remorseless waves of bombers which came nightly from France. Would her father ever stir from that deep pit of gloom in which he seemed to wallow? If and when he did, it would be because Julia had stayed with him. She felt angry with both her father and Alex—her father because he seemed unaware of his selfishness, Alex because she did not recognize the job that Julia did for them all. When the spring came—finally the spring—would it be any different?

The spring did come. The days grew longer. The fields all around Anscombe were dotted white with the new lambs. The hedgerows began to leaf and blossom. Michael watched his roses anxiously, and still refused even to accompany Julia on her shopping trips to the nearby towns. There was little to buy, and each trip made her more aware of the damage suffered by the coastal towns, battered and with their beaches ringed with barbed wire. They were a microcosm of what she imagined London must be like. Neither she nor Michael had been in London since her mother's memorial service in October. It began to seem as if she would never be free of her father or Anscombe again. Catching sight of herself in a mirror in a draper's shop in Tunbridge Wells, she stiffened with a sense of shock. Was this she?—Julia?—this too-thin girl with her hair dragged back for convenience and tied with a piece of tired ribbon, she with gaunt hollows in her cheeks, and an ungirlish look of weariness about her? At Anscombe there was never time to look in mirrors. But what did it matter? Everyone around her was tired and strained. She completed the purchase of a cardigan for her father, counting out the precious clothing coupons, and made her way back to wait for the bus.

The April afternoon had grown warmer as she walked the mile from the village green where the bus set her down. Anscombe Manor looked peaceful as she topped the rise from the wood, and looked down on it. The countryside around was pock-marked with the damage of the aircraft which had come down, as the fighter had descended on Anscombe itself. But the metal heaps of the craft, enemy bombers and fighters, and their own craft were always cleared away —useful for something, if only for scrap metal. The swelling green of spring covered the ugly gashes where they had fallen. She began to see some sense in her father's labour to remove the ruin of the oast-house, the struggle to make some little thing of beauty where ugliness and death had reigned. She even paused for a few moments by the rose garden to admire the rapid growth of the bushes, to recognize the promise they held for a June flowering. Then she went on to the kitchen to unpack her meagre bits of shopping.

Cook and Stella were in the kitchen, and so was a young man in a RAF uniform, wearing the stripes of a Flight-Lieutenant. He sat with a mug of tea in front of him, and a slice of bread-and-butter. As Julia entered, Cook thrust a jam pot close to him, but he either didn't want it, or was reluctant to accept one of wartime's luxuries. He rose awkwardly when he saw Julia.

"Well, here you are, Miss Julia," Cook said. "You look as if you could do with a cuppa . . ."

Stella said, "This is Flight Lieutenant James Sinclair, Julia. I found him hanging over the gate, looking at the house. I could see he hadn't known the road ended here . . . He'd got a bus over from Sparrow's Green—just wandering. He's in a convalescent hospital there. I thought the least we could do was offer him a cup of tea."

"Yes . . . yes, of course." It was tradition to offer servicemen whatever hospitality could be afforded—especially those who wore the RAF uniform in this part of the countryside which had been so savagely fought over. But never before could she remember a serviceman wandering down what was really a private lane from Anscombe. There was nothing in Anscombe except the church, and a pub, which didn't open until five. He probably didn't even know that there was no bus back to Sparrow's Green that afternoon. He looked not only lost, but very uncertain.

"Had any luck with the shopping, Miss Julia? Your father will be glad to see you back. He heard some flack over the coast, and of course he's always expecting another . . ." Cook turned away and got the kettle off the Aga, making a fresh pot of tea. "Well, Sir Michael's out with Harry Whitehand, looking over the lambs, I dare say. Don't know if he really sees them, but at least it gets him out of the house, and away from that bloody—" She caught herself. "Away from brooding over the roses."

Julia noticed that Stella was swiftly laying a tray,

even laying a tray cloth, a nicety they hadn't bothered with for a long time. Delicate cups and saucers replaced the mugs. The plate of bread and butter, the jam pot, and the addition of some raisin scones, were placed on the tray. "Julia," Stella said, with the ease of one who had been giving her orders as long as she could remember, "why don't you and the Flight Lieutenant have tea in the drawing-room? I opened up the windows, since the afternoon was so warm. It's pleasanter there. And you can let Cook get on with supper . . ."

What was Stella trying to do, Julia wondered. It was one thing to ask a stranger in for a cup of tea, another to begin entertaining him as if he were a friend, or would become one. Julia dropped her packages on her chair. "Oh . . . all right," she said, and realized her tone sounded ungracious. She was remembering the glimpse she had caught of herself in the mirror of the draper's shop. How long had it been since she had cared what a man's gaze on her could mean? How long since she had been aware that her hair was lank and stringy, her face without a trace of make-up, her nails broken and chipped, her body too thin underneath the good wool skirt and sweater which were relics from that time when it had been possible to buy such garments. She felt some colour come to her face, and was furious that she could not control it. She tried to avoid all airmen these days. They might have flown over, and defended their house and land a hundred times—a thousand times—since the battles began last year, but she wasn't yet prepared for the sight of any one of them in the kitchen of Anscombe. Then she looked at him fully, and some instinct told her that this was no ordinary young man who had just strayed down their lane. There was something in those clear blue eyes that was not quite so innocent, nor so young, as his age might be. He had straightened himself to his full height—she thought he was about six foot, as if he was bracing himself. As she let her eyes stay on his face she saw the scar down his left cheekbone, saw where the line of his blond hair grew in a ragged way, as if a bullet had clipped it. She felt some shame at her churlishness.

Stella carried the tray to the drawing-room. The French doors, which had had only half their glass restored, the rest boarded up, stood open to the lawn, and the rose garden. The sun revealed the dust on the old, once-polished boards, but brought out the silken sheen of the rugs. Stella laid the tray on a low table. "There, Julia—relax for a while. I expect your father will be back shortly. I've set a cup for him."

The young airman had followed slowly, as if he too were reluctant to make this move. Julia noticed now that he carried a walking-stick, but did not use it; he had a barely perceptible limp.

"Please sit down." He lowered himself onto the edge of a sofa. He was facing the open French doors, and sunlight fell on his face. Julia began to realize one of the other things which had flustered and bothered her. He was astonishingly handsome, with classic features which even the scar on his cheek, on which she could now see the fading marks of the sutures, nor the ragged crease at his hair-line could mar. It was the sort of face, photographed in profile, which managers like to place on the billboards outside their theatres.

"Will you have more tea?"

"No, thank you. Have some yourself. You look—"

She gulped at the tea. "Yes, I know how I look. As if I've been dragged through a hedge backwards. One forgets so easily . . . how things were. The way one used to look, and the things one did to look that way."

"You look beautiful to me," he said, simply. "I don't find it easy to flatter people, Miss Seymour. Perhaps that's the Scot in me. I didn't come here to flatter anyone. I'd rather not be here. I didn't walk down that lane by accident. Walking that mile from the village was about the hardest mile I've ever travelled in my life. It's the extra mile no one wants to travel."

She put down her cup. "What on earth are you talking about?"

He gestured with his hand towards the rose garden through the French windows. "I heard about it. I heard someone talking about it in hospital. About your father making a rose garden. Things that people as famous as your father—and your mother—do, get talked about. One can't help hearing things. Even my mother wrote from Scotland. A small item about the rose garden in a newspaper, she said."

"Yes—I suppose it would find its way into newspapers," Julia answered, her tone stiffened with hurt. "They think he's mad, of course. They think he's become a crazy old man, trying to bury his wife."

"Not crazy," he objected. "Loving. Grieving. Trying to do something to replace death with life."

"And what's all this to you? Why is it so special? Plenty of people are grieving these days."

"I have my own particular grief. Shame, if you

want to call it that. I killed your mother, Miss Seymour."

Her hand flew to her mouth, trying to stop a cry of pain, of disbelief. "You—"

"Yes. My plane. The one I bailed out of. I thought I was clear of all the towns around. Just open countryside. Chances of falling on a building are pretty remote. If anything, the wood up there"—he jerked his head sideways. "It should have stopped it. I had plenty of time to survey the land as I walked down the lane. But when I bailed out at that height, I really didn't have much idea what would stop it. I couldn't see very well . . ." The faintest gesture, which he immediately checked, indicated the furrow above his left eyebrow. "We all hope, with a bit of luck, that the craft will carry on out to sea, and hurt nothing and no one. I had no such luck that day. Survived, that's all. But I brought death to one of England's greatest families. I tried a dozen times to write to your father. But I couldn't. It's impossible to write to say you're sorry you killed someone. That you've killed a great talent as well as a lovely lady. That you've brought grief, not just to a family, but to the thousands she didn't even know, but who loved her. I couldn't write it. I had to come."

"You *didn't* have to come." Julia rose abruptly from her chair, and went to the security of the open window, where she could keep her back to him. "We didn't know your name. Didn't want to. Your CO came over, as you'd asked, but he never said your name. We never enquired if you'd survived—the operations. I suppose we didn't care. You needn't have come. You *shouldn't* have come. It would have been better if you hadn't . . . I don't think any of us thought about the man who was involved. But I can remember . . . yes, I do remember my father saying to your CO, that it was better than the plane dropping onto Canterbury Cathedral—or a whole row of houses where it might have killed a dozen women and children. Canterbury—yes, that would have been worse for the nation. But we lost *her*. I wish my father hadn't said that. People say these things when they are in shock. Naturally, he said something rather theatrical. But if it gives you any comfort, then believe it. He did say it. But still . . . you shouldn't have come."

Behind her, she sensed that he had got rather clumsily to his feet. "For my own sake, I had to. Since I couldn't find the words to put on paper, I had to travel the extra mile."

She rounded on him. "Is it because it was Ginette Maslova? Because it was Michael Seymour's wife? Would you have gone to a demolished row of houses and got down on your knees? Would you have made a pilgrimage to Canterbury? No! You wouldn't! That plane would never have made it to the sea, and you know it. If you had stayed with it, trying to guide it away from everything, you would have been burned alive. It was your *duty* to bail out. We all know that. We need pilots more than we need civilians. You couldn't have controlled that plane. I *saw it.* I saw it from this window. The propellor had been shot away. The tailplane section was half gone. The engine ended up ploughing into that beech hedge—shot to pieces. We knew that. We saw it taken away. You survived to fight another day, Flight-Lieutenant. You owe no one any apologies. You don't have to share our grief.

In fact—" She lowered her voice. "We don't want you to share our grief. I wish you'd go away."

He picked up his cap from the arm of the chair, and reached for his stick. "You may be right. But I shared a lot of your grief, and my own guilt as well. Because I knew Ginette Maslova in other ways."

"What do you mean?—you knew her?"

"Please don't make the mistake of thinking that because I'm wearing a uniform I don't have any thoughts except flying. We become anonymous in this uniform. What if I told you that my mother took me twice, when we were in Edinburgh, to hear her play? That we have some of her recordings at home? A couple of my chums from Scotland who were with me at Oxford joined the RAF Volunteer Reserves the same time as I did—we were learning to become flyers before war was declared. I never believed in the Munich pact, so I got ready. Well, that last summer before the war I dragged these two up to London to hear your mother play at the Proms. Yes—they liked her—the whole occasion, but they couldn't understand why I wanted to hear a particular pianist. I couldn't understand my own fascination with her, either. I don't know a damn thing about music."

"It isn't necessary to *know*—it's what you hear, and feel . . ."

He responded to the softening in her attitude. "I only saw your father once—in *Hamlet.* I suppose he was great. All the critics said so. I just know I preferred listening to your mother play. You come of a very extraordinary family, Miss Seymour."

She was looking at him very closely now, as he stood in the sunlight. He couldn't have been more than in his early twenties, but he was a veteran; the scars of battle showed on his body, and in his mind, in the twisted sense of duty which had brought him here this afternoon. Her first estimate had misjudged him; his features were far stronger than those belonging to young men posted outside a theatre. The gash cut into his scalp was much deeper than she had first noticed. If he had been hit a little further down his brains would have splattered the plane. For the first time, to her shame, she saw that the skin of his hands was mottled, with strips of fiery red where skin must have been grafted. The skin still looked raw.

"Sit down," she said, her words coming in a burst. "For God's sake, sit down. Here . . ." She was pouring tea into second cups. "Drink it if it kills you. I suppose I need to talk some more . . ." With immense relief she saw him sit down again on the sofa, cap and stick went on the floor. She heard the cup rattle in the saucer as she handed him the tea. "Of course it's taken courage to come here. It wasn't necessary, and—"

"And it wasn't wanted," he interjected. "Perhaps I did it for myself—as a sort of act of penance. As if I ever could be absolved."

"It's not for us to grant absolution. I see you're wearing quite a row of ribbons. Your CO said you were one of the best."

"Just a serving member of the RAF, Miss Seymour. We're all the same whether we get medals or not. I believe, and so do all my chums, that some of the best of us go down, and get damn all in the way of recognition. Medals don't matter when you're up there. They guarantee nothing. You trust your squadron to protect you, and you do what you can to protect them. We didn't think about medals in the days when they were trying to take out the airfields last year—Goering's big gamble. It was our job to shoot them out of the sky before they shot us. We didn't think much about the people below, either. Couldn't. You went up there to bring down German planes. Up and down again. Refuel. Wait for the next lot. Until one was numb. Killing on reflex action. But when I heard about Ginette Maslova I felt I'd killed too often."

"Please—don't! We live with it. My father called it a necessary sacrifice."

"But how I wish it hadn't been I who did it." He paused. "I expect in about three weeks they'll pass me fit for duty again. So I felt I must come before that . . ."

She felt herself shiver. The afternoon was not, after all, so warm. "You think you might be killed, so you came here while you still could. You didn't have to go through this awful business. *We* would never have known. Shame on us that you had to make this journey. We should have made enquiries. One of us should have gone to see you in hospital. I think war makes us selfish and hard. My sister, Alex, says so. She writes about it. So does her husband, Greg Mathieson. Heroes and cowards—they're all mixed up. I think we've been cowardly in not asking about you. It was something my mother would never have forgotten, or overlooked. Why didn't we ask about you?—she would be ashamed of us . . ."

"Never," he said. "Not *that* lady. I only heard her play. Saw her on a concert platform a few times. I don't think she'd be ashamed of anything any of you did. She was too warm and human a person for that—at least, that's how she came over to me. It was my choice to come. None of you said a word of blame or accusation. Your father . . . even in those first dreadful hours, was forgiving. Understanding. I'll go back to duty feeling a little better. I've at least talked to you. I've seen the rose garden. I think it was my mother writing about the rose gaarden that forced me to come. She is not a sentimental woman—far from it. She didn't actually *say* I should come. But now she will know I've done—"

"What she thought was your duty?"

"No. For her it would be a very personal decision. All she will know is that I have travelled the extra mile."

"So she knows—about Mother? You were able to tell her?"

"When I found I just *couldn't* write to Sir Michael, I wrote to her about it instead. It helped a bit. Then she sent me the little cutting about the rose garden."

"The rose garden has probably been his salvation. It's the only thing he's done since—since she died. That, and drink. He looks on it, of course, as a memorial to her. It means far more than whatever words we'll finally put on a stone in the churchyard."

She saw the pain in his expression. She got up and went to sit on the sofa beside him. "I'm sorry. We all share it. She would have seen her death as no more and no less than any other woman's. She was very much aware that great talent is something that is visited upon one. In most cases it is the most terrible burden—something which has to be constantly lived up to." She felt herself, almost without volition, extend her hand to him. "We accept her death. Won't you?"

He took her hand as if it were something precious

she offered. His hand in hers had the feel of something mangled, both rough and smooth. She felt the stretched tightness of the skin between thumb and forefinger. "*Will* you be able to fly again?"

"They say so. In ordinary circumstances they probably wouldn't put a crock like me back into a plane. But so many of the experienced pilots are gone. Because I was in the Volunteer Reserve I was ready when we were sent to France—got experience there until we got thrown out. Not all my chums were so lucky—even if they were damn good flyers. Now they're sending up raw kids who've just finished a very quick training course. They go pretty quickly, poor devils. Some didn't, at the worst time, clock up more than a few hours' combat. They hadn't learned the tricks of how to dodge death."

She looked down, and realized she still held his hand. "I'm glad you did—so very glad . . ." She felt the colour mount in her face. She busied herself with the tea things. "Look, do try the blackberry jam. I picked them last September. The lane is always loaded with them!" Without his consent she covered a piece of bread with the jam. The blackberries had been picked when she herself had been seeking any sort of distraction she could after her mother's death, as her father had begun to toil at the rose garden.

"We're lucky," she went on, trying to cover his silence. "On a farm, one can always cheat a little. Butter and jam. Sometimes we feel ashamed—and sometimes we just don't care. I hate to admit it's cheating, but that's what it is. I suppose we've cheated in quite a few ways. My father served in the First World War, and he hasn't forgotten how things were. They say actors are not practical people—but he certainly could see this war coming a long way off. He was convinced it would come. I can remember him giving us loads of money—more than he could afford, I suppose, and telling us to stock up on warm clothes. He stocked the cellars until they wouldn't hold another bottle. Hoarding. That's unpatriotic—now. But not then, before war was declared. He couldn't bear the thought that any of us would go without—not if he could provide. It was especially important to him that my mother would have everything he could possibly provide for her."

She saw with satisfaction that he actually bit into the bread and jam. She found herself smiling at him, something that would have seemed impossible just short minutes ago. "You see, he suffered from father-in-law trouble. He resented the fact that, in the early years of their marriage, my grandfather Maslov was so much more successful than he was. My grandfather, being Russian, enjoyed throwing money around. He seemed to have especially enjoyed, my mother told me, being able to shower his daughter with things her husband couldn't give her. So as soon as my father *could* afford it—whether he went into debt or not—he just lavished things on her. On us girls as well. Nothing was too much. To this day, I still don't dare ask him about the overdraft."

He put the plate aside, leaned towards her. "You're very kind to me—Miss Julia. You're as kind and forgiving as he was—in what must have been his worst hours."

"I think there's little or no sense of hatred—or malice—in my father. He's a very human being, full of faults. Rash, impetuous, given to fits of temper which blow over. But hatred or meanness isn't in him. In neither of my parents. They were, I suppose naturally, quite a bit more temperamental than most people. Rows were everyday things. Blow ups! But that was all they were. They loved each other deeply. Forgiveness was part of both their natures. They would think poorly of me if I didn't feel the same way."

"Thank you. I cherish those words."

"Then please eat up my jam." She had to do something to cover the emotion they both felt. In talking of her parents, in talking of forgiveness, she felt she had made a long stride in that direction herself. A sense of calm fell on her; she had taken a giant step in the direction in which their lives had pointed. She could face whatever came in the future with a touch of their maturity.

"I remember," she said, and her voice amazed her with the dreamlike quality of recalling, "I was trying to learn *Cordelia* at the time I picked the berries, and getting the lines all mixed up, and wishing there was someone to cue me. I was thinking of trying to be an actress then. That's sort of slipped away—over the winter. It seems pretty frivolous now. I think I'll join up as soon as—when Father's ready to go back to work. It isn't frivolous for him to act. He's needed. I'm not. My middle sister, Connie, is in the WAAF. She's stationed at Bentley Priory. In the Operations Room," she added, with pride.

"Operations Room! . . . Those girls do one hell of a job there. We owe them a lot. Those and the ones who are fluent in German and man the radar stations along the coast, and listen to the Germans talking on their intercom. That meant that at the worst time, we were warned in advance, and were up in the air, waiting, instead of being sitting ducks on the ground when they came over. But then we owe it to the girls in all sorts of ways. They kept the tea coming, and the bacon and eggs. Women have nursed and babied me all these last months. I love women," he said, simply. "They're the greatest."

"Some of them are. We all think Connie is. She never talks about what she does. It's almost saint-like the way she keeps her mouth shut about the big-wigs who come to visit. No one would ever know from Connie that Dowding was in charge. She makes me feel more than a little ashamed at times. And Alex—she's been in the thick of the Blitz. You might have noticed her by-line in *The Record*. She got her job there because Lord Wolverton—we call him Old Woolfie—is a good friend. She started as a glorified tea-girl, and then they began to send her out to report society functions, and things like that. But when the men began to join up, the women were given more important jobs. You probably know her husband's name—Greg Mathieson?"

"Most people do. I've read his pieces, and listened to him on radio . . . oh, since Dunkirk, I suppose. Quite a hero, I think—although he doesn't blow his own horn. I even caught that broadcast he gave from Washington after he'd interviewed Roosevelt. I've tried to catch him whenever he's been on radio. I've listened a lot to the radio these last months—there hasn't been much else to do."

"There isn't much else to do here at night, either. Just read—and listen to the wireless. Father put the wireless in the dining-room, so he could listen to *his* sort of thing. Cook had always had her own set in the kitchen. She listens to all the entertainment shows.

Stella decides where she wants to be. She used to be our nanny, and then she began to be a sort of dresser to our mother—as you've probably noticed, she still bosses us all around. We can only keep the Aga in the kitchen going, and one fire in the dining-room. It's hard to remember how warm and cosy this house used to be. My parents always had their comforts whether they could afford them or not. My mother needed to be warm to practise. My father doesn't mind who knows that it was her money that paid for the central heating to go in. He's always called it the Brahms central heating. My grandfather, Guy, inherited a load of debts from *his* father, and the farm needed so much spending on it, there wasn't really much left over for luxuries. But I do remember fires in all the bedrooms when I was small—I suppose because we had so many of the farm worker's wives who were glad of jobs here at the house . . . oh, I'm running on. Life's changed for all of us, hasn't it? Do you think it will ever go back to being what it was?" Her tone was faintly wistful.

He shook his head. "I don't expect it will. God, I can hardly believe how young and raw I was when I joined the Volunteer Reserve. Flying was a piece of cake. Even out in France. Good fun. Then when we got back here, and we knew we were fighting for our lives—well, it wasn't fun any more, and I'm beginning to wonder if there'll ever be times I'd think of as 'fun' again. No . . . I don't think things will go back to what they were . . . no more than they did after the last war. Even the rich began to notice then that not nearly so many young women were willing to go into service for almost no wages. And not many young men were content to work for a landowner without the hope of ever working for himself. My parents found that out. My father had had to let out most of the land to tenants—he farmed as much as he could himself, but it was never easy . . ."

Almost automatically he handed over his cup to have it refilled, a gesture of trust and intimacy that warmed her. "We had fires too, I remember—and someone to tend them, but not nearly as many as we needed. Now—like you, my mother heats just two rooms. The kitchen, of course, and what, in grander days, used to be the housekeeper's room. She lives between those two rooms—she and the dogs and cats, and in the scullery she puts the odd lamb or two when the ewes won't take them. She's got one 'treasure'—as we used to call them. Janet. She almost grew up at the castle. She's a marvellous cook—and will turn her hand to almost anything. Occasionally they get a bit of help with cleaning, but precious little. And that's all she has to take care of a bloody great pile that variously dates between the thirteenth and eighteenth centuries—a Scottish castle, towers and all. She goes to bed up in one of the towers with three hot-water bottles, and three dogs who sleep on the bed for warmth."

"A . . . a castle? With towers?"

"A castle. Not a pleasant, warm, charming manor house like this. My father might just as well have been Thane of Cawdor. That's what the place reminds me of. Tall, and big and cold, with dungeons, not cellars, and a guard room with an earth floor, and a portcullis that's rusted into place. It's on a small island a wee bit out into a loch. There's a sort of causeway, and then three spans of a bridge, and a drawbridge that's half rotten. My mother's farming a couple of thousand acres, but a lot of it is hill farming —land which will only carry sheep. She's as tough as they come, and she looks too old for her age, and too tired to care."

"Where in Scotland?"

"Inverness is our town—city, if you like. Capital of the Highlands. She's the daughter of an earl, and she married a minor chieftain of our clan. Obviously for love, because it certainly wasn't for money."

"You don't talk about your father."

"I hardly remember him. He killed himself in a hunting accident when I was about four. He was out looking for deer—for us to eat, not for the pleasure of the hunt. Nobody could understand how he'd been so careless. He'd been used to guns all his life. Must have slipped, or something. They found his body in the bottom of a sort of ravine in the forest."

She began to understand his courage in coming here. "I'm sorry. You have brothers—sisters?"

"No, worse luck. I had a brother. He was killed when he was young. If there'd been someone besides me, my mother would have had more to spread herself on. But I was the only one—the one who had to take my father's place. I had to inherit. I think she once had the chance to marry again—to marry well. She was—still is, I suppose, a very handsome woman. But that would have meant leaving Sinclair. She would have had to turn over the management of it to someone else, and I wouldn't have grown up there. I was meant to grow up there, and eventually take my father's place. There's a very strong streak of Scottish feudalism in her. Very clannish. She nearly lost the whole bet the day my plane came down."

Julia shifted her cup uneasily. He was very blunt,

this young man. He laid no aura of romance over a turreted castle and an ageing woman who kept guard over her son's inheritance. "She must be thankful you're alive."

"Thankful is hardly the word. She *expects* me to stay alive. I have to come home to my inheritance. I have to take over from her. She wants me married, and with children. She's even got the girl picked out for me. She was angry when I went into the RAF before I married her. She was angry with me for not going home to the Highlands as soon as they said I was convalescent. It would have been an excellent time to begin to court Kirsty."

"Why didn't you?"

"I suppose I wasn't sure that was what I wanted. I wasn't sure Kirsty would want *me*. Something of a crock. And I was having thoughts, too, about whether it was fair to marry a girl, and perhaps leave her with a child, when I knew what my life in the air was worth—I think I'll wait until after the war before I chance making any woman a widow."

"And this Kirsty—will she wait?"

He shrugged. "Who knows? She's a great girl, full of spirit. Intelligent. She grew up in the country, and knows a lot about farming, which is why Mother wants her. And she has money. That would be useful. In Mother's view."

"And yours?"

He looked at her directly, and his mouth twisted in a rather bleak smile. "Perhaps that's what I couldn't quite take. She was *too* right. I think I could have had her for the asking, so there must have been something that wasn't right for *me*. We were good friends. Nothing more. I thought there should be more than that. So that's why I didn't go back to Scotland when they said I could go to a convalescent hospital. I stayed at the hospital at Sparrow's Green listening to the planes going overhead every night. I would rather have gone to Sinclair. In my own way I'm as wild about it as Mother is. I love that crazy old ruin. I love the country. Perhaps I was keeping away from Kirsty—or perhaps I was just being practical and remembering that I'd get this leg in working order sooner if I stayed where the weather would let me get some walking every day. The snow's pretty deep around Sinclair. It would have meant sharing the kitchen fire with the dogs. Not what the medics were advising."

So the winter of their grieving, Julia thought, had been the winter of his struggle back to life, with the thought that at the end of it would be a return to his squadron, and perhaps only a few more hours of life in the air left to him.

"So you decided you'd come here. In case there wasn't another chance."

"That's about it. I didn't know whether it was the right thing to do. I just did it." Once again he reached down for his cap and stick. "But I'm glad I came." He pulled himself up off the sofa, and held out his hand. "I think I'd better be shoving off. Taken enough of your time. If you feel like telling your father—"

"I don't think I will. He's never mentioned the pilot . . ." It was impossible now for her to associate him with that flaming missile which had come down and obliterated the oasthouse and wiped out her mother's life. He had a life of his own. A name. A personality. A background. "Just those few things he said when your CO came. Perhaps . . . much later . . ."

The warmth of the April afternoon had left them. The late sun now lay slantingly on the floor. She went over to close the French windows, wishing, for no reason she could name, that she could invent a reason for him to stay a little longer. At the window she stiffened. "Oh God—here he comes." She turned back to James Sinclair. "Don't say anything—not about her. *Please* don't!" She raised her voice. "Father—you're late for tea. Shall I get some fresh?"

"I'd love it, darling. I'm parched." He was walking towards them from the direction of the rose garden.

"Father, this is Flight-Lieutenant James Sinclair. Stella found him in the lane—rather lost. So she brought him in."

A broad smile lighted her father's face. "So Stella picked him up, did she? Brazen hussy . . ." He held out his hand. "How do you do, sir? I see why Stella picked you up. Gave you some tea, did they? Good. Well, you can stay and have another cup with me. Do go off and make it, Julia, dear. I'll just take the Flight-Lieutenant to see the rose garden."

"Well, really, sir, I think I should be shoving off. If I miss that bus from the village back to Tunbridge Wells—and the connection on to Sparrows Green, I don't think I'll make it back tonight."

"What—have they got you locked up somewhere? Hospital?"

"A convalescent hospital. They're pretty free and easy though. They encourage one to get out, when it's possible. They just don't want us lost or straying."

"Well, as a matter of fact, I don't think there's another bus back to Tunbridge Wells this evening . . ." Julia knew that her father would be the last person in the world to keep bus time-tables in his head. "But our steward, Harry Whitehand has to go into Tunbridge this evening—some frightfully important farmer's meeting—more food for the nation. I think some big-wig from Whitehall is coming down to tell them what's expected of them. So using the petrol's all right. Harry can easily make a detour to Sparrow's Green. So you can stay and have some tea with me. And Julia, bring in a couple of glasses and some Scotch, will you? We'll take it into the dining-room. Start the fire. But first I'll take the Flight-Lieutenant and show him the rose garden."

Her father turned away, and for a moment James Sinclair looked back at Julia with an expression of near-desperation. But she simply nodded, and indicated that he should follow her father. He had come to face this, and now he must face it. Her father's voice drifted back. "It's quite new. I just began planting it this . . . well, last autumn. Everything else's been turned into vegetable plots. This is . . . this is rather special."

He stayed, having tea again with her father before the newly lit dining-room fire, tea which her father hastened through so he could produce the whisky bottle, and pour generous measures for them both. Julia had murmured something about going out to help Cook and Stella. "Nonsense, my dear. I've just enquired about dinner—supper, I suppose we have to call it. Cook's got steak and kidney pie all made up—rather less steak and kidney than we'd like, but rather better than they're getting in the towns. And apple tart. She's sitting here with her feet up, knitting. I told her to put it forward a bit so Jamie here—" He had already dropped the Flight-Lieutenant title, "—can stay and have a bite with us. I've telephoned Harry Whitehand, and I had Jamie phone his convalescent place. They know he's all right, and will be delivered back to the door. So you can just join us for a drink."

Unhappily, she poured herself a weak gin and orange. There was now no way to warn her father, to tell him whom they harboured in their midst, whom he willingly and cheerfully invited to stay and eat with them. There was no way James Sinclair could escape the hospitality heaped on him. It was the convention of the times—all servicemen were welcomed and offered hospitality. James Sinclair belonged to that very special group which Winston Churchill had forever labelled "the Few" who had saved Britain in her most desperate hour. Julia's father had been able to read some of the coloured stripes on his uniform. One of them proclaimed that he had won the Distinguished Flying Cross and bar. Michael regarded it as an honour to give the best the house could offer to an authentic hero. She noticed that her father did not mention his own medal from the war that now seemed so far away.

She went upstairs to wash, and to change her clothes, something she scarcely ever bothered to do now before dinner. Generally she was just too glad to slump in front of the fire, wiggling her tired feet, at last freed of their Wellingtons, in the thick socks which Stella had knitted. But now, after she had washed, she powdered her face, put on a little lipstick, brushed out her hair, which surprised her by springing back to some life. She even used a precious drop of the perfume she still possessed. Her mother's dressing table held at least a dozen crystal bottles of different perfumes, but no one would have dared to touch them, or suggest they be used before they evaporated. Her clothes still hung neatly in their built-in cupboards. Her concert wardrobe, swathed in muslin had always occupied a small room of its own. It hung there, untouched. No one would have dreamed of suggesting to Michael Seymour, even in this time of rationing, that anything should be given away. Ginette Maslova's possessions, like the rose garden, were something he must be allowed.

She slipped back into the dining-room, and her father rose to pour her a gin and orange. He glanced at her in appreciation. She wore a scarlet wool dress she had not put on for almost a year; she had found it surprisingly loose at the waist. "Very nice, dear. Have I seen that dress before?"

"Probably dozens of times, Father. You don't think I bought it in Tunbridge Wells, do you? Nor can you imagine how many coupons I'd have to give up for it. By the way—I bought you a cardigan. That sweater's seen better days . . ." She didn't mention that his chest of drawers was crammed with cardigans and sweaters, all of them cashmere, and not for digging the rose garden in.

He looked down at the edge of one sleeve, which had ragged threads hanging from it. "Seen better days . . . I suppose it has." His features contracted, as if in a momentary spasm of pain. It occurred to Julia that this was probably the first time for many years that anyone but her mother had bought clothes for him. "Thoughtful of you, my dear. I'm sure you should be using the coupons for something pretty for yourself . . ."

"You did all that before the war, Father. What do you expect me to buy?—two pairs of large navy-blue knickers with strong elastic top and bottom, which is all that's on offer now?"

The spell of his self-absorption was broken. "No, Julia. Not that. I would hope not that!" He was busy filling up the glasses again. While she had been upstairs he had gone to the cellar and brought up a bottle of claret which was open on the sideboard. She recognized it as one of his better wines. Obviously James Sinclair had earned some appreciation from him. Julia and the airman exchanged a long glance while Michael was busy with the glasses. Silently he shook his head, indicating that he had said nothing about his involvement in her mother's death. The small, but vital lie they had contracted to act out was now a pact between them. When Michael said, "Well . . . cheers . . ." they looked at each other, then quickly away, as if the moment were too intimate and fragile to hold against the reality of what they had done.

Stella brought in the steak and kidney pie, and the apple tart together, and laid them on the sideboard. There was whipped cream and a generous slab of cheddar cheese. His face alight with anticipation, Michael poured the wine while Julia handed out portions of the pie. "How nice to have an unexpected guest," he said, raising his glass to James Sinclair. "Come back again, young man, before they put you up in one of those infernal flying machines. We'll look forward to it . . ."

Too soon for Julia they heard the soft honk of

Harry Whitehand's car outside. They switched off the lights in the passage, and saw James Sinclair to the door by the light of a torch. They ducked around the black-out curtain. The night was still, and the sky clear. Suddenly, over in the direction of Dover, and then all along the coast they saw the search-lights of the anti-aircraft batteries pierce the darkness, and the too familiar drone of the aircraft heading towards London. The guns had started their pounding, trying to pick the elusive specs from the sky. Then, closer to them, they saw the dim glow that told them incendiary bombs were dropping when planes had been stricken and had not the fuel to make their target, which was London, and were turning again to try to make their haven in France. "Doubt there'll be much of a meeting in Tunbridge tonight," Harry said.

Michael grasped James Sinclair's arm. "You'll have to stay, old boy. Nothing else for it. Plenty of room . . ."

Despairingly Julia felt herself dragged further into the vortex of their lie as Michael went back and happily settled himself before the fire, after producing a bottle of brandy. He had reached the point where he had begun to tell one of the myriad stories of the theatre, always somewhat embroidered, sometimes out of context, but always delivered with the wit of an unsurpassed raconteur, and in the voice and tone which had made him famous. He continued while Julia and Stella went to make up a bed. "Nice for your father to have company," Stella said. "It's too lonely for him down here. He misses company—it makes missing your mother that much worse. He should shake out of it and do something . . . Well, I mustn't pass judgement. We all have our ways. That's a nice young man. I wonder why he wandered down here? Young servicemen usually stick to the towns when they're allowed out."

"He said he wanted to get out into the country. He comes from a country place. Scotland, of course—the Highlands."

Stella was silent for a moment as she tucked the pillow into its linen case, her grey hair falling in soft wisps from the severe bun she wore. She had a once-pretty face, gently worn with time. "Well, we all have our reasons, don't we? I would say he's had a hard time, that young man. I don't know how bad the leg was, but that scalp wound came near to putting an end to him. No hair will ever grow there again. And his poor hands. Nearly burned to a cinder, they must have been. Of course Cook dotes on him already. I remember he just stood there in the kitchen door, after I'd invited him in, as if he wasn't certain he should come in. She took one look at him, and put the kettle on the stove. And I'm sure she was glad she had the pie all ready. Plenty to go round. Sensed your father would want him to stay." She was laying out fresh towels, and a pair of her father's pyjamas; she had brought out a new toothbrush. "We'll sterilize it after he's gone. Can't waste it. Now you run on down and keep them company." She placed fresh soap on the edge of the wash basin. As Julia opened the door Stella threw a few words over her shoulder. "You look pretty tonight, dear. Got a little colour in your face for a change."

At eleven-thirty Julia went quietly upstairs, having contributed nothing to the conversation between the two men—hardly a conversation at all, but just an audience which her father craved. The level of the brandy bottle steadily diminished. The bombers and their fighter escort seemed to have finished their runs over London and had headed back out over the Channel. With the light out, Julia drew aside the curtain in her room, smelling the sweet sharp chill of the April night. In a far pasture there was the bleat of a restless lamb. She could see the fires of Hastings, and the glow of the sky over Dover. Would they never stop coming? Would there never be an end to this nightmare? Would James Sinclair live only a few hours, or a few minutes when next he flew up to intercept them?

It was very early the next morning when she came down to the kitchen dressed in her corduroy pants and thick socks, ready to put on her Wellingtons and go down to help round up the cows for milking. Cook, as usual, was ahead of her. "He's gone, deary. He found out what time the early bus left from Anscombe, and said he didn't want to trouble us any more. Pity—he could have stayed here just as well as that dreary convalescent home. He said to thank you —and Sir Michael, of course. Your father was sound asleep when I took him his early morning cuppa. Looks as if he needs to sleep off last night."

Julia nodded, swallowed her tea and chewed quickly on a piece of bread, unable to say anything. What had she hoped for—a cheery breakfast with James Sinclair when the milking was done, watching him devour a plate of fresh eggs and their own home-cured bacon while they talked? Had she no imagination not to realize what misery last night must have been for him, trapped with her and her father, acting out the lie she had fabricated? Acting out the silence because he had not dared to break the interdiction she had laid against him saying to Michael Seymour the words he had come to say? She had denied him the absolution he had sought. He would have been glad to have the words said, even if they had evoked a cold dismissal by her father. Instead he had received warmth and hospitality, and she had made his weight of guilt all the greater. He had walked the extra mile, and her own naïve good intentions had rendered the journey and the resolve useless.

She walked the half mile to where the cows were pastured, calling to them, and watching them come at a deliberate pace, glad to hear her voice, needing to be milked. She thought that she would never be able to work the sheep this way—she had no command of a dog, and sheep were reckoned to be obstinate, if not stupid animals. She patted the leader of the herd as she came through the gate. "Hello, Primmie." She thought the cow turned her head at Julia's doleful tone. "Well, Primmie—I think I blew it. I'll probably never see James Sinclair again."

But they heard from him—a thank-you note from the convalescent hospital, a little stilted in tone. What else could it be, Julia wondered. Only two more weeks before he went back on duty, she thought, if he passed the medical exam, and, given the need of pilots, that seemed more than likely.

Then something else arrived. It was a weekend when Connie had leave. She had brought a young man down to Anscombe with her, Flight-Lieutenant Kenneth Warren. Although he wore the uniform of the RAF, he peered at them myopically through thick spectacles. "He's an aide to Air Vice Marshall Dowding," Connie had explained in her telephone call alerting them of her arrival. "Intelligence—that sort of thing." He was a tall, stooped, dark-haired young man, with a forgettable face, his features straight and undistinguished, as if they had been arranged for a dummy in a shop window. Michael had waited expectantly for their arrival at Anscombe station. He drove a pony and trap with some style, but little expertise, and his face wore a bemused look when they all arrived at Anscombe in time for tea. It was the first time Connie had brought someone home on her brief leaves. "Can't make it out," Michael almost whispered to Julia when Connie and Kenneth Warren were unpacking in their separate rooms upstairs. "He hasn't a word to throw to a goose. Looks like a bit of a goose himself to me. But we'll see . . . Perhaps Connie's sorry for him. Can't be all empty up top, if he's an aide to Dowding. But Connie . . . a gorgeous girl like her . . . I thought when she finally did break down and bring someone home, he'd be a real killer, like Jamie Sinclair."

Julia winced at the word "killer", and then smiled. "He's got hidden qualities, Father. And he's probably terrified of you. You haven't forgotten that you're famous, have you?"

He returned her smile, a little ruefully. "Does it matter, Pet? Well, we'll do our best by Connie. Make this a nice weekend for her chum, Kenneth. I don't even like his name. I wonder if he'd mind if we called him Ken?"

The conversation through tea and supper was wooden. Michael got little help with lowering the level of the whisky bottle, and no comment at all on the fine burgundy he opened. Brandy later was declined. Ken, as he allowed himself to be called, was tight-lipped about his work, and refused utterly to speak his boss's name. He did, however, offer a precise and good analysis of the aims and mistakes of the Allied Forces thus far in the war—as good, though not so colourful, as Greg Mathieson would have done. He also had some predictions for the future, especially the desert war that the British were now fighting in the Middle East. "But we are doomed in the Far East," he concluded, dryly.

"What do you mean—doomed?" Michael demanded, almost angrily. "Why, we haven't even got a war going there. No one can take Singapore from the sea. The Germans can't spread their navy that far. They're too busy blowing up our shipping in the Atlantic."

"When the Japanese come in—as they're certain to do—they will take the whole of the Malayan Peninsula. They will *walk* down through it. They will enter Singapore by the back door."

"Look here—better not let anyone hear you say that," Michael objected, alarmed. "It's a preposterous idea. And you're not supposed to spread gloom and despondency."

"I only say things like that when I think the company can be trusted not to repeat them," Ken Warren answered. "You did ask my opinion."

"Yes—I see. Well, an interesting idea," Michael said, groping for words. "I hope for all our sakes you're wrong."

Ken Warren didn't reply, nor did he appear apologetic. They had learned that he was the son of an accountant, had a degree from Cambridge and the London School of Economics. He had joined the RAF a year before war broke out, having correctly predicted that that was what would happen, and sure that by joining up early, he would find his right niche. He had always known that his eye-sight would bar him from active service, but they began to understand that in his quiet way, he could well have been an invaluable, and also an almost invisible aide to whatever chief he served. He had known that he was destined to use his mind, not his body, in the service of his country, and his masters, swiftly realizing this, had placed him where he could do exactly that. Connie had told them that his only brother had been killed at Dunkirk. His parents had been bombed out of their house in Hampstead, and now lived in cramped conditions with his aunt in a semi-detached in Putney. "He seems such an incredibly ordinary chap," Michael had commented to Julia when they carried the last tray of glasses to the kitchen, and rinsed them. "What on earth does Connie see in him?"

"Perhaps having grown up in *this* family, she finds someone like him a nice, undemanding change," Julia offered. "And anyone with half an eye can see that he worships her."

Her father grinned at her, and shrugged his shoulders. "You mean someone nice and 'unstagy'—no big temperament, no big scenes. Peace and quiet. Can't say I blame her, really. But next time it'll be someone different. Beautiful girl like Connie can just lift her finger and they'll come running."

"She hasn't shown much sign of lifting her finger in the past."

"There'll be others," her father predicted confidently. "You just see."

The post came next morning when they were all

assembled in the kitchen at the sort of breakfast Julia had hoped for with James Sinclair—eggs, bacon, toast with generous mounds of butter, three different kinds of preserves from the pantry where Cook stored them from previous years, cream with the coffee. Ken Warren helped himself in a way that earned beams of approval from Cook. His thin, stooped frame looked half-famished, Julia thought. She found herself urging more toast and butter on him, and won a warm look of gratitude from Connie. It was then that Stella brought in the post. A few letters, bills, and two parcels.

"What's all this?" Michael said. Both parcels were addressed to him. He opened the first, rather clumsily wrapped and tied. From it he produced a thick, navy-blue hand-knitted sweater, and a note from James Sinclair.

Dear Sir Michael,

My mother is an indefatigable knitter, and seems to think I get through sweaters at the rate I grew out of my pants when I was a kid. I have three of these already. With your permission, sir, I'd like to offer this for work in the rose garden. Please do accept. It comes with my renewed thanks for your most generous hospitality.

James Sinclair

"Well, this is a great present," Michael said, fingering the thick, evenly knitted ribbed garment. "I wonder how many coupons the dear lady spent on the wool. I really don't need it, but it would seem churlish to refuse it."

Connie reached over eagerly and took the sweater

from him. "Well, *if* you don't need it, I know Ken does. He lost all his civilian clothing when his parents' house was bombed. I don't think I actually insult her if I say that Ken's mother isn't much of a knitter. He could use it . . ."

Ken Warren turned scarlet as they all looked at the sleeveless pullover he wore. Inexpertly and loosely knitted, it seemed to hang on his bony body in thin folds. Connie held up the new sweater, measuring it against his shoulders. "Yes, that would do very well. Winter may be over, but next winter is on the way. I'm sure it would fit under his uniform. Who did it come from?"

Between them Julia and Michael told the story of the night James Sinclair had spent with them. "Well," Connie said, "that's pretty good work on your part, Stella. Sweaters like this don't come with every lonely airman lost in the lane."

"Nor this, Sir Michael," Stella said. She had been carefully unwrapping a very expertly wrapped and tied parcel—several layers of brown paper, hard to come by now, and beneath that, many layers of newspapers which grew progressively damper as she went to the heart of the bundle. The very first shoots of a fully rooted rose bush had not even withered in the days it had taken for the parcel to travel.

Dear Sir Michael,

My son has written of your most generous hospitality to him. In return I offer this from my very northerly garden. If it can flourish here, as it does, it surely will blossom for you in that much kinder climate of Kent. It is, by the way, a deep crimson in colour, somewhat like the velvet gown your wife wore in one concert she gave in Edinburgh which James and I attended. I realize it's now a little late for planting where you are, but I have left a good ball of earth, and trust it will take well in its new home.

Sincerely, Jean Sinclair

On the outside of the packing the return address read: Lady Jean Sinclair, Sinclair Castle, via Newton, Invernesshire.

Tears stood out in Michael's eyes. "How incredibly kind of her. Jamie must have told her about the rose garden." Gently he touched the severely pruned bush, felt the dampness of the heavy ball of earth about its roots. "She didn't say what its name is. Looks as if it's a reasonably young plant, from the pruning cuts. Could have a lot of years left in it." He put butter on the last of his toast hurriedly. "Well, I'll get at it at once. Can't let it dry out when she's gone to all this trouble." His eyes screwed up in concentration. "Deep crimson. I think I know just the spot for it—among a couple of pale ones where it'll show well. Deep crimson velvet . . . you know, I do believe I remember that dress. She used to keep it for places where she thought the concert hall would be cold. It'll be out of date now, of course . . . But it's probably still hanging up there in her wardrobe room. She could never bear to part with concert gowns. Some were for Tchaikovsky, she used to say, and some for Beethoven. I can remember a lilac chiffon one . . . she looked like a lovely iris in it. I think that was for Mozart . . ."

Connie said briskly, "Kenneth and I will give you

a hand, Father. We could go and bring a barrow of manure from the barnyard."

Michael blinked, as if he doubted Kenneth Warren had ever seen manure. "Yes, and I'll make a start on the hole. Make sure you get right into the heart of the pile where it's well rotted. And bring some straw for mulch around it." His face had brightened, anticipating this addition to his beloved garden. "Maybe we'll call it the Lady Jean."

They had their morning coffee at the group of teak pieces of garden furniture which Michael had placed at one end of the rose garden. They had once faced the old rose garden, and so had escaped the fire. He eyed his new prize, standing nicely erect, the soil firm about it, and swathed in damp straw mulch, to which the manure clung. He raised his cup to it. "I think she'll do nicely, even if it is a bit late in the season. I'll see that she's kept well-watered to get her through the first spell . . ." Julia had the feeling that Lady Jean Sinclair had somehow taken over a corner of a garden in Kent. "We should telephone that young man and ask him over. It must be terribly boring in that convalescent place."

Ken Warren's lips curved in the first relaxed smile Julia had yet seen, and his face was totally transformed; it spoke of a quiet, almost hidden humour, a pleasure in unexpected things. She felt herself warm to him. "Not before I escape with this sweater I hope, Sir Michael." He fingered the good, thick wool with a gesture of possessiveness with one hand, as he raised the other to put in his mouth the last of the three scones he had eaten. "I've grown very attached to it in these few hours. I hope the chaps in the mess don't mind the smell of manure. I shall tell them I've been digging for victory."

Michael returned his smile, and his expression seemed to indicate that he also just might find the saving grace of humour in this rather unlikely young man Connie had brought home. "I'd bet—what's his name—James Sinclair?—wouldn't notice. And if he did, I'm sure he wouldn't begrudge it."

Connie leaned over and placed another scone in Ken's hand, which he acknowledged with a nod before starting to eat it at once. "It isn't," he said, "that my mother *wouldn't* knit something like this for me— but she's . . . well, she's not very gifted along those lines. She's a very sweet lady, and I love her, but she isn't a dab hand at well—doing things. She's never learned to cook. Before the war, it wasn't necessary. My father took pride in the fact that he could afford help in the house for her. She's always been rather delicate, you see. My father . . . well, he comes from a rather humble background. He is old-fashioned enough to think he married above himself. He wouldn't marry until he could afford a house—a good house—for her. He worked like a dog to get himself ahead, and even launched his own firm. Starting out on . . . well, sort of a wing and a prayer. Then my mother's father died and left her *his* house. It was a big Victorian pile. Quite an undertaking for my father, but he thought of it as something she had been born to, so we all moved there. I think it broke his heart to give up that rather sweet little place we had in Henley—on the river. The house in Hampstead has a big garden—that meant employing a gardener, as well as two maids and a cook. They went as soon as war broke out, and of course they couldn't keep on Cook when they were bombed out. I think my father's deeply ashamed that she's living with his sister and her family in a pokey little semi in Putney. But it's handy to his office in the City. He wanted to send her to a guest house they used to go to in Cornwall, away from the bombing, but she's refused to go. My brother's death hit her badly. She clings to everything that's left."

"So do most of us, old chap. Your father sounds like a splendid fellow. Not afraid to take risks. I sympathize with him. An actor's life is not noted for security. It's one long search for a new role, and not even bread and butter if one doesn't come along. When I remember the early days . . . and the days after the war when I was trying for better parts . . . if it hadn't been for my father and Anscombe, my wife and children wouldn't have had a roof over their heads. *Her* parents were dead against the marriage. I think she must have loved me, or she wouldn't have chosen a penniless actor. Strange what marriages turn out in the end to have made good sense—almost against reason."

"Well . . ." Connie's tone was almost muffled. "I promised Julia we'd have a good turn-out of the linen cupboard." The dishes clattered noisily together. "Of course we're not *throwing* anything out. But you did tell Mother to stock up before the war, Father. There are some sheets that are starting to get thin, and Mrs. Whitehand would be glad to turn the sides to the middle . . . With three kids she's . . ." She paused, listening. "I do believe our sister, Alex, has arrived." She dumped the tray back on the table. "It is! It's Alex and Greg! I telephoned her before we left with just the faint hope that she might get here. And Greg with her."

They all rose expectantly. "I didn't even know Greg was back in the country," Michael said.

"He wasn't—until yesterday. Flew back in one of those Lend-Lease bombers Roosevelt is sending us. No doubt it'll be a great story. I wondered if he'd have thawed out by now—or have the energy to come down here."

Alex was driving, and she brought the car to the kitchen door. She and Greg started across the lawn to them. After kissing and embracing her father and sister, Alex was introduced to Ken Warren. Briefly, the same look of puzzlement that had greeted him last night crossed her face, to be swiftly erased. "So glad to meet you. Connie asked especially for us to hurry to get here. Greg just had time to file his story. We borrowed the car from *The Record*. Greg's dying for some sleep, but we have three days, and he'll sleep better here than in London." Stella was already bringing a fresh pot of coffee and scones to the group at the table. "We didn't have any breakfast . . . came straight from Fleet Street."

It seemed to Julia that Greg, in his rumpled war correspondent uniform, his eyes puffy from lack of sleep, looked infinitely older than when she had last seen him. She made allowances for the journey by plane across the Atlantic, the stop in the Azores, the cold of the aircraft, and fatigue, the necessity to file the story about what it was like to fly in one of the stream of bombers and fighters which had started after the Lend-Lease Act had been passed by the American Congress. But he had aged beyond that. He gulped the coffee eagerly, and even more than Ken

Warren, he grabbed at the scones. "Great—" he said. "Food and fresh air. God, I'm going to sleep like a log." He stretched out in the chair, turning his face up to the spring-time sun, reaching for another scone, eating it at a more leisurely pace. "Great to be back. Great to know something like this still exists . . ." He looked around the three women, and a slow smile spread on his face. "Lord, Sir Michael, you have raised a bevy of beauties here. I brought a few little bits and pieces from Washington. Strictly forbidden. You've heard of nylon stockings, I suppose? Well, now you're going to be the proud owners of three pairs each."

Connie looked down at her thick lisle stockings. "I wouldn't dare bring them back to barracks. They'd be pinched . . . But still, they *would* be nice for the odd evening out." She glanced quickly at Ken Warren. His expression registered blankness, as if he tried to suppress near panic. "Well, I'll *make* you take me out dancing one night. We'll go into the West End . . ."

"You know what a rotten dancer I am."

Connie sighed. "Well, a girl can dream, can't she? I'd like the Savoy, and a chance to wear nylon stockings for my birthday." She looked across at Greg. "Any more goodies?"

"Greedy, aren't you? There are a few more things. Lipsticks. A fancy sweater each, nice smelling soap, bath salts. I ran out of ideas then."

Alex put her hand across his. "Forgive me if I look like the cat who got the cream. He brought me the most gorgeous underwear I've ever seen—except for Mother's. My belated honeymoon present, he said."

Ken Warren was blushing violently, biting his lips.

"Well—Constance, if you'd really like a night out . . ."

"I just said I did, didn't I? I'll take a pretty dress back to the station, and hide the nylons." She ran her hands through her hair which, now released from her service cap and the tight roll that the services demanded, shone like gold in the sun. "Oh, Lord, sometimes I get so tired of being patriotic . . . I long to kick up my heels. Have a party—"

"Then, why don't we?" Michael said. "With you all here—I met Archy Alderson at the station yesterday. Billy and Ted are home for a few days. I'll fix it with Cook and Stella—all the best things we've been hoarding. A welcome back to Greg. A toast to my lovely darlings who've kept me alive since . . . since August." His voice nearly broke, but he hurried on. "Greg, you'll help me pick the wine. The best the cellar has. Alex, where did you put those jazz records. . . ? I haven't been able to find them." They understood that that night there would be none of Ginette Maslova's records played. But there would be music in the house for the first time since that fiery day in August. "We'll roll up the carpets in the drawing-room. Light a fire there. I'll go and telephone the Aldersons right away." He hurried away from them to the house.

Alex gazed after him. "Poor darling—is he really any better, Julia? Or is he just putting on a show for us?"

"He's better—in spots. He brightens up when there are people around. And then there are days when he's in such a black mood I'm afraid to speak to him."

"If only he had something to do. If only someone

would *push* him back into the theatre. Surely there will be something for him soon. The raids are starting to taper off. People are coming back to the West End. I'll telephone D.D. See what's happening . . . what's around. D.D. hasn't been down recently has he?—well, petrol's getting a bit scarce even for *him*. Old Wolfie asked me the other day when Father was going to come back. I said 'soon'. That's all I could say."

"The trouble is," Connie said, "that being Michael Seymour he can't just take any old thing. It has to be a lead in a *good* play. Rack your brains, Alex. He *needs* it."

Later that afternoon Michael tapped at Julia's door. "Darling, everything in the kitchen and dining-room looks very festive. I'm so glad you got out the best china . . . Cook and Stella are thrilled. Billy and Ted Alderson are dying to see you again—a bit of luck they're both on leave. And old Algy and Milly are delighted to come. I've been a selfish old brute, keeping you buried away here, with no young company—no boy friends. What happened to all the young men you used to go out with at RADA?"

"Well—they're in the services, naturally. Some of them write to me. Any rate, none of them were special. Just boys . . ."

"I'll try to make it up to you, Pet," he said. And for a moment his hand rested lightly on her cheek. Then he held out a muslin-draped garment he had carried over his arm. "Here . . . just as a favour for me. Wear it, if it fits. You're just her height, you know. Connie looks more like her—but you have her expressions, her movements . . ." Slowly Julia uncovered the gown of deep crimson velvet.

"Oh, I couldn't! Not one of her concert gowns! No one should ever wear any of them!"

"*You* should. Her daughter. Her beloved youngest—the baby of the family. Do it for me, darling. Tonight. It won't be an unhappy memory for me, I assure you. I'd love to see you in it."

Julia looked doubtful. "If it fits . . ."

"That's my darling. Tonight we'll be a family again."

Being a concert gown, it had been made on classic lines by Molineaux. The armholes had been deeply cut, with many folds, and sleeves which tapered to slimness at the wrists. All her mother's concert gowns had had to have deep armholes to allow her easy movement at the piano. Julia peered at herself uncertainly in the mirror. Had she grown an inch in the past year?—her father was right. The length was perfect. It was slightly large at the waist, but a long tie sash pulled it in. She had washed her hair that afternoon, and let it hang loosely on her shoulders. The lipstick from Greg was a good match. She smudged a little dark powder on her eyelids, as they had taught her at RADA. It wasn't quite Ginette Maslova who stared back at her, but it certainly was her daughter. She experienced a faint *frisson* of apprehension. Whatever her father said, she was playing a role. Tonight she was supposed to bring Ginette Maslova to life again. Some part of her rebelled against it; she couldn't—wouldn't do it. Not even for her father.

But earlier than she had expected, she heard the sound of car wheels on the gravel drive. Now it was too late to change, to say the dress didn't fit. She was made up for her role; she would have to go through with it.

She ran downstairs, knowing that she was the official hostess of the evening, expected to be there to greet their guests. Her father waited in the hall, looking almost as he had done before last August. He was freshly shaved and bathed, his dark hair gleamed, he wore a black tie with his dark green velvet smoking jacket. His face wore an expression of expectancy and pleasure, which heightened as he saw her.

"My darling—you are *beautiful!* Almost the image of her. I really didn't expect . . . Oh, Pet, what a joy for this old man." He caught her in a quick embrace. "She would be so proud."

The knocker sounded against the ancient oak door. But Julia heard no sound of mingled voices, as there would have been if the four Aldersons had arrived—instead, just the sound of a car being driven away. "What. . . ?"

Carefully Michael switched out the lights and drew back the blackout curtain. "Come in, dear boy. Come in!"

A tall shape moved around the curtain, and the door was closed; her father put the lights back on. "Very good of you to have me, sir. Good of you to send the car . . . it's a great treat. I was going to Scotland early tomorrow, but my mother won't mind an extra day's wait. Not when I tell her . . ."

Michael was moving ahead of them into the drawing-room, bright and scented with the sprays of hawthorn Julia had taken from the hedgerow, warmed with the fire. "Come along, dear boy. What will you have to drink? Other friends are coming—two of their boys on leave. And my family around me . . . Just like old times . . ."

James Sinclair, walking now without his stick, managed to halt Julia before they entered the drawing-room. His face was anguished. "I almost said 'no'. Almost said I was leaving for Scotland tonight. I thought I just couldn't face him—or this house again. But I came—because I had to see you."

Michael was waiting for them by the drinks tray. "What shall I pour you? Nice we have these few minutes together before the others come down. Harry Whitehand was delighted to go and fetch you. We've seen enough of the war around here to know what we owe to you lot. A little petrol won't be missed in a good cause. Now tell me—what do you think of my Julia? Doesn't she look marvellous? You must tell your mother that we brought out the crimson velvet gown to honour the rose she sent, and her memory of my wife."

"Beautiful, sir. Beautiful. Very much like your wife. I've never forgotten *her*."

Michael turned his back, as if he needed a second's grace to control his feelings. "Will it be Scotch?" he said. "You're right. No one could forget her . . ."

The evening progressed as Michael had wanted it. Everyone exclaimed over Julia's appearance, and made her realize that in their eyes, before this, she had seemed hardly more than a child. They examined her with new eyes. She sat at the opposite end of the table from her father. The pâté, made from scraps in the larder was marvellously successful; there was leg of lamb, accompanied by Nuits St Georges, *pot au chocolat* was rich with cream and real chocolate. The Alderson twins, Billy and Ted, were both lieutenants in the army, and on embarkation leave. "Can't be anywhere else than the Middle East," they said cheerfully. "Could stand a bit of real sun . . ." They threw themselves into the spirit of the world they had hardly glimpsed before leaving school, and which they didn't understand would never return again.

James Sinclair danced with Julia, his foot movements slightly awkward, but his arms and hands expressively warm and close. "You smell like a rose," he said, his face brushing her hair. And then, "I thought I could never come to this house again. I thought I could never face him. But I'm deeper into this lie. But I couldn't help it. I had to see you. I made my mother send that rose bush. God knows what she really thinks about it all . . ."

"We've got to forget that we ever knew," Julia said. "It was an unknown plane that came down, and the pilot was saved. That's all we know. That's all we remember . . . from now on, that's all we'll remember."

Michael had had Stella secretly prepare a room for James, and he stayed the night. He left the next morning to catch a train from Anscombe station to London, to change there for a train to Edinburgh, and on to Inverness. Stella urged a large breakfast on him, and Cook had prepared sandwiches, fruit, and a wedge of cake. "No knowing how long train journeys take these days—what a long way home, young man. Stella showed me on the map." They, all of them, including Stella and Cook, gathered at the door when Harry Whitehand drove the car around. There were handshakes, good wishes. James Sinclair looked as if he wanted to bend and kiss Julia, but he had never kissed her, and would not do it for the first time before an audience.

"You'll be posted back to Hawkinge, I suppose," Michael said. "It's only round the corner, more or less. Let's not lose sight of you. Julia and I will be here . . ."

They waved him off. Julia had thought of going to the station with him, but that would have proclaimed feelings of which she was not yet certain. But she felt a wrench of loneliness, of depression, tug at her as they returned to the breakfast table. She helped Stella fill the cups with another round of coffee, urged more toast on Ken Warren, which he eagerly accepted. Cigarettes came out. Michael did not smoke, because he was afraid it might affect his voice, and Julia followed his example. Ginette had not smoked; she had so disliked the nicotine stains on her father's fingers, and she thought cigarette holders affected. Julia had once or twice seen Connie puff awkwardly at a cigarette, as if she regarded it as something which made her seem older, but Julia noticed that now she did not, and she guessed it was because Ken Warren did not smoke. Greg and Alex very nearly chain-smoked, in the fashion of most journalists. Chairs were pushed back. The warmth of a sunny May day drew them to the garden. As Julia and Connie helped Stella with the dishes, short stabs of conversation drifted through the open window. "Those Alderson boys . . ." Greg's voice. "Going off to war as if it was going to be some lark . . . It's no joy out in the Western Desert."

"No sense of history," Michael said. "Haven't they read anything about the First World War? That's the way we went then."

"They haven't been blooded," Ken Warren said. "If they'd ever been in France . . . But then, who am I to talk? I'll probably never be near the front lines, no matter where they send me. I'll always be at my boss's side, getting on with the paperwork."

"Someone has to," Greg interjected. "And don't think that behind the lines is always safe. You've been in as much danger at Bentley Priory as anyone who's seen out the London Blitz . . ." The talk drifted to possible theatres of war. Ken stuck to his argument that Singapore was a target, and that the Japanese would eventually come through what were believed to be the impenetrable jungles of Malaysia. Greg gave him some sharp arguments—the need for the battleships to remain in the Atlantic and not being needed for the defence of the Far East. "But I give you that there's lots of talk in Washington that the Japanese will give it a go, despite all their reassurances to the contrary. But to go through Malaya . . . well, that's a bit far fetched. They'd have to have huge land forces, and fight off the American Navy . . . If they try . . . Well, the only good thing would be that it would bring the Americans firmly into the war . . ."

Julia and Connie went upstairs to make beds and tidy rooms. It never occurred to either of them that Alex might come and help. She was no longer totally part of a woman's world; she had moved beyond it. It was her right to sit outside with the men and argue the possible ebb and flow of war. "I've never even heard her mention a ration book," Connie said. "She's always so well-dressed . . . or she can make herself *seem* to be. She and Greg are well matched, aren't they? I sort of feel she could go anywhere with him. Almost do his job . . . Alex has toughened up, and she's growing away from us . . ." They heard again the voices on the lawn as they moved into the room Alex and Greg shared. "Oh, God," Connie burst out. "I do wish they'd stop talking about the war. I'm sick and tired of it. Last night was such fun, wasn't it? Almost as if the war had never been. Except Mother wasn't there. But you looked marvellous, Julia. For a second . . . when I saw you, I almost believed she had come back. What a strange, but rather beautiful idea of Father's . . . He likes James Sinclair, doesn't he?" She said the words with no particular emphasis, though she might have asked it directly of Julia.

"It seems so. But then, he likes anyone who turns up and gives him a few hours of conversation, and takes his mind off . . ."

"Did Stella really pluck him out of the lane?" Connie asked. She was holding up against herself the silk crêpe-de-chine nightgown Alex had tossed on the bed. "I suppose this is one of the spoils of Greg's trip . . . Very sexy, isn't it?"

"Yes, of course she found him there, and brought him in. It was a lovely afternoon, and he was just riding buses around the country. He just happened to get off at Anscombe and he wandered down the lane." She was further into the lie.

"He's terribly handsome," Connie said. "And a hero. Poor Ken. I think he feels quite swamped by all these glamorous people around him. I had the hardest time persuading him to come. I think if he'd dreamed that Greg and Alex would show up, he'd have backed out."

"He seems to be holding his own pretty well," Julia observed, laying the precious nylon stockings Alex had dropped on the floor across the arm of a chair, giving the last pull to straighten the bedspread.

"Oh, he's not a dummy. It's just that . . . well, he doesn't seem to know how nice he is . . . once you get past the thick glasses and the scholarly stoop. I thought it was so touching what he said about his father and mother. He'd be just the same with any woman he married. Always looking after her—wanting to give her the best."

Julia looked at her sharply. "Is that what you want, Connie? Do you want to marry him? Does he want to marry you?"

"Good God! He'd never dream of mentioning marriage. Certainly not yet . . . not before we'd known each other much longer. And I don't think he'd ever marry as long as the war goes on. He wouldn't want to think that he could turn a wife into a widow—or God forbid, there would be an orphaned child."

"You love him?"

Connie avoided her gaze. "I don't know. I think if he asked—"

"Oh, Connie, you're the best of us three. You're beautiful, and kind and sweet. There have to be other men you'd look at. Someone—someone a little more exciting."

Connie turned from the dressing table, where she had been wiping up some of Alex's spilled face powder. "Exciting!" Her face was flushed, her expression almost angry. "Don't you think we've had enough excitement in this family? Our grandfather Seymour was the only sane man I ever knew when I was growing up. Everything else was chaos. Quarrels and rows and make-ups. Lavish presents, and always the bills that couldn't quite be met. Grandfather Maslov behaving like every stage Russian even Father could think of. The ups and downs—the swings and roundabouts. I've seen it all, Julia, and so have you. Alex is starting down just the same road. I hope I don't . . ."

"What about me? What do you think will happen to me?"

Connie shook her head. "I have no idea. Father is dragging you behind him, and *he* doesn't know where he's going. You'll have to break loose, Julia. Somehow. He won't come out of his dream reverie about Mother until someone shakes him out of it. Julia, you have to watch out—think of yourself a little. Perhaps it was a mistake to wear that dress last night."

"It was a mistake. I *know* it. Perhaps I'll join one of the services. But it seems so cruel to do it abruptly. And if I discuss it with him, he'll try to talk me out of it—"

"Hey!—you up there. You two chambermaids." Alex's voice reached them from the garden below. "When you can drag yourself away from your gossip, drinks are served." She stood on the lawn with a tray of bottles and glasses. From the kitchen drifted the smell of rabbit pie. It could have been any peaceful Sunday in the country.

After lunch they went their own ways—Alex and Greg to their room—"Got to catch up on some sleep," Greg said. But before they slept they would make love, Julia knew. Connie and Ken Warren set off to walk the country lanes, fragrant with Maytime blossom. Michael dozed over a book in the drawing-room, the French windows open to the view of his rose garden. Julia experienced a terrible sense of aloneness. She pictured James Sinclair on his long train journey north, a journey to see his mother and his home before he went back into active service again. She went to her room and lay on the bed—like an old woman, she thought, having her afternoon nap. From Alex's and Greg's room she heard the stifled sound of laughter—the laughter of loving friends. Hard not to feel envy—even jealousy. She buried her face in the pillow, thinking of James Sinclair. Time soon to go down and help Stella make tea. Cook had the afternoon and evening off. Cold lamb and baked potatoes for supper. After tea she would go and bring the cows in and help Harry Whitehand with the milking. There was always the milking . . . and the dozens of other chores that made up her day. And when they were all gone, there would be her father alone again, retreating to his silence and his drink. Her hands clenched in futile revolt. How much longer could she stay here like this? James Sinclair could be killed, and she might never see him again. Did he think of her as he journeyed northward? How infinitely remote and far away that Scottish castle seemed to be. He would be lost to her behind that portcullis rusted into place; he would cross a rotting drawbridge to a world where she could not follow. Uncharacteristic tears slid silently down her cheeks.

She did not see the Rolls because she crossed to the kitchen door from the milking parlour, but there was a bustle within the kitchen from Connie and Stella which alerted her that something had happened. And down the passage from the drawing-room the sound of the voices reached her. Not the somnolent early evening voices, when drinks were just being poured, but animated voices.

Connie jerked her head in the direction of the drawing-room. "He's come."

"Who's come?"

"D.D. Don't you recognize the voice." Julia saw for the first time that D.D.'s driver sat at the big table; he was drinking tea and munching scones contentedly. He grinned at Julia, and half rose to his feet. "Miss Julia," he said politely.

"Go in," Connie said. "He's been asking for you. Stella and I are getting together some supper—and a few extra touches. There's plenty of pâté left over." D.D. was a noted gourmet. Her father's stock of precious wines would be raided further, Julia thought as she hurried along the passage in her thick-stockinged feet, having shed her Wellingtons in the kitchen porch.

"D.D.!"

He got heavily to his feet. "My child! So good to see you!" He embraced, and kissed her on both cheeks. His Hungarian accent was still strong. Julia privately thought that he cultivated it as part of his flamboyant style. "And what part are you playing now, darling? Is it Rebecca of Sunnybrook Farm? Or Heidi? No, too old for that. Is she one of those Russian servants from Chekhov? What do you say, Michael. Are there, or are there not, hayseeds in her hair?"

"Don't tease, D.D. Julia's been doing her share around the farm—like everyone except me. All I've done is make a rose garden."

"Then shame on you, Michael, for letting this rose grow wild! Have you never heard of cultivation, my friend!" The bulky figure in his expensive suit stood back from Julia a little, but he kept one hand on her shoulder. "Unpruned, untended, she will straggle into thin shoots running off in all directions, with hardly a bloom to be seen. For heaven's sake, she could even go off and marry some farmer, and then the theatre will have lost something precious."

Julia felt a flush invade her face, and sense of anger rising. "For heaven's sake, D.D. I haven't even finished at RADA yet. The theatre's lost nothing but another clumsy ingenue. If the theatre still exists . . ." She went and gratefully took the glass of Scotch which Greg had poured for her.

D.D. shrugged, and resumed his seat. "The theatre will always exist, child. We old hands know that. And it must have its fresh blood. For the actors, the producers, the directors—always the lure of just one more curtain rise, one more production that might mean fame and fortune. Like children we are—I acknowledge. Always playing our games. But what a splendid game it has always been. Such risks—such chances—and such rewards!" He raised his glass to her solemnly. "But you are both blooming and running wild at the same time. Don't wait too long, Julia. You should have been on the stage long before this. You've not been blooded by even a one-line walk-on."

"Not my fault," she muttered into her glass, wishing someone else in the room would help her. "With what's happened in our lives . . . the theatres closed, and half the West End in ruins, or so they tell me. Where would I get a one-line walk-on, to start with? I haven't been wasting my time," she added defensively.

"Nor has she," her father said, at last trying to come to her rescue. "The times are hardly normal, D.D."

"Nothing is normal, and it never has been. There will never be the perfectly right time to do anything. We have traditions and a culture which must be kept alive, no matter what. That is what our Prime Minister believes. We will carry on—no matter what happens. Already, since the bombing is less, the people are coming back to the West End, hungry for what the theatre can offer them. Escape from the grimness of their lives. They want—no *need*—the play to go on. What a propaganda coup for our enemies if the theatres should be permanently dark for the duration. It would be conceding a defeat where they have no victory."

Julia sipped her drink. "You're right. Of course you're right about that. I just don't see what it's got to do with me."

The big man's shoulders went up in another exaggerated shrug. "If you and Michael choose not to hear me, darling . . ."

"Well, you haven't *said* anything yet, except that I'm going to seed." She looked around the others assembled in the room. Alex rigidly controlling her expression, so that her handsome face was unnaturally cool and uninvolved, Greg smoking and watching as if some new, amusing game was being played out for him to watch, Ken Warren determinedly staring at the carpet, his shoulders hunched over the glass held with both hands. She suspected he wished he were anywhere but here.

"Well, darling, I have this little idea . . . no, I have this *big* idea. I want Michael back with me. He owes me a production, since he walked out on the last." He raised a hand to stifle any protest that might come. "All right. The circumstances were understandable. What is not understandable is that he should betray such a wonderful wife by letting his talent, like yours, Julia, go to seed. I propose to him something. He turns it down. He turns it down, not only for himself, but for you. I find such selfishness hard to forgive. Almost cowardice –"

Greg cut in. "That's a bit strong, Mr. Davidoff."

The big, fleshy face turned to him. "And what do *you* know about it, Mr. Smart Guy! Go and interview your Presidents and Prime Ministers, and leave those who know *this* end of the business to run it. If I say 'selfish'—if I even say 'a coward' that is what I mean."

"*What* do you mean?" Julia demanded. "What do all of you here know that I don't?"

"Only, darling, a lovely idea I have, and which Michael rejects out of hand. Not just for himself, but for you. I come here to him to say we are reopening the St James' Theatre. A bit bomb shaken, a bit dusty—but usable—perfectly usable. I propose to him that he make his return to the stage in one of his greatest roles, and that you should play with him."

A coldness engulfed Julia. She gulped at her drink, and started to choke. Tears streamed from her eyes. "Need I say that I propose to open with *Lear*, with Sir Michael Seymour starring?"

"And me?" Julia managed to gasp out between her choking breaths.

"You? Why my dear, you'll play Cordelia, of course. Who else?"

Julia put her drink on the low oak stool beside her. "You're mad, D.D.! I've never set foot on the stage professionally, and you expect me to play *Cordelia!* I'd be laughed off it. I'd disgrace Father. What a field day the critics would have. You said it yourself. I haven't even had a one-line walk-on yet."

"And what will you do instead? Spend your life here? You and Michael together. Marry your farmer. Or grasp your chance—which I think is your destiny. What actress in history has ever played Cordelia to her own father? I tell you, it will be a sensation! What a return for Michael. What a chance for you!"

"A chance I can't take. A chance to be laughed off the stage." She swung to face her father. "You were right to say 'no' for me. But not for yourself. Someday you must go back. If D.D. thinks *Lear* will be wanted at this time, then you must do it. You must do *something*. But you don't have to carry me on your coat-tails. In time I might be able to do something on the stage. I've always dreamed of it, and meant to work hard to get it. But *this* is preposterous! Fail or succeed, I'll have to do it on my own." She turned to look at each of them. "Can you imagine Father's return to the West End ruined by the amateurish performance of his daughter? I would be glad to take the humblest role at the Old Vic if they'd have me, but I won't let my father be made a laughing stock of—they will call him a fond and foolish old man for staking so much on an untried actress. Even worse that it's his daughter."

"Understudies have stepped into roles and become famous overnight." D.D. neglected to name one.

"Understudies have the indulgence of the audience. I would meet only the critics with their knives out. You'd literally be throwing me to the lions."

With an air of great sadness D.D. took up his drink. "I thought you had more in you, Julia. You refuse this challenge—this *great* chance, because you lack courage. You have been a good and dutiful daughter, helping her father through his most tragic hour. Now I see that that is *all* you have been. It is easier to stay here, going to seed with him, than return to the world.

"Yes, my dear, the world is hard and cold. It is tough. Who ever said different? It will be tough no matter what you do. Who needs the easy path? Go—join the Old Vic, if they'll have you. Do your walk-on parts, and know what a coward's heart you have. Or will you stay and live with your father in his retreat, which is a shameful waste. But you will not venture out for him . . . oh, come, I am ashamed of you. You—like a daughter to me. My very own idea of what Cordelia should be. But I have been proved wrong. You have not Cordelia's love, nor her courage. I am mistaken, after all. You are a pale image of Cordelia. Not her stuff at all.

"Tell me, my dear, why did you bother to go to RADA at all, if you don't know what chances you must take? I am willing to employ you, at a beginner's salary. It will be merciless on you. There will be no charges of nepotism, even if I do regard you like a daughter. Can you imagine someone like Julian Tredwell agreeing to direct this production if he thinks a rank amateur is going to ruin it for him? Your own father will train you—you will be, *are*, Cordelia. You have shared his pain and his sorrow and exile, and become a woman because of it. Go out and show the world that it is so. Prove you are no coward. If Ginette Maslova sat here she would urge you to take this chance. I knew Ginette. I knew her heart and soul. A child who first faced an audience at twelve years of age, under the baton of that old tyrant, her father. Are you her daughter? Are you Michael's daughter? Or are you some changeling left on their doorstep? If so—well, then you'd better wait until someone is ready to do *A Midsummer Night's Dream*. But don't expect to play Titania. You might be offered the role of a fairy in her entourage. You disappoint me, Julia. I thought you were made of different stuff. You are letting down both your father *and* your mother."

Julia looked around all the faces again, only Ken Warren avoided her gaze. She now read Alex's expression more truly. Did it say, "I dare you?—I dare you to go out into the world as I did—to grow up." And Greg Matheison, man of a thousand encounters, worldly wise, a shrewd judge of character and of a situation. Was he sitting there, as he had sat at the ringside of so many spectacular events, waiting to see if this little, quite unimportant domestic tangle would sort itself out? Had she really grown into a woman, as Alex and Connie had? Last of all, her father. Here she expected support for her arguments. He knew the theatre through and through. He knew what misery could lie in wait for her, the beguiling trap she might let herself walk into. Surely he could see for himself how D.D. was playing this? Even if he was throwing her to the lions of the critics, he must surely know that D.D. would reap a tremendous publicity coup. Success or failure, she would be written up in every newspaper and magazine. Success might please their friends, her failure would give satisfaction to so many of those who envied Michael his success. It was unfair to be compared to both father and mother at the one time. Not even Alex had had to experience that. Connie had shown her courage in her own way.

But what she saw in her father's face was not the determination she had expected. D.D. had said Michael had already declined, but she suspected it had only been a faint protest. He wanted her to do this thing which could destroy her. He *needed* it. He needed a reason for going back to what he had been born to, but since last August he had lacked the will to face it. She saw it now. She would be there, with him, as she had been with him all these months at Anscombe. She would be both his Julia, and his Cordelia. Ah, but D.D. was clever—and cunning. When it came to the storm scene, she would truly be Cordelia. Her father needed her to help him back. He would lean on her, and rant against the storm, and the unkindness of fate and ungrateful children. It didn't much matter what she did, *he* would triumph. He would grope his way back to his old world, and he would lean on her all the way. And she would support him.

"Father? What do you think?"

Carefully he rose and went to the tray to refill his glass, so that he did not have to face her. "It's up to you, Pet. I don't want you to do something you don't feel you're ready for. But I can't stand in the way of a brilliant chance . . ."

There, that was it. If she didn't go with him, he would stay behind with her. He would go only if she did. It was he who was throwing her to the lions, the lions now being her conscience.

"Well, if you think it can be done . . . If you really want to take this chance with me . . ."

The tension visibly relaxed, as if a collective sigh had escaped them all. Greg lifted his glass to her, and came out with a phrase he must have collected somewhere in the world. "Good onya, mate."

She gulped the rest of her drink, and mutely held out her glass for more.

3

THE weeks that followed—the nightmare weeks Julia forever labelled them in her mind—went by in a blur of work, tears, and the all-pervasive smell of dust. Sometimes she woke from a few hours of sleep, sleep disturbed by nightmares of apprehension—to find the dust choking her, and she was back again in the hours and days that followed her mother's death. It was a different sort of dust—dust mingled with the ancient soot of a city, as if someone constantly stirred the embers beneath a devil's brew pot. After seventy-six consecutive nights the bombing lessened, and the last major raid on London had come on May 20, 1941. After that the raids were spasmodic. The Germans had failed in their attempt to break the spirit and morale of the people, but harassed them intermittently, so that an air of uncertainty hung over a tired population. Exhausted people went about their work with grey faces and half-alive expressions, living in make-shift accommodation, still taking to the shelters at night, not believing that the raid they had come to think of as inevitable would not come. In June the Germans had broken their pact with Russia and turned their forces eastwards, so the pressure on Britain was eased; most people would not believe they were now allies of the Russians. They only knew that they went about their jobs and their work. They produced more and more aircraft. They listened to news of their armies in the Western Desert, listened to news of the shipping sunk in the Atlantic trying to reach a nation which could not feed itself. They counted those numbers against the numbers of German submarines reported sunk, and the figures did not make sense. They shook themselves slowly from the apathy and shock which was the aftermath of the Blitz, and did not know whether to trust what their leaders told them—that they would, in the end—prevail, and would not go under to tyrany, or whether their exhaustion was just the dying gasp of their whole endeavour.

Julia began, privately, to think the whole exercise D.D. had dreamed up was totally mad. She saw the devastated city, and wondered who on earth had the will or the wish to fill its theatres. Whether she did well or badly in D.D.'s scheme seemed hardly to matter now. Who would be there to see it? And yet she put their flat to rights; miraculously untouched except for some shattered windows, learned which shops she must register at for food rations, and went through the motions of an opening of *King Lear* planned for July. She went before her former teachers at RADA—those who were too old for call-up, or were female—and read, rather than played her part. She still didn't know it perfectly. They passed her out "with merit". Did they have much choice, she wondered. A student with a ready job guaranteed, the daughter of Sir Michael Seymour, protégé of David Davidoff, she would not have been failed unless her work was atrocious. With them, also, there burned the need, as D.D. had said, to keep the theatre alive. It was their own life's work, their own effort. They did it along with all the other duties that life entailed —the alternative nights as air raid wardens, their work with the St John's Ambulance, the Red Cross, the sheer drudgery of their day-to-day living, the necessity to keep going. As Julia did her half-playing, half-reading before them, prompted by her father, she wondered if some of them were not asleep there in the darkness beyond the stage.

With Michael she attended a number of plays, amazed at the audiences they attracted. Tired people in their office clothes mingled with the no less tired who had dressed for the occasion. She had dinner at the Savoy with Alex and Greg, and realized that half of the dining-room had been partitioned for diners who could not get home that night, and would sleep there. The cellars of the hotel were available as an air raid shelter. All around her she saw the law of the austerity meal which must cost no more than five shillings being flouted—the extra was simply added to the wine bill. It was at the Savoy they had their dinner with Greg and Alex, Connie and Ken Warren, which Julia sensed was their leave-taking. Greg said nothing, but Alex's air of apprehension and heightened gaiety betrayed that another parting was imminent. "Do you remember our wedding-reception here?" Alex said. "Father and Mother thinking I had made a dreadful mistake, but putting a good face on it." She smiled across the table at Michael. "You were wrong, of course, and I'm still thankful you made a jolly occasion of it. It's something I'll always remember." Around them, other diners became aware that the table was occupied by the Seymour family. It was the first time, since the memorial service, that Michael Seymour had been seen in public. Julia saw how the occasion revived him—the very fact of being back in the city which had given him the motivation for his work, given him fame, had at last touched in him the tap root from which he drew his strength to live and to go on. Julia began to understand even more deeply that whether she did well or badly as Cordelia, her consent to play with him, to continue her support, would be his salvation. The fact that she had brought her father back to the stage, that she was there if he should stumble or falter, was of prime importance. D.D. had had a stroke of genius in casting her in the role of Cordelia. She was that in real life.

In the midst of the dust and rubble she began to long for the peace of Anscombe—especially now since the bombers and the fighters no longer went over with numbing regularity. She longed for the sweet, warm smell of the dairy, she wanted to rest her head against Primmie's broad side as she squeezed gently at the teats which gave so willingly, so plentifully of their milk. She longed for the scents and sounds of the country. She, the daughter of two parents who had made their lives and fortunes from cities, from crowds who came to see and hear them, began to feel that she was lost. Ambition, which had once propelled her to the Royal Academy of Dramatic Art, was gone. She was here to serve her father. Sometimes she telephoned Anscombe, to enquire from Stella and Cook how things were. She denied to herself that she also telephoned with the need to know if James Sinclair had ever again shown up at the kitchen door. He had not. There had been no letter from him, apart from a note from Scotland to thank Michael again for his hospitality. Sometimes there was enough petrol to allow them a visit back to Anscombe. Nothing waited for her—no letter, no word. She ate the good food

—the eggs, the butter, the rabbit stew. Her father enthusiastically tended the rose garden, although Stella had taken it on as yet another task. For her, there was nothing. James Sinclair might be at Hawkinge, or anywhere else in the country they might have stationed him. But he sent no word. He was gone, in the classic pattern of men in war time.

Julia believed that her father worked himself back into the theatre through her; she had much need to be coached, rehearsed, given behind the scenes direction which did not come from Julian Tredwell. Her father spared nothing of himself or his knowledge. He taught her every trick in the book which would serve this role. He even taught her how to upstage himself. "Pet, try to forget it's your own dear old Dad. Go for stealing the scene whenever you can—and good luck to you. If you can steal it from me, you're no amateur, because I certainly won't play down to you. This is a highly professional business, Pet. And a greedy one. We all snatch for the limelight. Don't you miss a moment's opportunity for that. It comes your way rarely. But it's sweet, Julia. It's sweet. Wait until you hear the applause . . . We will work together, you and I, Julia. But I won't carry you. With whatever is left of integrity in me, I have promised myself that—and you. In the end, you will do it on your own, or not at all."

With her stomach twisted in a tight knot of nerves Julia faced opening night with her father. At the last moment he gave her a glass of champagne. "You're going to be great. Think of yourself first, but don't forget to react to the others. They'll be watching *your* face as you listen to the others. And your old Dad's here with you . . ."

It was an interminable night. To Julia's amazement the theatre was packed. Yet, it was a fine night in July. The raids now were intermittent. People badly needed entertainment in any form, and Sir Michael Seymour's name was enough to draw them. In her need to perform well, she lost her feeling of being thrown to the lions. She was one of this company, and together they had to make a success of this production. Whether she sank or swam hardly mattered. She was one of many. During the intermissions her father refrained from saying anything of any significance to her, except a murmured, "You're doing just beautifully, Pet." Her greatest encouragement came from a stagehand she knew only as Bert. "You just go on giving it to 'em, Miss Julia. They're with you. I seen too many in my time not to know. Big and small. I can smell an audience. You got 'em!"

The applause afterwards was mostly for her father, but as always he gestured the other members of the cast on to share the bows and curtain calls with him. Cook and Stella were in the stalls, along with Alex and Connie. Lord Wolverton had brought his wife, and a party of friends. There were many friendly faces out there to welcome back Sir Michael Seymour, to watch with no small interest the debut of his daughter. But it was from none of these known, friendly groups that the first insistent cry went up. "Julia . . . *Julia!*" Somewhere far back in the house a familiar voice called her name. Gradually it was taken up by many in the audience. Finally, in response to the insistent demands, her father beckoned her to come and take her bow alone with him. Tears were in her eyes, and nearly broke through her make-up. The first crimson rose landed at her feet. She picked it up, kissed it, and handed it to her father. The house erupted with roars of approval. At last she knew what it meant. Single red roses continued to land at her feet. She tried to gather them all up. Then the flowers in sprays and baskets were brought on. Her father summoned back the whole cast to take another full curtain call. The whole house seemed to be in an uproar. Desperately she searched beyond the footlights, trying to find the face of the man who had first called her name.

They all came backstage. More than her father's dressing-room could accommodate, and much more than the humble one Julia shared with two other members of the cast. The party, and champagne, spilled out into the corridors. Her father embraced and thanked each member of the cast. There was a glass of champagne for them all. Julia went and found Bert, who was on the stage with the rest of the stage crew cleaning up. She toasted him, and offered him his own glass. "I'll never be able to thank you . . ."

He grinned at her. "Nufing, Miss Julia. At my age if you can't smell 'em, you ain't been in the theatre. You got the stuff of the old man in you. An' you look like your mother. Don't get many combinations like that . . . But don't you forget there's tomorrow night, an' the night after . . . an' the night after that. It's learning to go on, no matter 'ow you feels, that sorts out the men from the boys . . . in a manner of speaking, like."

It was there, on the almost empty stage with Bert, that James Sinclair found her. "'ello, 'ello," Bert said. "If it ain't bloody Romeo come to fetch you, deary.

Enjoy your night. It ain't always like this. Bloody hard work, and sometimes little thanks for it . . ."

Jamie's arms were around her, and he was kissing her, the thorns of the huge sheaf of red roses in his arms piercing her shoulders. "'ere, mate! Watch it! Crack Miss Julia's ribs, and she won't be able to take a deep breath tomorrer night. There's more than one night in the theatre, y'know."

Jamie behaved as if Bert didn't exist. "God, I love you," he said. "I cried like a baby for you. I didn't know if I dared to come backstage, or if they'd let me. But in the end no one could stop me."

"I think I died a little when I heard your voice. You started it, didn't you? You came up the aisle and threw the roses, didn't you? Jamie, how I've missed you! Why didn't you write? Why didn't you telephone?"

"Not fair," he answered. "I had to leave you alone. When I read you were going to play in *Lear* with your father, I kept out of the way. You were going beyond my world, Julia. You were following your parents. Into places I don't belong."

She caught his hand firmly. "You belong. Come and join the party." But before she left the stage she bent and kissed the wizened cheek of the stumpy little stage hand. "I know you brought me luck, Bert." She did not add that, carefully wrapped in a silk scarf, in a drawer in her dressing-room was the worn grey rabbit her mother had carried with her to each concert.

He winked. "I'll be seeing you, deary, in a lot more parts, and you won't have your Dad to help you through them. But you done him proud. You'll sign a photo for me, won't you? The missis—she hates all the photos of the beauties I bring home, but I says to 'er, I says 'Look 'ere, me girl, that there's a star. An' don't you forget it.' An' tonight I'll go home and tell 'er a star brought me bleedin' champagne, and kissed me. A few others 'ave done it, mind you. But only a few . . . I'll remember it forever, deary. Now you get on with your Romeo . . . One day I'll see this little lady play Juliet—only her Romeo ain't goin' t'be 'alf as 'andsome as you. Flyer-boy, ain't you? And lots o' medals to prove it. Good luck to y' both." The experienced old eyes had taken in Jamie's scarred hands, the cleft through his skull which had nearly ended his life. "Guess yer must be one 'o them 'eroes Mr Churchill talked about. Well, why wasn't y' there when they bombed me little house in the Whitechapel Road. Been living with me bloody sister ever since then, and it's bloody 'ell. But get on it, Flyer-boy—sir!" He gave a tiny, almost mock salute, then strolled over to his mate, where a piece of scenery needed moving.

At the party D.D. gave at the Ritz, which included Lord Wolverton's group, Julia unashamedly revelled in the role of a woman in love. It was something she was incapable of hiding now. She insisted that Jamie be seated at her side during supper. D.D. was on her other side. He often interrupted their conversation, as if somewhat jealous of the attention she gave to the young man. "It's all very well to be in love, darling. I've been in love hundreds of times myself. Such a nice feeling. But you mustn't let it stand in your way. Marriage and babies . . . the babies come whether one has thought about them or not. Hardly the life for a young woman who has only just started to make her mark. I have plans for you . . . this *Lear* has been a great success, but no Shakespeare runs forever. We must find something a little lighter for you next time. And then, I read an interesting film script the other day. Not a great thing . . . but properly produced and played, it just might make it. A young girl . . . like you—in love, with war all around. It would be inexpensive to produce . . . there's a growing market now in the States for those kinds of films. Heroes . . . unsung heroines . . ."

She hardly heard him, but she smiled. "Yes, D.D. But who said anything about marriage? Jamie and I hardly know each other."

"Darling heart, that is not how it appears to me. Any man who can cause the sensation in the audience he did tonight . . . You are both madly in love with each other. Do be careful . . ."

She heard her own laughter. "Careful! What's there to be careful about? In a world like this? A bomb could fall on us right at this moment—just like the Café de Paris. This could be my last night, as well as my first night." She piled what was probably prewar caviar onto toast, and gulped it greedily. "I'll take life just as it comes—like this!" Then she turned back to Jamie, and raised her glass. "Here's to us. Don't stay away again. Not ever!"

In the flush of refinding Jamie, in the remembered glow of the applause, she was hardly conscious that the early editions of the newspapers were due, and the reviews. All hailed the return of Sir Michael Seymour; all seemed to intimate that the personal tragedy he had suffered since his last appearance on stage had heightened his powers, gave more weight to the giant role he had played. For his daughter, the reviews were mixed. Some welcomed "a bright new talent". Some seemed to withhold judgement:

> One would wish to see her again in a role where she did not play so personally to her father's image. In some aspect she is the perfect, unforgettable Cordelia. It remains to be seen if she can play any other role.

"You will play a hundred roles—and more, darling," D.D. assured her. "You have got away with it, you know. I feared so much they might just take out their wicked little knives and carve you up just because you *are* his daughter. It was a risk I had calculated. We won, darling. We won."

She turned her head and looked at Jamie. "Yes—we won!"

In the ladies' room, where the sisters went to collect their coats, their party being the last to leave the hotel that night, Alex touched her cheek lightly. "I'm so proud of you, my love. I wish Greg had been here to see you. He was more than a bit sceptical that you could carry it off." Greg had been sent to Egypt, and was working closely with General Alexander's staff. Dispatches from him, written from a forward position in the desert, were regularly appearing in *The Record*. Alex carried on with her own work, her by-line appearing more and more as she reported the home front. ". . . except for what the censors won't let me write," she had once said, with some bitterness. And now, "This James Sinclair—it's serious, isn't it?"

"Serious? It's serious with me."

Alex laughed. "Well, I can't see a Scot going off

his head and scattering roses at your feet unless it's serious with him, too. But don't pin too much on it. It's war. He's flying again, isn't he? I rather think flyers have a somewhat shorter life expectancy than war correspondents—though God knows, Greg's just as likely to be blown up as the soldier beside him."

"Oh, don't!" Connie almost wailed. "Why do you make it seem so inevitable? Plenty of men survive war. Why even Father . . . imagine surviving four years of that horror in the First War."

"And Ken Warren," Alex asked. "Do you love him, Connie? He doesn't seem half good enough for you, but is it serious?"

Connie's face tightened. "I don't see that that's any of your business. He may not be glamorous, or even good looking. He doesn't do a glamorous job. But it's just as essential as any other. Why do you keep running him down, Alex? What's it got to do with you? You married the man you wanted. Why can't you leave other people's lives alone?"

Alex snapped the lid of her power compact closed. "Sorry, Connie. I should keep my big mouth shut. But I can't help thinking . . . well, even in that dreadful uniform, you're by far the best looking of us all. And the nicest. You'd have made a great Cordelia to our poor father, half-crazed with grief, if Julia hadn't been there to do it for us all. But I can't help seeing how men look at you. I hope before you make up your mind about marrying Ken Warren, you'll come and have a good talk with me. I'm the old married sister, remember? Wickedly wise in the ways of the world."

"Kenneth and I aren't even thinking of getting married. He's far too responsible to marry in wartime, when one or the other of us could get killed . . ." A faint blush spread on her delicate skin. "Neither of you understand him—or me, I think. And what's more, I don't care."

"Easy . . . easy," Alex said gently. "It *is* none of my business. Except that I care about you. Sorry, Connie." She slipped on her coat. "I wonder why the most extraordinary things get said in the Powder Room." As the other women of D.D.'s and Lord Wolverton's party entered the room, she closed ranks with her sisters. "It's been a most marvellous night, hasn't it? Seeing Father back up there on the stage, and our wonderful little Julia with him."

"There you go, again," Connie muttered. "There's nothing little about Julia. Or me. Don't be so damn patronizing—" She tugged her cap further down on her head, and marched out of the room. Alex stared after her, her expression startled. "Well, she's certainly grown up while my back's been turned. Never thought I'd hear Connie use a word that was even mildly blasphemous."

"When one thinks of what she must hear used all around her every day, I'd hardly wonder . . ."

"And you, too, little one—Oh sorry, I mustn't use that word again. Difficult to get used to the fact that the baby of the family is also grown up." Then she turned her full attention to Lady Wolverton. "Yes, I hear from Greg as regularly as the mails allow—and as much as the censors will let him say. Actually, I learn rather more of what he's up to from the dispatches to the paper. I haven't the faintest idea when he'll be home . . . if he'll be there for the length of this campaign. I suppose events—and Lord Wolverton—will decide that."

Lady Wolverton turned to Julia. "You must be so pleased with this evening. But it's just the beginning, my dear. And what a handsome young hero to come and throw roses at your feet. I remember once meeting his mother on a visit we made to Scotland. Years ago. Our hosts took us over to tea at the castle. He was a little boy then . . . and what a handsome woman she was. Still is, I suppose. With a family history that takes in the whole of Scottish history. How lucky he was to get out of that crash with his life. One can see from that head wound it must have been a pretty near thing. I don't know how these men do it. I mean . . . climb back into those planes and go up again . . ."

Her words caused Julia to shiver slightly. Lady Wolverton touched her hand. "You're tired, dear. No wonder, after such a night. Your father's waiting outside." She kissed Julia's cheek affectionately. "How you've brought him back to life, my dear. A double triumph for you. We're all so pleased . . ."

Lear ran for three months, which was considered a great success for a play of that nature in the middle of war, when audiences were mostly looking for something to laugh at, or with. The tightened knot of stomach muscles became a familiar thing for Julia before she went on each night. "Not to worry, Pet," her father counselled her. "It happens to almost everyone. The good ones, that is. Once you begin to feel it's easy, then you're going to slip. Every performance counts. Some nights you don't feel like it . . . it's the last thing in the world you want. Those are the nights when you must give it all you've got."

She and her father continued to share the flat, and

their lives continued in the routine dictated by the theatre. "I wish you could have a place of your own, Pet. You're old enough, and you should be breaking loose from the Old Man. But with the city bombed half to bits, it would be hard to be as comfortable as you are here. Especially with Agnes to look after us." Agnes was a middle-aged cook-general who had worked for a family not only now dispersed by war, but whose London house had been bombed. "She's the most delicious snob, isn't she?" Michael had remarked, after the first interview. "She was so busily weighing up whether working for us who are just mildly famous equalled working for a baronet's family who are filthy rich."

But Agnes did keep them clean, and as well-fed as the rations and supplements from Anscombe would allow. Julia and Michael stayed out of each other's way as much as possible, knowing that they must come together each night, and for the Wednesday and Saturday matinées. They were scrupulous in trying to avoid any questions about whatever private life the other might have. Julia began to understand what Michael had meant when he'd said she should have a place of her own. Before, there had only been Anscombe, this flat, and her mother and father. She had wanted nothing else. But before there hadn't been James Sinclair.

He came to London whenever he had sufficient hours off duty. He would telephone her, and she would leave a ticket for him at the box-office. Afterwards there were always roses. She chided him for his extravagance. He laughed at her. "What else do I have to offer you?" They found a few small restaurants where they could eat quietly, and most people did not recognize her. "That's good, Pet," Michael would remark when she said she was going out to supper after the show. "Enjoy what you can."

Slowly he was easing back into life with his friends in London. Julia knew she no longer had to sit with him, and the whisky bottle was no longer his constant companion. She sensed that with the prospect of the play, he had gone back into training, like an athlete. Her time as companion-nurse was over. She blessed D.D., and, once or twice, when he insisted that she join him, with other friends for dinner, she told him so. "Darling child, think nothing of it. Selfish of me, really. I wanted Michael back at work. He's made a lot of money for me, you know—now, and in the past."

"And you've produced one or two flops with him in the lead which have cost you money, D.D. We all know about them."

He waved the thought aside. "It comes out about even. One doesn't count in friendship. I just happened to have the right idea about you two at the right time. But, of course, you must now begin to do things by yourself. We cannot have too much of this father-daughter act. Not good for either of you. What do you say to playing in *The Importance of Being Earnest?* As Gwendoline, of course. You're not up to Lady Bracknell, yet. I think it's just right for the West End now. Lots of laughs and style. We'll dress it as lavishly as we can."

She drew her breath in. This time it would be alone, unaided by her father's presence, his strength on the stage, his ability to get her through a scene when she might falter. "When?"

"In time to catch the Christmas trade. When people

come up to town again for shopping. When they're feeling in the mood for a good time."

"I've never played anything but this role. Do you think. . . ?"

"Yes, I think. Otherwise I wouldn't be suggesting it. It isn't a *big* role, Julia—but I think you will do it very nicely. A touch of class and wit. I want you back on stage as soon as possible. Before people have had time to forget there's a Julia Seymour as well as a Michael. We would go into rehearsal late October—early November."

"That means—if I took the play—I'd have a few weeks off."

"Of course you'll take the play. What else is on offer? Or is there something you're not telling your old D.D.? Don't ever keep me in the dark, Julia. I'm willing to act as your unpaid agent, as well as your producer, but you must always tell me what offers come your way. If your career is properly guided, you could really make something of yourself—in your own right. And yes, of course there would be a few weeks break. Any special plans?"

"No, nothing. Perhaps just a quite time at Anscombe—learning the part. I'm still not used to the raids starting up at any old time, just when Goering thinks he'll give us a night's shaking up. The Luftwaffe don't bother with Kent much, now. And surely—surely lightning can't strike in the same place. We've *had* our bombing."

"Well, Anscombe's very convenient to Hawkinge, isn't it? That's where James Sinclair is stationed, I think? Dear heart, I hope you're not really serious about this young man. Oh, yes, it's a wonderful thing to be in love. I expect you'll be in love many times.

Part of growing up. But what can he give you? A mouldy old castle in the depths of the Highlands! How could you manage that, and a life on the London stage?"

"Perhaps he can give me love."

"Ah yes . . . love. How long does it last when the children come, and the boredom sets in, and the lights of the London stage are very far off? Don't rush into anything, Julia. Talk to your old D.D. first."

"I won't forget," she said curtly, feeling as Connie must do when her relationship with Kenneth Warren was questioned.

But when she told Jamie of D.D.'s plans for her when the run of *Lear* was finished, he was quiet, and thoughtful. "I'll be at Anscombe, Jamie. We can see a lot of each other . . ."

"Yes, we'll do that. You need a rest, Julia."

"I'll get it at Anscombe. Stella and Cook will put me properly back in my place. There's no 'star' treatment at Anscombe. I'll be out gathering up the cows early in the morning, cursing them when they're slow to milk, mucking out after them. I suppose I'll just do whatever Harry Whitehand tells me to do. And *he* does what he's told, too. The Ministry of Agriculture just comes around these days and tells you what you've got to plant, and what animals you can keep. And let you buy ammunition to keep down the rabbits. Do you know how many acres of food a good size warren of rabbits can consume, if you just let them breed? And to think I've been raising rabbits for food . . ."

He smiled. "Yes, Julia. I know. I'm supposed to be a farmer. Or I will be if I get through this war."

"You'll get through it," she said fiercely. "You

will! You've had your one big chance to get killed, and you didn't take it. It's a special sign. You're going to come through everything now. You're going to go on right to the end."

"If you say so . . ."

"I do say so. You just listen to me."

But when *Lear* closed she spent only a few days at Anscombe, and then was on her way north to Inverness with Jamie. He had managed ten days' leave. "I know rather too well where you live, and how. It's time you came to see where *I* live."

She was almost reluctant. "Must I? Couldn't we just stay here at Anscombe?"

"Why? Why don't you want to come to Scotland?"

"I'm afraid," she said, frankly. "I'm afraid to meet your mother. I'm afraid of how she'll compare me with that girl, Kirsty, she wants you to marry. Just afraid, that's all. I've never been to Scotland . . . I don't know how things are done there."

"Well, we're past the stage of being savages," he said, his tone almost rough. "We don't eat strangers. We're nearly civilized, I think you could say."

"I'm sorry," she said. "I know what you have in Scotland, and that it's produced some of the greatest scholars and scientists. It's just . . . well, I wish we could have this time at Anscombe."

He signalled for the check from the waiter at the small Italian restaurant at which they had eaten dinner. "You don't want this to go any further, do you? You want to keep your girlish, uncommitted love. You want the romance, but not the reality. You want to stay safely with Father at Anscombe, in a world where you're known and secure. Well, my dear, that's what you shall do. But not with me. I have my leave, and I'm going north. I'm going to *my* home."

So she sat with him through the long, weary hours of the train journey which took them overnight to Edinburgh. It was a slow journey, with many unscheduled halts on the way. They missed the morning train to Inverness. As they had crossed the River Tweed, and were in the Border country, she couldn't repress a shiver, which Jamie instantly noticed. "Yes, Julia, we are a different race. You lot—especially you lot down around London, are Anglo Saxons. We're Celts. Up in the Highland we're Gaels."

"And I'm half Russian," she retorted. "My grandfather was a revolutionary—or almost."

"Well, then, we'll make a great pair, won't we?"

"Who said anything about making a pair, great or otherwise? I've accepted your mother's kind invitation, which you extracted from her, I'm sure, to take a little break in the Highlands. Such a polite invitation, and warm as a cold hot-water bottle. How can she thank us for such generosity as we have given you, etc . . . Of course she doesn't want me with you. She doesn't want me at all. She wants you alone, or with the Kirsty girl."

"I may love and admire my mother, but I'm *not* tied to her apron strings. I don't intend to live my life to please her. And whom I love, I love."

She remembered the words, holding them to her like a shield, as the train was finally drawing into Inverness station, two hours late. But the woman who stood waiting for them on the platform neither mentioned the wait, nor the raw cold of the October day. She gladly accepted her son's embrace, and then turned to hold her hand out to Julia. "Welcome to Scotland. I understand it's your first visit. I do hope you'll enjoy your little time with us."

She had very fair skin, the delicate kind of skin which wrinkled early if not indulged and protected. Hers had not been. But her jaw-line was firm, and the bone structure of her face very beautiful, Julia thought. She had clear blue-grey eyes, to which the smile on her lips did not quite carry. She had a slight, and delightful Scottish accent, which made her voice seem warmer than she may have intended.

She was very restrained. It was only the second time she had seen her son since her one visit south when his life still hung in the balance after his crash. But she did not exclaim over how he looked, nor note the improvement in his movements since that brief trip back to Scotland when he had been passed fit for active service. She led them from the station to a dilapidated shooting brake which stood outside. The real welcome came from the three dogs—two Border collies and a golden labrador, who flung themselves out when the door was opened, and leapt over Jamie in an ecstasy of delighted barking. He half-squatted to let all three put their paws on his shoulders, to lick his face, to muzzle the breast of his uniform coat.

"Well, they certainly haven't forgotten you," Lady Jean said. "Of course, I told them you were coming, but one is never sure of what an animal remembers." Was this her subtle reproach for the long months of his convalescence when he had stayed away from Scotland?

"These old devils would never forget. I sneaked too many goodies to them when they were puppies. Julia, these are the hounds who will bother you all through your stay. The collies are Angus and Duuf, and I don't expect you to tell them apart. The Labrador is Rory. And you lot be careful with this young lady. She's a great star of the London stage, and not used to rough and tumble."

"What do you mean?" Julia demanded. "Wasn't I up every morning with Harry Whitehand milking the cows, and mucking out, and doing all the odd jobs? . . . not quite up to repairing the tractor, but near enough."

"Well, my son didn't tell me you were so multi-talented, Miss Seymour," Lady Jean said, as she supervised the loading of the baggage. She directed how they would be seated in the car. "You'd better sit beside me, Miss Seymour. We'll put Jamie in the back with the dogs, because they'll give him no peace if they're not with him."

The old car rattled into shuddering life. Slowly they drove through the city, with its Victorian castle on the hill, a mixture of medieval streets and lanes, old houses and new ones. "We've had such a lot of battles through the centuries that not much of the old survives," Lady Jean said to Julia. "But you must come in with Jamie one day and see the worthwhile things." They were heading out of the city, meeting much horse-drawn traffic. "Though I hope you've no ambition to keep Jamie standing out in the hope of seeing the Loch Ness monster. But then, old Nessie's been a great attraction for tourists to Inverness—that is, in the days when we had tourists. Even then, not many ventured this far north. Except for those who came to shoot or fish, we're a mite chilly for your average tripper. And a mite strange, too. They don't feel quite comfortable here, those from south of the border."

And that told her, Julia thought, exactly where she belonged, and should stay—south of the border.

Forever Julia would remember her first sight of Sinclair Castle. They had gone south of Inverness, and then turned off the main road that continued on to Elgin and Fraserburgh, driving through a forest of mixed conifers and broadleafed trees, with outcroppings of rock, and a narrow stone bridge which spanned a white rushing stream. It was near to sunset when they emerged into the relatively flat land which lay around a small and now tranquil loch. The road had twisted through the forest so they approached from the east, and the castle was silhouetted against the last of the pale, low sun. It was approached along a narrow causeway which jutted into the loch, and this in turn gave way to another narrow, three-arched bridge. Part of one of its towers, almost a ruin, stood gauntly against the sky; the rest, a huddled tall dark mass of stone showed only one light to the approaching travellers. All around the loch the flat land gave, in some places gradually, in others sharply to the lower slopes of hills, with a range of mountains standing far behind them. Across the still waters of the loch Julia could discern two lights in locations which seemed to be miles apart. It was a scene of breathtaking beauty, and of extreme desolation and loneliness. Instinctively Julia reached up and drew her scarf closer about her neck.

The dogs, who had been dozing in a pile over Jamie's legs and lap, suddenly came to life, as they scented home, recognizing the sound the wheels made as they crossed onto the bridge. They sounded a deafening home-coming cry.

"You're home again, Jamie," his mother said. "We know one day it will be for good. You'll come back to us forever."

"Well—of course," he said dismissively. "I never think otherwise. It's where I belong."

His mother said nothing, but in the growing darkness, as they rattled over a wooden drawbridge which led from the last of the stone arches, Julia could almost sense her smile, an inward smile, the smile of possession. They passed under the portcullis Jamie had once mentioned. Julia had thought it figurative, but it actually existed, and undoubtedly, as he had said, rusted into place. Lady Jean gingerly eased the shooting brake between walls that could, Julia thought, have been eight feet thick. They were in a small, inner courtyard, and a light over one door was the one they had seen when they had emerged from the forest.

Jamie had the far door open, and the dogs tumbled out. He opened the door on his mother's side, and then ran around to Julia. "Don't be afraid. In the morning it's bright and beautiful, and all the ghosts have gone to their rest."

"How many ghosts?" Julia asked.

"It depends," Lady Jean said. "It depends on how sensitive one is to these things. We've had one or two guests here who were reputed to have 'the sight'—they reported not only ghosts we knew about, but a few extra as well. Those we put in the doubtful category."

One half of the double entrance door which had a weathered coat of arms engraved in the stone above, was opened, and light spilled out. Jula realized that here, in the isolation of this situation, they had little care for the blackout. What bomber would be headed for a target so far north, a lonely prick of light at the edge of a loch in the wilderness. Above her, reaching high into the swiftly darkening sky, three high towers rose. A light touch of wind blew from the loch, and sang against the castle walls, like an ancient sigh. "Welcome back, Master Jamie," a woman's voice called. "Aye, 'tis grand to have you home again."

Jamie's arms enfolded a woman Julia judged to be in her forties. "Glad to be back, Janet. Julia, this is Janet—Miss Julia Seymour."

Julia found her hand grasped by a strong, rough one, and she was half led, half pulled towards the light of the open door. "He said you were a bonny one. I never knew him to lie."

Jamie carried the bags, the dogs preceded them, and they went first into a smallish stone hall, which in turn opened into a very large room, with a carved wooden staircase leading to a gallery which ran around three of its stone walls. The ceiling of this room was lost in the darkness above. A few sconces on the walls were lighted, and a small fire burned in a huge fireplace.

"Extravagance, Janet," Lady Jean said.

"Well, it's only a wee bit of a welcome. It isn't every day we get Master Jamie back home." Despite the fire, the great stone hall struck chill into Julia's bones—or was it her spirit? "You'll be wanting a wash, I'm thinking. And I've set the whisky by the fire. There's jugs of hot water in the room, all ready."

Jamie carried the bags up the stairs, and led the

way along the gallery. "The Red Tower Room," his mother directed.

He looked back in disbelief. "Oh, Mother, not that! Julia will be lost in there."

"It is our principal guest bedroom," Lady Jean replied. "I wouldn't offer her less."

Shrugging, he led the way along a short passage, and then up a few winding stone steps. His mother moved before him to lift the heavy iron latch on an oak door. It swung open to reveal a room which commanded the whole space of one of the towers which Julia had seen from the courtyard. Three large windows were clothed in red silk which was faded, and beginning to shred. The four-poster bed was hung in a similar fabric, the bedcover was red velvet, and stiff with ancient embroideries. The bedhead was carved with the same coat of arms as in the courtyard, and this was repeated in a shield carved in the stone above the fireplace, where the fire that burned did almost nothing to cut the chill. There were chests and stiff dark chairs of the Jacobean era, and one massive wardrobe, a concession from Victorian times, Julia guessed. On the washstand a flowered china bowl and jug stood, with a pile of towels, and a cake of soap in a cherry-red patterned dish.

"The bathroom, Miss Seymour, is a rather long hike. Back down this little passage, and it's the second door on the right—or you can go through the dressing room and on into the bathroom, which connects with it. But the dressing room is very dusty —we have very little help. Everyone's gone into factories or the forces. Janet has only one young girl, Morag, to help. I'm afraid Scottish castles are a proper muddle. The few bathrooms we have are the last word in Victorian modernity. Sometimes the hot water gets here, sometimes it doesn't. The Sinclairs stopped putting in bathrooms about the turn of the century, when the money started running out. At least, before that happened, they had the good sense to put in a bathroom downstairs where some of the servants slept—so that's where *I* have my baths. To have a few water closets back in those times was a great thing, considering the difficulty of getting the plumbing into a place like this. Mostly the family took their baths in front of the fire—but then there were legions of servants to bring the hot water. Jamie wrote me that your house is very old—like this. But then you never had quite the need to fortify yourselves in the way the Scots did. All these towers—very good for repelling the enemy, but rather awkward to live with now. Both the weather, and the peace you enjoyed down there have made life easier for you, since your Elizabeth's time."

"Ours is a quite unimportant small manor house," Julia said, thinking of it longingly, for all its narrow twisting corridors, with bathrooms and cupboards squeezed in wherever space existed. With the central heating that the Brahms concertos had paid for. "No one would have thought of fighting for it. It was never a fortified house." She resented the allusion to "your Elizabeth". Until Queen Elizabeth had died, and James the Sixth of Scotland, Queen Mary's son, had become her heir, there had never been a joint ruler of England and Scotland. Would her whole stay here be one barrage of small barbs about the differences of their cultures?

Jamie laid her suitcase on top of one of the oak chests. He cast a last, dispirited look around the room. “Not the cosiest place on earth, Julia. But don’t worry—they’re all rather friendly ghosts.”

“I rather suspect,” Julia replied, “that it depends on which side of the border you come from.”

He tried to smile at her, and failed. “Well, when you’re ready, we’ll be waiting downstairs in the hall. If you need anything, give a shout. And you’re not quite alone up here. My mother sleeps in a room almost as big as this in one of the towers opening off the gallery, and I’m on the floor above her.” The thought gave her little comfort.

They left her, and she raced to the fire, holding her chilled hands to it, daring to add some extra coal from the scuttle. Ancient cast-iron radiators stood beneath the windows, but they were stone cold. She hung up the clothes she had brought—good, sensible, warm clothes, as Alex had advised, and the long velvet crimson gown of her mother’s, in case Lady Jean had planned some dinner party. Now that she had met her, she rather doubted that would happen. She went cautiously along the narrow stone corridor, and found the second door on the right. She opened the mahogany door to a bathroom of sumptuous Victorian size and fittings, and icy cold. There was an empty fireplace, and what was meant to be a hot towel rack, which was cold. For a few moments of bewilderment she couldn’t find either bath or toilet in the midst of the mahogany panelling. Then it occurred to her that the magnificently worked window seat was, in fact, the lid of the toilet. Above it hung a chain with a ceramic pull, decorated with a blue *fleur de lis* pattern; the cistern, too, was encased in mahogany. The pan of the lavatory was also decorated with the *fleur de lis*. After she’d used it, and pulled the chain, the noise of water seemed to gurgle and plunge through an unimaginable labyrinth of pipes, eventually, she supposed, to arrive in the loch below. Only a large mahogany-framed mirror above what looked like a chest of drawers, directed her to the washbasin. The lid she raised was also mirrored underneath, and the same beautiful blue and white pattern greeted her. The water that ran reluctantly from the tap at the washbasin was cold. But the soap was fresh and sweetly scented, as if left over from the days before the war . . . A blue and white handle on what looked like a very large wardrobe allowed her to slide back a mahogany panel which revealed a huge bathtub, again in the magnificent *fleur de lis* pattern. It occurred to her that whichever laird of Sinclair had installed the bathrooms, and the attempt at central heating, still had had strong Jacobite leanings, favouring the ancient French cause of Mary, Queen of Scots, and Bonnie Prince Charlie.

She went back to the Red Tower Room, keeping her hand on the stone wall and treading carefully, because it was so poorly lighted, and the stones beneath her feet worn. The room looked no cosier than before, but on one of the chests, she saw a small, prettily arranged bowl of asters—she supposed the last of the autumn yield in this far northern place. She washed in water from the jug which was now lukewarm, and changed her skirt and sweater—defiantly wearing a red which almost matched the colour of the room. She added a paisley-patterned cashmere shawl, something else from her mother's wardrobe that her father had insisted she take. He had been very concerned about this visit to Scotland, anxious that she enjoy herself, and yet worried that she would not be warmly welcomed.

"I have a feeling about Lady Jean," he had said, when she had offered the letter of invitation to him. "Despite the rose bush, and this invitation, I have a feeling that she would rather that Jamie did not bring an English girl back to his home. But, Pet—it can't hurt." Then he shook his head. "Or perhaps it will. I think I see what Jamie is doing. He's showing you what it's like up there—even if it is a castle. He's madly in love with you, but he wants you to know what his life after the war will be. He'll never desert Scotland. You do know that, Julia? And you are set on an acting career. You can't manage that from Inverness."

"You talk as if we were married. We haven't even talked about it ourselves."

"But you're both in love," he said, with great gentleness. "In war one makes hasty decisions—because you don't really believe there will be a future afterwards."

"*You* married Mother in wartime."

"That's exactly what I'm talking about. We married and we both knew I had only a slim chance of not getting killed. But at least I was sending her and her parents to safety. And close to a city where they both could pursue their careers, whether I was there or not." He shrugged. "I presume too much. James is a gentleman in that he's showing you what *his* home is like. When he asks you to marry him there will be no surprises."

"You do presume rather a lot."

"I do, Pet. I do. Forgive your interfering old

father. Your trip should be a very . . . a very enlightening experience."

These words were in her memory as she came down the great oak staircase to the dim hall, the light of the fire the one bright spot. But then Jamie came forward and took her hands, and the atmosphere seemed to alter, or her courage was renewed. The dogs, too, added their welcome with whipping tails which threatened to upset the glasses on the low oak stools about the fire.

Lady Jean had changed into a severe green gown with a high neck, with suited her magnificently. "Do come closer to the fire, my dear. Have a dram, or would you . . ." she looked doubtful, as if just remembering where her visitor was from. "I'm sure we could produce a gin and tonic if you'd prefer it."

"Whisky, please," Julia murmured. She wrapped her shawl closer about her, and leaned towards the fire.

"Are you frozen?" Jamie said, as he poured the whisky. "Water?" She nodded; she noticed he drank his neat.

"It's a pity about the heating," Lady Jean said. "We used to be reasonably comfortable when we were allowed enough coal—and when we had help to stoke the boilers. Now, of course, there's not enough of either. But it's nothing to the misery some people suffer, so we just try not to notice it. And say less about it. Here, do try some of these—we call them Scots Toasts. Janet has made them especially for you. We don't get them every day. I haven't decided if it's Jamie's homecoming, or the daughter of a famous actor and a musician which has inspired this activity, but enjoy it while you can. Of course—I should have added a famous actress. Janet saw a write up of your father's return to the stage in *King Lear*, and the . . . the glowing reviews about you. Of course it was she who helped me dig up the rose bush . . . Janet will do anything for something or someone who interests her."

The Scots Toasts turned out to be small pieces of fried bread, spread with a mash of finnan-haddie, or kippered herring, or flaked salmon, all done in thick cream. Julia murmured her appreciation. "Janet will be pleased," was all Lady Jean said. Jamie filled her glass again.

Dinner was in the long, formal dining-hall, again hung with the ancient regimental banners, smoke-dimmed portraits of stiff-faced ancestors, the antlered heads of stags, an array of swords and shields which decorated the Great Hall. The dogs went obediently to cushion-lined baskets before the fire. Cock-a leekie soup was served by a young girl Jamie introduced as Morag, and fried venison collops, tastes which were totally unfamiliar to Julia—not at all like the dishes which went under these names for her before. When she commented on this, Lady Jean replied, "Ah, well —Janet is an excellent cook, and she uses the traditional Scottish recipes and ingredients. Fortunately we can still get most of them. The Scots have never been big meat eaters—except for venison and game. We sell our beef to the English, and live off what the rivers and the sea give us, as well as the forest and the moors. Scotland was, and still is in many ways, a poor country."

Perhaps she discerned Julia's glance at the silver candelabra, the silver flatware engraved with the Sinclair crest, the faded splendour of the panelled room about her. "There were times when the Sinclairs had much more land. Some of it went to pay debts. Some of it just fell into neglect. We could have much more fine acreage for cattle if we could find the money to drain the land. It's gone so boggy in places, and the cattle won't stand that. We have some hill-farming in sheep, and Jamie's father did plant out a great deal of acreage to forestry—the land was too poor for anything else. But that's a cash crop that takes many years to grow. We must wait for our reward on that."

Jamie shifted in his seat uncomfortably. "Mother, you paint the worst picture. We're not quite on the point of being sold up, and after the war, when I get going on the place . . . well, it will be different then."

"Yes, Jamie—I think of the time, and wait for it. Wait for your energy and youth to come and do what I cannot. In the meantime, Miss Seymour, we are short of everything as well as money. Don't imagine we dine in this state every night. There's a house-keeper's room next to the kitchen which is our living and dining-room—at least that, and the kitchen we can keep warm. For the farm, we are left with middle-aged and old men, and a very meagre ration of petrol to run the farm machinery. But then, you probably know all this, since you live on a farm your-self. We've dust-sheeted and closed off a number of rooms—those we don't have to walk through, such as here and the Hall. There's a drawing-room, but it's too damp for use, and a fine library. The whole of the North Tower has been closed off . . . but then it should be closed off. It's in a rather dangerous state of decay. We have to be as self-sufficient as possible here. The snow drifts in winter can keep the road through the forest closed for weeks . . ."

Jamie had cleared the plates, and Lady Jean went to serve the pudding. "This is called Holyrood pudding, and Janet must have been highly excited at the thought of Jamie's homecoming to make it. Milk and semolina, butter, egg-whites—all the rationed things, of which we have plenty. Janet never hesitates to raid the food we send to market. And it's covered with her almond sauce, which is sheer luxury. I dread the Ministry of Agriculture turning up one day to ask why we aren't producing more, or—God forbid—taking a poke around the pantry."

They had shared a bottle of good red burgundy with the meal. "There's little enough of it left, though," Lady Jean said. "We're not short of whisky—one has one's contacts, and one's friends. The Highlands, of course, are dotted with distilleries, and it's not a labour intensive industry. Old men serve it perfectly well. But it's getting the barley that's the trouble. We're supposed to export the whisky, though, to pay for the guns as well as butter. But one cannot expect the Highlanders to go without their dram. It's been both the blessing and the curse of this country. Children and wives go hungry because men must have their whisky . . ."

"If you're finished, Mother . . ." Jamie scraped his chair roughly back on the wooden floor. "I must say I'm damn sick of hearing the long dirge about how meanly we live here. It's a good life, when there isn't a war on. We have enough of everything we really want or need." He looked almost pleadingly at Julia. "You're giving Julia such a bad impression. All deprivation and poverty. It's a damn good inheritance, and when I come back I'm going to borrow money to put it to rights. I'll clear land and drain it. I'll double the cattle herd. There are new strains of hill sheep I want to experiment with. There's still enough land if one has the will to work it. It's just that you've been without Father so long . . . it's a tough job for a woman . . ."

Lady Jean rang the silver bell to indicate to Janet that she and Morag could clear the table. Jamie pulled back her chair for her. "Yes, Jamie, I'm sure you could do all those things—given the money. It *does* need a young man's freshness and enthusiasm, so be sure you do come back."

The dogs rose as they left the table. They returned to the fire in the Great Hall. Julia watched as Lady Jean seemed to bite back words of reproof as Jamie added more logs. It was quite deliberate, of course, this tale of poverty. It was probably true, in many respects, but the point was being made that if she and Jamie married, she would not bring with her the money that this place so desperately needed. Julia was filled with a sense of desolation. She dropped into the seat before the fire she had had before, and pulled the cashmere shawl closer about her. Then suddenly leaping flames lighted the Sinclair crest on the back-plate, and on the fire-dogs. Jamie was filling small glasses from a decanter. "Here—try the aristocrat of whiskies—this one's The Glenlivet. You'll surely sleep soundly after that." Julia sipped, and tasted her first malt whisky. It was very strong, but a drink of incredible smoothness and sublety. "You mustn't take all that Mother says too seriously. She was brought up in a far less comfortable house than this—although the history of her family embraces about every famous event you can name. But somehow they always seemed to back the wrong horses—and not much money, or land stuck to the fingers."

"Poverty is no shame, James," his mother said tartly.

"No—just lack of money. I can remember the wind whistling through broken panes in your father's castle. I'll bet it's in an even sorrier state now."

His mother's stern expression softened to something near sadness. "Your uncle doesn't care for the place—he's more comfortable at the farm in Ayrshire. With no money spent on the castle, it's falling down. It breaks my heart to think of it. Only a couple of old women and a caretaker there now, and they're threatening to move to the mainland when the war's over. The place will be abandoned then. We gave plenty of men to our Scottish causes, but we seem to have been unlucky in the women they married. Hardly an heiress among them. Married for love . . ." She turned to Julia. "I'm one of the Macdonalds of Clanranald, and the castle is in the Western Isles. At one time we held sway along most of that coast. But it's all gone. Ruins against the sky . . . Very picturesque . . . for the tourists—"

"Oh, for God's sake, Mother! Those days are gone . . . finished. A hundred or more years ago."

"One's pride is not."

"And one can't eat history or pride. After the war I have to get on with the job here. It's not impossible. I'm reading everything I can lay my hands on about agriculture. We've come out of the age of crofting, you know . . . It was a mistake for me to go to Oxford, to read history like a gentleman. I should have learned something about agriculture instead."

"An education never hurt. I was determined you should have those three years of your youth to enjoy. Mentally, you would have been better prepared for the task you faced here. But . . . yes . . . I mustn't keep returning to the past. It's a vexing habit. Of course you will do all you say. I have no doubt. It is hard to wait until this war is over. But it seems we have hardly begun the battle yet. What does your brother-in-law, Mr. Mathieson say, Miss Seymour? How does the tide of battle really go?"

"He isn't allowed to write that, Lady Jean, even if he knew. Alex hasn't had a letter for some time. She thinks he is on the move somewhere, but not even her boss, Woolfie—I'm sorry, Lord Wolverton, will tell her where. We just hope it isn't Russia . . ." They all now lived with the dread of what a German victory in Russia could mean. The Germans were pressing on relentlessly; Leningrad was cut off, some reports said the Germans were almost at the edge of Moscow.

"We will hope he is safe, my dear. And not in Russia." Her tone was kinder than Julia had yet heard. "Of course we must wait for the Americans to come in . . . surely it cannot be too much longer."

"It will take something to *force* them in," Jamie said. "There's so much isolationism in Congress, Roosevelt can't stir a further inch without seeming to be pushed."

"Then we will hope for a good hard push," Lady Jean said, with more spirit in her tone. "I *cannot*—I refuse to believe we will go under, and yet if we don't get America as an ally soon . . . Ah, well, what's the use of talking about it. We must all do our various jobs, and get on with it." Julia had the distinct impression that for Lady Jean, acting on the stage in time of war was no real job at all.

Janet entered with coffee. Jamie poured more of The Glenlivet. When Julia demurred, he simply handed her the glass. "Drink it. We had a miserable journey here. I want you to sleep like a log tonight, and wake up ready to see this small bit of heaven that I think this place is."

"I'm thinking, Master Jamie," Janet said with the confidence of a long-time friend as well as servant, "that maybe it's no wee bit of paradise to others who are used to maybe a wee bit more excitement. But still and all . . . a fair enough place it is. Not that I've been much further than Edinburgh, Miss Seymour, but what I do see at the cinema . . . ah, well, now that's another world."

When she had gone, Jamie laughed softly. "Is she still as mad as ever about it, Mother? The cinema and the film magazines, and all that?"

"Absolutely. Every Wednesday, without fail, unless the snow drifts are too high, she walks to the main road, and picks up the bus into Inverness. And next morning I can't get a cup of tea until I've heard the whole plot of whatever picture she's seen—and if it isn't that, it's the latest on the private lives of the newest stars, or her favourite stars, or those she's betting will become stars." She looked at Julia. "Don't be surprised, my dear. Under that plain exterior lurks the heart of a true romantic. All that Janet never had in her life, and all that she will never be, is up there for her on the screen. Truly, I think she lives a fantasy life in the darkness of the one-and-thrupenny seats. The Wednesday matinée, and the end of the war is all she lives for. *You*, through your father, are the closest she has come to such glamour. She knows your father's films by heart. He didn't make many, did he? I'm not too well up on these things, but whatever he has made, you can be sure she's seen them all—probably three times, as they come round again."

Jamie rose, and snapped his fingers. All three dogs got up eagerly, tails wagging. "I'll take them out, Mother. Bed, Julia. You look all in." But instead of leaving her at the bottom of the stairs, after she had said good night to Lady Jean, he climbed the stairs to the gallery with her, which, lit by only one light, was nearly in darkness. There, where his mother's gaze could not reach them, he bent and kissed her lips tenderly. "Don't think for a moment that I feel as restrained as that seemed. If I had my way, I'd carry you to bed. But I've been patient this long, and I intend to go on until you're sure. Julia, do you think you could stand this place?—I mean, if I were here with you all the time. . . ? Unfair question. But think about it? Sleep on it. It's nothing to what you could have if you went on in London. You know . . . something like Janet's dream of a star. I wonder why I even brought you? I should have lied like a trooper, and tried to marry you to some romantic image of the life of a Scottish lady of the manor—or the castle. Well, now you know the castle, and you can pretty well guess what life is like here. Yes, I was a fool. I should never have brought you—"

"If I've fallen for a fool, then you're an honest fool. Kiss me again, dear fool. I think I shall love you forever."

This time his hands pressed her shoulders against the stone wall, and his lips searched hers with growing passion; one hand slipped down to her breast. "Dear God, Julia, I'm dying for you . . . Go and dream uneasy dreams. But you needn't lock your door. When it is time I will love you with all my heart and my body. Will you ever be mine as I want you, Julia? What can I offer except this run-down place, and a life of hard work?"

"Yourself," she whispered.

From far below his mother's voice drifted up. "Jamie, the dogs are impatient. And I'm longing for you to come back here to the fire so we can have a good, long talk."

A talk, Julia realized, from which she would be forever excluded, the intimacies of mother and son. She groped her way up the twisting steps in the half-dark, fears, and a despairing, almost last hope in her heart. Hope about what? She would be a disastrous wife for Jamie, and they both knew it. The one who knew it best was Lady Jean Sinclair.

She finally went to sleep with tears still wet on her mother's grey rabbit, which she had brought as her good-luck mascot.

But she woke in the morning from a deep sleep which had contained no hint of presences strange to her, no violent dreams had disturbed her, no ghostly visions had penetrated it. She woke to Janet's cheerful presence, a tray with tea and a thin slice of buttered bread on the table beside her, and the sound of the curtains being pulled back on huge wooden rings which rattled together with an almost musical sound. Swiftly she thrust the rabbit under the pillow.

"Ah, there, isn't it a very fair day you've brought with you?" Janet made it sound as if the weather was within Julia's gift. Ignoring the tea, Julia sprang from bed, without bothering with her robe, and ran to the windows. Bright sunlight poured in. The loch and all the land around glistened with colours which made it seem a new creation, born in that very hour. The water was still, and as fresh as a mirror into which no one had ever before looked. The pasture lands about it were the gentle grazing ground of cattle, rising to the hills where the white dots of sheep could be faintly discerned. And behind the hills, the mountains she had been barely able to see last evening—the peaks of some of them dusted with early snow, the sight of which brought no foreboding to her. It was part of the enchantment of this scene; a new, fresh world laid out before her. No wonder it so tied and chained Jamie's heart.

They ate breakfast in the more cosy atmosphere of the housekeeper's room. It was a large room—perhaps several rooms thrown together when there had been money to do it. It contained a dining table and chairs, and drawn near the fire two long sofas and several upholstered chairs. In a passage opposite the housekeeper's room, were a number of small rooms—the estate office, rooms for Janet and Morag, the unbelievable luxury of the bathroom for the servants which Lady Jean had mentioned—the whim of whichever laird had put in bathrooms in the towers, and attempted central heating. Lady Jean's greeting to Julia was civil, but lacking in warmth. Perhaps the good long talk with her son last night had not been much to her liking. The morning newspapers had not yet arrived, but the radio brought the news. The fighting in the desert war, the siege of Leningrad, the nearness of the German troops to

Moscow, the dread possibility that it might fall, were all there. Openly Jamie kissed her when she knocked and entered the door Janet had directed her to; then he turned off the radio. "The news will come when it does," he said to his mother. "We'll have our days together, won't we, Julia?"

He said it with the defiance, with the lack of care they had all adopted. Life had to be lived now—that was the creed for them all; she saw it everywhere about her, the frantic embraces of lovers, of greetings and partings. She looked at Jamie with love, and the happiness spilled out about her. The dogs rose to greet her.

"Do you take porridge?" Lady Jean asked.

"No—I hate it," Julia answered. Why should she pretend, and choke down something she had loathed from babyhood?

"A pity," Lady Jean said dryly. "Scotland lives and grows on oatmeal. But then—there's always toast . . ."

Happily Julia piled her toast with butter, which seemed to be there in abundance, and Janet's marmalade. But there was also bacon and eggs. Whatever Janet stole from what was designated for the Ministry of Agriculture, she made sure that they themselves did not go short.

Jamie planned a picnic for them both, but before they left the castle, Julia demanded a tour. "Oh damn—must we?" he answered. "It's such a great day—not raining, for once." Reluctantly he showed her some of the principal bedrooms—one called the Blue State Room. "Far too grand a title . . ." It had once been a State Room. The curtains and embroidered bedcover told that, but it was otherwise bare and spartan. He took her on to what was called the Culloden Room, and the Prince Charles Suite—both grand in size and style, with intricately panelled walls laid over the old stone which was their foundation. The Prince Charles Suite had an ante-room, with a beautiful stretcher table and upright wooden chairs, of the Jacobean period. Everywhere the furniture was shrouded in sheets, and dust was thick on the hand-pegged wooden floors. But all had magnificent views across the loch, or into the road through the forest. "There's a tradition—unconfirmed—that Bonnie Prince Charlie spent a few days here before he moved on to Culloden House—which is only a few miles away—to meet with his generals to plan that battle. And pretty badly planned it was. I'm sure you know most of it—the slaughter of the clans—the end of the Stuart cause. Well, whether he did stay here or not, of course my family was involved in the cause. And when the battle was over, we were as heavily penalized by the English as any family. We lost the incumbent laird of the time—he died in the battle. His younger brother was only nine. The best land we had was fortified. The object was to reduce those who had supported the Stuart cause to poverty, to break up the clan system as fully as they could. We were forbidden to wear the tartan. Oh, it's all the sort of thing my mother dwells on too much. Look—do you really want to see the other rooms? These are the so-called grand ones." He showed her some of the rooms that were reached by steeply pitched stone stairs in the upper parts of the towers. One of them was his, strewn carelessly with his possessions, the bed unmade, the view over the loch of stunning impact. "Yes—I know," he said. "From here it makes one feel as if one owned the world. All very well. But think of what it means to bring wood and coal up here for the fire. My brother's room is in this tower—my mother keeps it locked. There's an ancient bathroom—but these days I have to go down to Janet's bathroom beside the kitchen to get any hot water. Whichever laird put in all these modern conveniences, depended heavily on a ready supply of coal, and a hefty man to stoke the boiler. I hardly need say the boiler is on its last legs. There isn't any hefty man, and there's precious little coal. Above your room—the Red Tower Room, there's a couple of rooms like this—but they've been abandoned to the dust and the spiders." Lastly, after knocking, he put his head into the room his mother occupied. "I don't think she'd mind. She's never here this time of day . . . it's called the Rose Room. A pretty faded rose, as you can see." Like the other rooms, it had its four-poster bed, but the furniture and curtains were covered in chintz—just discernible as having a rose pattern. An ancient rose-patterned carpet lay on the floor. The room was tidy in the most extreme fashion, almost the only indication that it was occupied was the array of silver-framed photographs on the chintz skirted dressing-table—photographs of Jamie's father, in uniform, his brother Callum, dark-haired and handsome, a photograph of Jamie as a baby, held by his mother, with Callum, wearing the kilt, beside her. She had been a very beautiful young woman, Julia thought. There was a photograph of Jamie when he had been at Oxford, seated with a cricket team. "My friends—the Hendersons," he pointed out. And then a single photo of him in his RAF uniform, a young and tender, untried Jamie, not marked with the scars of combat, nor the death of friends.

"She comes up here as soon as the snows have melted, and only retreats down to a little room near Janet's when the winter cold drives her out. As you can see . . . the view . . . Faces west. As far north as this, she is often in bed before the sun sets—she gets the last of the sun."

They retreated, Julia feeling that she had indeed intruded on someone's very private sanctum. Hastily Jamie showed her the drawing-room. It was a long, narrow room—squeezed along the side of the Great Hall, and with only the aspect of the front courtyard. Then they went to the library, reached by another stone passageway off the Great Hall. Julia expected nothing better than the drawing-room, but she gasped when she saw it. It was a full two storeys high, and at one end might have connected two of the towers, but the end was closed off. The narrow gallery ran about the upper level, and the whole room, except where the three great mullioned windows gave an unexpected view of the loch, was lined with books. "Well, the laird who completed this must have had a bit of spare cash, and a yen for books. Some of them are pretty good." Julia gazed at the thousands of leather-bound volumes, many of them showing signs of mould. There were two great fireplaces in the room, but it was evident that neither had held a fire for a long time. The chill of the room was deep and intense; but it was possessed of a lonely kind of grandeur, a thing of beauty at the end of a narrow, dark passage. "I've never had time to go through all the books," he said. "I suspect there are some that might bring quite a penny or two at auction—but of course

Mother would never hear of selling anything. Like selling the family silver. What I see in some of them is a couple of new tractors. Had enough? . . . let's get going. This is all the past. It will be the future when I have enough money to do something with it. For the moment, we just leave it to its dust sheets and the spiders . . ." He pulled at her arm hastily, and slammed the door behind them. Something about that beautiful room upset him. Whether it was that its neglected splendour troubled him, she could only guess.

Jamie had arranged to borrow the shooting brake, and it was filled with petrol he had taken from what was meant to be reserved for farm use. "Oh, what the hell! I've earned this one little fling." It had been packed with a picnic basket and two rugs, woven in the Sinclair tartan. The dogs waited expectantly. "This is going to be *our* day—just us! Before we have to go visiting the neighbours, or they come to us." Unspoken between them was the thought that he might be returning to an overseas posting. They had shared the good fortune that since his return to active duty he had not been posted to the fighting in the desert. Perhaps his slight disabilities had not allowed that; perhaps he was still being assessed for his fitness. But his squadron, made up now mostly of newcomers, was still based at Hawkinge. So few of the original members were left, Fighter Command perhaps rightly thought of it as a novice squadron, no matter its brilliant and blazing record of enemy kills. Only a few—a very slim few of Churchill's famous "Few" were left. The squadron was kept in place because the raids on London, and other great cities continued erratically, the Luftwaffe dispatched by

Goering to keep Fighter Command off balance, although they knew that most of the German thrust had been turned east in an attempt to crush the Russians before the winter froze machines and men into inaction, if not death. As the autumn days had grown shorter, Julia knew that something of great import must soon happen in their lives, dictated by the Russian winter. But now she deliberately cast it from her mind—whatever it might be, finding her delight and comfort in Jamie's company, in the beauty of the world he opened up for her.

The island in the loch on which the castle stood was bigger than she had realized last night. There were two more inner courtyards overlooked by the three towers; there was extensive stabling for horses, though it was now tenanted by two oxen and two donkeys.

"Horses are a pre-war luxury," Jamie said. "When the tractor breaks down, we use the oxen. The donkeys are just for odd jobs—bringing in firewood, carting things from here to there." But there was one horse left. "Catriona," Jamie called her, stroking the dappled grey head, opening up the stable door to run his hands over the smooth shining grey flanks. "How are you, old girl? Looking pretty good to me. She was the one thing we could not part with," he said softly as he fed the mare an apple. "Actually, she does do her bit—we almost always use her in a trap, but she doesn't consider it beneath her dignity to pull a cart, though she's not, and never will be, a cart horse. There's a bit of thoroughbred in her, and she enjoys a jump—more than a bit mixed up, I'd say. My mother used to ride her—and she was my great joy before I went to Oxford. William Kerr's kids—

he's the steward, keep her exercised, if there's no work for her to do. She's as gentle as a lamb, and the kids adore her. And they take good care of her."

Julia had already noted how beautifully she was groomed, the fresh hay and water in the stall, the fresh straw on the ground.

"My mother likes to think she has some Arabian blood in her—that's because her sire was a stallion Mother brought with her from the West when she married, who was almost pure white. Mother dreams of Andalusian horses—the Lippizaners of Vienna—she likes to think there's some of that strain in Cat. The countryside around here is littered with a lovely mix of off-colour horses that Catriona's father sired. My father never charged stud fees. He liked the fact that the commonest old mare could be mated with a blood sire. He was a great believer in raising the level of everything—and everyone. At least, that's what I'm told."

He gave Catriona one last pat, blew gently against her nostrils, and closed the half-door of the stable. "So old Baltazar used to have marvellous summers out in the meadows with as many mares as he cared to cover. They seemed to like it. Catriona is probably his grand-daughter. We didn't keep records. I have just the vaguest memory of being taken out to see him—at work, let's say. Oh, look, here's William Kerr, come to bid you welcome."

A smallish, wizen-faced, middle-aged man approached them from a neat white dwelling which formed part of the stable complex. Julia had already noted that the parts of the castle which were not in ruins, were well kept, a policy of money wisely spent, she thought.

The two men shook hands. The welcomes said, Jamie introduced Kerr to Julia. "Ah, hasn't Janet already flown over to tell us that the loveliest creature she's ever seen outside of the cinema had come to grace the castle."

"Well spoken, Mr. Kerr," Jamie said. "I've been struggling for months to find words like that."

They were taken to William Kerr's house to meet his wife, a stern-faced woman who civilly offered them a cup of tea. "We've just finished breakfast, Mrs. Kerr."

Julia felt herself being scrutinized with care, but reserve. "It's well you're back, Master James. The last visit was far too short . . ." The reproof was clear. Jamie chose to take no notice of it. Julia realized that she was being blamed by more than one for keeping Jamie at her side.

Jamie enquired politely about the children. "Rachel and Colin are naturally at school now." He gestured with a slight show of affection and pride at the little boy who peered shyly from around the back of a chair. "Dugald, here, our late-comer, has a few years yet before he joins them." When Jamie commented on how well Catriona looked, William Kerr replied, "But she's their great love. On weekends we have to say, 'No one rides Cat until the homework is done . . .'"

They exchanged some talk about the farm. "I'll come and have a real talk with you later, Mr. Kerr," Jamie said, with a hint of impatience. It was clear that he did not want to waste this radiant morning in domestic discussion when the world he wanted to show to Julia still waited.

They drove over the bridge and the causeway, and

into the forest. About half way along what Julia later judged was about a two-mile stretch, near to the little bridge which spanned the stream, she noticed a small cottage, half-hidden in a clearing which was being encroached upon relentlessly by young saplings. It had the deserted air of a place which is never used. No smoke came from its chimney; no family washing hung on an outside line.

"It's been empty for years," Jamie replied to her question about it. "We couldn't keep all the workers we would have liked—someone who might have lived in that cottage. It's just used now as a sort of shelter when we're out gathering windfalls from the forest. Although I get angry every time Mother brings it up. It is true, of course, that the whole estate needs a lot of money spent on it. But I'm damned if I'll spoil this leave by worrying over what I can't do anything about until the war's over . . ."

"Everything will happen when the war's over, is that it?"

He shrugged, as if disturbed by her comment. "Don't see how it can be otherwise. I *have* to come back here, and work the place myself. Mother has done her best all these years, but she's tired—you can see that. She's been alone too long. It's not that she isn't very capable. But somehow the whole thing seemed to wait for me to grow up. And the war has further postponed all that. So the waiting goes on. I have to survive, Julia. You can see that. But that wasn't why I bailed out of the plane that day . . . if I could have hung on, I would have . . ."

She placed her fingers lightly on one of the scarred hands on the wheel. "We agreed not to talk about it, Jamie. Do you imagine it would have made any one of us feel better if another life had gone with my mother's? Everything from that plane was shot away. Leave it alone. It's done. It's our secret—shared with your mother. And I don't think she'll ever want to talk about it."

They drove on in silence until they emerged from the forest, and onto the main road. Jamie nodded towards the fields of stubble on one side of the road. "Those are ours. Some of the best land we have." They passed a cottage where a woman rushed to the door to wave. Jamie returned her wave. "One of the tenant farmers. I'll have to stop and have a word with her on the way back. I'm afraid they'll all expect to be visited, and they'll be frankly curious about you . . ." He nodded again to the land on each side of the road. "Here's where we grow barley and wheat. When my father was young we used to own all the way to those far hills. I suppose we were prosperous then."

"What happened?"

He sighed, and the old engine almost covered the sound. "The usual. No, not gambling, for once. Not the usual sort of gambling. My grandfather was certain he was a financial wizard. He put his money into fly-brained schemes. He had a ready ear for every crack-pot who swore he could turn dross into gold. He wasn't content to be just prosperous. Oh, no—he meant to be the richest man in Scotland. I don't say that everyone he trusted with money was a rogue, but there must have been a fair few in their number. He didn't like being a minor little local laird. He wanted to be a really important man—not just a gentleman farmer. A vain little poppycock, I suppose is how I'd characterize him, although I never really knew him.

I remember an old man. A bit touched, was what they kindly said about him. Quite mad, I would have said. Still poring over schemes to get rich, while he continued to sell the land which would have kept us at least comfortable. In the end my father had to act to take power of attorney from him, before we were absolutely ruined. He didn't live long after that, and of course people blamed my father. I don't, myself, thinking about it, see what else my father could have done . . ."

They drove a number of miles along the road, mostly passing small cottages. Sometimes there were large stone pillars and wrought iron gates which marked the entry to some grander property. "We won't go calling on neighbours today, Julia. Today is just for us."

Then he turned off the main road onto a rough track, which Julia thought was certain to bog the old vehicle down. But Jamie drove skilfully, slewing the car from side to side, avoiding the places where pools of water had settled into the ruts. Here the land was open and uncultivated; heather, now past its August glory of purple, was brown. "Good shooting—or it used to be when we had game keepers. My mother used to make a little money by letting out the shooting before the war. If people were willing to pay, she would even put them up at the castle, and she played the lady of the manor very well—at the same time helping make up the rooms in the morning, and giving a hand in the kitchen." They were climbing quite steeply, and finally reached the place he sought. They were on high ground, a steep bluff which overlooked the loch. They went to the edge, which gave a view of the castle on its island.

"We're actually on Sinclair land here, but you can't reach the castle except by a long hike along the shore . . ." Julia saw from a different aspect the scene which had so enchanted her that morning. There were patches of cultivation, and pastures for the cattle, the same white dots of sheep stretching up into the hillsides. The sun glowed warmly at its noon zenith. There was a mirror vision of part of the castle reflected in the stillness of the loch.

"Jamie—it's so beautiful."

He took her hand. "I almost wish it weren't. If it were pouring with rain, and shrouded in mist you'd get a truer picture of what it's usually like. But there it is—my whole world, Julia. All I have, and all I ever want. Apart from the money to make it a bit better. But I'll earn it. I know I will. After the war things will be different. My father pulled it free of debt, but I'd gladly mortgage the whole thing again to give it new life." He sighed. "Well, that's what I say. That's what I dream. One can always dream, I suppose."

"Only very dull people don't have dreams," she said softly.

He went back to the car, and started carrying the picnic basket and rugs to the place where they had stood. The dogs ran around sniffing in the heather for rabbits and hares, their waving tails sometimes the only mark of their presence. "Aren't you afraid they'll get lost—wander off?"

"Not them," Jamie said as he spread the rugs. "They'll always have an ear cocked—perhaps looking for a handout from the basket because you're a stranger, and they've already reckoned that you're soft-hearted. But at the first sound of the engine starting up, they'll be jumping into the back, no matter what. They know where they live, and who feeds them. Country dogs don't often get lost. If they decided to make their way back along the shore, they'd be waiting for us with tongues hanging out when we got back."

They ate the ham and cheese sandwiches Janet had packed, the chicken legs, the Dundee cake. They washed it down with small tots of whisky poured from a silver flask and drunk from small silver cups. Jamie produced these from a leather container made especially for them, a relic, Julia thought, from more lavish times.

When they had finished, and after Julia had shared some of the sandwiches with the dogs, who had come back to claim space on the rugs, Jamie lay back, put his hands behind his head, and stared at the sky. A hawk of some kind circled above. "We have a pair of Golden Eagles nesting here," he said. "Our own special treasure." He fixed his eyes on the bird. "Now that I've told you all my poor dreams, Julia, what do *you* dream of? Tell me. Do you dream of seeing your name in lights above the title—when the lights go back on again? Do you dream of being up there on the screen which Janet thinks must be very heaven?"

She shrugged, and looked down at him. "I wish you hadn't asked. Or I wish you'd asked some night when we were having dinner in London, and the answer would have seemed obvious. I spent years studying at RADA with just that thought—but because of Father, I wanted it to be the stage rather than the screen. He didn't . . . well, he didn't enjoy Hollywood, or filming very much. But it paid well. I thought I would follow him, and I would fight like a tiger to get the parts I wanted. Well—you know what happened. I got a plum part, and I'm lined up for another, and I'm not at all sure that's what I really want. I prepared all my life to be my father's daughter, but when it came to playing that on the stage, that's all it felt like—a stage, and I was only there to support him. He doesn't need me now, and I wonder if I need the stage, or the name in lights. I'm not a great natural, as he is. He strides the stage, and he dominates it, as he does the audience. His is the face and the figure everyone watches. Even in the few films he made, it was the same. A natural photogenic quality. A gift of presence. I don't believe I've got it, and I don't think it can be learned. And somehow, now, I don't care very much. I've enjoyed the applause—and the red roses. Oh, I loved the red roses from Jamie Sinclair. But I don't think I care *enough*. I hate the thought of a life-time of discipline—of keeping up ballet classes, and voice classes, if it isn't going to get me right to the top. The top is a long way off, Jamie, and I may never make it. I'd mind that—just being mediocre. I'd hate people—worse, I'd hate critics saying 'What a pity, with a mother and father like that.' Sometimes I envy Connie. It isn't that she isn't ambitious. But she's ambitious for much simpler things. I think she would like a steady husband and a family. A modest measure of happiness. *That* isn't easy to achieve, either."

He was silent for some time, absent-mindedly playing with Rory's soft ear. Then he sat up, and stared down at the castle on its island in the loch below. "And I am bound here. I can't live anywhere else, or for any other reason. I was born to this, and

I can't shake it." He paused, then he said, "It would have been different if Callum had lived."

"Callum?"

"I told you I had an older brother. Years older than I. We weren't companions. Too big an age difference. But everyone adored him. He would go shooting and fishing with my father. *They* were companions, more like brothers than father and son. It was really for his sake that my grandfather realized that he would have to hand over affairs to my father, or there would be nothing for Callum to inherit. My mother thought the sun rose out of him. I was an unexpected afterthought. I think they were quite pleased when I was born, but in their hearts they already had the perfect heir."

"What happened?"

"We're not sure. Just the empty, capsized boat in the loch. He often went fishing alone, and was perfectly capable. But storms here get up very suddenly. The wind sweeps down from the mountains, and there are waves enough to swamp any small boat. They never forbade him to do anything, you see. He was so capable—so damn good at everything. Even if there'd been someone else with him, it could have happened just the same way. It nearly killed them—my parents. Even as young as I was I can remember that they were seized with a kind of rigor. Hardly able to think, or give directions. It was the steward we had at the time who organized the search of the shores of the loch—every man and woman on the estate joined in, and every neighbour sent their help, and came themselves. It took about three days to find him. Washed ashore on the other side of the loch. His hands were tangled in fishing lines. My father could not understand how Callum got himself into that situation. For months after that Father hardly spoke. He didn't want to talk to the children of the estate workers. He didn't want even to *see* me. I wasn't very old, but I knew what it felt like to feel guilty. I was alive, and Callum was dead. I think I realized later that if I lived three lifetimes I couldn't make up for what they had lost. My father drank quite a lot, I remember—something he hadn't done before. My grandfather died—some say of the shock. And then my father went off and did the same thing that had killed Callum. He went shooting alone in the forest—it was deer-hunting season, and he was used to stocking up the larder. But this time he didn't ask his friends—it had always been a sort of social occasion before. And he didn't take a ghillie with him. To go shooting alone is against the rules. Just as it's against the rules not to break your gun when you're walking through the woods. He hadn't broken his gun—or perhaps he was stalking a deer and was into the kill. We don't know about that, either. We think he slipped from a craggy place in the forest. They found him at the bottom of a sort of ravine with half his head blown away. Of course there was talk. Some people said he was a crazed man. Others just said he was a damn fool. But whatever—it left my mother alone, with just me. A poor enough legacy."

Julia felt anger. "Jamie, I won't listen! You're worth more than that. You're her life. She hangs on every word you speak."

"More's the pity. She should have something more to anchor her life to. The war might have been bad for me, but if I go—then I go! Death doesn't bother me. It's what I leave behind for her to carry on. I sometimes wonder if I didn't let the Spitfire go that day just a fraction too soon, thinking that somehow I had to survive . . . for her."

Julia began quickly to pack their plates and the remainder of the food back into the basket. "We agreed we wouldn't talk about that. You're morbid, Jamie. It's nonsense to think you have to get yourself through the war just to come back here to have care of an inheritance. You have to live for yourself! Not for a castle, or a sacred trust. Not for your mother." She got to her knees, but he pulled her back down beside him. This time his kiss was more urgent, more demanding than last night's.

"Damn!—I want you," he said. "I ache for you. But it can't be yet. Not until I'm sure that that's what *you* want. Not just a quick roll in the hay, but forever. So, if you don't mind, I'll try to live for you, if for no other reason."

She disengaged his hands from her shoulders. "Jamie, we'll take it one step at a time. Being as sure and careful as two people who are in love can ever be. People in love aren't careful. Love makes you reckless, not sure and careful. One day at a time . . . Come on, let's go. I'm tired," she added striving to keep the tension out of her tone. Perhaps her mood was over-laid with disappointment. She wanted him, and he would make no move to take her. "Honourable Jamie. Not taking advantage . . . Perhaps you expect *me* to wait forever. I'm not Connie. I really don't know how to be sure and careful. I'll grab at just a little time—if that's all we've got. But now—now I'd like to go back. I can still feel the aches from the train. It's getting cold . . ."

Her mood had changed from peace and equanimity

to doubt and mistrust. Michael had been right. Jamie had brought her here to show her what he was committed to, what he would return to if he came through the war. There was no woman stronger than this legacy of sadness and dwindling hope. He lived only to struggle upwards from the depth where the deaths of his father and brother had left him. She began to wish he had never come to Anscombe that day in spring. She wished she had never seen his face, wished she had never laid her eyes on his hands. Just then a chill wind whipped up from the loch. Looking around for the last time she saw that mist had come in to obscure those far, snow-touched peaks of the mountain range. Jamie whistled the dogs into the back of the shooting brake. They drove away in silence. When they passed through the forest it seemed darker than before. She knew now that somewhere near to here his father had died. She had a further, quick glimpse of the forlorn little cottage which the forest had almost overtaken. It had become a place of sadness. Then the vision of the loch and the castle came to them. Here his brother had died. Physically she tried to shake off the thought and memory of death. Then, as if he had known the wild mixture of her emotions all along, his hand reached out to take hers briefly as they rattled over the drawbridge. "I'm sorry, my love. All these wild outpourings. Just put it down to my coming back here. Coming back—well, I wish sometimes I need never come back. They all expect too much. I know it. They expect too much of any woman who's fool enough to marry me. And yet I'm stuck with this. There's no need for you to be buried here, Julia. The world holds better things for you. Don't let all this trap you, as it's trapped me."

That night dinner was in the housekeeper's room, as breakfast had been. Lady Jean had not changed, so neither did Julia. She drank her whisky with her legs stretched out to the fire, where all three dogs lay. The talk was mostly between Jamie and his mother—talk of friends and neighbours, or cousins and more distant kin. Inevitably there was bad news of deaths and injuries, things his mother had not told him in letters. There had been some deaths and injuries among those who fought, and among those too old or too young to fight. The Glasgow docks had taken a fearful hammering from the German bombers, and a young cousin had died as his ship berthed at Strathclyde, having survived yet another perilous Atlantic crossing. Another cousin, a girl of twenty, had died from shrapnel wounds she received as she helped man an anti-aircraft gun post. And there had been births. More young kin scattered all over Scotland. Photographs to show. All the things of a family life Julia could not share.

Dinner was soup and fish and beef, pudding with heavy cream. "Janet really does not take much notice of the austerity measures—and most certainly not when Jamie is home. She cannot see that the little she keeps back will make any difference."

"She isn't far wrong," Julia said. "In London, if you know the right places, there's always enough—and not as well cooked."

"Don't tell her." Lady Jean managed a smile. "It will only encourage her. Dear knows, she eats little enough herself. But at times like this her pride is involved. You both must eat the best she can provide, and she's ingenious about where she gets it—and rather unscrupulous. Barter is the great thing. Fish for eggs. Ham for game. That way, you see, no ration coupons are involved. She thinks she's inside the regulations."

This evening, as they sat around that simple table, without the silver candelabra and dishes, the mood was more relaxed. Often Julia found Lady Jean's eyes on her, but she asked no questions about their day, except where they had picnicked. "Good for Jamie to have a day off. But we must try to visit a little—and invite some people here. His last visit was so short, there wasn't time for any of that. But people will expect to see him this leave." She seemed to be indicating that Jamie did not belong to Julia alone.

The whisky and wine seemed more potent than the night before. Julia said, "If you don't mind—perhaps I'll go to bed. The journey up here—or perhaps just the bracing air today . . ."

Jamie was on his feet immediately. "You won't take a walk by the loch first? Clears the head. You'll sleep marvellously."

"I think I'll sleep marvellously, in any case."

Lady Jean nodded in approval. She couldn't keep them apart, but she welcomed every sign that perhaps they were not as close as she feared. "I know Janet has already put hot-water bottles in your bed. Put more coal on the fire," she added expansively. "Would you like a brandy to take upstairs?" The solicitous hostess, eager to be rid of her.

Jamie saw her, as last night, to the top of the stairs. Without last night's blazing fire, the Great Hall seemed vast and cavernous, devoid of life, and yet haunted by too many centuries of history. He kissed her gently, almost absently, as if he knew the doubts that swirled within her, and would do nothing to assuage them. "Sleep well." She might have been one of those numerous cousins and lesser kin they had talked of.

In the silence of the Red Tower Room she pulled back the curtain a little. Utter blackness greeted her. No sign of stars, no sheen of water. As she stood there, the first spatter of rain hit the glass. Soon it lashed more strongly. By the time she was ready for bed, the lead, handmade gutters and downspouts, stamped here and there with the Sinclair crest, as she had observed in the courtyards that morning, were already running with water. She slipped into the huge bed, and gratefully felt the touch of the hot-water bottles against her feet.

Her sleep that night was troubled and fitful. There was a dream of hands lifted desperately from the water of the loch, hands entangled with fishing lines. She woke shivering from that dream, and sensed that she was not alone in the room. The fire had died, but its red embers remained. Was there some vague image there by the great carved mantle? something in a flowing robe, man or woman she couldn't tell? But the gentle sigh she heard which seemed to be the end of a sob was that of a woman. Or was is nothing at all? The wind also sighed about the castle, and moaned in the chimney. She half sat-up, and the image was gone. Then she lay down and pulled the blankets about her ears, willing to hear no more of what this place might reveal to her.

But she was still awake in the morning when Janet brought her tea. The curtain rings rattled back as before, and the cheerful voice was telling her there was a wee bit of rain, but that it would clear by evening. She didn't need to look from the windows to know. The mist and rain pressed against them, and the ashes were dead and grey in the hearth.

"Janet, was there . . . was there ever someone in this room who was very unhappy? Someone who wept?"

"Ah, if you go back over the centuries there might have been scores, Miss Seymour. But the one they see most—those who do see or hear her—why that could be the Lady Ellen. Very young, she was. No more than fourteen. The laird of that time abducted her—ah, it was always happening in those days. Hundreds of years ago. They plundered and murdered and abducted—all for the money, or because they thought *they'd* be murdered. Terrible harsh times they were, and these old walls have seen the lot."

"What happened to—to Lady Ellen?"

"She was fatherless, poor bairn. Her lands went to the laird. She died in childbirth. But her son lived. Myself, I've never seen nor heard her. But some say they do." She peered more closely at Julia. "Master Jamie didn't tell you, did he?"

"No, nothing—he said nothing."

Janet poured tea into a dainty china cup. "Then it's best you say nothing. It will not please them to know that you have been disturbed. Or perhaps that you even know anything about Lady Ellen. I'll get a tongue-lashing from Lady Jean. Ah, but mistress—" she had slipped back into the old Scottish form of address, "it would be a strange house that has stood as long as this one without its tragedies." Her face brightened as her habitual cheerfulness came back. "But then we've had our times of joy and happiness as well. Like every other family . . . Well, mistress, Morag will be up in a few minutes with the hot water. And a good hearty breakfast will take away any wee stirrings in the night."

The days of Jamie's leave sped by, and they seemed hardly ever to be alone together. If someone did not come to lunch, then they were bidden to lunch at some of the adjoining estates. Dinner parties were given for Jamie. There seemed an anxious wish on the part of those who entertained them that Jamie should have the best sort of welcome. It was evident that the Sinclairs were a popular family. Many of the people to whose houses they were bidden were of Lady Jean's generation. To welcome back a young man was part of the yearning, sternly suppressed, to see their own sons and daughters back among them. In Jamie's case there seemed a special warmth, Julia thought. He was one of the famous "Few" of the Battle of Britain. He had been decorated for gallantry and service. He was an air ace who had barely missed death—Lady Jean must not have told her neighbours and friends the full extent of his injuries, but they could be clearly seen in the first minutes with him.

The welcome for Julia was somewhat more reserved. Firstly, she was a stranger. They were polite enough to welcome her because Jamie had brought her. But their good manners were overlaid with just the faintest hint of mistrust. She was not one of them; she came from that far-off world of the stage, and her mother, though famous in her own right, was, after all, a Russian, and therefore totally strange. Her father might be a Knight, but was one of those "stage fellows"—a breed they scarcely met and who were generally thought of as being of the unstable kind. But she evoked an amount of curiosity also. The story of her *Cordelia* to her father's *Lear*, his disappearance from the stage after his wife's death, and his return with his own daughter as his support had penetrated even the Scottish papers and magazines. Julia wondered what the reaction would have been if these Scottish gentry, these welcoming neighbours and friends had known the full truth of the complex relationship between herself and Jamie, the secret she had said must not ever be talked about, even though she knew Jamie was tortured by it.

Even the story of the rose garden in place of the oasthouse was known—though Lady Jean was hardly likely to have talked of the rose bush she had contributed. But somehow the news had got out. One day of glorious autumn weather, as Julia strolled in the rose garden which graced a fine Georgian house built when the need to fortify great houses had gone, the owner, a courteous, handsome man, with a disconcerting straight gaze from his grey eyes, in his mid-fifties, she judged, talked to her of it. "A lovely idea of Sir Michael's—to make a memorial rose garden. I keep this one up myself. Can't spare a gardener for purely ornamental things like this—but we've put as much ground into vegetables as we can manage. This was my wife's great passion. I keep it up for her. The only thing that comforts me about her death was that she didn't live to know about our sons' deaths." He paused for a moment. "I'd be extremely honoured if Sir Michael would accept a bush from here. Now might be a good time to lift it, as everything's pretty well gone dormant for the winter. You might take it back with you, perhaps . . ."

It was the first time she had felt genuine warmth and sympathy among those who had been her hosts. Tears were close to her eyes. "That's extremely kind of you, Sir Niall. At first we—the family—thought his obsession with the rose garden was somewhat morbid. My sister, Alex, was really firm that the area should just be seeded into lawn. But now we see the point. Perhaps it kept him sane through those first months after her death. Certainly the labour of clearing the site—preserving whatever materials were left after the fire for when he can build walls for the rose garden, was the best thing he could have done. Otherwise, I'm afraid, in the hours when he wasn't working, the whisky bottle was his companion. That's passed now . . ."

A kindly hand, obviously worn from his work in the garden, touched hers. "I understand, perfectly, my dear. We all seek escape from tragedy in our various ways. It is good to know Sir Michael is working again—trying to put it behind him. Here in Scotland, although we don't get much chance to see these things, he's regarded as having played the best *Macbeth* of modern times. We're not quite out of the world, you see."

As they walked quietly among the now pruned and leafless bushes, he spoke again. "Does Jamie ever mention my boys . . . the Hendersons?"

She whirled to look him fully in the face. "The Hendersons! Of course. Oh, how stupid of me! But I've met so many people in these few days . . . His best friends . . . not just chums. Friends. They were in his squadron . . ."

"They'd been friends all their lives. Jamie and my younger son, Ian, were the same age. The elder one, Gordon, was only a year older than those two. They grew up together. Gordon went to Oxford a year before the other two followed. But they all joined the RAF Volunteer Reserve. My sons . . ." His voice wavered a little, and he looked firmly at the well-tended earth about the roses bushes. "Gordon was killed first. And then Ian—just a few days later. It was the day after Ian was shot down that Jamie came to grief. I often wonder if his concentration wasn't disturbed by his feelings about losing his friends. They were going so quickly then . . . during the Battle of Britain. It must have been a desperate situation. Watching your squadron shot to pieces . . . and losing your two best friends in such a short time. Jamie has some hard memories . . . You can hardly imagine what it was like for Lady Jean and me in those days. Just to know he survived, never mind how badly he was shot up. We had to have something left to live for. I'm afraid I stake a large claim on Jamie's affections, because he's just about all I've got left. I pray he survives this wretched war." He lifted his head to look directly at Julia. "Do you care for him?"

"I love him."

He nodded. "That's all the answer I need."

For Julia the most difficult day was when they were invited to Darnaway for lunch. Since the day was fair, and no rain threatened, they hitched Catriona up to the trap. "She must be seen to earn her oats sometimes," Lady Jean said, but it was said lightheartedly. Julia suspected that she was looking forward more to this luncheon than any of the others. Darnaway was the home of Kirsty Macpherson, the girl Jamie had told her his mother preferred for his wife to all others. The girl with beauty and money.

The family had gathered in the hall of a splendid eighteenth-century Robert Adam house to greet them. Behind the house was the remainder of an ancient Keep which had once sheltered members of the family, their servants, their cattle, and any who swore allegiance to the chieftain in times of trouble, just as at Sinclair. But here they had been able to abandon the discomfort and inconveniences of the ancient building, demolish the outhouses, and leave it, restored, but not inhabited, to represent their former fighting history. They had been fortunate in the lands that surrounded the castle, good arable and pasture. There was no hill-farming at Darnaway. They had been fortunate in members of the family who had sought their fortunes abroad—investing in sugar plantations in the West Indies, Lady Jean said. That also would have meant enjoying the profits from slavery, Julia thought. They had made wise investments in the Scottish ship-building industry, unlike Jamie's grandfather who had gambled everything on new inventions which had failed. The family owned two whisky distilleries. "Best of all, I suppose," Lady Jean said, when she had come to the end of the recital of good fortune which had made and kept the Macphersons rich, "was that at crucial moments in their history they made good marriages. Some families have a genius for it."

Embraces were exchanged as the two families met. Julia was introduced to Sir Allan and Lady Macpherson; then to Kirsty. Kirsty's welcome to

Jamie had been cordial, but not excessive. Julia found marvellous green eyes turned upon her. "We're so happy you could make this long journey up here. Jamie's letters have been full of how kind your family have been to him." She really was beautiful, Julia thought. The pale, perfect oval of her face was framed by shining auburn hair. She was slim and of more than middle height, with a long neck and jaw-line which was accentuated by the crew-necked cashmere sweater she wore above a pleated skirt—the Macpherson tartan, Julia didn't doubt. She wore no jewellery, except a silver brooch which probably represented the clan badge and motto.

"We didn't ask anyone else," Lady Macpherson said. "I'm afraid, selfishly, we wanted Jamie to ourselves for these few hours. We haven't seen him for such a long time." Julia had already been told they had a son, Harry, serving in the Navy. "We suspect, though of course he can't tell us, that his ship is heading for the Far East." She gave a little sigh as her husband poured the drinks. "And now that I'm over my little illness . . ." Julia had been told on the way there that it had been a major operation from which she had taken a long time to recover, "I think Kirsty will be joining the WAAF. That leaves only our little Una, still at school. But if this wretched war goes on much longer, even *she* will be old enough to join up." She beamed a false smile at Julia. "But you, dear, don't have to think about such things. You will be in demand on the stage, and even if you did join up, they'd just send you around entertaining the troops. Quite necessary, no doubt . . . How very dull life has become here in the Highlands since the war. No one visits any more—never further than a few miles. Most of the servants have gone, they help on the farm—or at least the sons have gone, leaving us only the middle-aged men. You haven't noticed problems like that, I suppose, Miss Seymour. Such a glamorous world you live in—"

"Julia lives on a farm which was right under the action in the Battle of Britain," Jamie cut in. "And she works in London. There's precious little glamour in it, Lady Macpherson."

"Oh, dear." The lady looked flustered. "I've put my foot in it again. Allan, dear, fill Miss Seymour's glass. Can't you see it's empty? Kirsty, pass those little things, whatever Cook's dreamed up. All the servants, Jamie, have asked me to tell you how glad they are you've been able to manage a visit. And that you're well again. Won't it be wonderful when it's all over, and life's back to normal."

"I wonder if it can ever be," Kirsty said. "Any rate, I don't intend to be left out any longer. I want to be able to look anyone in the eye when it *is* all over, and say I did my humble bit."

"I keep telling her there's absolutely no need to join up. It's not yet compulsory. She's doing so much work here with the Red Cross and the—"

They still managed to retain an elderly butler. "Luncheon is served, m'lady."

As they drove back to Sinclair the weather turned, and rain poured down. Julia could only think miserably that Kirsty Macpherson was indeed beautiful and graceful and fully at home among her people in the Highlands. And she was rich. Because of the dark sky, the castle loomed over them suddenly. Julia felt her shoulders, already shrugged deeply into her raincoat, hunch even further. Water was trickling down the back of her neck. She thought she hated Sinclair, and all it stood for, a world in which she would never belong. She would be glad when the visit ended, which would be the day after tomorrow. She would go, gladly. She would never come back. They drove around to the stable yard, so that Jamie could dry and feed Catriona. The kitchen door opened to admit them. "Ah, it's drowned you must be," said Janet. "Shall I pour a wee dram, Lady Jean, to drive out the cold?"

Julia unwillingly shared a glass with Lady Jean in the housekeeper's room. There was a spurious friendliness between them. "Such a lovely house, isn't it—Darnaway? And don't you think Kirsty is beautiful? Augustus John painted her portrait. It wasn't commissioned. He saw her once in London—her coming-out year just before war broke out. He asked to do it. Such a pity there wasn't time to see all their paintings. And they have such a wonderful ceramics collection. Oh, I've been to such grand balls in that house. You didn't even see the ballroom, did you? There are portraits of Victoria and Albert presented to the family after they had stayed at Darnaway . . ."

At last Jamie joined them. "Cat's beginning to show her years, I think," he said. "More than happy to see the stable."

"We all are, my dear," his mother answered. "I so much want tomorrow night to go off well, but it's been a big burden on Janet and Mrs. Kerr and Morag—"

"What the devil are you talking about?"

"No need to be so affronted. I just planned a little dinner party. I would have done it last time, but you couldn't spare more than two nights here. It's your last night here, Jamie—for heaven knows how long. I just asked to dinner the people who have been kind enough to entertain us." Her tone dropped to a reproachful note. "Your last night, Jamie . . ."

He tossed back his whisky, and went to pour another, silently taking Julia's glass from her, and refilling it also.

"You'll wear the kilt, of course, Jamie," his mother said.

"Damn and blast . . ." was all he answered her.

The kitchen was in a flurry of activity all the next day. Jamie grabbed Julia's hand after they had eaten a cold lunch of ham and Scotch eggs. "Come on—get your coat. If I see or hear any more of this I might just decide not to turn up tonight."

He was silent as they made their way through the old walled garden, which presented a picture of neglect, weed-choked and faintly melancholy, and into the vegetable garden, which the Kerrs kept up, and divided the produce with Janet. "Something else to do after the war," Jamie said dismissively.

They made their way around to the drawbridge, and the causeway. The dogs had followed automatically. "She must *know* I didn't want any of this nonsense. I said I wanted a quiet leave, and it's been nothing but tea parties."

"Your friends haven't seen you for so long." Julia felt she had to say it, though the words came unwillingly.

"I haven't enjoyed being peered at quite so closely," he answered. "They've all been gauging how close a call it was for me. One of the reasons I stayed away so long—I didn't want them to see me shuffling along with the stick. But I'm back on active duty. That tells them I'm well. One of the things I most baulked at, though, was that Sir Niall had to see me alive and well—when he had lost both Gordon and Ian. They were great chaps. I was lucky to grow up with them. The whole place feels so odd without them around . . ." He turned off at the end of the causeway. "You haven't walked along the loch yet—well, I grant you, there's not been much time between lunches and tea parties, and so on . . ." He gestured to the three dogs. "Come on, you lazy brutes. What a dog's life you have. No one now to keep you from getting fat and lazy." Then his mood of complaint seemed to break. He bent and fondled the labrador's head, and as the two collies pressed around him, he stroked them all. "Oh, you're not such a bad lot. Can't be helped that there's nothing doing here these days. Look, Julia, look at Rory. What a wonderfully soft mouth he has—a great retriever. Well, my pets, it's a long and boring war for you, too. But we'll get through it. I'll work your tails off when I get back . . ."

There was a touch of winter in the wind that blew off the loch; a dark, lowering sky hung about them. Jamie pulled Julia to him as they walked. "Too cold for you out here? The first snows will be on us soon. It's lonely up here in winter, Julia. I suppose you've imagined that. Perhaps that's why we make such a song and dance about being together when we can . . . it was churlish of me to begrudge Mother her little party. She has long months alone."

His train of thought seemed to flow on naturally. "I suppose this damn castle adds to it—being stuck out here on the loch. Now, if we'd been placed like

Darnaway, or Finavon, Sir Niall's place, all this might have been fertile, arable land. As it is, we have to go miles just to herd the cattle. Lambing time is very rough. I suppose the Sinclairs thought they'd got themselves a nice secure spot when they built where they did, but it's damned awkward now. Even the drawbridge is breaking up. I suppose you've noticed that the arches of the bridge from the causeway are starting to crumble. These old places . . . a real pain in the neck."

"Oh, shut up, Jamie. You do love to grumble. You wouldn't have it any different, even if you could."

He laughed, and bent and kissed her. "Well, a *bit* different." Then he whistled to the dogs. "Let's climb up into the forest. Now that most of the leaves have fallen, it's rather a beautiful place."

They scrambled through the rocks of the shore-line, and into the steep side of the forest. Conifers mingled with oaks and beeches, and underfoot was a carpet of damp leaves. The dogs ran joyously ahead. "If we're lucky we might spot a buck or a doe. That is, if those rascals don't frighten everything within earshot. They've really got very undisciplined. No one to keep them in check."

The magic of the forest closed about them, and they walked in silence, Jamie giving her his hand over the steep and difficult places. There were great outcroppings of rock to which trees precariously clung. "Needs a bit of clearing out," Jamie observed. "Not very good wood-management, but then we don't have the men for it. One clean sweep of the deadfalls here would give us wood for a couple of years for the fires."

"I didn't realize what a nagger you are," Julia said.

"You've hardly stopped complaining about things since we arrived. Can't you just accept what is, and know nothing can be done about it until . . . until later."

He caught her and swung her around until she faced him. "I just need *you* to know that. Nothing can be changed until later. But that doesn't mean I don't see what needs changing. I wonder if you can bear it here? If you can be patient through all the years while I try to change it?"

"Are you asking me to be here then? Are you really asking me?"

"I keep putting it in roundabout ways. I'm afraid to ask, because I'm afraid of the answer. Just take it as said. You'll answer in your own good time."

He walked on, and she had to hurry to catch up. "If that's a proposal of marriage, it's the funniest I've ever heard."

"Had many proposals of marriage, Julia? I suppose you have. Some must have been hilarious. Some must have been quite tempting. Those years at RADA—you must have met some interesting men."

"Boys," she said. "Not very interesting. Boys hoping to be men, hoping to be actors. And most of them terrified of coming near me because of who my father is." She shrugged, and added laconically, "No, Jamie, I can't say I've had a proposal of marriage that was quite meant to be that. So we'll count yours as the first." She tugged at his coat sleeve. "Want to say it again, just so I'll be sure."

As they kissed, the first drops of rain fell through the remaining leaves. "Oh, damn! You'll get soaked again. Look, we'll have to make a dash for it down to the road. It's pretty steep here. Think you can manage it?"

"Yes . . ." But she sensed his reluctance. He whistled to the dogs, and then turned quickly through the trees until they came to the edge of the steepest part of the forest they had yet travelled. He half-lifted her through the worst places, leading the way in others, showing her where to hold the limbs of trees, where to place her feet. The rain grew steadily heavier, but his features expressed a feeling that had nothing to do with discomfort. His look told her this was a place of special significance, somewhere he did not want to be. "Was it here, Jamie? Was it here your father . . . fell."

"Yes," he said tersely. "A place I never meant you to be." They had reached the bottom, where a narrow stream ran, and began the ascent of the other slope. "Not so far now," he said, "not such rough going." His mood seemed to brighten as they reached the top. "You know—you're in very good shape. You look so ethereal . . ."

"Oh, for heaven's sake, what do you think we train for? Titania's fairies? How much energy do you think it needs for my father to put on one of his fight scenes? Hamlet isn't always languishing around, you know."

"From the feel of you, I think you could probably manage an army assault course. Good, we're getting there. Do you see the road? It's easy now . . ."

"There's the little house," she said. "Can't we stop there? It's a good mile back to the castle. Perhaps the rain will ease off."

He looked at her wet hair sticking to her cheeks. "Well—perhaps we'd better. Not that I can guarantee it's much dryer than out here." He touched the door of the cottage, and it gave under his hand. He looked dubiously at the roof. "Well, it's still almost in one piece."

She was surprised to find a slate floor beneath her feet. "I don't know why I imagined it would be an earth floor."

"No, not this place. It was the usual old Scottish butt and ben—just two rooms, and one tacked on the back later. There's the remains of an old wooden bed in the other room. The man, McBain, who had it was a game-keeper for my father. He added the other room as the kids came along, and dug a well. I suppose he did the floor as well."

"What happened to him?—if he put in all this work he must have expected to stay."

Jamie shrugged. "I don't know. All I know is that he went off to Canada rather suddenly, with his family. It was sometime close to when my father died. I wasn't paying much attention to anything else then—ah, look, there's dry wood still. Before the war I used to come with the men when we did a few days timber cutting in the forest. We always used to come here to eat our lunch if it was close enough. It was generally chilly enough for a fire—nearly always is in Scotland by the time the leaves have fallen. We'd make a fire, and eat our lunch, and I don't think food ever tasted so good to me. I remember the flasks used to come out. Come to think of it, this was probably the place where I first got just a little bit drunk. I seem to remember they wouldn't let me handle an axe or a saw that afternoon. Self-preservation." While he talked he was breaking off little twigs from the slim dry branches, and he put a match to them.

"Hope the chimney still draws, or we'll be smoked out." But the thin smoke spiralled upwards, and he laid on bigger sticks. "In a minute I'll chance something heavier, and we'll have a decent fire, and a wee dram."

"You haven't got a flask with you!"

"Hardly ever without it up here. *Uisge-beatha*. Water of life, we call it. Ah there . . ." The fire was gaining on the dry wood. "We always made it a rule that whatever we burned, we put back the same amount, cut and ready for the next time. But the forest's grown too damn close now. This used to be a nice open space. I can remember that man's kids playing in the sun." He looked more closely at the roof. "I'll have a word with Kerr, and see if he can't spare a couple of men and a few hours to see to the slates. Pity to let it all go. Though God knows, there are enough of these old places dotted over the estate —empty, just falling apart. But this is close enough to the castle to perhaps be of some use in the future. When the war's over—oh, damn the phrase, but there's no other way to say it—when the war's over, I think there'll be men and families looking for jobs and some place to live—almost any place."

He looked around more closely, though the curtain of rain cut off almost any sight of the road or the forest; the glass of the small windows was filmed with the dust of years. "I had some pretty good times here, Julia—with the men. I wasn't the young laird when I worked with them, and shared their smoked sausage and their dram. They talked to me as if I were a man, and said things to me my mother would never have said. These were the people I wanted you to meet, Julia. Some of them are dead now. But enough are still around—probably their kids are in the forces, too. Yes, it would have been better if we'd gone through the whole estate, drinking tea and eating scones, and drinking whisky and listening to what they had to say to me. Far better than these bloody tea parties. Well, next time . . ."

He added another stouter log to the fire, and filled the cap of his flask and gave it to her. "Just toss it back—don't sip. It'll get right down into your bones." He eased the raincoat off her shoulder. "God, you're soaked." He took off the woollen cap she wore, and fluffed up her hair. "Lean into the fire, you silly fool." He took off his scarf and tried to dry her hair. "Can't have you going back with pneumonia."

She dropped her coat on the ground, careless of the dust of the years, the mud brought in on their shoes. Jamie had dragged up some old rush matting, and Julia sat there before the fire, reached out a hand to give back the flask cap. "Fill it up for yourself, and come and sit by me, and keep me warm, Jamie."

He spread his own waterproof on the matting beside hers. He refilled the little silver cap, and eased himself down beside her, the movement of his injured leg still not quite easy. He tossed back the drink. "Want another? And then perhaps we'd better go, rain or no rain. Because if we stay . . ."

"Yes, Jamie. If we stay we'll finally make love to each other. What do you think, Jamie? I think we'll stay . . . it could be that we'll stay together forever?"

"You'd stay here—with me—forever?"

"Forever. I have no home except with you. You're in my heart, Jamie, however inconvenient it may be. However difficult, and perhaps not very sensible. Even foolhardy. But I love you, and I can't help it.

I can't bear the thought that you'll go away, and maybe you'll be killed, and I'll live forever with the thought that you never had me as your own—and that I didn't have the courage to give myself to you. I want you, Jamie, just the way you want me. There's a war, and maybe our time is very short. I want to remember . . ."

He stifled her words with his mouth. "You can't know how much I want you," he said, his lips moving against hers. "Fiercely, terribly. But loving you with it . . . always loving you, I'll love you until I die, Julia."

She lay back on her coat. "But you won't die, Jamie. You'll live because I need you so much. You are my future—and my past. We'll love together all our lives. And we'll begin right now."

"You'll freeze . . ." he said as he began to undress her.

"Not with you, I won't. You'll be gentle, Jamie? I know you will. For me, it's the first time."

"The first time . . . in a humble, rather dirty little bothy in the middle of a wood. I had planned much better than this."

"A palace could be no better . . . Ah . . . Oh, so beautiful," as he stroked her breasts, as he bent to kiss them. "Look how beautiful the fire is. How the rain sounds on the roof . . . Ah . . ."

He was slow and gentle the first time, and then later, after they had lain wrapped in each other's arms, heads pressed into each other's shoulders, the second time was more tumultuous, as if they were aware not just of the day passing, but time itself, the very era in which they lived. They had to use time as it hurried away—a phantom leaving them as the woods grew darker. Each second together seemed to be marked off on a finite clock. Neither could say how much time was left to them. They used what they had. The witnesses to the passion of their coupling were the dogs, who pressed their wet coats against the naked, entwined bodies.

They got back to the castle when it was fully dark. "We took shelter in the old McBain cottage," Jamie said carelessly, without apology. "But we got wet, in any case."

"I was beginning to worry . . ." Lady Jean said.

He shook off Julia's wet outer clothes in the little porch of the kitchen door. "Ah, don't you remember I know every inch of this place like my own hand? I took Julia in out of the rain, and built a fire. Must ask Kerr to try to get some more dry wood put there . . . It was like the old days, but much better with Julia." He looked his mother straight in the eyes. "Oh, yes—better in every way."

"I see . . . Well, you'd better go up and get changed. You just have time. We've fired up the boiler, so there should be plenty of hot water."

"Time! Oh, yes, we have plenty of time. All the time in the world, don't we, Julia?" They had come in through the kitchen, and Janet had offered them a cup of tea in passing. Surveying the flurry of the dinner preparations, Jamie declined. "Maybe we'll take a drink up to our rooms."

"The fires are lighted. Your hair, Miss Seymour . . ."

"Her name is Julia, Mother. Surely you know that now. And I'm sure she can dry her own hair . . ."

He paused in the Great Hall, where a huge fire

burned, to fill two glasses. "I'll be drunk before the evening even begins," Julia said, and then giggled. "Do you think she knows?"

"Who cares? She'll know soon enough."

"Dear heaven," Janet called out to them as she came sweeping across the hall with another tray full of glasses. "And haven't you let the dogs bring all their mud onto the floor Morag spent half a day cleaning!"

Boisterously Jamie put his arm around her shoulders and kissed her cheek with a loud smack. "Now you can't be angry with me, Janet . . . my last night. Is this the way to send a warrior back to battle."

"Oh, shush now, Master Jamie, getting around me with your tongue. Aren't I a stern enough body when I have the mind to be?" She slapped the tray down, and turned back to look at them both. "Well, you make a bonny couple, you do, at that. Miss Julia looks as if she's been dragged through a hedge backwards, but a bonny sight, for all that. You really should be in the moving pictures, Miss Julia, where *everyone* could see you, instead of those poor few who pack into the theatre. But you will, mark my words. I'll look for the day."

Calling to the dogs, she scurried briskly away, and Jamie gently took Julia's arm and led her upstairs. "Are you all right, my love? Did I hurt you? I would never hurt you, if I could help it, Julia."

"The divine hurt of a woman's life—if it's the right man. I've been pawed and grabbed at, and I've landed a good right-hander from time to time. Today, I invited you, Jamie. You came home to me, and it was the most wonderful feeling in the world. The McBain cottage will be the palace of my life."

There were actually a few inches of hot water to run into the huge bathtub. Julia bathed quickly, and rinsed out her blood-stained pants in cold water, not caring what anyone thought. Let them think what they liked. Soon she would marry Jamie. Nothing mattered beside that—no one's good opinion, no one's disappointment. She could fight them all now. She dried her hair, and sang; experiencing a light-heartedness she had not known since she had entered this castle. She swept her long hair up on top of her head, and thrust a few pins in it, letting little tendrils trail on her cheeks and neck. Did they think that merely getting wet hair would stop an actress from looking good? Very discreetly she applied make-up, using the techniques of the theatre, so that her eyelids were faintly shadowed, and her mouth appeared to have no lipstick on it, although it was very defined. Then she took out her mother's crimson velvet gown—the rose gown she now called it. Janet's cooking had added the few pounds she lacked, and she filled it nicely. Her breasts swelled warmly at the neckline. Just before she turned away from her mirror she paused, touched those breasts. Jamie had kissed them. Forever they would be different.

And far below, in the Great Hall, she heard the first, rather unearthly sound, as a lone piper warmed up, a sound both plaintive and melancholy, and in this ambience, heart-touching.

For several minutes she remained in the darkness of the high gallery, taking in the scene below. About eight of the guests had already arrived. They had expected, in the depth of war time, a festive evening in their own tradition, and had dressed for it. Every man wore a kilt and a velvet jacket, with buttons of silver. They wore sporrans of soft fur, and silver buckled shoes. The women wore either a tartan pleated silk skirt with a white blouse and sash of silk tartan pinned to the left shoulder and tied at the waist on the right, or a dress of plain colour, again with the sash. The clan brooches were of silver, and some, by the flashes of light from the fire, had their heraldic symbols discreetly outlined by tiny jewels. Lady Jean stood in their midst, wearing a severe black dress, the bright Sinclair tartan slashing it with colour. The piper had moved up to the other side of the gallery from where Julia stood. He strode back and forth, the tune brighter now. Julia realized that her hand shook just a little on the banister as she descended into the light. Jamie looked up and saw her, and at once came forward. He wore the kilt, as his mother had asked, his velvet jacket was black, his frilled and ruffled shirt had obviously been freshly laundered and made ready for this occasion. "This is too much, Jamie," Julia whispered to him. "It looks like something from a stage set—or more, the cinema. Even the piper . . ."

"Sometimes I'd like to curse my mother. But you have to understand that it's no great thing here for them to dress like this. They do it naturally. The man up there with the bagpipes is one of the farm workers, who happens to have a talent with the instrument. If we seem to be in fancy dress, I assure you we aren't. But Mother does carry her little schemes a bit far. I had hoped for a quiet last evening—" He dropped her hand, as more guests arrived, "You'll have already met them all. It's Mother's thank-you for their hospitality. Her one chance for a little festivity. She won't be going out all through the winter, and there'll be precious little chance for any of these other families to have something to celebrate. So be tolerant with her . . ."

The last arrivals were the Macphersons. Lady Macpherson wore a little tartan vest above her pleated skirt—perhaps for warmth, Julia thought. Her clan badge holding the silk sash in place was set entirely in diamonds; diamonds were on her delicate hands. She greeted Julia. "What an English rose you are among all we thistles, my dear. Allan, doesn't she look divine? Such a gown . . ."

"It was my mother's . . . used for concerts. My clothing coupons would never stretch to it."

"And you don't have a tartan, do you?" Kirsty said. She wore long diamond earrings which blazed against her auburn hair and long white neck. She wore a white crêpe gown which showed no sign of having been inherited from anyone, with the clan sash tied about it. The badge which held it in place, like her mother's, was jewelled, but the figure of the cat with upheld paw at its centre was picked out in tiny emeralds and rubies. "The tartan takes we poor Scots through so many occasions. All you really need is a skirt and a blouse and the sash, and you're perfectly dressed."

Julia bit back the tart response which rose to her lips. Instead she said, smiling, "No, we don't have nearly such a neat and decorative way of getting through every social occasion. May I ask what your clan badge stands for? It looks remarkably fierce."

"Most clan badges and mottos are fierce," came the

reply. "We're a fighting nation. The motto of the Macphersons is 'Touch not the cat, bot a glove'—really means 'without a glove'."

"Remarkably apt," Julia answered. "I can see one should take care in dealing with the Macpherson—"

She was interrupted by Sir Niall Henderson. "I brought it, my dear. The rose bush. For you to take with you tomorrow. All wrapped up in wet sacking. I say, you do look splendid. You must forgive we old fools for dressing up this way. We don't have many legitimate excuses these days." He glanced around the Great Hall, the shining floors, the bowls of early winter jasmine which brightened the corners, the pieces of shining family silver which Lady Jean had brought out and polished. He cocked his head to the skirl of the pipes above them. "Oh, it does my heart good . . . pray God we'll see the old times back again, whatever the sacrifices we must make. Jean, my dear, did anyone tell you that the young Robertson boy was reported missing in action in the desert the other day? We can just hope he was taken prisoner. Those Italians are worthless, but I fear what the Germans may do."

"I'll write to Margaret," Lady Jean said. "Her most loved child, I think. He came so late to her . . . how sad . . ."

"Now, I shouldn't have told you. Don't want to spoil your evening . . ."

Julia was served whisky from a tray carried by a man wearing a kilt whom she belatedly recognized as William Kerr. Jamie was back at her side. "Well, Mr. Kerr, I didn't expect to see you here—doing this. A little beneath you, isn't it?"

"Not if it's for Lady Jean, Master Jamie. I would

pitch in and do anything to give her the evening she's been hoping for since the news came that you were shot down. I think that day she never expected to see you alive again. This is the evening she's dreamed of. Why should I not help out? Mrs. Kerr's going to be waiting on table to help Morag."

Jamie stayed at Julia's side all through the drinks period, but they were separated when William Kerr finally, with a faint show of embarrassment, announced dinner. Lady Jean was seated at one end of the long table, Jamie at the other. Lady Macpherson was on his right, Mrs Gilcrest on his left. Kirsty was placed almost opposite Julia.

Julia found to her relief that Sir Niall was next to her. She thanked him again for the rose bush. "Father will be thrilled. I know he'll rush down to Anscombe to get it planted . . ."

He asked her carefully, courteously, about the intensity of the Battle of Britain as it had raged in the skies above Anscombe, being careful to avoid any direct mention of her mother's death, but avid for details of the last days of both his sons. "It must have been terrible—living right under it all. I understand the bombers and Messerschmitts had only the fuel capacity to stay a short time on the raids, so they must have been coming and going endlessly . . ."

"I can remember," Julia said, as she described what it had been like, "one of the farm workers saying to me. 'Looks like we had a real fine harvest of Messerschmitts this year.' We didn't really admit that so many of them were Spitfires and Hurricanes."

"Well, thank God Jamie survived his episode." He was silent for a while, perhaps thinking of his sons, who had not. Then he turned his attention to the soup, as they were finishing it. "Now this to you, my dear, may seem like any ordinary beef soup, if a bit hearty, since it's nearly a stew. But the old Scot's name for it is 'Skink'. Tell them that when you go back across the border."

They were being served now by Morag and Mrs. Kerr with smoked salmon. "Don't look so surprised, my dear. This may not be the Savoy, but these are salmon from our own rivers, and we all have our own smoke houses. We turn a blind eye to a bit of poaching, so long as some is left as a wee gift at the house. Ah—look at Lady Jean! How radiant her face is . . . for this one evening, at least, she's a happy woman . . . Now what's this . . . ah, well, she's done us proud. Her Janet must have worked like a dog . . ."

When the salmon plates were removed, the piper had descended the stairs and placed himself by the doors to the kitchen passage. Morag and Mrs. Kerr held them open as Janet, in a severe black dress and starched apron marched out to his tune, carrying a great silver dish which contained something Julia had never seen in her life. "Haggis!" Sir Niall exclaimed. "Well, that's a treat. Can't seem to get anyone to make it these days. Now don't be frightened of what you think is in it. Just enjoy the taste."

"Sheep's stomach, isn't it?" Julia said, dubiously.

"Sheep's stomach is only the skin that holds it. It's a sort of sausage. The 'haute cuisine' of all sausages." After it was served, he tasted it anxiously. "Haggis Royal, I'd say, from all the different things in it." They had been drinking good wine, and their glasses were never empty, but they were now served small glasses of whisky. "Pour it over the mix, my dear," he advised her. "Ah yes—this lovely nutty flavoured brown oatmeal, mutton, lights, anchovies, cayenne—Janet's got it all." He raised his glass to Lady Jean. "Marvellous, my dear. A real treat."

Julia took the first forkful, aware of Kirsty's eyes on her. Even if it was hateful, she would eat it. To her surprise, it tasted very good, and had a marvellous texture. It was accompanied by mashed potatoes and swedes. "That's traditional," Sir Niall assured her. "Trust Janet to get it just right."

Julia felt she was being challenged when the haggis was withdrawn, and the dessert served. It looked something like trifle, but tasted richer, and she wondered if her stomach could stand it. "'Tipsy Laird', it's called," Kirsty said, across the table. "A mix of sherry and brandy."

"Potent," Julia gasped. "And terribly filling . . ."

"I suppose an actress has to watch her figure very carefully," Kirsty remarked.

"What's wrong with her figure?" Sir Niall barked. "Looks perfect to me. And I'm no mean judge, Kirsty."

Julia smiled her gratitude. There began a little round of toasts, and short speeches—mostly to wish Jamie well. Other names were recalled. "Jean, just for one magic night, has brought back the good old days. May they and peace soon return to us all. May our sons and daughters—the sons and daughters of Scotland—return in health to us. May this war, finally, forever, end wars."

Julia never knew how anyone summoned the energy for it, but after dinner, the piper played reels, and that little company formed up to dance. Julia hung back, refusing even Jamie's request to partner her. "I haven't any idea of how it's done. I'd only make a fool of myself."

"Oh, come on! Everyone is half drunk. No one will notice." But she still refused, and saw him take Kirsty as his first partner. They all performed what seemed to Julia some intricate patterns, and was more than ever glad she had refused even to try them. But she was aware of Jamie's disapproval, as if somehow she had let him down. She kept her seat by the fire, and Sir Niall gratefully retired to sit beside her. "Old leg injury plays up when I start this sort of caper. Getting a bit long in the tooth for this sort of thing, but it does make a grand sight, doesn't it? In the right setting, among friends. The only better sight would be if all our young men were out there with Jamie. How we miss them—especially the ones we'll never have back."

William Kerr continued to circulate with his tray of drinks. The cries of the dancers grew wilder and louder, but somehow no one ever went beyond the bounds of correctness. There was no careless swinging of partners, no one raised their arms above a certain level. It was revelry, but not carousal. Janet and Morag and Mrs. Kerr had lined up at the end of the Hall to watch the dancing, glasses served to them also, as if it were an understood thing that they all belonged to this one festive evening in the darkness of war.

It took Julia a long time to fall asleep that night. She knew she had eaten and drunk too much, but it was the glow of her happiness in the memory of having become, finally, Jamie's lover which lighted a spark in her much more potent than the spirits she had drunk, something that the heaviness of the food would not blot out in sleep. "I love him . . ." she murmured in the stillness of the Red Tower Room. "I'll love him forever . . . forever. Come hell or high water . . . or the bloody Highlands, for that matter. They won't take him from me."

She slept at last, but when she woke it was not yet dawn. Once again she thought she heard the sobbing that trailed away to a deep sigh. She raised her head from the pillow, and once again a vague shape seemed to stand by the mantel, only discernible by the last red glow of the embers of the fire. Her head spun from the effects of the wine and whisky. Did the shape move, almost turn in her direction, an imploring hand outstretched? "Ellen. . . ?" she whispered. "Lady Ellen. . . ?" She felt no fear, only compassion. Did the figure turn away—shrink back on itself? No, it was not there at all. She told herself she had heard nothing, seen nothing. But she did not sleep again.

4

THE world Julia returned to made her feel that she had forever suffered a sea-change. The rites of passage had been made. For ten days she had lived in a world of supposed peace, the landscape untouched and beautiful, and yet full of tension. She had known hope, despair, and love. She came back to the present tension of a world very much at war, the streets only partly cleared of rubble, the barrage balloons, the ever-flying dust, air raid shelters, queues for food, and for every other necessity. It was a world in which war, and the talk of war was ever-present. A world in which death was beside one on the street, as well as in the Western Desert, and in the Atlantic. She realized she was returning to the world of theatre where competition was as keen-edged as the war itself; pride, envy, generosity and greed were its hallmarks. She had begun to question the concept of what a hero was in her father's world.

Since it was Friday, she continued her journey on to Anscombe, saying goodbye to Jamie at the platform of the station where the line split, he to report back to his squadron at Hawkinge. She kissed him, and knew that she had grown older by as many years as she had already lived. She hadn't telephoned ahead to Anscombe, so there was no one to meet her. She walked the two miles from the station in pitch dark, carrying her suitcase and the rose bush. Stella opened the kitchen door to her, the blackout curtain carefully drawn. She had returned to the world which was no longer carefree, nor careless.

She was drawn into the warmth and welcome of the kitchen. Stella and Cook exclaimed over how well she looked, even after the long journey. But even as Cook examined her face, and asked questions, she was frying egg and bacon, scraping butter onto bread. "You've gained a little weight," Stella said. "Which you needed. I thought, myself, at the end of *Lear*, if that child doesn't get some rest, she's going to collapse. You've borne your father's burden for too long. It looks as if you've put it off now."

Cook turned from the spluttering frying pan. "Not a child any more, if you please, Stella. She's a grown woman. Proved her worth. She isn't in your nursery any more."

"Yes," Stella said, with surprising humility. "I keep thinking back to the days when you all needed me in one way or another. Even your mother. I once remember when I went with her on one of her tours when her secretary was ill . . . Well, you'd better eat that, Julia, while it's hot. I'll go and telephone the London flat. I can't imagine why you didn't stop there to see your father."

"I wanted to come home . . ." Julia replied, and cut into the egg, dipping bread into the running yolk. She ate, and tried to answer Cook's questions about the food she'd had in Scotland, and how the kitchen at Castle Sinclair had been appointed.

Stella returned. "Your father was home, for once. Had a couple of friends with him, of course. One was Mr. Davidoff. You're expected for rehearsal on Monday afternoon. He hopes you've learned your lines. Just as well I 'phoned, because Sir Michael will be here tomorrow. He'd forgotten to let us know. I told him about the rose bush . . . He's bringing Mr. Davidoff with him, and possibly someone else . . . He said not to meet him at the station. He'll come by car . . ."

"Isn't it amazing how some folk always manage to get things other folk can't . . . such as petrol," Cook remarked dryly. "We'll have to hustle in the morning, Stella, to get rooms ready. I just wish we had some nice soap to put out . . . like it was in the old days. Now, let me think . . . I'd better make some pâté from the scraps . . ."

She made it sound as if the old days of careless plenty were a hundred years ago, and would never return.

But it was not D.D.'s Rolls-Royce which turned into the driveway at Anscombe the next morning. It was a stately Daimler, with an old man in chauffeur's uniform at the wheel. There was D.D.'s voice as he emerged. "Dear child . . ." Her father's arms were about her. "How wonderful you look, Pet. It's done you a world of good . . . Ah, and this . . . Luisa, may I present my youngest daughter, Julia. Julia, Mrs. Henry Radcliffe."

An immaculately gloved hand was extended to her; the face, clothes and figure seemed to have sprung instantly from a fashion magazine. How could any woman in England at this moment be so well turned out? Her shining dark hair, under a neat, veiled hat, seemed to have come directly from the hairdresser. Her make-up was subtly applied. There was the warm scent of good perfume.

"My dear, I am so happy to meet you. I admired

your performance as Cordelia. I was asked by D.D. to the first night, but unfortunately my job—it's the Red Cross, and it does often keep us up late at nights—prevented me from being there that evening. But I made a point of seeing *Lear* later. What a wonderful beginning to what I'm sure will be a great career. Following your father . . ."

"Luisa, please . . ." Her father's tone begged jokingly. "No more of that. Welcome to Anscombe." The chauffeur was bringing suitcases, and the food hampers which D.D. always seemed able to procure, from the boot of the Daimler. Julia still stood speechless, hardly able to take in this vision of perfection. It was another shock of returning to a world where it was still possible for a woman to look as Mrs. Henry Radcliffe did. A jerk on her arm from her father focused her thoughts on the moment. "Oh, yes . . . welcome to Anscombe . . . Please do come in."

She was acutely conscious of her worn and dirty corduroys. That morning, in the cold darkness, she had presented herself at Harry Whitehand's cottage, and then helped him bring in the herd. "Old Primmie's hanging on," he had said by way of greeting, "and damn me if she's not in calf again. I thought she was past it now. Well, now you've finally come down from the footlights, I'd be grateful for a little help. We're training another Land Army girl, but she's a bit thick. Or perhaps I should have said citified . . . You look well, Julia. Had a good time up there in those Highlands? You'll have to tell me about how they manage their farm . . ."

A million miles, or years away. Julia was now conscious that probably she still smelled of the barnyard. Stella and Cook had come to the door, both, by virtue of long standing, being introduced to Mrs. Radcliffe. D.D.'s hand restrained Julia as the others moved inside. He whispered to her, "Darling, be nice to her. She is rich. *Rich!* She has a lot of interest in the theatre, but I have succeeded in interesting her in this little film I plan for you. I've been gathering up front money, and the most comes from her. Now I shall go to work on the Ministry. Mostly a propaganda film, of course, and it may do very good business in the States, where, of course, we need box office money. Dollars. Your role isn't very large, but it's one of only two female roles. Very important. The world will see your face, instead of a few thousand on the London stage. Darling—do you have to look so *dirty* as this." Then he flicked his hand impatiently. "No—I'm wrong. You look almost exactly as you should look for *Return at Dawn*, or whatever we shall call this film. All you have to do is see off your hero, and gaze at the planes as they return, counting them. I'm not sure whether your hero survives or not. We haven't got that far with the script. But we will photograph you very nicely, and I wouldn't doubt that offers of other films will come pouring in."

"Who is she? . . . Mrs. Radcliffe?"

"She comes of a very grand Spanish family. She married a Frenchman—the Comte de . . . oh, something. One of the wine families. Wine was a sideline with him, but it gave them a nice château for entertaining. He was primarily a banker, considerably older than Luisa, and he wisely transferred as much money as possible to New York. He became very ill just before it became evident that France would fall. He sent her, and loads of jewellery—and probably money—to England for safety, and died in his bed in Paris, just a little after the Germans arrived. She married Henry Radcliffe—surely even *you* must know his name? Another banker—they tend to move in the same circles. Widowed. He got himself killed in the Blitz, being a hero. No children of either of Luisa's marriages, and no step-children. Quite—or almost quite—alone in the world. Sad, a woman so beautiful . . ."

"With all that money—sad," Julia said sharply. "Most men would be afraid to marry her now, in case he just happened to die. Or does she only marry rich men?"

"The rich of good families marry the rich of other good families, you know that, darling. After all, they seldom meet anyone else."

"Then what is she doing in *your* world—in Father's world?"

"She's a woman of great culture. Brought up to the theatre and music—finishing schools. You know how *grand* grand Spanish families are —"

"No, I don't really. Never met any."

He tapped her chin. "Naughty girl! You must be nice to her. She could be a great help to your career."

"And Father's career."

"Now that is quite uncalled for! Your father's career needs no help. He is just coming back into his world. The companionship of a woman like Luisa Radcliffe is good for him. Don't be jealous, Julia. It's not like you. Now please organize some coffee, and go upstairs and change those disgusting garments."

"Can't—I'll have to be out in the rose garden helping Father in half an hour. Cook will already have coffee on the way."

"Well—I can see your little stay in Scotland has put more than roses in your cheeks." Then he smiled at her fondly. "Well, darling, you were bound to grow up some day. I hope you haven't thoroughly neglected to learn your lines. You're supposed to be a professional now . . ."

A short while later they were all in the rose garden, watching Michael planting his new rose. "I wonder what it's called? Very nice of that man—what's his name—to send it. Nice ball of earth on it. Did he say what colour it is? No? I suppose you forgot to ask. Well, we'll just have to put it in this spot, and hope it won't clash . . ."

"What a charming idea, Michael," Luisa Radcliffe said. "This garden in memory of your adored wife. I do predict that in the future you will become a great rose-grower . . ." She gestured expansively. "I think after the war, when they let one do these things, you should take in part of that next field. One garden opening into another—a touch of mystery." She glanced back from where the oasthouse had been to the manor house. "What a charming place this is. So sweet . . . so English . . ." Except for her very dark hair, and her faint, attractive accent, she looked, Julia thought, exactly as the lady of the manor might have done before the war—though perhaps just too expensively dressed. She had changed into a skirt and sweater of fine cashmere, shoes not too high-heeled, a subtle gold chain around her neck, plain gold earrings. All the understatement which money and good taste could buy. She had even pulled on pigskin gloves to hold the bush steady while Michael shovelled earth around the roots, and trampled it firmly into place. D.D. surveyed all this from a bench. He still wore his grey flannel Savile Row suit. Gardens, for him, were things to be looked at, strolled in, if the grass was not wet.

Julia washed and changed for lunch, recklessly dabbing on a little perfume to restore her confidence. Luisa Radcliffe puzzled her. Her charm and overt good manners were undoubted. She was handsome, rather than beautiful, but she carried herself as an undoubted aristocrat. No doubt her Spanish pedigree was as long as her beautifully coiled black hair. Would she be near to forty years old, Julia wondered? If so, then a forty with the agile, exercised body of a girl half her age. She had seen such faces in books of paintings from the Prado. Haughty, confident, long pale hands emerging from lace, and limply holding a fan. A Velazquez face. Nothing resembling the rather daubish faces of the Seymour ancestors which hung at Anscombe. It proclaimed them English country squires, and nothing more. Luisa Radcliffe could move in any circle in the world she chose, and would, probably, make another wealthy marriage. What was she doing amidst the rough and tumble of the theatre world? Of course, it amused the rich to dabble, but Luisa Radcliffe did not look the kind to waste her time merely dabbling in anything. Then as Julia went downstairs, it occurred to her that her father was not only a great and famous actor, he was an extremely handsome man. Sometimes, women like Luisa Radcliffe fell in love. Having all the money she needed, perhaps she now sought something that had eluded her.

A fire had been lit in the drawing-room. Dark November clouds scurried across the sky. D.D.

poured champagne for her. "Enjoy it, darling—hard to come by now. Next time we drink it, I hope it will be to toast you on the first night of *Earnest*."

"Supposing . . . supposing there's nothing to toast. Supposing I don't live up to it."

Luisa Radcliffe's voice was calm and even, but it almost carried a threat. "The daughter of such a man as Michael does not even entertain such thoughts."

Julia wanted to retort that she was her mother's daughter also, but in the presence of this woman, her mother's spirit seemed to have been banished from the house.

They listened to news from the BBC at one o'clock, which was both sad and good. The Germans were attacking Moscow, but the 8th Army seemed to be regrouping for a fresh campaign in the desert. More shipping losses in the Atlantic. "Has Alex heard from Greg?" Julia asked as they went into lunch.

"Not recently. There haven't been any dispatches recently in *The Record*. She says she suspects he's on the move to Singapore. Not even Wolverton will tell her."

Lunch went on until it was almost dark; they lingered over the wine Michael had brought up from the cellar, and then port. Julia took little part in the conversation, trying to stifle her yawns. It had taken a whole twenty-four hours to travel down from Inverness. She slipped away to check that all was well in Mrs. Radcliffe's room—the principal guest room. The room was fragrant with pot-pourri, and she had clipped some *immortalis*, and arranged it with the last two blooms of the climbing rose which draped the kitchen door. They had long since used up their pre-war supply of scented soap, but she had raided

Stella's special storeroom for some bath-salts. The sheets were linen, the towels still thick and plentiful in the adjoining bathroom. She hoped the hot water supply would hold out. They had dared to turn on the central heating—for which extravagance they might be cold later in the winter. But she felt her father expected this from her.

Then she went and changed back into her corduroys to go and help Harry Whitehand with the milking. He had the cows already herded into the barn, and was washing them off. "Bit late, Julia," he said. "But you've got fancy guests this weekend."

Mrs. Radcliffe's chauffeur was lodged over the garage, and Mrs. Whitehand had had to scurry to get the apartment ready. He would take his meals in the kitchen with Stella and Cook. It was evident that Mrs. Whitehand already had learned some of Mrs. Radcliffe's history.

Julia leaned against Primmie's side, and pulled rhythmically at the teats. Her thoughts were on Jamie, and the fierce ache of missing him. All day she had heard no planes overhead. Was he thinking of her now; did he feel this strange emptiness? "Julia—Primmie's been dry for the last five minutes. You're no more help than that ruddy Land Army girl." Harry Whitehand's voice came from close behind her. She sprang up from the stool, and knocked over the pail of milk. "Oh, damn!" Then she burst into tears.

Instantly Harry's arm was about her. "Here, there's no need to get so upset. There's more where that came from. But it's not the milk, is it? Look, don't worry about the rest. Go back to the house and have a bath—if they've got the water. You looked great this morning, and now you look all done in." She was grateful for his kindness, and didn't attempt to explain her tears. But she paused for some minutes outside the kitchen door in the windy November darkness, making sure there would be no sign of tears for Stella's discerning eyes to see. She was greeted by Cook when she entered. "You missed a telephone call from Squadron Leader Sinclair . . ." Squadron Leader. He had been promoted. He would lead his squadron until the war was ended, or he was shot down. No matter where they sent him now, he would be out in front, expected to lead, no matter if it was to death.

Next morning Alex caught one of the few Sunday trains from London, and arrived in time for lunch. It was raining, and she was wet, and looked cross when she reached the house, having walked from the station. "I don't know why I bothered. I should have stayed in bed. But I rang the flat, and Agnes told me you were all here. I suppose I just got a yen to be here with you. I haven't seen Father for weeks . . ." Julia followed her upstairs to her room when she went to wash. She carried a glass of sherry for her.

"Here, this will warm you up a little. It's wonderful to see you, Alex."

Surprisingly, her sister leaned over and kissed her on the cheek. "You look good, Julia. A bit changed. I suppose you're still hopelessly in love with that Scot? Was his mother the gorgon I've been imagining? The Scots can be so . . ." She shrugged. "None of my business." She sipped the sherry appreciatively, and then started to comb her hair, and apply powder and lipstick. "I suppose I'd better go down and make the acquaintance of the particular gorgon we've got downstairs."

Julia gasped. "How can you say that? You haven't even met her."

"I hardly need to. She's in the newspaper columns every other day. Doing her bit for the war effort, of course. In a very well-tailored Red Cross uniform. Neat as a pin. But always, it seems, in some very glamorous company. Mostly taking care of the needs of generals—that is, when she isn't at a night club. She's been seen quite often with Father. I suppose that's what got me down here today . . . curiosity. I suppose she plays the country lady just as smoothly as everything else . . ."

"She can't be *that* bad. She's very elegantly turned out, I'll give you that . . ."

"And she's a self-centred bitch," Alex snapped back. "Did D.D. give you some story about her being sent away from France by her loving husband to England and safety? The way I hear it is that she left behind a very sick man, who hardly knew what was happening to him. She's happily drawing on all the dollars he left her piled up in New York, and wearing as much of the jewellery as is appropriate to wear in war time. I expect most of *it's* in New York where the bombs can't get at it. What I can't understand is why she isn't there herself, having a nice, comfortable war. Oh well, she did happen to meet Henry Radcliffe when he was just poking his head up into the world after his wife's death. He stayed on in banking, since he was too old for active service, but one heard bits about him being one of Churchill's unofficial Cabinet. He was a *very* clever man—as well as being a nice man. I met him once. He had to go and make a hero of himself in the Blitz, when he should have been minding his own business, instead of dashing into some building and rescuing some family who were too dazed to move. Went back for the bloody dog, and the whole place toppled in on him. *She's* come through it smiling, though—or so it seems from the newspapers. And a whole lot richer. As if she needed to be. Is she angling for Father?"

"I don't know. I'm not as quick at spotting these things as you are. Any rate, if she's like that, would he want her?"

"You can never tell. You have to realize, Julia, he's not going to stay married to our mother's memory forever. He's still, in the eyes of many people—well, a relatively young man. And handsome as the devil. Famous, distinguished. He may be Father to us, but he cuts a figure in the world. He's going to find a woman, eventually. I just wish she would be a gentle little nobody."

"You don't like competition, Alex."

"I don't think I'm going to like Mrs. Henry Bloody Radcliffe." Then she shrugged, and drained the last of the sherry. "Well, nothing I can do about it, if that's the way the land lies."

"You may not have to do anything about it. Father has taste. And don't forget whom he was married to."

"Father is a man—like all men."

At the head of the stairs, Julia stopped her. "Alex, I've never known you quite like this. What is it? Not Mrs. Radcliffe . . ."

Alex shook her head, and quickly passed her hand across her eyes. "Of course it isn't Mrs. Radcliffe. Father will do as he likes, when he likes. I just wanted to see you both today. I get so lonely. I haven't heard from Greg for weeks. It seems months. I won't know where in the world he is, and I don't think the Boss really knows, either. Last dispatch was from Hong Kong, but that was weeks ago. He seems to have vanished. Or forgotten about me. Oh, God, Julia, I do miss him. I've discovered that there's something terribly sensual about me that Greg completely satisfied. Without him, I'm hungry all the time. I would snatch at any man—except that it can't be just any man. Not after Greg. I just wait—and hope he's alive. You know, of the three of us, Connie's the smart one. It would only be by accident that Ken Warren got killed. He'll always be in some relatively safe place." She started down the stairs, then looked back. "Well, Julia, that's you and me. The risk-takers. What would anyone expect? Look who our parents are."

Before they entered the drawing-room, from where the deeply accented voice of D.D. held forth, Julia stopped her again. "You know who you looked like just then—all fierce and angry and tense. You looked for all the world like Grandfather Maslov."

Alex's face broke in a grin. "I hope not, moustache and all!" She was laughing as she entered the room.

They returned to London late that afternoon, Michael, D.D. and Luisa Radcliffe: Alex went with them, grateful not to have to endure the cold, slow journey by train. Julia declined the offer of the ride. "But, darling, you are to be at rehearsal tomorrow afternoon," D.D. protested.

"I'll be there," Julia said. "And I'll know my lines. I feel I owe Harry Whitehand a little help. It's Sunday. The Land Army girls don't work . . ."

"What nonsense," Michael said sharply. "Harry is getting on perfectly well without you. You'll have to get up at the crack of dawn tomorrow to . . ."

"Leave it, Father," Alex said crisply. "When did Julia not do what she said she'd do." He shrugged and accepted what he could not alter. He must have sensed Alex's attitude towards Luisa Radcliffe, although she had been restrained and civil to their guest. Julia had been more guarded. She had seen them off, already wearing her clothes for the milking parlour. All she wanted was to put some distance between herself and this new situation which had developed. She needed a few more hours alone, conscious that she would have had to return to her father's flat. Tomorrow she would return to the theatre and to work, but that was tomorrow. She opted for one more night of independence.

She worked solidly with Harry Whitehand for the hours it needed to bring the herd in, wash and milk them, feed and water them. He thanked her for her help, and offered her some lanolin for her hands.

She ate in the kitchen with Stella and Cook, mostly left-overs from D.D.'s hampers. They were companionably silent, or was it, Julia wondered, that neither of the other women wanted to comment on this new guest at Anscombe—perhaps hoping that there would not be another visit? Why should there not be, Julia wondered? Alex was right. Why should anyone expect their father to remain in perpetual mourning for Ginette Maslova? Nothing stood still . . . In the hall the telephone rang. Julia ran to it. "Julia?" Jamie's voice.

She knew why she had waited here.

"I wonder how soon we can get married," he said. "Have you thought about it?"

She felt dizzy with joy, and hungry with wanting —the sort of hunger Alex had spoken of, hunger and an emptiness she had never experienced before.

"Soon, Jamie . . . please. Soon."

Three weeks of adjusting to the disciplines of the theatre again, the direction of a man to whom she was a well-known stranger, finding her way with the new cast, all without her father's comforting, protective presence. At first she groped her way through her part, in awe of the great lady of the stage who was playing Lady Bracknell. In the beginning she played a humble and fluttering Gwendoline, and knew she was doing it wrongly. All the experience of *Lear* seemed useless; she was a raw amateur fumbling her way into a new character. She was miserable and confused. At last she begged her father to come to a rehearsal.

He waited until it was over, and then took her for a drink to the Ritz. "Not at all bad, Pet. A little bit stiff in places. No use telling you to relax. One owes it to the audience to give a performance—even if it's only a couple of lines. But you'll have to leave Julia behind, and step into the skin of the character you're playing. You'll have to *be* Gwendoline. Seemingly demure, engagingly pert, determined to have her own way, even with Mama. Remember how I taught you not to miss any chance of upstaging anyone? Even if this is Dame Lillian Kenton. It's just possible to steal a bit of her thunder here and there. You can't let yourself be afraid of her. Respectful of her formidable talent, yes. But afraid—no. It isn't easy. It never will be. Not even your old father does it without some anguish, and a lot of mental preparation. We'll have an evening alone, tomorrow night, you and I. Run through it. I can't tell you exactly how to play your character, but there are a few tricks this old dog knows which may help you . . . I have to run now, Pet." He rose, and signalled the waiter. "You stay and have another. Less lonely here than at the flat. Agnes isn't the best company. Where's that Sinclair fellow these days?"

"On duty. He's around, but I don't see him. He telephones me. We're going to get married soon."

He sank back into his seat, and asked the waiter for a second drink for himself. "I thought it might be that. Want to tell me about it?"

"What's to tell? We're in love. He's asked me to marry him. I want to. I want to very much."

"I never really asked you about the time in Scotland. You've looked alternately radiant and sad ever since."

"Isn't that what being in love is like? I thought it was supposed to be a grand passion. I remember once that you wished me the sort of feelings you and Mother had for each other."

"At your age, it has to be a grand passion, or it doesn't exist. When I married your mother—well, we seemed to be the oddest pair in the world. But we were perfectly in tune with each other. It didn't matter a damn what anyone else thought. If it's not that way between you and this Sinclair chap, then don't do it. Be his lover, if you must be, but don't marry him unless you believe you can't live without him. Saves a lot of heartache in the end. I wonder if he's considered what it's like to be married to an actress. You're not going to be the little wife at home all the time, Julia. You're going to be a woman who works. After the war, when he goes back to his Highland castle—"

"We'll come to that when it really is 'after the war'. All that matters is *now*."

"If you hadn't said that, I'd have said 'forget it'." Then a smile broke across his face. "What can I say, Pet? Good luck!" He raised his glass to her. "In my mind it's less than ideal, but it's you who'll live your life. And to Jamie Sinclair—happy landings. He doesn't know what he's taking on. But then, none of us do. Want to come to dinner with me and Luisa tonight? Just to celebrate . . . there'll be a few other people . . ."

"No, Father, thank you. I'll celebrate when Jamie can be with us."

He swallowed the rest of his drink. "It's a hell of a risk. A hell of an adventure." He leaned over and kissed her cheek. "Well, Pet, to live is to take chances. Somehow I think I fancy him more than that fellow Connie is determined to wait for. Too safe and solid. Perhaps that's what she needs, poor sweet. None of you ever did have a safe and solid childhood. You're more like Alex than I thought. She's going through hell over Greg. *That* wasn't a suitable marriage either. It just might work—after the war."

"Does everything have to wait until after the war?"

"More or less. We're all on 'hold' now. Not our emotions—our loves. But we can hardly say we can shape our own destinies. That's being done out there, somewhere—by forces and events we can hardly imagine. Take what you can, while you can, Julia. Sort it out afterwards. When there's time. Time is compressed now. Don't be like Connie. Grab at life.

Take the risk. Now, that's the worst advice a loving father could give. But I'm damned if I know how to say anything else, and not sound like a pompous and hypocritical ass." He kissed her again, and left.

In a mood of defiance she ordered another drink. It would be cold in the bus queue. Next week she would open on stage with one of the greatest actresses of their time, without the help of her father. Her slender talent would be shown up for the insubstantial thing it was, or she might just pull it off. But there was one certainty. She would marry Jamie, and love him forever.

Julia went down to Anscombe on the Sunday before the play opened. She went because she needed one last day of peace, and because Jamie had a twenty-four hour pass, and they would have that time alone together. She had begun to feel the need to escape the confines of the London flat, fearing that she impinged on her father's privacy, although he was seldom there. He did not speak much of Luisa Radcliffe, but she suspected that he spent most of his free time with her.

Mrs. Radcliffe lived in a large, elegant house in Wilton Terrace, off Belgrave Square, and she still retained those members of her husband's staff too old to be called up, such as her elderly chauffeur, who gladly acted as substitute handyman, and when pressed to, as a sort of butler. He also gave his two nights a week as an Air Raid Precaution warden—everyone seemed to have a second, voluntary job, except the people who formed Julia's world—the people of the theatre. Many of the men had gone, joined up. Productions still continued all over the country, but young male actors were hard to find. The one who played opposite her in *The Importance of Being Earnest* was there only because he had what he called, "a dicky heart".

"My career will do just fine out of this war, ducky," he had once said to her, "if I don't keel over on the stage one night." He was on call every Sunday as an ambulance driver.

Jamie arrived at Anscombe before lunch, and they ate with Stella and Cook in the kitchen. But Stella brought them tea in the dining-room where a fire burned, and left them to themselves. Later Julia carried a tray of cold supper to the dining-room. They talked. How many hours did they talk—and of what? Hands and arms entwined. The talk of lovers, which could have sounded trite and banal to anyone who listened. But the words, and more particularly the silences, had a meaning that only lovers would have recognized.

Jamie went out to say goodbye to Stella and Cook just as the BBC nine o'clock news came on. The announcer's voice carried the confirmation of the surprise air strike of a Japanese air force on Pearl Harbor. Casualties and losses were not known, but they were thought to be extensive; there were unconfirmed reports that capital ships had been lost, moored at their berths. The loss of their crews was not calculated. Jamie, who had been waiting with his coat and cap on, suddenly swept Julia into his arms and kissed her. "God help the poor bastards, but they're in now. The Americans are in the war, hook, line and sinker. Sorry if that's in poor taste." In turn he went and hugged Stella and Cook. "You understand what it means? No more lend-lease. We're in it together. We've got an ally. We're not alone any more. God, how did the Japs manage it? Was everyone asleep because it was Sunday morning?"

When he was gone, the three women sat together drinking cocoa, speculating what it was like out there in the now-important Hawaiian Islands. They hadn't even thought of the American Pacific Fleet having its base there. For them, the war at sea was the Atlantic. Julia went and got an atlas. "Well, they can't invade America! That's preposterous!" Her finger traced along the islands of the Pacific, the Philippines, the long trail of land that led from India through Burma, through Thailand, down to Singapore, island group by island group even down to New Guinea and Australia. Before this, they had only been names in geography lessons to her—lessons which Stella had started her on.

Alex would have seen this long ago, and her anguish over Greg came sharply into focus. Stella's lips twisted sternly. "If they've already inflicted so much damage, it will be a longer war than anyone ever thought of."

But outside, in the cold darkness when Jamie had kissed her goodbye, she remembered his words. "It is the beginning, but only the very beginning of the end. We *will* come through it Julia, you and I and all the rest."

She wanted to believe that very much.

The play opened the following Thursday night with a greater success for Julia than she had dared hope. The whole production was warmly praised, and she had a few lines in the notices to herself.

Julia Seymour shows an unexpectedly nice flair for the comic.

Another paper said:

It is good to see that Julia Seymour can hold her own on the stage without also holding onto her father's coat-tails.

Naturally, the bulk of the praise went to the great actress whose name headed the cast, the bouquets were hers, as Julia knew must happen. She had warned Jamie well in advance that there must be no repetition of the red roses being thrown, no calling of her name. He had obeyed, but applauded with wild enthusiasm from the stalls, where he sat with her father and Luisa Radcliffe, D.D., Alex and Connie. But Julia's tiny dressing-room, which she shared, was filled with so many red roses it was difficult to move.

They had gathered for supper afterwards, waiting for the first editions of the newspapers, at Mrs. Radcliffe's house. But they had already sensed triumph from the reaction of the audience, and it was a relaxed group who drank champagne and ate food from the cold buffet which contained many delicacies not now usually seen in the shops.

Ken Warren had managed to get to the theatre for the second act. "Last minute hold up," he apologized to Connie. But her expression was made radiant just by his presence. His long, rather lugubrious face, melted into a shy smile as he congratulated Julia. "You seem well on your way now. I hear there's a film coming up." Behind his thick glasses, his eyes seemed both kind and concerned, as if he wondered what possible attraction the uneven, uncertain future of an actress could hold. Then he engaged in an animated conversation with Alex about the results of the Japanese entry into the war. By now they knew more of the extent of the devastation at Pearl Harbor, the massive losses the US Navy had suffered. "Of course now the factories will start pouring out material," he said, "but I wonder how far the Japs can get before there can be a turning point. I think it would be a terrible mistake to underestimate them . . ."

Alex's face seemed pinched with anxiety. "I agree. No one I talk to is very optimistic about any quick victories. Greg's managed to get to Singapore. *The Record* got a dispatch from him this afternoon. It will be in the morning editions."

Everyone was trying to forget what the week had actually been like, for these few hours to forget the stunning disasters which had followed Pearl Harbor. The day following the Pearl Harbor attack, Japanese bombers had destroyed British air power in Hong Kong, and this morning's news had been of the British battleships *Prince of Wales* and *Repulse*, steaming from Singapore to cut off the Japanese communications, being sunk. It was a disaster none of them had yet quite absorbed. Julia wondered if some of the laughter in the theatre tonight had not been to gain release from the tension and dread the week had brought.

Julia whispered something to Jamie, and he had nodded eagerly, and put his arm about her shoulders. Julia asked her father to make the announcement that she and Jamie were engaged and would marry "soon". The champagne glasses were raised, and toasts and congratulations offered; but Julia sensed that some of the good wishes heaped on them seemed hollow. "Darling," D.D. said, "you haven't forgotten that you have a run-of-the-play contract? And after that there is the film. You know I count on you for that. After tonight no one doubts you are an actress."

"Most actresses get married sometime."

"For you—better later than sooner. Give yourself a chance to get really established. Waiting a little can't matter."

"I don't *want* to wait. Jamie and I have waited long enough."

D.D. shrugged his heavy shoulders. "Well, darling—just remember not to get pregnant. It does seem to cramp an actress's style." He turned away, his face registering disapproval.

Alex put her arm around Julia. "Well, my love, you've done it. And who's to blame you? Your flyer boy is handsome enough to take any girl's breath away. And don't listen to D.D. Now that Greg's so far away, I wish I'd had the courage to go ahead and have his baby. It would give me something to hold on to—some part of him. But, of course, I thought there was plenty of time for babies. But not everything can be postponed. Especially in war." She gulped at the whisky she had exchanged for champagne. "God knows when I'll ever see him—now that all this has happened. But he's safe in Singapore, at least. He'll wangle transport out of there, somehow. But knowing Greg, he'll just want to get closer to the war, not further away."

Luisa Radcliffe came to offer her congratulations. She exclaimed prettily over the modest ring Jamie had given Julia. For some reason she looked more pleased over the announcement than anyone else in the gathering. "Well, don't you see," Jamie said quietly to her when their hostess had left them. "You'll soon be out of her way. Alex is married, and Connie is blindly committed, and firmly in the WAAF. There was only you between your father and her. She'll be glad to see you safely removed."

"I've never stood between my father and Mrs. Radcliffe . . . or anyone else."

"Yes, you have. You symbolize the mayhem of that day. You were the closest thing on earth he had, after your mother was killed. No—after I killed your mother." He stopped her protest. "He's felt he had to look after you the way you looked after him in those months when he was like a helpless child. Now *she* will take over."

"You really think she wants him? It's not just a little flirtatious distraction for her?"

He smiled at her, and smoothed a wisp of hair back from her forehead."You're still an innocent, aren't you? Maybe that's one of the reasons I love you so much. Of course she wants him. She's got everything else. She is bored with the world of safe, dull marriages in the banking world. Now she'd like to move onto something more glamorous. She'd like a bit of glitter in her world. She's a young woman, Julia—comparatively. Though at your age you don't think so. She likes first nights. She would like Broadway and Hollywood. She's got enough presence and enough money to outshine any actress she's likely to come up against. She's not afraid of competition. To notch up three marriages before you're forty—without a divorce—that's quite an accomplishment. She doesn't need money from your father. She wants status and recognition. She doesn't just think she's a worthy successor to Ginette Maslova. She's going to single mindedly promote and help your father's career far more than any woman who had a career of her own ever could find time to do. Why do you think she's investing in this film of yours? She might want you out of the way, but she'd like you famous too."

"Jamie!—I didn't think you could be so cynical. You sound like Greg—or Alex."

"I'm not stupid, Julia. But she might not be the worst person in the world to trust his interests to. She'll take very good care of him, and his career. I don't doubt that for a second."

They were married three days after Christmas. Julia wondered if Jamie even noticed the ceremony. In his mind, he was already married to her. It was held in St Paul's, Covent Garden, a church much loved by the acting community. It was the first occasion Jamie had been able to arrange a three-day leave. Her father had offered her her mother's wedding dress, but Julia knew how this could affect Jamie, so she borrowed the simple white silk suit Alex had worn for her own wedding in a registry office. As many of Jamie's friends in the squadron who could get leave attended, but they were few. "Can't leave the place denuded," he had said. Other army and navy friends stationed in the South turned up, some his distant cousins. There seemed a solid phalanx of uniformed men on the groom's side of the church, all of them invited by telephone, hurriedly. Lady Jean came down from Scotland, and occupied the front pew on that side accompanied only by Sir Niall Henderson.

That there was a wedding in a church at all seemed

unreal. They were among the darkest days of the war; the desert war seemed a stalemate, with the British retaking a place called Benghazi, but with every possibility that it would be taken back from them by the Germans. On Christmas Day Hong Kong had fallen to the Japanese, and they had invaded Burma. In an atmosphere of tight-lipped tension, which might have disguised near-panic in those who could read the maps, and had some idea of the paltry numbers of British aircraft guarding the Malayan peninsula, Julia was married in a ceremony arranged and made beautiful, she recognized, mostly by Luisa Radcliffe. The right things had been done; there were flowers, there was organ music, enough guests were assembled to make the occasion festive, and seem important. She had even reminded Jamie of something he had forgotten—a wedding ring. Afterwards the reception was at the Ritz. Julia felt guilty about what this must cost her father—there were all the little extras which only Mrs. Radcliffe could have thought of. It was as unlike a war-time wedding as any could be, with flowers and a three-tiered cake, and an official photographer. They would eventually have their scrap book, like any other married couple.

But after the kisses and congratulations, the speeches, the toasts, as Julia moved among the crowd, there was the ever-present talk of the war. The Japanese were hitting all along the Malayan Peninsula, and there was some talk, among those who might know, that the air-fields had been practically denuded of planes in order to serve the battle in the Western Desert. With Jamie beside her, Julia realized she was being kissed by the Wing Commander who had come that terrible day to try to convey the sorrow and anguish of a young pilot whose plane had taken Ginette Maslova's life. He held her shoulders for an unexpectedly long time, and looked her fully in the face. His words were low, and intended for her and Jamie only. "A most happy and unexpected outcome of a tragic day, my dear. I'm sure your mother would have blessed this marriage. And never worry—I'll never speak of it to a soul."

But a little coldness went through Julia as she realized there were many others who must have known—the person who had told Jamie in the beginning, stretching on through how many others who had nursed him, men in the squadron, not all of them dead. But she looked across to her father's face, bright and animated, laughing, remembering other weddings, accepting good wishes for her and Jamie. He was a long way removed from the man, stupefied and drunk on brandy after the shocking news of his wife's death on that terrible day. If he ever were to learn of Jamie's involvement he would now see it for what it was—entirely accidental. But she still hoped he would never learn. Surely no one could be so cruel as to tell him?

Lady Jean and Sir Niall seemed an island to themselves. They sat together at a small table on little gilt chairs, forking the food, drinking the champagne sparingly. Lady Jean's face wore a mechanical smile, behind the smile was a sort of mask of desperate resignation. What she had thought could not happen had happened. This stranger to their country and to their whole way of life had become the wife of her only son. All her hopes, plans about Kirsty Macpherson were gone. She looked at the world of show business about her, of cheery young men in uniform laughing at jokes she could not understand, of malicious little bits of gossip on which the theatre thrived, and Julia knew that to her it was a world totally without substance. From it Lady Jean Sinclair could expect nothing. And what would she expect of the children of this young woman her son inexplicably had chosen to marry? The doubt, the dislike, even the fear was plainly there behind the smile.

Alex kissed Julia and left early. Julia knew that she would go straight back to the office where the wire service tapes might tell her something more about Greg. Connie was there, and in the absence of Ken Warren, who hadn't been able to get leave, she was, with some bewilderment, trying to cope with the numbers of young men who pressed her with champagne and more wedding cake, and tried to get a telephone number where she could be reached.

Then D.D. was at Julia's side. "Almost time to say goodbye to your guests, darling. Two hours to curtain time. No doubt there'll still be a few left even after the show's over—but I don't suppose you'll be interested in coming back here . . ." He lingered for a moment. "By the way, did your father tell you? I've managed to persuade him to take on the Professor Higgins role in *Pygmalion*. I've got the theatre and the director. He'll go into rehearsal next month. Now . . . don't look like that! He's had long enough being idle since *Lear* closed. And *no*, I should not have waited for you to be available to play Eliza. That would have been too much of a good thing, right after Cordelia. The critics would have nailed you. They'd be saying forever that you couldn't do a thing without him. Far better where you are, darling—and the script for the film is coming along nicely. You'll have plenty to occupy your time."

"Somehow," Jamie said, as they quietly left the reception, "I never imagined my wife would have to work on our wedding-day."

Julia chose not to take the remark seriously. "That's the world you married into, love. Do you think I'd let the understudy take over . . . she just might be better than me."

He sat through the performance. He had invited his mother and Sir Niall to attend, but Lady Jean pleaded fatigue from the long journey the day before. She would leave again early the next morning, while Sir Niall stayed on at his club for a few extra days. He had been delighted when Julia said she would send a ticket for the show. "I'll turn up with flowers, just like those stage-door Johnnies, even though you are an old married woman now." She went through her performance with more verve than she had thought was left in her. It had been the greatest day of her life, and the glow remained with her. They returned to the Ritz, and were amazed to find that the tag-end of the reception guests were still there. Had she really been away at the theatre, taken on another skin, played a part, and still the old life continued, as if she had never been absent? They had a late supper with her father and Mrs. Radcliffe, D.D., who had been at the theatre to monitor her performance, and Sir Niall. They were in the suite booked for them for three nights, the bills paid for by her father. "You'll want your time to yourselves," he said, smiling on her benignly.

"Except for the evenings, and the Saturday matinée," D.D. added.

"Jamie will be gone by Saturday," Julia reminded him. "This is a war-time wedding, D.D. We're lucky to have even this time . . ."

Her father gracefully dropped his own key to the London flat into the middle of the table. "Well, my darling Julia, I think you're entitled to more than that—as long as you can have it. Your old Dad won't be coming back to the flat for a while. Mrs. Radcliffe is kindly putting me up. So whenever Jamie has leave, he knows where to head, and you have the place to yourself. Except for the dragon lady, Agnes."

Her marriage had signalled his complete return to a life of his own. Ginette Maslova would not be forgotten, but she had taken a step backwards into the shadows of his life. The past was the past, treasured memories, but like old photographs, in still life. Luisa Radcliffe, handsome, smiling, supremely assured was the present, moving, living. Feeling her own happiness with Jamie, their future together, how could she begrudge her father his own future, no matter with whom it lay? She remembered Jamie's words. "She'll take very good care of him, and his career." She put the key into Jamie's hand, and smiled at Luisa Radcliffe. "That's very kind . . . yes, very kind. My father is lost without someone to take care of him."

Better to make peace now. Better to let her mother slip into the shadows. Her father was a man who needed a woman, as she needed Jamie. They would keep of the past what they most cherished, his memories of an extraordinary wife, she of a mother who had been like no other of her knowledge. On this, her wedding night, she was vividly reminded of her time with Jamie in the cottage in the forest of Sinclair. Back to her memory also came that vague shape by the mantel in the Red Tower Room—the shape which had no substance, the sob which might have been a sigh, or merely the wind in the chimney. She leaned over and kissed her husband. "Never leave me, Jamie," she whispered.

"I never will. Never on earth—or in heaven. I will never leave you . . . We promised forever—and that doesn't mean only 'till death us do part'."

Death was the reverse side of his life. Death had brought them together. Her father and Luisa Radcliffe seemed to fade out of the room as they looked only at each other.

Their coming together in bed had the feverish longing of two young people in love, conscious of time and war inevitably ticking away their deadly seconds. To Julia it was different, it was still miraculous, and they made love many times that night, sleeping briefly, and coming together again. But the first time had been unique. She remembered the cold flagstones, the brief pain, the smell of the woodsmoke, the bodies of the dogs pressed against theirs. The first, greatest, unforgettable love lay back there.

Through January and February Julia played every night, and every night prayed Jamie would get leave. There was little of it, and Sundays, without the theatre and without Jamie, were hard to bear. Jamie had told her there was talk of the squadron being moved to Lincolnshire. "Just guesses," he said. "The Russians are screaming for us to open a Second Front, as you know. That would mean fighter escort for bombers. Of course we can't open a Second Front at this time, it would be suicide. In theory, we're still guarding the narrowest strip of the Channel, but the Germans have sent just about everything they've got to the Russian Front—and are locked in there. And what's not there, has gone to North Africa. But we still have to maintain a defence force here. Goering just might take it into his head to send over a thousand bombers one night, and there has to be someone minding the shop."

"Do I detect a trace of boredom?" Julia asked lightly. "You want more action? Haven't you had enough. You want more medals? More campaign ribbons?"

"I want you . . ." Their time together was short and precious. Agnes served their food silently, and with more graciousness than Julia had thought her capable of. At the wedding she had spoken briefly with Lady Jean. While she mistrusted actors and their world, she knew quality when she saw it, she had once remarked to Julia. "Your husband doesn't have a title, does he? He's not a baronet . . ." The last words were spoken with snobbish hope.

"No, Agnes. His mother is the daughter of an earl, but he's just the local laird."

"But after the war—when he's home, you will be mistress of Castle Sinclair, won't you?" That seemed to satisfy her needs.

After the war. It seemed an almost unimaginable future for Julia.

The unimaginable future seemed to grow to an unimaginable nightmare. They had welcomed their American ally, but the thought of defeat was still there. The German advance had bogged down on the Russian front, but they were not defeated; in the Western Desert they continued to fight over, lose, and retake outposts in an eternal attrition. But the Japanese advance in the Pacific was frighteningly swift. It became a possibility that the American Pacific Forces would be broken before their aid in Europe and Africa could contribute much of substance. Horrified, Julia traced the swiftness of the Japanese rush down the Malayan Peninsula. She returned from the theatre one night in the middle of February, smiling to herself as she saw the light in the sitting-room still on. Jamie had had unexpected leave? But it was Alex who sat there, smoking, the remains of a glass of whisky on the table at her side.

She didn't rise, just looked with a kind of despairing numbness at Julia. "Singapore's fallen," she said. "It's come over the wires. General Percival had been forced to surrender. There's no news of Greg. He filed his last story from there only half a day ago. It's possible . . . it's possible he didn't get away. Bloody fool! He could have got out. War correspondents aren't combatants. They don't have to stay to surrender."

Silently Julia took Alex's glass and refilled it. She poured a small drink for herself. "How can you say that until you know? There were plenty of ships leaving in these last days. He could—"

"A cable from him to *The Record* would have priority. He wouldn't need to send a message to me. I would know he was alive."

"He *is* alive—until you know differently. He could have got out on anything. A plane to one of the nearby islands. A small boat without radio." She spoke brightly, and yet she felt fear. A smell of fear and defeat seemed to hang about Alex like the cigarette smoke. She went to the kitchen where Agnes always left a plate of sandwiches prepared for her return, and brought them back to the living-room. "Here—have some. I'll bet you haven't had a bite . . ."

Alex shook her head, and lit another cigarette from the butt of the last. She held out her glass silently, and Julia went to refill it. "He didn't have to bloody well *stay!*" she said vehemently. "Some pig-headed idea of being a hero, filing dispatches while the ship goes down. That would be so like him . . ."

She talked—it sounded more like raving to Julia—until her words became slurred and almost meaningless. All the resentment of her long separation from Greg came to the surface. "The most I know about him comes from what he writes for the paper. His letters are little scraps—a few lines. He loves me. He's very busy—very rushed. There's lots of action. He isn't allowed to say any more. *'Keep your chin up, lovely. I'm counting on you.'* They're the last words he wrote to me."

"Oh, Alex, come off it!" Julia cried. "Those aren't the last words. You talk as if he's dead. He isn't dead. He's just in some place where he can't get through to you—or the paper. Have you looked at the maps? There's the whole of Sumatra and Borneo—all the Dutch East Indies. Thousands of little islands—"

"And they'll be the next places the Japs take." Alex spilled ash over her dress and the carpet when she waved her hand dismissively. "His only chance was a ship to Australia. And the last of them would have gone days ago. Oh, damn him—*damn* him! How I hate heroes . . ."

Eventually Julia got her into Michael's bed, wearing a pair of pyjamas her father had left behind. She took the last cigarette from her fingers, and put it out firmly. "Sleep. There'll be news in the morning."

In the morning there was no news of Greg, only fuller details of the appalling surrender of the ninety-thousand garrison of British, Australians and Indians at Singapore, in what had been thought of as the impregnable fortress. Its useless guns faced out to sea and the enemy had come overland.

Alex stayed at the office for long hours each day, refusing to return to the flat she had shared with Greg. Each night Julia found her waiting when she returned from the theatre. She ate almost nothing, smoked and drank too much. Her face grew gaunt, and if she had not known differently Julia would have thought the lines on her face had been put there with greasepaint. "Old Woolfie walked through the newsroom this evening and saw me. He practically fired me. Said the copy I'd been turning in was lousy—they haven't used any of it, that's for sure. He told me to go home, and straighten myself out. But before he did that he took me up to his office, and someone produced smoked salmon sandwiches—how *do* these people keep getting such things? We had a couple of stiff drinks. He talked about what he thought I should do in the future. Something about America. Washington. We have a bureau office here, and staff, but no women. He'd like a regular column on the war seen from Washington—by a woman. Human interest stuff, I suppose. Not too important. But you know he's the patriot *extraordinaire.* He wants a woman journalist to interpret events in Europe and Russia and North Africa as *she* sees them. Stories about women in the armed forces, women in factories—and ordinary mums coping with rationing and bombs, and bomb-blasted houses. I'm to be ready to go on radio, or on lecture tours at the drop of a hat. Anything to spread the word that there's the European side of the battle to be won. Not to let them forget. Not to let them think that it's all out there in the Pacific."

"But that's great. You'll do it perfectly . . ." Julia's voice trailed off as she saw the tears begin to run down those haggard cheeks of Alex.

"Don't you see? Don't you understand. He thinks Greg is dead, or captured. He doesn't think we'll be seeing Greg very soon—perhaps not ever. Not a word since Singapore. Java's surrendered. We lost the battle of the Java Sea. We're losing and giving way everywhere. If the Japs get to Australia, it'll be a goner. If Greg were free, he'd have found some way to get in touch by now. He isn't free, I know. And he's probably dead. I told Old Woolfie I knew he'd been trying to find out something through the Red Cross. But it's all chaos, and no one knows anything. I said I'd think about Washington. And he sent me home in a staff car. Or rather, I said I'd come here. I can't stand the flat any more—with Greg's things around—and silence. Julia, how would you feel if Jamie were killed? If he were dead?"

No comforting words came. Only the truth. "I think I'd feel dead myself."

In March D.D. replaced Julia in the play; he had decided that the script for the film was now ready, and they would begin filming at Pinewood before the end of the month. "You need a little rest, darling. Looking a bit peaked. Go down to Anscombe where you can be near that flyer husband of yours. We'll be arranging a few visits to Bomber Command stations—just so you'll get the background feeling. He'll explain anything you need to know. Might as well make use of a hero while we've got him . . . Now, don't look like that! I didn't imply he's going to die. He just may be transferred abroad . . . Though where there's left to send him, God knows." His gloom reflected the continued advance of the Japanese in the Pacific, apparently unstoppable, a sort of weary stalemate in North Africa, and the sense that the Germans were only waiting for the spring thaw to begin swallowing up further huge territories in Russia. "But the film will be good. The Ministry is very anxious for it to make . . . good propaganda."

"The trouble is that I don't believe in the script," Julia said dispiritedly. "I just can't see us making any raids into Europe at all, never mind one of that size."

"We will, my dear," D.D. said through a haze of smoke. "Only a foreigner knows the British as well as I do. They are quite mad."

Before filming started on *Return at Dawn*, as the script was called, Michael Seymour married Luisa Radcliffe. It was a surprise to no one. It had simply been a matter of time. "It can't go on like this, Pet," her father had said quietly to Julia. "I know this war had turned convention on its head, but I can't go on living with Luisa without marrying her. Don't mistake me . . . she's made no demands, set no deadlines. We're just two lonely, rootless people who have come together, and are trying for our own little bit of personal happiness in a very doubtful time—like you and Jamie. We're keeping it very quiet. A registry office, and just our friends at Luisa's house.

Luisa doesn't want a big fuss—Ginette's and her husband's deaths are too close. But I'll want my three girls around me. Try to bless this marriage, Julia. Somehow I care more about what you think than about Alex and Connie. Perhaps because you were Ginette's favourite. Connie would be loyal, no matter what I did. Alex will never be reconciled to it, because she doesn't like Luisa—oh, don't think I don't know that. I thought life ended for me that day Ginette was killed. A large part of it did. But somehow my body didn't die. I need a woman, a marriage, a home. I suppose I'm hopelessly old-fashioned . . ."

Very gently she reassured him. "That's what I want with Jamie. Connie wants it with Ken Warren. Alex is hurting because she doesn't have it with Greg any more. You're entitled to your piece of happiness, Father. Grab it. Don't let it go."

"Bless you, Pet."

The ceremony and reception was a low-key affair by the standards of the wedding Luisa had arranged for Julia. But the press got wind of it, and jostled each other, and the three sisters on the steps of the registry office. But Michael and Luisa smilingly posed for photographs, both there, and at the entrance of Luisa's house. The ghost of Ginette Maslova took one further step back into the shadows.

"Well, she got him," Alex said with some bitterness to Julia at the reception. She looked worn and tired, and had taken little trouble with her clothes, but she still retained the indefinable air of chic and assurance that had always been hers, despite the general air of shabbiness and "making-do" that marked most people's clothes these days. She had lost pounds in weight as the weeks had gone by, and there had been no news of Greg. Lord Wolverton was urging her to take up the post in Washington, and was growing impatient with her refusal to make up her mind. Julia had a sense that Alex believed that if she waited here in London news would come sooner of Greg, as if leaving here was a betrayal. But Alex did not speak very much of Greg any more, though she continued to use her father's bedroom at the flat.

"I don't think it was a matter of 'getting' him," Julia answered. "It is something he wanted. He's entitled—"

"Of course she got him. She always meant to. It was a matter of waiting, of making herself indispensable to him, of always being there, the way Mother never could be. That—and pots of money. Just as well Father's talent is incorruptible, or she'd begin to manipulate his career. Rather the way she's doing with yours."

"*Mine!* What the hell do you mean?"

"Well, it's mostly her money in the film, isn't it? She'd like a nice success for you. It would look good for Father. An acting dynasty, sort of thing."

"Rubbish!—it's D.D.'s film."

"And D.D. takes the money wherever he can find it."

"And why not? That's always been how the theatre keeps going. You're jealous, Alex, and more than a bit stupid. It isn't like you. Don't begrudge him whatever happiness he can manage to grab. You're too old to be resentful of a stepmother, for heaven's sake. Did you expect Father to live like a monk for the rest of his life? And if she has money to make his life easier, then all the better. He's always been short of money—you know that. Most actors are. They don't handle it very well. And any rate, he spent an awful lot on us. Fancy schools and university don't come cheap."

Suddenly Alex gave a wry little laugh. "You know, you've touched a sore spot. I *am* jealous—just a bit. When I don't have Greg, I want to keep Father for myself. I expected him to hold my hand. But he's holding Mrs. Radcliffe's instead."

"Lady Seymour's hand," Julia corrected. "Better accept it."

"Yes—Lady Seymour. That used to be our mother's name . . ." She broke off. "Oh, damn, I can see Old Woolfie bearing down on us—beaming. It makes me sick. Everyone's so damned pleased. He'll say the usual things about how good it will be for Father to be settled—and then he'll start up again about Washington. I really don't want the job. It sounds a bit too much like cutting and running. I'm not even sure of what I'm supposed to do . . ."

"You'll make it your own, as you've done with everything. It would be a great experience. You'd be mad not to take it."

"What you're saying is that Greg won't be coming back, and there's no point in my hanging around here."

"I'm not saying anything of the sort. You're turning sour inside, Alex. If you can't have Greg back for a while, then accept the challenge of this job—even if it's only as a distraction. *Grab it!* How many women get offered anything like that. Greg would despise you for being unprofessional."

"Unprofessional! No one ever called me that!"

"Ours is a professional family. We've always been.

You know what Greg would expect of you. Go and do it."

Alex deposited her empty glass on a waiter's tray and requested whisky. "I need fortification," she said. "Not only is Old Woolfie pushing his way steadily here, but here's Connie with her long drink of water in tow. I can't, for the life of me, think what she sees in Ken Warren. I hear that after Dowding left Flight Command, Ken was transferred into some hush-hush job in the Ministry of Defence—a Whitehall job. Intelligence, no doubt. That should keep him nice and safe for the duration."

"You really are turning into a witch, Alex. Can he help it that he'd never be allowed on active service with those eyes? In his quiet way, he's probably quite brilliant, and someone has to do the desk work. Only he would never talk about it."

"Oh, I don't doubt it. He'll follow in the shadow of the mighty, and take care to make himself indispensable. He'll be one of those faceless, anonymous people who suddenly end up getting knighted for no good reason that anyone can see except the Prime Minister. At the end of the war he'll slide into the Civil Service, and end up as someone's Permanent Under Secretary—"

"And what's wrong with that?" Jamie was beside them. "Not my style, but old Ken has a lot going for him, behind those glasses. Don't underestimate him, Alex."

"Not you too, James Sinclair. I really can't take any more flak."

"Then stop making yourself a target for it. Try smiling, just for a minute. You used to be a good sort, Alex." He kissed her briefly on the cheek to take the sting out of his words. "Now *smile!* It's your father's wedding day. Smile for him, if for no one else."

She did manage a smile as Connie and Ken Warren pushed their way to them through the crush. "Here's Ken," Connie said breathlessly, as if they hadn't noticed him. "He managed to get away, after all. Doesn't Mrs. Radcliffe . . . I mean . . . well, what are we going to call her now?"

"Try Luisa," Jamie said. "Asking her gracious permission, of course. Somehow, I don't think she'd object."

"Yes, I'll do that," Connie answered. "I do think she looks lovely, don't you? And I think she'll make Father happy. It must have been such a lonely time. Now he has a home—a base—someone to look after him."

Julia looked at the smiling Luisa across the room, and knew what Connie said was right. But something in her still longed for her own beloved, temperamental mother, the one of brilliance, near genius. The one whose house or life was never quite as orderly as it might have been, but who had been capable of flashes of such warmth and love that no one had ever taken seriously her erratic flaws. Her encompassing talent had reached out to hundreds of thousands of people. Her laughter had been rich and true, her tears had been from the heart. She had had all the tempestuous passion of her Russian ancestry. She may have retreated further into the shadows on this day, but Julia could still hear her voice, hear her softly sing the almost forgotten lullabies of her own childhood, feel herself held close to that warm, scented breast, know her kisses, feel the ache of her frequent departures and fervent joy of her returns. She had neither Alex's jealousy, not Connie's calm acceptance of this marriage. For her, no other woman would touch the memory of Ginette Maslova.

She reached for Jamie's hand and held it tightly. "You must go and congratulate Father. And wish the bride happiness. She did her best to give us a lovely wedding . . ."

"She did her best to shove you out of the nest," Alex said. She turned and faced her employer, who had at last made the passage to her side. "We were just discussing what we should call our step-mother . . ."

Michael and Luisa left for three days in a house in Somerset which a friend had lent to Luisa. Jamie and Julia were packing for the journey to Anscombe, where they would spend the rest of Jamie's three days of leave. Agnes hovered about them with the coffee pot. "It doesn't taste like much, I'm afraid. But the best we can get these days. Wasn't the reception beautiful? Isn't Lady Seymour's house beautiful? Exquisite taste—anyone can see that, although they told me so much had been put safely away until the war's over . . ." She was once again enjoying the association with wealth, but still a little anxious about her own position. "You'll still be keeping on this flat, Miss Julia? I mean, you're sure to be back on the stage again once the film's over."

Julia wished she had not mentioned it. She guessed that Jamie was still of two minds whenever he was reminded that his wife had a job, a career almost, even if a fledgling one. The time beyond the war was not settled in their own minds. The question of how one carried on a career from a remote Scottish castle was still not resolved. She guessed he welcomed the film because if she continued in that direction, there could be long gaps between films, and therefore she would be at home with him. But it all belonged in a realm almost beyond their imagination—the end of the war.

Alex quietly entered the flat just as they were about to go to the station. Something utterly desolate in her expression made Julia rush to her side.

Alex spoke one word. "Changi."

"What?"

Alex allowed herself to be guided to a chair. Agnes poured coffee, but Jamie went to the drinks cabinet and brought her a brandy.

"I—we—the paper's just had word through the Red Cross. Greg was captured with all the others when Singapore fell. It doesn't matter that he's non-combatant. No one gets out. He's in a prison called Changi. That's all we know."

"He's alive . . ." Julia said tentatively.

"Alive," Alex repeated. "Yes, alive. I'm grateful. But when will I ever see him?" She swallowed quickly on the brandy, and turned to Jamie. "When will the end of the war be? Your guess is as good as mine." She continued to ramble on in that vein for a few moments, asking unanswerable questions. Then Jamie touched her shoulder.

"Come on, it's time to go, or we'll miss the train. Julia, can you throw a few things into a bag for Alex. A toothbrush—whatever else she'll need."

"To Anscombe?" Alex protested. "I can't leave London. There might be more news. Woolfie sent me home—but I don't know what I'm supposed to do. I suppose he didn't want me weeping all over the office. Bad for morale. I'm supposed to be such a sympathetic but tough reporter of other people's misfortunes. I suppose he thought it would be better to have me out of the way."

"He sent you to your family, Alex," Jamie said. "You're with us. To swear or weep or curse the gods. No matter what. Any news they get will come to Anscombe. You're coming with us."

"I don't—" She stopped. "Well, you *are* family, Jamie, and you bear the scars of war. Until this minute I didn't think of you and Julia as quite real. I mean . . . a real marriage. Just something that came because of the war. But it's more than I thought." She reached for the brandy again, and then fumbled for a cigarette, which Jamie supplied. "OK . . ." It was said a little grudgingly. "I'll come. Better there than back at Greg's flat . . . alone. I suppose I've got to get used to the feeling that 'alone' could be a long time."

"Yes," Jamie said. "That's what you've got to get used to, Alex. Like a lot of other women."

"I've never been like other women."

"You are now."

Alex stayed at Anscombe through Jamie's remaining two days of leave. Julia wondered what was wrong with her own feelings that she had a sense of resentment that Alex took all their time and attention, a time she had wanted so badly with Jamie. But she was there—either telephoning the office, or the Red Cross, or going on long walks with them unwillingly. "I never was a country person. You know that, Julia. I hate walking . . ." They avoided the village of

Anscombe, where she would encounter too many people who knew her, and would ask about her husband. When questions were asked, Julia or Jamie answered them, and let Alex walk on. Once Alex did pick a few daffodils which were still tightly in bud, and asked that they go to their mother's grave. She laid them there. "I'm a simpleton," she said. "I haven't got any time or place for grief. I didn't know how to handle it when Mother died. I still don't. I think of Greg as dead—and yet he isn't—not yet. One hears the Japs aren't too kind to their captives. Too many mouths to feed. And we haven't got any Jap captives to strike some *quid pro quo*. Sort of 'You be nice to ours, and we'll be nice to yours'. Well, belatedly, I've laid flowers on my mother's grave. I wish, instead, I could send a few tins of bully beef to Greg. Let's go home, before I get more maudlin. Let's raid Father's cellar tonight. A couple of bottles of his best. I don't suppose it will matter. From now on Mrs. Radcliffe will replenish his cellar. I'm beginning to see how her money might be useful—but I hope to God he didn't marry her for that reason."

Remembering her talk with her father before he had married, Julia cut her off sharply. "No more of that, Alex! They are two lonely people who found each other—who needed each other. They have as much chance of happiness—as much right to it, as anyone else. Father has never done anything purely for money in his life. No one goes into the theatre for money. No one marries a young musician for money. He needs money, but he's always scraped it up from somewhere. But he would never marry for it."

"Well . . . well! I stand rebuked." Alex put her

arm through Julia's and began to lead them all from the churchyard. "My little sister's grown up since she married, Jamie."

"And you'll realize it even more when you stop calling her your little sister."

She smiled at him, the first attempt at a genuine smile they had seen since before Michael's wedding. "You know, Jamie, I don't think I ever can. I don't mean it patronizingly. In many ways Julia's much wiser than I. But she was such a sweet and pretty little thing—with her golden hair that I so much envied. I once thought I was jealous of her because she was the youngest, and my parents adored her. But I really wasn't. I always knew that if something big came along which threatened her, I'd be there to protect her. She doesn't remember the times when both Mother and Father were away, when I really was the Big Sister. Connie was never any trouble. She was always so supremely sure that everything would be all right. But Julia used to fret—she doesn't remember that, but she did. And I tried to make her understand that they would always come back." She gave a last glance to her mother's grave, with the unopened daffodils. "Of course it doesn't always work that way . . ."

That night, as they drank two bottles of white burgundy, with jugged hare and apple pie, Alex grew pensive, less frenetic than she had been. "Well, I suppose I have to make plans—if anyone can make plans. Greg is in a Japanese concentration camp. I can sit and mope here, where everything and everyone in the office reminds me of him. I can push myself on you two, and move into the flat, play on your good nature and sympathy. Or I can do as Julia said Greg would want me to do. I can take the Washington job and make what I can of it. I have no specific brief from Woolfie. Just do what I can to make the Americans remember that we have a need over here—and that we, too, have lost thousands of serving men in the Pacific. I can write things for *The Record* so that people here will understand our new ally better. The fact that I have a husband in a prison camp could gain me a little extra entrée. I could use his name with all his old buddies in the Press Corps. I can use Father's name. God help me, I'll even use Mrs. Radcliffe's—no, Luisa's name, if it will get me anywhere. Those banking circles are as tightly knit as our little worlds." She raised her glass to them. "I'll choke off this self-pity that I'd so much despise in another woman. I'll make you—I'll make Greg proud of me."

"I'll drink to that," Jamie said. "And I'll hold you to it."

Jamie went early the next morning to catch the first bus from Anscombe. "How quiet it seems without him," Alex remarked when she came down to breakfast in the kitchen. "I think I'll miss him, though he isn't exactly the rowdy type. I like your man, Julia."

"Thanks," Julia said, and scraped butter sparingly onto her toast. She looked down again at the newspaper, and then back at her sister. Alex's appearance was better than Julia remembered it since the news of the fall of Singapore, and Greg's dropping from sight. She looked, for once, as if she had slept. The end of doubt had seemed to bring its own relief. Perhaps her half-decided plans of the night before had cracked the hard shell of her pain, had given her a kind of future, however tenuous.

"I think I'll telephone the Boss today, and tell him I'm taking a little break here—telephone Father with the news about Greg." She had refused to allow anyone to telephone the house in Somerset where her father and Luisa were staying. "It isn't fair to break in on them. After all, there's nothing they can do. They should be back by this evening. Father's only four days away from the play—and D.D. was stretching it to do that. I suppose he thinks the publicity made up for it. Have you noticed how the public loves a wedding in war time? If it's someone notable, it always makes the front pages. I suppose they think it's a sort of guarantee that other people —important people—are expecting this mess to turn out all right in the end . . ."

"Stop talking, Miss Alex, and eat," Stella said, thrusting a plate with a fried egg and one slice of bacon at her. "Of course it's going to be all right in the end. Whoever thought otherwise?"

To Julia's surprise, Alex began to eat the food in front of her, and didn't start to argue.

Alex stayed all through the remainder of the two weeks Julia had before starting on the film. She telephoned her father daily, and even asked, occasionally, to speak with Luisa. She had a long conversation with Lord Wolverton, and accepted the job offered in Washington. "I think they're all very relieved," she said. "Old Woolfie really has been very patient with me . . . humouring me. Perhaps because he liked and respected Greg so much . . . now I'll have to do the best I can for him." She laboured over the very short letter she was permitted to send through the Red Cross to Greg. "God knows when he'll get it." She made enquiries about sending food parcels, but the Red Cross was uncertain of deliveries. "No one seems to know how to handle the Japs just yet. It's all too new to them—to us. I can't remember when we've had an Asian enemy before."

"Half of Russia is in Asia," Julia remarked. "They weren't declared enemies, but they weren't friends until Hitler broke the pact."

"Sometimes you surprise me," Alex said. "Those are the sort of things *I'm* supposed to remember. I've grown up thinking everyone in the theatre lived inside their plays, and weren't really aware of half of what was going on about them. That's a notion I'll have to drop. Though with Father . . ."

"Father is different. He's very special. He is a very special actor. Don't expect him to be ordinary."

"Perhaps it's just as well he has Mrs.—Luisa. She seems an extremely practical type. Have you noticed . . . I mean how careful she's been not to come charging down here, full of solicitude, and beginning to take over? Do you realize it, Julia? This is probably the last time we'll ever be alone here together. After this, it will be Luisa's home, as well as Father's. I think she'll tread carefully, but I think we can expect changes—in time. Of course there are some things she'll never change." She gestured through the window at the rose garden. "Perhaps she'll even be clever enough to enhance them. Well, Father made something of beauty where other men might have left a firewood ruin. You realize, don't you, Julia, that with all her money she's never going to shift him out of this place? Even when the war's over, there's never going to be a grand country house somewhere. Father will never let go of what the Seymours have held for all these years. At one time he would have done it—but not now. Heritage and history have overtaken him. She'll have the ghosts of the Seymours as well as Ginette Maslova to fight."

"She's clever enough not to try to fight either. But you're right Alex. We'll be guests at Anscombe from now on."

Alex shrugged. "Tough luck. We were born and mostly grew up here. Not a bad beginning. She can't take that away from us." The clock struck six, and instead of going to turn on the news on the radio, Alex rose and went to the drinks cabinet and poured two whiskies. "We'll let it go until the nine o'clock news, shall we? I've thought war all day, trying to write that pitiful little letter to Greg. What is there to say to someone who probably feels as if he's there for eternity." She handed Julia her drink, and indicated the film script Julia had been studying. "What's it about?"

"Why don't you read it?"

Alex shook her head. "I tried a couple of Father's scripts a few times. They didn't make much sense to me—so disjointed, with all those film and stage directions. Not my sort of thing. I'm strictly non-fiction, as a matter of taste and training."

"Well . . ." Julia began slowly, groping for words. "Well you have to understand it's a low budget picture. Big on emotion, short on props. Made strictly with the co-operation of the Ministry of Defence. In fact, we've all been told to keep pretty quiet about the subject, but of course it will get out. D.D.'s got permission to do some shooting inside Bomber

Command bases—so you can guess the theme. It's set in a little village somewhere on the East Coast—Norfolk—Lincolnshire. The script doesn't say. The village had been virtually cut off by the expansion of the base. Only people who live there—people who have passes, can get in or out. It throws them together, whether they want it or not. No petrol to get out—no cars. Just bicycles. And a delivery van twice a week." She sighed. "I really don't know how to make something so slight seem like a film—even if it is a low budget one. D.D. keeps insisting that it's the quality that matters."

"And who do you play—the village horse?"

Julia smiled. "Maybe the village idiot is what I'll turn out looking like. No—I'm from outside. Only allowed to rent a little tumbledown cottage because I'm married to a pilot. Oh, yes—D.D. cast me well, though there's a very big difference between fighter and bomber pilots. Well, I'm just there—pregnant, and trying to get used to that cut-off village. Waiting every night with the hope that my husband will be allowed home for a few hours. My neighbour is the local aristocrat, whose house has been taken over as officer quarters. She hates the whole situation, but takes it in a sense of *noblesse oblige*. She doesn't like me, and she doesn't like the young Canadian navigator from the base who turns up and insists that he's related in some very distant way. He also insists on coming and helping her with her vegetable garden, and bits and pieces around the place. It isn't patriotic to send him away, and anyway, she needs the help. She isn't used to doing for herself—"

"Sounds like this lady has got the whole film for herself."

"When I tell you that Dame Audrey Fellowes is playing the role, then you *know* she's got the film."

Alex gave a low whistle. "How did D.D. land her. She's a big fish."

"The way he lands everyone. An appeal to their sense of patriotism—or whatever ruse he used before the war. Believe me, when he can find the right film for Father, he'll have his services for nothing. Luisa will see to that."

"So—go on—you're pregnant and waiting for your man, and the old aristocrat is trying to fight off the kindness of the young Canadian, whom, I'll bet, is as lonely as hell, and would rather be working in *your* garden, but he can't because your husband's a buddy."

"Why don't you write the rest of the script?"

Alex held up her hand. "I'll stop interrupting."

"The old lady has cancer—is beginning to be aware of it. The audience knows, but no one about her knows. The bombers are training over the North Sea almost every day. Sometimes there's a fighter escort. Neither I or the old lady ever know if it's training, or maybe, one day, the real thing."

"No one has made a bombing raid on the Germans since we gave up in France."

"Didn't I tell you it was a propaganda film? D.D. will be using plenty of free clips of training missions from the MOD. Well, one night they take off, much later than usual. Both the girl and the old woman are aware of it. And more bombers than the base carries join up with them. Fighter escort goes up—stays as long as their range will allow. But the bombers are away much longer—hours and hours. Just before dawn the fighter escort goes up to meet them, to beat off any fighters going up from the German side. We —the old lady and I, know it's been the real thing. They've been on a real bombing mission pretty deep into enemy territory. We both stand at the wire fence of the base. We'd counted them out, and now we try to count them in. They come in ones and twos. But we see from the way they're landing that they've been shot up. There's no formation. Some land there which don't belong to the base. We lose count. It gets lighter. We see the ambulances. Then all the sound is gone. No more planes approaching. Mechanics already starting to work on the planes they've got on the ground. It's full daylight. The planes are a long way off. Some of them askew on the runways. Some right off it. We can't read numbers. So we go back into my cottage and make tea. It grows into a really beautiful morning. We leave the door open . . . waiting. I see someone cycling up the lane. It's the Canadian. They've been on a *huge* bombing raid deep into Germany—just to show the Germans we can do it. He tries not to tell me, but he can't get out of it. It's been reported by other bomber teams. My husband's plane had been seen going down in flames. No one reported anyone bailing out from it. So he's reported missing. No one says 'presumed dead', but I know it. I put my hand on my belly because the baby had just given its first kicks. The Canadian takes the old lady back to her cottage. I wait through the day. One of my husband's pals comes to tell me—more or less officially. And I just sit there in the long twilight watching the Canadian working on the old lady's vegetables. She's going to die, but she's still got him."

Alex seemed to take a long time before she spoke.

She refilled both glasses. "It sounds like the sort of film where you're going to have to do a lot of looking at the sky, and the old lady's vegetable garden, and down the lane."

"That's about it."

"You'll do it beautifully. Just keep thinking of how Connie would have stuck it out, and you'll do it beautifully." Was Alex's voice husky? In the growing dimness of the room Julia thought she saw an unusual brightness in Alex's eyes, as if there were tears to be shed—tears she had denied herself all these weeks of waiting for news of Greg.

They went into shooting, and Julia had to be coached in every scene by the director. She found herself confused and depressed. The closeness of the cameras distracted her, the sense of many people clustered just beyond them, people who were all professionals in their particular work, not a theatre audience. She only ever had a few lines to say at a time, but they were done over and over, as the director called for another take. She felt as if the camera were boring down into her very nerve ends, and sometimes the director was only feet away from her. Dame Audrey was friendly, but slightly distant; she passed out no tips on acting before the cameras, but she evidenced no displeasure at having to work with a novice. During takes she sat and knitted socks—navy and khaki socks. "Used to do it when I was a young girl. Soldiers always need socks." In the end the director had her knitting socks as she observed the young Canadian toiling in her vegetable garden, unwanted, unbidden. She and Julia were filmed frequently at the wire fence, and the painted backdrops of the bomber base. The scene came when they stood there, each trying to identify the planes as they came in, but saying nothing. When the director called "Cut! Print it!" Dame Audrey nodded to Julia and smiled. "Well done, child. The hardest thing of all in acting is saying nothing."

Two days after the filming was finished, and ready for the cutting room came the news of the first one thousand bomber attack by the RAF on Cologne. D.D. was exultant. "We're dead on time! And on target!" There had been minor, less heralded sorties by Bomber Command, but never anything of this strength, and never had they penetrated so deeply into enemy territory. For Julia the news only brought a sense of horror, and nightmare-ridden sleep. She saw herself clinging onto the wire, counting.

For the first time since filming had begun she went back to Anscombe. She could be near Jamie, and they might have time together. But she remembered her talk with Alex. Never again would Anscombe belong entirely to them. Luisa was there, mistress in her mother's place, her father's wife. She approached warily.

She found only small changes. Some furniture had been rearranged, some strange pieces had appeared, probably from Luisa's Belgravia house. There were some small luxuries—good soap, rather more abundant hot water—though she didn't see how Luisa had managed extra coal supplies. Food parcels came regularly from America. "I am so fortunate," Luisa said. "So many good friends are so kind." There was tinned foie gras and caviar, and large tins of good biscuits. Cook looked at them rather askance, but since she lacked the ingredients to make them, she was forced to accept and serve them. She became clever at disguising the taste of tinned stew. Anscombe had always had a small herb garden, now tended by Stella, which was made full use of. It seemed Luisa was no stranger to cooking, and she was tactful in making suggestions to Cook. "They sent me to a school to learn how to cook so that if I married a poor man I'd always know how to make a dinner from almost nothing," she explained to Julia. There had been little chance, Julia thought, that she would have married a poor man—until she had the money to afford to marry Michael.

Her father had now finished the run of *Pygmalion* and was enjoying his time of quiet at Anscombe. The relationship between him and Luisa seemed calm and almost uneventful, as if they had been married a long time. He spent many hours with Harry Whitehand, talking over farm matters, proud that they were making their production quotas, and even, in some things, surpassing them. In the early summer morning and the evenings Julia went back to her task of herding and milking, helping the Land Army girls get through their tasks more quickly, and earning them more time off. Jamie came over and spent three nights. She felt her marriage renewed, and the nightmares began to ease.

Daily her father tended the rose garden, and often Julia saw Luisa, gloved and with secateurs, helping him. But whatever she did, pricking out seedlings from the green-house, putting a hoe skilfully around the potatoes, gathering and hanging herbs to dry, making a last-minute sauce with a smoothness and flavour which even Cook had to admire, she was always the immaculate figure who had first appeared at Anscombe. The black hair, caught into its classic chignon, never had stray tendrils, her hands were soft, her skin nourished by good cosmetics she freely acknowledged came from America. "I'm at a sensitive age, my dear," she once acknowledged to Julia. "Every woman approaching forty with a husband like Michael is." She laughed lightly. "I'm still afraid of every beautiful and brilliant young actress who crosses his path." But she did not mean that, Julia knew. She was still the utterly self-assured creature they had first known. She feared no one, so she could afford to be generous. But Julia noticed that there were few times when she could be alone with her father. There was no talk that did not include Luisa. Luisa actively encouraged Jamie's visits, however short they had to be. Julia must be occupied, and Michael must not be left alone. She had a way of managing Stella and Cook, lavish in praise, but equally firm in dictating how *she* liked things to be done. The days of Ginette Maslova were over, though her memory would be honoured. The reign of Luisa Seymour was not only begun, but well established.

A precious letter had finally reached them from Alex while Julia had been filming. She had made the journey to Washington through neutral Portugal, and taken the risk of the Atlantic crossing, with life-jacket always at the ready. She had almost the status of an accredited war-correspondent because of the mission Lord Wolverton had entrusted to her. He had written letters to his friends and business acquaintances, to his military contacts, asking that Alex should be granted any courtesy within their power, that she was not to be regarded just as "a woman's writer", but a worthy successor to her distinguished husband. He wrote to the President's Press Secretary reminding him of the interview the President had granted to Greg Mathieson, and suggesting that at some time Alex Seymour might be given the same privilege.

> It will not be time wasted for the President. All our newspapers will carry it front page. Anything to cement the alliance.

And, fatefully, he had written privately to his friend, Elliot Forster, the proprietor of a large empire of newspapers and radio stations.

> Look out for her, please. She's had a bad knock, but she's as tough as they come, and she's a good journalist. Open doors where you can.

5

WITH the filming done, Julia was in time to witness the late summer blooming of Ginette Maslova's rose garden. Luisa had already made sketches of how it would be extended. "We shall use the bricks from the oasthouse for a wall, and there will be gates—very beautiful wrought iron gates with a long walk stretching back, perhaps to a gazebo and more high walls so it will trap all the warmth, and keep out the winds. This—" She nodded to the long strip of garden, "is just the prelude."

Michael smiled at her in gratitude. "What a lovely idea, darling. I shall look forward to working on it with you."

Julia then knew that Luisa had already divined the truth about Michael Seymour. He knew little about the land, and could never have endured the life of a gentleman farmer, but he could not now be parted from the Seymour lands. Luisa would add and build on, and do what she wanted, when it was possible, but it would be at Anscombe, and nowhere else. Sensibly, if she wished to keep her husband, she would accept that; she appeared to have done so. By now Julia had seen pictures of the castillo in the hills near Granada where Luisa had been born; she had seen the château amidst its vineyards which Luisa had inherited from her first husband. She knew there was a Georgian house, now a convalescent hospital, within its seven hundred acres in Gloucestershire which belonged to Henry Radcliffe, and which was now Luisa's. Whatever she chose to do with the château, and the stately Georgian pile, she seemed to understand that this far more modest house would be her country house so long as she remained married to Michael Seymour.

With the summer had also come the sickening news of German successes in Russia—the siege of Sebastopol began, and in North Africa the 8th Army once again retreated before Rommel. But at midway in the Pacific the American navy had sunk four Japanese heavy carriers. *There is the faintest feeling here*, Alex wrote from Washington, *that in the Pacific now we just about have parity with the Japanese, but, dear God, there's such a hell of a long way to fight back—all that territory to be retaken.*

The battle of the Coral Sea in May in which the Japanese had been defeated, seemed to have marked the limit of their advance, and Australia had been saved. *By a whisker*, was Alex's comment.

She seemed to have thrown herself into her new life in Washington with vigour; when the almost unknown General Eisenhower was appointed Commander in Chief, Europe, she had a piece about him ready, and it was meant for popular consumption in the British press. She had well researched his background, his family—skated over his lack of combat experience. He became for the British the boy of a simple background from a place called Abeliene in Kansas, who had won out over all the more famous names to take the supreme job of the reconquest of Europe.

Elliot Forster arranged for me to interview Mamie

Eisenhower. She doesn't seem to have the faintest idea what her husband's heading into. A nice enough, but rather unsophisticated woman.

Julia noted how often Elliot Forster's name cropped up in Alex's letters, but then, she wondered, why shouldn't it? As the owner of several hundred newspapers in the States, of radio stations, and the influential magazine *Insight*, and therefore a power in Washington, he had seemed to have taken seriously his friend, Lord Wolverton's, request to "open doors where you can". Greg's name was seldom in Alex's letters, because there was little or nothing to write about him.

We hear now about what hells the Japanese prison camps are. All I can hope for is his survival until they finally give in, and I know that's years away. I've only had two letters from him. I've written dozens myself. They don't seem to get through. I can't tell him how the war's going, to raise his hopes, because those letters would certainly be stopped. And what can he tell me about life in Changi that isn't perfectly awful—and they certainly wouldn't let that through. I feel so powerless to help him. I just work as hard on my stuff as I can, and hope he'd approve. I keep cuttings of everything I write. I tell myself one day he'll read them.

She described her small Washington apartment in a house in Georgetown.

It's near enough to the centre of things, and I'm

very lucky to have it. Washington's crowded to the skies, as you can well imagine, and housing's difficult. I wouldn't have got it if Elliot Forster hadn't put in a word with the woman who owns it, and who's decided to let off the top floor while her husband's serving in the Navy. Elliot took me to the Washington Press Club where he addressed a luncheon yesterday. I was thrilled to be his guest —even though, naturally, with all the big-wigs there, I wasn't at the top table. There's so much going on here—I really feel as if I'm part of things. I was one of a dozen reporters allowed into one of Roosevelt's "off the record" press conferences in the Oval Office the other day. We can only report "unofficial sources" but everyone knows what that means. I love being here, living in a city that hasn't been bombed to pieces. But I do feel terribly guilty when I think of how comfortably I'm living, and Greg's probably half-starved.

And then her old anger broke through again.

But why the hell didn't he get out while he still could? He knew what his job was. It was to report the war, not moulder in a prison camp. And I always thought he was such a clever man. Always more than one step ahead of the others in knowing which way the wind would blow. He was always such a restless soul. I can't bear to think of him caged up . . .

Michael read the letter with some sadness. "She's trying too damned hard. I'm glad she's not in London. Being in Washington she's not encountering memories of him around every corner and pub in Fleet Street."

Before she had gone, Alex had given up the tenancy of the London flat, and stored Greg's belongings. "It would have been requisitioned for someone else," she said. "You can't leave empty flats in London." Julia remembered the book-lined warren of rooms in an old house near Covent Garden, and knew that its absence would be something else of a changed world Greg Mathieson would have to adapt to when he eventually returned. They also learned from Lord Wolverton that Alex had instructed that Greg's salary, which *The Record* still paid, be turned over to support his child by his first marriage. It was so easy to forget that Greg Mathieson had ever been married to anyone else but Alex.

Michael was preparing for a film—"another propaganda venture by D.D."—was how he described it. "He's so certain yours is going to be a big hit, Julia, he's got much more ambitious . . . It's the navy, this time. I'm supposed to be descended from a line of old sea dogs—the skipper of a destroyer escorting convoys across the Atlantic, doing the whole dramatic, heroic thing. I hope no one finds out I get slightly sick in a rowing boat on a mill pond on a still day. Most of it will be faked, of course, but there'll surely be times when I'll have to get out on the water. The navy likes the idea, so we're getting full co-operation. I shall feel such a fraud. They'll have to make me look a bit younger . . ."

There was, however, nothing for Julia at that time. Nothing in the West End was offered to her—there was no play suitable. And there were no film scripts with a part for her. "One of those empty periods," she said to Jamie. "I suppose if I were truly patriotic I would join a touring company. Get out into the provinces. It would be very useful experience. The sort of experience I've never had. But that would take me away from you. I'm a bit of a help here on the farm, and as I'm married, they can't conscript me. I can't sing or dance, so I'm useless to the ENSA concert parties. Can you imagine me standing up and reciting *The quality of mercy* . . . etc, to a hall full of soldiers dying for a good laugh, or the sight of a shapely leg."

"They'd whistle the roof off for your legs, my darling," Jamie said. "But I rather doubt *The quality of mercy* . . ."

"I could formally join the Land Army instead of just giving Harry Whitehand some help when it's convenient."

"And bureaucracy being what it is, you'd probably be sent to deepest Wales instead of being left right here where you belong. But of course the money would make us rich—what do they pay Land Army girls, anyway?"

"One pound eight shillings a week," Julia said promptly. "I ought to know. I hear enough about it."

Harry Whitehand now loved his Land Army girls. He had shaken his head over them at first. "What will these townies know?" Later he said to Jamie, "They're wonderful with stock—just the way Miss Julia is. I've taught some of them to drive a tractor in a day. All the jobs we thought women couldn't do. They've worked alongside me ditch digging, and hedge laying, up to the top of their gum boots in water. I never thought I could work with women on a farm. Now I'm shouting to the Ministry for every one they can send."

Jamie was still leading his "circus" squadron. He didn't like the lightness the name implied, but he well understood the importance of keeping the enemy engaged and whole squadrons pegged down in France to counter the bombing raids. "We're strategically useful, and we do shoot down our share. But still, it doesn't seem like real fighting. Not like the old days . . ."

"You want to leave me, then?" Julia teased him. "Go where the big action is. You'll be here, Jamie, when it's time to invade France again. You'll get your own back for the time they pushed all of you out of France."

"I hope so," he said fervently. "There's a lot I want to get my own back for."

Michael was on location in Northern Ireland, filming the necessary background shots for *Atlantic Approaches*. Luisa had not asked to accompany him. "I wouldn't dare. Think of what they'd say about a useless wife cluttering up the scene, when she should be at home doing her job."

For all the fact that she seemed always present when Michael wanted her, she did manage to keep up with the Red Cross committee in London, and when at Anscombe, she attended the village hall to help with the Women's Voluntary Service. "They don't mind what you do there, or who you are, so long as you do something useful." She was often at the convalescent home where Jamie had spent so many months, helping in the kitchen, writing letters for those whose injuries would not permit it, supporting those still unsteady on their feet to walk in the grounds.

"She isn't what I first thought her," Julia admitted to Jamie. "She's so much tougher, and ready to work. I thought those marvellous hands would never go into dishwater, but they do more than that."

But it was a different Luisa she discovered one morning as she started down to the kitchen for early breakfast before going out for the milking. She heard strange sounds coming from Luisa's bedroom. She hesitated a long minute before tapping on the door. There was no reply, but the choking, gutteral sounds went on. So she opened the door gently and looked in. The great double bed which Luisa and Michael shared was empty, the sheets thrown back in disarray. The sounds came from the connecting bathroom. Very quietly, ready to retreat, she tiptoed forward. What she saw at the bathroom door stopped her. Luisa, in an exquisite satin and lace nightgown, was on her knees before the toilet bowl, retching almost convulsively, but her stomach now only yielding a little bile and water. As she watched, Luisa's hand went up to flush the bowl once more.

"Luisa . . ." Julia's voice was very hesitant. Perhaps it would have been better if she had not come in. Whatever was wrong, perhaps Luisa would prefer to remain private.

The dark head turned; for once her hair was not restrained, and fell about her shoulders and body with luxurious warmth. But there were stray tendrils which Julia thought could not exist, and they clung to her face, wet with sweat. She collapsed into a sitting position on the floor, one hand still holding the bowl for support; with the other hand she weakly gestured Julia to come to her. Julia knelt beside her.

"What is it, Luisa? Can I help?"

Julia lifted the light, slender body easily under the armpits, and supported her back to the bed, straightening the sheets and blanket, plumping up the pillow. "Are you feeling terrible, Luisa?—forgive me, but I couldn't help hearing—I was just going past the door . . ." Without thinking, she put her hand to Luisa's head, brushing back the sweat-soaked hair. "Just a minute . . ." She went to the bathroom, and wrung out a face-cloth in cold water, and grabbed a crystal jar of such size she guessed it must have contained cologne. Very gently she bathed Luisa's face and hairline, her neck and shoulders. Then she lavished cologne on the cloth, and wiped her again.

"Ah—how kind," Luisa breathed. "How much better that feels. I think it's over. For this morning, at any rate." Her large brown eyes, slightly hollow and dark-ringed, looked directly at Julia. "I think . . . I hope . . . I believe I am with child."

That curiously old-fashioned expression struck Julia to the heart. "Oh, Luisa . . ."

One of the long pale olive hands sought hers. "For me, it is the most wonderful thing. All my life I have wanted a baby—a child. I hope Michael will be happy. With my first husband . . ." she shook her head. "Then with Henry . . . for about two weeks I thought it was possible I was pregnant. But I hadn't consulted a doctor. And then he was killed. If I had been carrying a child, it left me then. I was never sure . . ."

"Shall I send for the doctor. . . ?"

A weak smile lightened Luisa's face. "What?—for

a little morning sickness? He has many more demands on his time. I saw a doctor just when Michael left for filming in Northern Ireland. He was almost positive, but we are having tests done. From what I now know, we really don't need them."

Julia was almost without words. "It means a great deal to you?"

"You cannot imagine. I love your father. I know Alex finds that difficult to accept, but it is the truth. I have longed for a child—but most particularly by Michael. But, you see, I am very old to be having a first child. It will be difficult. It will be difficult to carry this child. I realize I must be a—a sort of invalid for the whole time it takes." She gave a wan smile. "I so hope it will please Michael, when he returns, to know that he will be a father again. I hope for a strong and healthy child, so I shall be very selfish, and rest as much as possible, as the London doctor told me I must, if I am to carry it to full term."

She touched Julia's arm. "I see that the idea does not dismay you."

"Why should it? It's the most natural thing in the world. A happy thing. Of course Father will be delighted. Why shouldn't he?"

"One never knows, my dear. At his age—at my age. Perhaps he just hoped for years of contentment, with nothing to bother him. But I so much wanted . . . But . . . ah, Julia . . ." She relaxed back into the pillows. "I am of a Spanish family. They regard women without children with scorn. My sisters married Spaniards, and between them they have many children. They pity me. At last . . . at last, with

Michael's child . . . There is nothing more on earth I could wish for."

Julia sat back on her heels. "Let me help you. Let us all help you." How could they have ever doubted this woman—she and Alex? She absolved Connie from that judgement. This was a woman who loved her husband, and longed for a child. Everything in Julia cried out in sympathy for this last hope of the exhausted woman lying in the bed.

"We shall all help. I promise you. You will have your baby—a healthy, happy baby. And my father will be so delighted. I hope it will be a boy. It would make a nice change for us all."

The thin hand gripped Julia's again. "You are very generous—kind . . ."

"I'll bring you up some tea. Some toast—without butter. You'll perhaps be able to keep that down. At other times . . . well, that old saying, 'You'll have to eat for two.'"

She went downstairs, faintly bemused, wondering, as she made the tea, what sort of difference this would make to her father's life—to all their lives. But fervently, with all the death she had witnessed, had read and heard spoken of around her, she uttered little prayers for this child's life.

After a month her father returned from Northern Ireland. He took the news of the baby with, at first, a silent wonderment, and then with boyish enthusiasm. "Good God!—at my age! What an old goat people will call me. It's the most marvellous thing." He said later to Julia, "Dear Luisa . . . I had no idea she wanted a baby so badly." He touched his daughter's cheek. "She tells me you have been very good to her.

I would have known it, Pet, even if she had not told me."

He was working for the next two months at Ealing, finishing the film. Then her own film, *Return at Dawn*, was released. It had instant praise from the critics, and there was almost as much praise for Julia as for Audrey Fellowes. Luisa came up to London for what was called a "première"—but was really just a first showing.

Afterwards, at a quiet supper—Michael insisted that everything now be quiet—at her Wilton Terrace house, with only D.D. present, Luisa observed, "I didn't realize what a good actress you are. Forgive me. Perhaps it's that I don't understand the language as well as you think I do. But in the theatre I get so distracted by the people around me. I can't get lost in the play—and the intervals are a complete distraction. But there in the dark at the cinema I felt you very much. You have so little to speak—and yet so much to say. Being pregnant, the growing love for the old woman who would soon die, for the young Canadian. And that country lane, with only one figure cycling down it. The expression on your face. You photograph very beautifully, Julia. Some women who are beautiful do not photograph that way."

D.D. was exuberant. "Didn't I see it all along? Once I saw the screen tests, and the first rushes, I knew we had it made. I just feel in my . . . my guts, that it will be a hit in the States. And when Michael's film follows that . . ." He beamed on them all.

When Jamie came to Anscombe two weeks later, he was smiling and shaking his head. "Well, of course, it's all over the base. What did the Old Man do to deserve a film star as a wife? Really, Julia, you're impossible to live up to now. Being a stage actress is one thing—a lot of the chaps never went to a theatre in their lives. They've vaguely heard of your father, and that's about it. But the cinema—that's something different. They've all taken their girls to the one-and-sixpennies on a Saturday night. That's the big time. And your pictures in the papers and magazines. I swear that if my squadron didn't think I might spot it, some of them would have you as a pin-up."

"I'm not Betty Grable yet—nor likely to be."

"I'd swear on oath that your legs are as good. And *she* can't act her way out of a paper bag. I wonder when I can get to see it? It wasn't very nice of you not to invite me to the first night."

"There wasn't a 'first night'. No glamour. Did you tell them at the base that I get just as mucky every day as any other farm worker?"

"No. Why spoil the image of the beautiful Julia Seymour."

"My name is Julia Sinclair, remember?"

A shy little note came from Castle Sinclair, from Janet.

> Oh, I thought you were lovely, Mrs. Sinclair. I've been twice into Inverness now to see it. I cried my eyes out—such a sentimental body I am. Lady Jean said she would go to see it when she collected enough petrol coupons. Then Sir Niall swept up and took her off one afternoon. She didn't say very much, except that she thought it was all very good. And that you were very talented. From Lady Jean that's praise indeed. I don't think she ever expected to have so many famous people in the family—

remembering your mother. Quality was what she wanted—she doesn't know what to do with fame as well.

Jamie got a week's leave in the late days of September, and demanded that they travel down to a hotel in the depths of Cornwall. "We've never been really alone, Julia. The flat in London is fine, but it still belongs to your family. And the same at Anscombe. We never had a real honeymoon. I refuse to go to Sinclair. I won't have you deferring to my mother again—though Scotland is beautiful at this time of year. But we must have a time to ourselves . . ."

They had a week of almost perfect weather; from their small hotel they walked the lonely beaches and coves, or the cliff tops where the barbed wire kept them off the beaches. They were drenched when they took a picnic lunch on Dartmoor; they lay among the heather and made love, careless of the wet and the sudden chill. They came back to dry off before the fire which the hotel keeper had decided to light in their bedroom. He had recognized Julia from pictures in the newspapers and magazines; he respected the ribbons Jamie's uniform bore. He even sent up a complimentary bottle of champagne. "You'd think we were young lovers instead of an old married couple," Julia said.

"We *are* young lovers. Always will be."

She smiled. "Remember how it was the first time? The little cottage . . . the fire you made. How you taught me to make love."

"Remember it, dearest. Every precious moment of it. Remember it when I'm away from you."

"You're going away?" Her voice was suddenly sharp with anxiety.

"I think so. I didn't mean to tell you. I think this is sort of embarkation leave. Only they don't tell you. You just notice a few signs of preparations for us to move out."

"Where?"

"I don't know. And if I did, I couldn't tell you. It can really only be to North Africa. There's nowhere else to send us. The Americans are running the show in the Pacific. I sort of sense they're getting ready for a big push against Rommel in the desert. But I've been at Hawkinge so long, I expected to be there when it was our turn to invade Europe. I wanted that, Julia. I wanted finally to be back on French soil again."

"North Africa! Oh, God, I won't ever see you. It's so dangerous."

"No more dangerous than what we do almost every day here. Tempting the Luftwaffe up to meet us. I know that blasted coast so well, sometimes I almost wished I were in Bomber Command and had the chance, some day, to smash the hell out of it. The range of the fighters is so short . . ."

But they tried as little as possible to speak of war. Rommel's destruction of Tobruk with thirty thousand men in June had been felt as a national disaster only second to the fall of Singapore. The Germans had advanced all summer along various fronts in Russia, thrusting towards Stalingrad and Rostov. But the first major victory had been won in the Pacific when the airfield the Japanese had built at Guadalcanal in the Solomons was taken. To Julia, studying the maps, it was a deadly see-saw with Jamie's life in the balance.

"When . . ." But she let the questions about the future die on her lips, and gave herself up to the joy of solitude with her husband, of loving him, of learning as much of his mind and body as she could. She sensed what she was doing—trying to store up all she could of him against a time of parting, of absence. She had begun to hate any mention of the film, *Return at Dawn*. In that film her love, her husband, had not returned.

It came two weeks later, a telephone call early in the morning when Julia had just come in from milking, and was hungrily eating breakfast. "Julia!" In the background there were sounds as if Jamie was making the call from the mess. "This is it, my darling. What we talked about. Can't talk about it now. I'll see you soon—sooner or later."

"I'll be waiting." There were no other words she could find to say. "I'll be waiting—for no matter how long."

With Jamie's going a strange lassitude fell on Julia. She went about her tasks on the farm routinely, finding little now to talk to the Land Army girls about, she did the milking, drove a tractor and mucked out, and spread the muck on the fields, with her mind a strange blank. She discovered after two weeks that a vital element was missing—she had nothing to look forward to. If Jamie had been sent to North Africa then there could be no forty-eight hour leaves, not even a few hours when they could meet in a Folkestone tea shop. It might be an endless time before his first letter came. She was hardly interested that *Return at Dawn* had opened in New York to extremely good notices. D.D. was ecstatic, telephoning her that the film had been booked into one of the major circuits. "There'll be some journalists coming down to Anscombe to interview you, darling. Don't dress up for them. Just wear those awful Land Army girl things. I want these pictures and interviews to show you as close to the girl in the film as possible. No glamour."

She went through the interviews as routinely as she did her everyday job, sometimes wondering if she wasn't playing the part of the hayseed rather too heavily. There were questions about Jamie, his DFC won in France, the bar added to it during the Battle of Britain, questions about her relationship with her father as an actor, about her future role when she went to live at Castle Sinclair. Ginette Maslova was mentioned. Sometimes she was obliged to take some particularly well-prepared journalists on a tour of the rose garden, which was becoming famous. But the hayseed atmosphere vanished when Luisa entered, quietly announcing lunch or tea, immaculately groomed, radiating her air of distinction and sophistication. A few times her father was at home, and every interviewer craved a little time with him, wanting his opinion of *Return at Dawn*, delighting in the added spice his presence gave to the interview.

Alex wrote from Washington:

You were wonderful. I've seen it three times, and even the great Elliot Forster came once, and pronounced that you were pretty good—especially playing beside someone as formidable as Audrey Fellowes. He didn't tell me, but I know from "other sources" that he's given the word that all papers and magazines are to feature articles on you. And I don't believe he's doing it because of his friendship with me. He's got too much integrity as a journalist himself for that. It would be rather the other way about. He'd almost bend over backwards not to do that if he didn't believe you've got great talent. I'm proud of you—and you're still my little sister, no matter what anyone says.

Her letter did not mention Greg.

The first letter came at last from Jamie.

You can guess where we are because of the sand in the paper. Not the most comfortable bivouac, but then we got rather spoiled at home. Rather different kind of flying too—new tricks to learn.

Then some sentences heavily inked out by the censor. Jamie had not yet learned the restraint that writing to her imposed; there had been very few letters during their marriage—mostly hurried notes or telephone calls arranging meetings.

She now followed the North African campaign with special care, learning what she could from the censored dispatches from the war correspondents, learning to interpret some of what they could only hint at, but not say. It was, in the main, tank warfare, and it was evident that the British had been heavily supplied with American vehicles. They heard a great deal about a place called El Alamein, and finally, a great victory there. Then came the great operation they would learn was codenamed *Torch*, the invasion of northwest Africa in a joint exercise by British and American troops under Eisenhower. Julia wondered where, in all of this great operation Jamie was. She had only one message to send him. *We are going to have a baby.*

The news was received with hoots of laughter by her father. "My dear, how absolutely wonderful! But it's the damndest thing—both my wife and my daughter pregnant at the same time." But he was delighted and solicitous at the same time. "Pet, you must stop all this farm work at once. It's too heavy. I won't permit it, and when I told Harry Whitehand, he was absolutely in agreement. If one of his Land Army girls got pregnant, he'd send her straight back home. Can't have you dropping the baby in a field like a calf. Take up knitting, like Luisa—that will have to be your war effort until the baby's born. And put away those scripts D.D. keeps sending you. Filming's tough work. There'll be plenty of that after the baby's born. Think of it—my first grandchild!"

Luisa heard the news with a gratified smile, and the hint of tears in her eyes. "Ah, my dear—so wonderful. Jamie will be so pleased." Luisa was having a difficult time as her pregnancy advanced, and had given up going to London altogether, and even to her WVS work at Anscombe village hall. On the orders of her Harley Street doctor, she rested most of the day. "He told me," Luisa confessed to Julia, "that that was not what he told most of his 'mothers'. A healthy amount of exercise was desirable, even helpful. But I am an elderly—oh, I can't remember what word he used, but it means that I'm very old to be having a first child. And there's been that little bit of 'spotting'—which is a bad sign. Michael is for putting me to bed altogether until the baby's born, but I have insisted that a gentle walk in the garden every day is necessary, and I shall not die of it. So I walk around the rose garden several times, and wherever else I am permitted that's within sight of the house. And I always know Stella is watching me from one of the windows. You must follow my diet—it seems to work." Luisa ate a number of small meals a day, as much fruit and vegetables as could be managed. "Never let yourself be hungry, my dear, it only brings back the sickness . . ."

However cheerful her talk, Luisa did not now look well. Her faintly olive skin had grown sallow, her eyes more deeply recessed, with dark smudges under them. She kept saying that she felt well, and she ate her small meals regularly, without protest. Her slight body seemed overburdened with the weight of the child. She found it difficult to sleep, appeared always weary.

But the first weeks of 1943 were brightened with the news of Allied victories in North Africa and Russia, the collapse of the Japanese resistance in Burma. Michael had refused any further stage or film work so that he could be with Luisa.

Two letters came from Jamie by the same post, one written weeks before the other.

> We're pretty busy, as you probably know, but unless I'm in the thick of it, I hardly think of anything else but you and the baby. Do take good care of yourself, my darling love. I wish more than ever I hadn't been sent abroad. I find myself imagining all kinds of things—teaching him to ride and fish, walking in the forest with him. Almost for the first time in my life I'm glad of Castle Sinclair. It begins to mean something other than a

burden which my mother has carried for me. Now I'll work it cheerfully, because it will be for our son.

"Supposing it isn't a son?" Julia wrote.

His next letter, which didn't reach her until almost the end of January replied, *Don't worry. There'll be others. One of them's bound to be a boy.* She worried about this deeply clannish streak in him, hitherto unrevealed. He did care far more about his inheritance than she had suspected. It would figure very prominently in the way their child was brought up. This had been no light, war-time marriage, made in haste, with the future still to be discovered. The future lay there ahead of them both, in Scotland, at Sinclair.

Letters came from Alex full of her doings in Washington. They often read her pieces in Wolverton's papers at home; she sent the cuttings of the pieces she wrote which appeared in American newspapers. She had sent cuttings of the articles published about Julia and *Return at Dawn*. The letters were bright, growing more hopeful as she studied the turn of events in the Pacific, North Africa and Russia. *Some day*, she wrote, *some day we'll wake up and find the tide really has turned. I hear so little from Greg. I suppose it's as much as he's allowed to write. But one hears such horror stories of the Japanese prison camps . . .*

In a letter to Julia, she added a page marked *for you only*. It was a cry of pain and guilt.

Don't tell Father or Connie. But I can't keep it to myself another moment. Elliot Forster separated from his wife two months ago. They have agreed on a divorce. I really don't think she cares very much, just so long as she gets enough money. He wants to marry me as soon as the divorce is final. And I want to marry him. I'm so ashamed and sickened by my betrayal of Greg. I thought it could never happen. Wasn't my love strong enough to bear this time of separation? I thought it would last forever. I am miserable, and yet everything about Elliot compels and commands me. He's so dynamic, and I suppose just sheer sexual hunger, the sense of aloneness, was too much for me. I don't feel proud to be writing this. I find myself praying about it, trying to rationalize it—square it—with God. And yet all I hear is the cry from the Garden of Gethsemane "Could you not wait and watch one hour with me?" I have loved two men, but Elliot is here, alive, in the flesh, my lover. Greg has become a shadow. I look at his photo every day, and know that that man no longer exists. Whatever emerges from that terrible place, Changi, will be a different person, someone I no longer know. He cannot have come through that experience unchanged, and I also have changed. But one thing I have promised myself, and told Elliot. I will not, until Greg is released, either write this to him, nor will I divorce, and marry Elliot—not if it takes years for Greg to be free. Not even if I lose Elliot over it. I just cannot write that sort of letter to a man in a prison camp. But it is becoming harder and harder to write to him at all, knowing that I am lying by not telling him. So I will have to go on lying. But most of the time I despise myself—except for the times when I'm with Elliot. Then

Greg slips even further into the background. But I am a woman in love, and I don't know how to deny it.

Julia found tears both of anger and pity in her eyes. How their destinies were all shaped by the men they loved; such different futures stretched before her and her sisters. Perhaps Connie would be the only one to experience an untroubled love, an unquestioning faith, the only one not to see any life apart from her husband's stretching before her. If they both survived the war, she and Ken Warren would marry, and thereafter Connie would happily submerge her identity in his. Julia found herself almost envying the thought of such an uncomplicated future. For Connie there would be no storm of torn loyalties, or conflict of ambitions or interests. If Ken Warren were lucky enough to keep her, he would have the perfect wife.

Although Luisa's baby was not due until February, in January Michael moved her back to the Wilton Terrace house, so that she could be near her doctor. There was an unspoken anxiety in Michael and Julia about her; she looked so frail and thin, despite the mound of her belly. Her cheeks had long hollow lines drawn down them. "She looks as if she's starving," Stella once whispered to Julia. "And yet I know she chokes down every mouthful she can. I've never known a woman to want a child so much. And I think she's really a little older than she says . . ."

At the end, Luisa asked Julia to come to London with them. "I've grown to depend on your company. I know I am such poor company for Michael—but at least in London he will be able to see his friends. I am selfish—yes? I want to take you away from the good country air, and back to London. But it's only for a few weeks. I would be forever grateful . . ."

But it was not for weeks. They had been installed in the Belgravia house, with Stella and the old butler-chauffeur, along with Agnes, who had been taken on by Luisa when Michael had given up his flat, for only a few days when Luisa went into labour, which was four weeks premature. Michael rushed her to the Harley Street Clinic; she laboured there almost a day and a half, with Julia and Michael taking turns to sit with her, bathing her face and shoulders, trying to comfort her, she panting and sometimes crying out in pain. In Michael's presence she tried valiantly to stifle the cries, because his sense of guilt and fear was very plain. "I should never . . ."

Luisa smiled weakly. "I shall soon have my heart's desire. I shall have our child."

Finally the doctor said he could no longer postpone a Caesarean section. "She just doesn't have the strength to endure any more of this. The baby seems well—alive, kicking, struggling to be born. In the right position. I don't like a forceps delivery. Might damage the child—and your wife's not up to it. Just one swift cut, and it will be all over."

Luisa had been afraid of an anaesthetic harming the baby, but Michael made the decision for her. The baby, a boy, was born well and healthy, though weighing just less than five pounds. Luisa woke from the anaesthetic, and tears came when she learned she could not hold her baby, or nurse him. A day later she viewed him in the incubator, and held out her arms imploringly towards him. "Not yet, my darling," Michael said. "He must be a little stronger—and you must, also."

There was more anxiety about Luisa than the baby. "Has she ever had rheumatic fever?" the doctor asked. "If so, she never told me. Her heart always sounded healthy enough. But she's been seriously weakened by this struggle—just the struggle to hold on to the baby all these months. Of course she must never try to have another."

But two weeks passed, the baby gained weight, and Luisa came back from the pale and shadowy world she had seemed to inhabit. Remembering the quick recovery of Ginette after the births of their three children, Michael was puzzled and upset. Luisa became strong enough to laugh at his anxieties. "Oh, don't worry, my darling. I come of a strong line. It's just that I am so old. Older than I believe I told you. Old enough to make it a kind of madness to have a first child. But perhaps age and longing has made me . . ." She laughed, for the first time with the sound of real laughter. "Perhaps I am a little mad. But now . . . now I shall have the joy of you and the baby as well."

"If a baby was all you wanted, you should have picked a younger man," Michael said, his tone gruff with emotion.

"I wanted you first," she said. "The baby is an added blessing." Neither of them seemed to care that Julia was present as they spoke.

They stayed two more weeks in London so that Luisa and the baby could be seen by her doctor. Then he ordered her back to Anscombe. "And if you know what's good for you and the baby you won't come back here until things are very changed. Stay where the air is clean, where you have plenty to eat, and there's no chance of air raids."

Occasionally the Luftwaffe did return to the major cities, to shake and send the population back to the hated shelters. But over the south east coast the fighting had virtually stopped, except when the fighter squadrons went up to intercept the enemy. They still heard the planes overhead, but they were no longer troubled by the rain of falling planes in the fields about them.

Tentatively, Michael had suggested to Luisa that they take up the small part of the Gloucestershire mansion not occupied as a convalescent hospital. She firmly refused. "You would never be happy there, and we would probably be very uncomfortable. It is large . . ." She shrugged. ". . . difficult. Anscombe is small and warm, and we have all the things there that our child will grow to love. It is *your* home. It will be his greatest, best inheritance . . ."

She could have said, Julia thought, nothing to please Michael more. The affection he had had for Luisa now turned to a kind of adoration that included the child so unexpectedly brought into his life. "A son . . ." he mused to Julia. "I had always thought it would be a girl. An addition to my family of girls. I hardly see myself as the father of a baby son. What shall I do with him. . . ? By the time he's twenty I'll . . . I'll be an old man."

"He will keep you young. You will never be an old man."

And once he knew that Luisa and the child were well, he went vigorously back to the stage. He went into a new comedy by an author who was well tried and popular. "Just for a change . . ." He played the part of a man many years younger than he, and played it convincingly. Julia marvelled at his youthfulness, his light-hearted attitude on stage and off. "You have renewed him," she said to Luisa. "You and the baby." Michael could now only come to Anscombe on Sundays. In London he attended a gym every day, reshaping himself for the role D.D. had persuaded him it was time he played once more, *Hamlet*. "You now truly understand what madness and death is, my friend. You can make yourself look like the young Hamlet. But you will play him as the veteran actor of—dare I say it, or will you demand twice the money?—an actor who approaches genius."

"You Hungarian liar," was Michael's comment. "You are a flatterer of genius."

Julia waited out the days and months until the birth of the baby early in July with patience and serenity. She liked to be with Luisa and her baby, who had been called John Carlos. "There cannot be two Michael Seymours," Luisa said. "John is a good English name, and my father will be very pleased to be so remembered." Julia eagerly watched the development of the baby, and helped to care for him, glad of the chance to learn how to care for her own.

She hardly seemed to notice when it was announced with some excitement in the press that she had been nominated for a Hollywood Oscar for the best supporting actress. It also came as some surprise to her when fairly sizeable sums of money began to come to her through D.D.'s office. At the time she had been making the film she had been paid the nominal scale, and had expected nothing more. It had been part of learning her trade, and she had been grateful for the experience. She had barely noticed the clause in her contract which gave her a tiny share of the gross, once the initial investment had been earned back. The unexpected success of the film in the States had made the vital difference. *I'm glad to hear you're earning some money while you're sitting still waiting for the baby*, Alex wrote. *But don't forget that Luisa is earning far more, since she put up about half the backing for it*. Julia privately thought Luisa was entitled to every penny of it for backing such a dark horse. She put the money into the bank, thinking of what things it would buy for her child. Luisa scolded her for being so simple. "Let me introduce you to some of my friends who understand money. They will increase it for you, I guarantee. It is only a small amount, but they will do it as a favour for me."

Julia agreed, but would part with only half the money in each cheque. She realized she was naïve about money, but the local bank seemed so safe; she hated to see so much of it disappear into other hands, to be invested in ways she did not understand. Both her father and mother had always spent whatever money they earned; she vaguely remembered that her grandfather, Guy, had by long years of thrift and modest living finally paid off the debts his father had accumulated. Perhaps her mother had inherited something on the deaths of her parents, but as they also had been prodigal spenders, she doubted if it could have been much. Now, for the first time, she realized she was close to someone to whom money meant large amounts, amounts to be worked and manipulated, amounts that turned into ever larger amounts. It awed her slightly, and made her take the advice Luisa proffered. But she said nothing about money in her letters to Jamie. She knew instinctively that it would upset him; he wanted to be the provider for his wife and child. He accepted the fact that she lived at her father's home, and he knew the allowance from his salary as squadron leader would provide anything extra she needed. That part seemed normal to him, just as if she had been at Castle Sinclair. He was, in that respect, she thought, just as old-fashioned as Ken Warren.

March, while it brought encouraging news from all the theatres of war, was also the worst month recorded for the sinking of Allied shipping in the Atlantic. So much of naval support had been diverted to the North African campaign, trying to protect the vital supply lines, that the Atlantic convoys were more and more at the mercy of the vastly increased German U-boat packs. Julia knew that Jamie must be somewhere involved in the Allied thrust to take Tunisia, but he never wrote from which point. Roosevelt's declaration at the Casablanca conference with Churchill that only "unconditional surrender" would be accepted had served to strengthen the German resolve—both in fighting and enduring the increasing bombing of their homeland. This time, unlike the First World War, there would be no armistice.

But March also brought to Julia the nearly unbelievable news that she had won the Academy Award for the Best Supporting Actress. The news came on the first bulletin they listened to while they ate breakfast in the kitchen. Julia's mouth dropped open with a look of such complete surprise that Stella began to laugh. "Didn't you ever think what's bred in the bone won't come out? It's early days yet for you to be winning awards, but remember your father and mother were winning them all their lives. Remember it, my girl. You have a lot to do yet in life to come up to your parents. But still . . ." She rose from her seat and came around the table to plant one of the rare kisses Julia could remember from her on her cheek. "But perhaps I didn't remember to tell you that *I* thought you were very good, too. Of course, my opinion counts far more than any of those people out in Hollywood. Who do they think they are, anyway? Just a lot of film people. You are an actress—"

The door burst open, and Luisa, who was still ordered by her doctor to rest in bed each day until at least ten o'clock, was there, hair flowing, her dressing gown open, the baby, Johnny, a yelling bundle in her arms.

"It is marvellous—*marvellous!*" She flung an arm about Julia, and nearly dropped the baby. Julia rose, and pushed Luisa down into a chair. "You mustn't excite yourself, Luisa."

"Why not to excite myself?" she demanded, momentarily losing her almost total command of English. "It is a moment of great excitement! Stella, perhaps some champagne? With orange juice, of course." The tinned orange juice, as carefully guarded as the champagne in the cellar, came from the States. "Oh, I am so delighted. Michael will be overjoyed. You—his favourite child."

Julia laid her hand on the yelling baby in Luisa's lap. "Not any longer. And I don't mind giving way to this one."

D.D. telephoned almost at once. "I realize, darling, that you didn't seem to think a thing of it when you were nominated. But that you *won*—it will be a big help at the box office."

Dame Audrey Fellowes telephoned. "You thoroughly deserved it, child." Calls came from other actors, and even some she barely remembered from RADA. After the six o'clock news, Connie rang. "I've known about it all day, but I've been on duty, but bursting to talk to you. Ken has just telephoned. He sends his congratulations. I think he was too shy to ring you directly. He says he's beginning to get rather frightened of our family!"

"Frightened?"

"Too much talent—and money around. In a way I'm glad I have him to myself because I feel he doesn't mind that I'm not like the rest of you."

"Oh, Connie! You're the best of us! The brightest, the nicest—the most beautiful."

"Oh, I don't hold a candle to any of you—but I'm so happy this has happened. So proud. I'm so happy Father has Luisa and the baby. There's so much unhappiness in the world, I'm so grateful for the precious bits of happiness we have. If only Alex had Greg back . . . Do you think Jamie knows about it yet? They must listen to news broadcasts wherever he is. It's been on every news broadcast today. Something to cheer people up. Britain can make it—as well as take it, sort of thing. Must go, darling. There's a queue waiting for the phone, and I've run out of change . . . I'll be down to see you all as soon as possible."

Did Jamie know, Julia wondered? He must, in some way. She knew he would be pleased, and yet a little troubled, as this must seem inevitably to draw her a little more into the world of theatre and films, and further from the world they intended to inhabit together. But he would put his doubts aside, as she would. In time, everything would be worked out.

The surprise call of the day came from Lady Jean.

"I am told by Janet that she will immediately hand in her notice if I do not congratulate you at once. Truth to tell, Julia, we *have* been trying at various times during the day, and were never able to get through. The news is all over the estate. It's been on the local Inverness news. Now that is real fame, up here, Julia. Believe me. I never thought I'd care a hoot about who won what in Hollywood, but so close to home, it's different. Sir Niall also sends his congratulations. He's been trying to get through to you, also. As excited about it as a schoolboy. You have won a true friend there, Julia. I hope you will remember that in the future—if you should happen to need him."

"I'll remember it," Julia said, a mood of sombreness suddenly falling on her with the realization that in some way she had managed to touch the imagination and pride of a people so far away, whom she had barely met, but people who would be a great part of her life in the future. It seemed as if she had been partially forgiven for not being Scottish. She went to bed, and was unable to sleep. Someone unknown to her, one of D.D.'s Hollywood friends, had been present to accept the award, in the unlikely event that it came to her. D.D. had believed and hoped for what she had barely thought about. What had it been like, she wondered? A glittering occasion, or quiet, because it was war time? But a humble little British film, made on a shoestring, was, momentarily, famous. She was momentarily famous. It was almost dawn before she slipped into sleep, exhausted by excitement and emotion. In one sense she felt fraudulent; the director, whom she had resented because he had demanded so much, should have had the award, not she.

The renewal of life came, as always, with the spring. Daffodils, planted many years ago and multiplying into thousands, bloomed beneath the swelling buds of the orchard trees; the lambs born in January and February, and now independent of their mothers, gambolled across the spring-green meadows. Julia listened to her mother's recordings, and hoped the baby within her would bear some imprint of Ginette Maslova. Luisa's baby thrived, and so did Luisa. The gauntness of her pregnancy had left her; the bloom that should have been hers then, now came to her. She was kind to Julia, heaping the best of the things that came in the parcels sent from America by her friends, and by Alex, upon her. She herself washed Julia's long hair in luxurious shampoo. One of her friends, whose children had outgrown their nanny, sent that lady, Brenda Turnbull, to help with the care of Johnny, and the baby that soon would be born.

Stella was indignant. "Doesn't she think I'm capable of taking care of children?—I've done it all my life—from the day Miss Alex was born, and before."

Remembering how many years ago that was, Julia was, for the first time, struck with the fact that Stella herself had aged. Why did one not notice this in the people one was always with?

For a few days there was constraint and a sense of resentment around the kitchen table. But gradually Stella relinquished what had been her first job at Anscombe, since Luisa now always referred to her as "our housekeeper". Brenda Turnbull was wise enough to bide her time until Stella's hostility had dampened. With skill and ease she looked after Johnny, and talked eagerly of the time when Julia's baby would be born.

"My father was Scottish," she said. "How Lady Jean must be looking forward to having a grandchild."

She appeared to know the history of that branch of the Sinclair clan well. Again, Julia marvelled at how the rich could still find servants such as Brenda Turnbull at a time when more and more women were directed into factories, if not drafted into the forces. Stella and Cook were beyond being drafted into anything, and their tasks in helping run a farm were "reserved". Somehow Luisa must have got Brenda Turnbull into this favoured position. Michael didn't ask questions about this; he just rejoiced that Luisa could enjoy her hours with their son without being overtired, and there would be someone to help with Julia's baby when it arrived, and would be there if Julia should, when she was ready, take another stage role, or another film. They had a smooth time, Julia thought, for people in the midst of war, and felt some guilt over it. Agnes and the aged chauffeur-butler kept the Belgravia house running for whenever it was needed. It was a little world of privilege that Julia slightly mistrusted, feeling it could not last.

April came—Julia wondered again why T. S. Eliot had called it "the cruellest month". Everything about her bloomed and flowered, and her spirit felt at ease. Calmly she awaited the coming of the baby, reading and rereading Jamie's letters. The first which related to the Academy Award reached her.

I don't know quite what to make of it. Marriage to

a film star was something I hardly bargained for. Will you ever be content with the humble life which is all I can offer you? Was I ever the callow youth who rushed up the aisle and threw roses to you at LEAR? Now I would lay them at your feet, if I could find them in this roseless, war-blasted land. But the rose of our love grows within you, my darling.

Then he quoted from memory from Yeats, something which surprised her. *Had I the heaven's embroidered cloths . . .* And on to the end. *Tread softly, for you tread on my dreams*. She saw from the first word that the censor's hand had hovered over the whole poem, perhaps wondering if it was some kind of code. But he had relented. She savoured it. How much she didn't know yet about Jamie. She remembered how he had talked of his dreams as they picnicked on the bluff overlooking the loch and Castle Sinclair. The prospect of the years of discovery before her seemed only the sweeter. She didn't care if she never stood on a stage again, never made another film. She had a husband and a child, and an abundant future.

How could anything so cruel come out of the perfect peace of a warm April afternoon, when she and Luisa, with Johnny, in the antique cradle in which all three sisters had been rocked, at their feet, sat having afternoon tea on the bench by the budding rose garden? They didn't see whomever it was who brought the telegram. All they knew was Stella's hesitant walk across the grass towards them; she held the envelope behind her back until the last moment. Silently she handed it to Julia.

The Ministry of Defence deeply regrets to inform you that Squadron Leader James Sinclair has been killed in action . . .

His death had occurred on the fiercely fought Mareth Line only weeks before all vestige of Axis resistance in Africa ended. Later, Julia found it impossible to forgive time for what she considered a monumental blunder.

When Julia became aware of external things beside her dry grief, April had handed to them its own fickle punishment. Rain storms swept across the green meadows. Ewes and lambs huddled against the hedgerows for shelter. But the air was sweet and clean, rain-washed, as if no ugliness such as death could breathe its purity. She lay on her bed, her hands placed against the child in her belly, guarding it as if death could strike here also. She hoped Jamie's death had come in one rapid burst of fire. She hoped he had not lived to ride with his stricken craft down to the inevitable end in the barren soil of such a foreign place. He had been a man of mountains and of a green, but harsh land, a man who had known the loch in its calm and savage moods. But his death had come in the desert. The same kind of arid hardness grew in her, as the tears of grief refused to come. She had to endure for the child's sake, because that was all of James Sinclair that survived, she had to endure so that one day the child might know the land of its father.

They were very quiet in the house at Anscombe. After the first few hours they did not attempt words of sympathy, because the words seemed to fall on stony ground. Gestures were made towards her—an extra effort to tempt her with little luxuries at meals. The very best wine was brought from the cellars. She ate and drank because she knew she must. Her father took two nights off from *Hamlet*, in which he had just scored a triumph—two nights which he could not afford, since his understudy was not what the audience had paid to see. What it all lacked, Julia thought, was the ceremony which usually accompanied a death. There was no body to be laid in earth. That, if there had indeed been a body left in the wreck of the plane, had been done hastily, and with scant ceremony, which the war raging about them, and the heat of that alien place demanded.

At last, Julia consented to a memorial service in the church in Anscombe, but a service of her own devising. The vicar, with some puzzlement, agreed. It had enough of the traditional things to rank as a religious service. They sang the twenty-third psalm, Julia choking on the words. The lesson was read—she had asked Harry Whitehand to do this, and his broad Kentish accent seemed to bring them close to the land she loved, and for which Jamie had ultimately died. Then her father went to the pulpit and read the last words Jamie had written to her.

> Had I the heaven's embroidered cloths
> Enwrought with golden and silver light,
> The blue and the dim and the dark cloths
> Of night and light and half light,
> I would spread the cloths under your feet;
> But I, being poor, have only my dreams;
> I spread my dreams under your feet;
> Tread softly, because you tread on my
>   dreams.

After that, on a portable gramophone at the back of the church, was played Ginette Maslova's recording of Chopin's second piano sonata. When it was ended, Julia rose, walking between her father and Luisa. The village congregation was puzzled and disappointed. Where had been the words to commemorate one of the heroes of the Battle of Britain, James Sinclair, DFC and bar? Where had been the rousing, stirring music, the music that made everyone feel that the sacrifice had been worthwhile? This eccentric ending to the service upset some, and convinced others that Julia had hardly cared about her young husband. It was said she had not yet shed a tear over him. She had been the waxen image of beauty as she had walked from the church; the late April sun returning as if to grace this strange event, bathed her face and dark-golden hair with warmth. Her swollen body and palely etched features gave her a Madonna-like look. She carried late Easter lilies in her hands, and wore no hat, but some dark, veil-like thing of lace which did not cover her face. They were not to know it had been borrowed from Luisa, and was a symbol of Spain. She laid the spring flowers on her mother's grave, and set off to walk the mile back to Anscombe.

At Anscombe they served tea and sandwiches and discreet whisky to those who had come a long way, from London and further. A number of the press had followed the walking procession to the house, and some of them had managed to pass themselves off as Alex's or Greg's friends. They wanted to know the reason for, and the origin of the poem Sir Michael had read. Some of them had managed to take it down in shorthand; it would appear in some of the papers the next day. Julia sat on a sofa flanked by her father and Luisa, and would talk to no one.

D.D. and Lord Wolverton were there, Connie had a forty-eight hour pass, and Ken Warren had managed to get away from London to be present. He gravely took Julia's hand, and said nothing, which she thought displayed exquisite taste. Slowly the people left. The late April evening light flooded through the windows where Julia had stood when Jamie's plane had ploughed into the oasthouse.

When they were all gone, and only her father Luisa and Connie were left, Julia said, "Now that is done, I will go to Scotland. Our baby will be born where Jamie was born."

Nothing they said could dissuade her—arguments that the journey was impossible for a woman in her stage of pregnancy in the war-time crowded trains, that she would be better to rest at Anscombe, surrounded by the people who loved her, who had cared for her since childhood. Her baby would be delivered at the cottage hospital when the time came, or, if she preferred, at the Harley Street Clinic where Luisa's baby had been so skilfully delivered they argued. She just shook her head. "It is what Jamie would have liked, though he never did ask it. It is what I want. When our child grows up, I want it to know where it belongs."

"Surely any child of yours belongs as much here, as up there." Her father's jerk of his head indicated what he considered a barbaric land beyond reaching or understanding.

"None of you understand. I have to go to where its home will always be. Jamie's only child. If it is a girl, that branch of the clan will have died with him. If it is a boy, that is where he should grow up. It's better that he comes into the world knowing that."

Her father said, "Then there's nothing I can do but take you up there myself . . ."

"I'll manage. You can't be away from the play that long. I wouldn't permit that."

"Then why, for pity's sake, are you doing it at all? Driving me out of my mind with worry."

"Brenda would be glad to go with Julia," Luisa said, "if that's what she's determined upon. Though I wish . . . Ah, the two babies could grow up here together, like brothers. Why take him away from all this, Julia?"

"Because he belongs up there. He has to know his inheritance."

The matter was solved when she telephoned Lady Jean to tell her of her decision. "You and your child would be welcome here, of course." Nothing in her tone to indicate pleasure, nothing to tell Julia that she was not making a mistake. With Jamie's death, perhaps Lady Jean had thought her life completely finished. She did not speak of the child's inheritance, or the continuation of a name. Her last words were, "I will see what arrangements can be made."

An hour later, Sir Niall telephoned. "I will be privileged," he said, in his old-fashioned manner, "to come to London to escort you to Sinclair. These war-time trains are no place for a pregnant woman without a man to fight for a seat for her." Then he added, "Lady Jean is almost beside herself. She thought all that was Jamie was gone from her forever. Never for a moment did she consider that you would actually wish the child to be born at Sinclair, in Jamie's home, in his country. She made the mistake of thinking of you as a foreigner. If she sounded strange to you, my dear, think no more about it. She is dumbfounded. She has no words to say to you. I know her so well . . . I will telephone when I know my final arrangements. But it will be within days. We cannot have you delivering the future laird of Sinclair in Durham waiting-room."

Sir Niall came and spent one night in Luisa's Belgravia house. Luisa came up to London for the occasion, and was with Michael when they went to the train together very early the next morning. They hoped, with luck, that they might reach Inverness the same day, though Sir Niall was definite in his promise that if they were held up by heavy military traffic on the lines, or even a bombing raid, he would take Julia off the train and find hotel accommodation somewhere. He was wearing an immaculately cut suit of ancient vintage, in tough Harris tweed, and he carried the stick he usually used when he walked the hills and moors. "You see," he said jokingly. "I am ready to defend her, and her seat, from all comers." He looked askance at all the luggage which came with her.

"I couldn't help it. Those are mostly things for the baby. Luisa got so much from American friends—good warm things. Shawls, nappies, blankets. And people had given up coupons to knit things. I couldn't leave them behind—"

He nodded, and he and Michael pushed their way into a first class carriage with the bags, which took up a whole luggage rack. Other people scrambled on after them. But Sir Niall had triumphantly secured a window seat for Julia. She kissed her father and Luisa goodbye, and asked them not to wait. Trains were so often late in leaving.

Julia saw her father's eyes bright with threatened tears. "It's not too late. You don't have to go . . ."

"I have to go."

It was a long day in the train, with people crowding the corridors, and waiting in line for the toilets. Very occasionally it was possible to buy food at the stations, but Luisa had packed a bag with food which could have lasted them two days. She had provided several thermoses of tea, which Sir Niall tried to get refilled at every station buffet, and four half-bottles of wine. Sir Niall offered sandwiches and biscuits around the compartment, but most people, seeing the obviously pregnant woman who might have needed them, refused. Some were offended by the sight of so much food, and disdained to touch any of it. Sir Niall had no difficulty in disposing of it to the rows of service men, with their kit bags, who stood in the corridors. Then someone recognized Julia, linked her with the face in the papers. Many did not know her husband had been killed, and pieces of paper were passed in for autographing. Sir Niall wanted to protest, to ask for her to be left in peace, but she refused that. "It's part of the whole thing," she said. "They stand out there, hour after hour, probably hungry and thirsty, and look in at us eating and drinking. A lot of them have seen *Return at Dawn*. All they ask for is a signature on a scrap of paper. Jamie would be ashamed of me if I didn't give at least that."

He nodded, but then added, "I hope, my dear, that you won't live your whole life by some idealized pattern of what you think Jamie might have wanted. He was a remarkably brave and likeable young man, but in most respects, quite ordinary. You're not going to put him on a pedestal, are you?"

She had no answer.

They changed trains at Edinburgh. The last train to Inverness was getting up steam as they hurried towards it, Sir Niall having commandeered the only porter in sight by the sheer act of bribery—of holding out a pound note. When the guard, in the dimness of the platform, perceived that it was a pregnant woman trying to keep up with the porter, he held his flag and his whistle until he was sure she was safely on board, and seated. They had no difficulty over seats. Few people were travelling at that hour of the night from Edinburgh into the heart of the Highlands.

It was after one o'clock when they reached Inverness. Sir Niall's hands helped Julia from the train, but she soon, in the darkness, felt Lady Jean's hand under her elbow. With surprise she felt her cheek brushed with the swiftest of kisses.

"Welcome home."

She passed the next two months in an almost dazed state. Her body grew almost unbelievably heavy and clumsy, her ankles were swollen. She attended a specialist in Inverness, and made arrangements for the baby to be born there in hospital. He had refused her urgent request that the baby be born at home.

"This is war time," he said brusquely, as if Julia hadn't known it. "We are very short-staffed. I could not make that journey myself, and we cannot spare a midwife to wait around . . ."

It was the local general practitioner, Dr. MacGregor, from Langwell who saw her regularly.

"You're good and strong—well nourished—a young woman. The right time to be having a baby."

Julia spent almost all her time in the housekeeper's room, where they both sat and ate their meals. Janet kept a fire going there, whether it seemed necessary or not. Each day Julia set off on a walk across the drawbridge, and the arched bridge that led to the land, along the road through the forest to the little cottage where she and Jamie had sealed their love. She would have preferred to be alone, but Lady Jean insisted on accompanying her. "Exercise is all very well—and beneficial. But this is such a pot-holed excuse for a road. If you fell—or—or something else happened, there's only the faintest chance of any casual traffic—only the farm machinery, or Mr. Kerr in the car. I should only be waiting for you, in any case. You have not come this far to miscarry. I cannot have your family say that you have been neglected. Not cared for . . ."

That was about as far as Lady Jean could let herself go in expressing her feelings. She never mentioned Jamie's name, but Julia thought that it was from stoicism, an indulgence she would not permit herself. Julia shared with her the letter she received from Jamie's Commanding Officer, giving a brief description of the action in which he had lost his life.

> He took protective action to shield a brother officer whose plane was already under attack from two enemy fighters, at very great risk to himself. He paid for that act of gallantry with his life. His brother officer, although badly wounded, managed to bring his plane down safely, and has survived. To mark this action of extreme bravery, witnessed

> by several other men engaged in the battle, I intended to recommend that he be decorated posthumously. Since he had already been decorated with the DFC and bar, I think the Distinguished Service Order might be considered. May I add, along with my deep sympathy, the certainty that he was not only respected and admired by the whole squadron which he led so outstandingly, but was held in true affection by most of them. He is missed, as the brave and the true always are. Had he survived this campaign, I am certain he would have received promotion to Wing Commander.

Julia saw Lady Jean's lips twist, as if she struggled to control their trembling. Silently she laid the letter on the table, and left the room.

Almost all of the last month Julia spent sitting with her legs, which were becoming alarmingly swollen, propped up on one of the sofas in the housekeeper's room. Janet came frequently from the kitchen to enquire if she would like a cup of tea . . . "A wee bite to eat?" Almost daily parcels arrived from Luisa and Alex—more baby clothes, tins of jam and biscuits. "Do they not understand that we are a farm here, and not short of a thing or two?" But Janet did exclaim over the soap and shampoo and talcum powder and some of the exquisitely lace-trimmed baby garments. *All my sisters are knitting ferociously for this first grandchild of my husband*, Luisa wrote. Julia wondered how these women found the energy or inclination to do so for an unknown woman, when they had all just come through their own tragic, bitter civil war in Spain.

Letters as well as the parcels came from Alex.

I am very busy, and just as well, because I don't have much time to think of anything but the job. If I think about Greg, I grow frightened and guilty and depressed. I've not heard from him for over five months. Does he sense my letters are mostly fakes? He's quite clever enough to be able to divine that, however I labour to make them seem normal. But can I pretend I live here like a nun, when he must guess I don't? It's difficult not to bring Elliot's name into every other sentence, and yet never to mention him would look wrong too. I'm so in love, Julia—I really believe that. And yet so unsure. Elliot keeps pressing me to tell Greg. A divorce would be swift if I wanted to make it so. But it also could kill Greg. I just hope one of his Fleet Street pals, over here on assignment, doesn't take it into his head to write about the gossip that's all over Washington about me and Elliot. Surely no one could be so cruel. I think of you often, my dear little sister, bearing your child and your sorrow, and wish I could help. Part of me thinks you mad for rushing off to your Highland wilderness, and yet I do believe I understand the reasons why you have done it. It is just the romantic, foolish, wonderful gesture you would make. If, some day, I have Elliot's children, I hope I will love them to that degree.

After the first night, Julia, at her own request, slept in the Red Tower Room.

"Would you not be more comfortable in a room—well at least a *smaller* room. Even one of these down here, near the kitchen, and Janet, even though they're really only servant's rooms."

"Ah," Janet interrupted. "Let her have her way. Pregnant women do have strange fancies. I always knew Mrs. Sinclair had strong feelings for the Red Tower Room, as if she had known it for a long time. But I'll just be taking up residence for a while in the wee room beyond—and the bathroom's only a step beyond that. I'll leave a wee bell, so you can ring if you want me during the night."

"Well," Lady Jean said, "as it's summer, I can see your preference for a light, airy room, with the sight of the sky and the loch. And with Janet near you . . ."

It had been Janet who had told her about Lady Ellen, without knowing, with certainty, that Julia had heard or seen anything in that room. The details had been told reluctantly, as if Janet did not wish to believe the story of a haunting spirit. She had not mentioned it again, perhaps afraid that it was no fit subject to discuss with a pregnant woman—the story of a woman abducted for her money and her lands, married against her will, dead in childbirth. Night after night, as the fire died to embers, Julia tossed, trying to find some comfortable position for her grossly uncomfortable body. Once, waking when the song of the birds about the loch told her that it was dawn, she thought she glimpsed that vague shape against the great chimney-piece, carved with the Sinclair arms. This time, there was no sobbing to remember, just that faint, almost unheard sigh. Did it forebode well or ill for her and Jamie's child? She had chosen to come to this room where another woman had suffered, so that her silent, nearly dry weeping would have companionship. Had she deliberately opened herself to another tragedy. Would this truly be the end of this branch of the Sinclair line?

But it was not so. A week before she was due to go into the Inverness hospital she woke to the feeling of wetness. The waters had broken, and she already, too soon, felt the first contraction. She reached and rang the bell. Janet came. "What is it, Mrs. Sinclair? Are you not well?"

"It's come, Janet. The waters have broken. I'd better dress, and you'd better tell Lady Jean we'll need to go now." She indicated the bag, packed and ready. "I've a feeling it won't be long . . ." She had been sitting on the edge of the bed, and then suddenly fell back as another savage pain gripped her. It was the sort of pain she had never experienced before, as if her very insides were straining and tearing, and wanted to come apart. "Oh, God—I didn't think it would be as bad as this."

Janet had drawn back the curtain to let in the growing light of dawn. She came back and peered closely at Julia. "How long since the first pain?"

"Just a few minutes. It came before I rang the bell."

Janet swung her legs back onto the bed, and covered her with the blankets. "I've not much experience in these things, never having had a bairn myself. But I saw all my brothers and sisters born. It seems to me a wee bit soon for the pains to be coming so fast. I'll go and tell Lady Jean. I'll not be more than a minute," she said reassuringly. "You'll not be alone . . ."

Lady Jean came, wrapped in a shabby gown, her hair in a long thick plait falling across her shoulder. "Janet tells me the pains have started." She took

Julia's hand, and stroked the damp hair back from her forehead. Just then another contraction seized Julia. She managed to hold her mouth shut against the cry that wanted to come. Lady Jean looked at the watch on her wrist. "How long between the contractions, would you say?"

Julia shook her head. It seemed that she had barely time to recover from each searing pain, a chance to draw breath, before the next came. In silence Lady Jean waited, her eyes on her watch. The pain came soon again. Julia turned her head away, clamping her lips on the sound that wanted to tear itself from her. "I must ring Dr. MacGregor. I cannot think this is a false labour, even though it's a first child. And it may be safer to keep you here. I'll have a word with him. Janet, you know what to do with the bedclothes. Please make her as comfortable as possible. I'll call Mrs. Kerr. Perhaps she can help . . ."

She left quickly, and Julia, through a haze of pain, felt there was a slight sense of panic. Lady Jean had had only two children, and both of them would have been born here in Castle Sinclair. But she was no more experienced than Janet. Dimly Julia tried to remember what she had read to expect at this time. She sensed it was all happening more swiftly than anyone had anticipated, especially for a first child. She felt she wanted to go to the toilet, but Janet forbade her to move. She brought a bedpan, and with swift, neat movements, managed to move Julia to the other side of the bed while she rolled back the sheet and the underblanket, and inserted fresh ones, moving Julia once again to do it on the other side. She inspected the contents of the bedpan. "There—that will make you feel better." She was moving with great efficiency. "Why, we all did First Aid Classes when war was threatened. And they included childbirth when and where it wasn't expected. I prepared myself for this—if it happened." She rushed to the bathroom, and came back with a jug full of water. "Ah! we must have it hotter. But I'll just wash my hands, and then give you a thorough wash—all over, Mrs. Sinclair. A blanket bath, it's called. That will see you easier before I go and ask Mr. Kerr to start stoking the boiler—but I'm sure Mrs. Kerr has already thought of that." She paused as Lady Jean re-entered the room.

"Dr. MacGregor said to stay where you are until he gets here. It may be false labour, in which case, when the pains ease, we can call the ambulance. But it's a risk now to try to get you to the hospital in a car. Not even he fancies a delivery in those circumstances, though I'm sure he's known worse . . . How are you feeling?"

"Like hell," Julia answered truthfully. "When the pain comes, it's like hell. And when it's over, I think I'm in heaven."

"Yes, my dear. The most wonderful—and terrible—experience of a woman's life. I was sure I was going to die myself. Do not be ashamed. It is better, I think, to scream than to bottle it in. There's no one but ourselves to hear. This old place has heard the cries of many a woman in childbirth—and cries of torture, I'm sure, if the whole truth were known." She checked that the sheets and underblanket were dry. "Janet is so good—clever and quick. As soon as she's back, I'll run and throw on some clothes. And I must wash up, thoroughly. Oh, dear God, why don't we have running water in all the rooms? I would never forgive myself if there was an infection."

"My fault." Julia smiled at her feebly. "I did insist on having this room. I felt—feel—at home here."

"Not your fault, my dear. We'd have had to lodge you permanently in the housekeeper's room to have you near running water. Sometimes I curse this old place—as much as I treasure it."

Julia could hardly believe what she had heard. Janet entered the room with another jug of hot water and a basin. "Mrs. Kerr is in the kitchen, opening up the dampers on the Aga, and Mr. Kerr is at the boiler."

"Stay with her a moment while I get dressed," Lady Jean said. "And I'd better get the car out . . . But surely a first baby cannot be coming as quickly as this. She's not built for it. Those narrow hips . . . Ah, well, we'll see . . ."

She was gone, and Julia felt the pain rip through her, and gave her first cry. "There," Janet said, "'tis better to let it out. But, oh, my dear lady . . . if only men knew . . ."

"If men knew, there'd still be babies," Julia whispered.

"You are right."

Lady Jean was back, and Janet went to the room next door and dressed swiftly. Then she stripped off Julia's nightgown and washed her thoroughly; Julia could smell the disinfectant in the water. Then a clean nightgown. Mrs. Kerr knocked, and put her head in the door, wishing Julia a brief, "Good morning", and then pausing to look at her. "Good luck, Mrs. Sinclair." She had brought yet another jug and basin. "We'll have the water good and hot in no time."

Then surprisingly she added, "You have a fair morning for a birth." She indicated the radiance at the windows, the reflection of the light that came off the loch with the rising sun.

Julia heard the heavy, deliberate tread on the stairs. This was no hurrying woman. Dr. MacGregor paused in the doorway. "Ah, well, I suppose film stars always do things differently. But in the end, Nature is all the same, isn't it, lass?" His tone was gentle, very calm. He removed his jacket, and rolled up his sleeves, going to the basin of clean water and scrubbing his hands. "Aye, it's a bonny morning you've chosen for it. How many times have I tried to get through snow drifts to a woman. Poor wee things. 'Tis not their fault, nor choosing. Now just let me have a look at you, lass, and see how things are going . . ." He felt her pulse, placed a thermometer between her lips, and then firmly, but with practised hands felt her bulging belly, placed a stethoscope to listen to the baby's heart. "Spread for me, a little, my dear. Ah, yes . . ." Another contraction, more powerful than any of the previous ones, racked her. When it was over he put the bedclothes back in position. "I think we'll just hold on here, Mrs. Sinclair. Everything seems normal to me, except the speed with which your young one is coming. I expect he'll be in a hurry all his life. The uterus is beginning to dilate. A journey to Inverness might not be good for you now."

"Then it's a boy?"

He smiled. "Bless you, my dear. It will be some time yet before doctors have that kind of knowledge—if ever. But whoever it is, is in the right position, and should not cause too much trouble. Except that no man ought to say that to a woman in labour. It is a particular pain we men will never experience."

"How long?"

He shook his head. "I cannot say. An hour or two . . . a bit longer. You're in the first stage. I take it you've been having wee preparatory contractions for the past few days?"

"Yes—but it wasn't due for a week, so I didn't want to bother anyone, or to go to hospital before I had to. But this . . ."

"Well, we'll not fuss you. There's some time to go. When we reach the second stage, you'll have to do some work for yourself."

"Well, then, Doctor, I think you could maybe do with a wee bite of breakfast, if there's time," Janet said.

"There's time. But someone must stay with Mrs. Sinclair."

"I will stay," Lady Jean said. "Of course."

In the time that followed, the time that was timeless to Julia, Lady Jean sat in a chair by the bed, reaching to take Julia's hand when there was a contraction. Many times she bathed her face and neck and arms, replaced a pillow which had become drenched with sweat. She administered a few measured sips of water. Dr. MacGregor came back, a large cup of tea in his hand. He finished it, mostly staring out at the loch. Then he scrubbed again, and examined her. "Not quite there yet . . ."

For the first time Julia felt frightened. Why had she spurned the idea of the hospital? She should have gone two days ago. "They would probably have sent you back home again," the doctor answered calmly.

"And you would have had a bone-wrenching journey for nothing."

The second stage of labour was even swifter than he had anticipated. She pushed and relaxed at his command, wanting to push until she had freed herself of a burden which had become almost unbearable to her. Several times she heard her own cries, but it was all mixed in a terrible confusion of fear and pain; did she see the light from the loch reach its noon zenith, or was that all part of the alternating light and dark through which she seemed to pass? "Steady now . . . the head is well through, and I must position the shoulders. Well, then, relax, my dear. No more pushing. Coming nicely . . . coming . . . coming . . . Ah, there now. You have a fine young son, Mrs. Sinclair. And here he is, ready to bawl his lungs out." Swiftly he cleansed the mouth and face of the baby. "Listen to him! His first breath, Mrs. Sinclair. He no longer needs you for oxygen. Well, I'll just attend to the cord. There . . . so." Once again he wiped the baby's face and head, and his mouth. Then a quick wipe over the baby's body with a warm cloth. Janet had a blanket, newly warmed before the fire, ready. The baby was wrapped in it, but Dr. MacGregor moved it down from his head. "Place his ear close to your heart, my dear. He will be missing the warm, dark comfortable place he's been growing in all these months. Let him hear his mother's heart-beat again, so he knows he's in the right place—that the new world isn't all cold and frightening."

Softly she kissed the soft fair fuzz of his small skull, striving to make some sense of the tiny, wizened features. She felt Dr. MacGregor's hand pushing upwards on her abdomen, while he pulled to release the rest of the cord, helping to remove the placenta.

"There—as clean and neat as I've ever seen. No tearing!"

"Oh, he's beautiful. Oh, Jamie . . . Jamie . . . You will never see him." She had cried out, screamed, even swore, she remembered, while the terrible pain had gripped her. Now in the peace that followed she felt the tears begin to slide helplessly down her cheeks.

"You have your son, my dear. So far as I can see, a very healthy son. And you are a healthy, strong young woman. You will go on from here, and make his life, as well as your own."

Afterwards, after she had been washed and had fresh sheets and nightgown, after she had fed her child for the first time and he lay sleeping in her arms, when drowsiness was beginning to overcome her, Lady Jean brought roses to the room. "Just to help get over the smell of the disinfectant." She bent to look at the baby. Her lips twisted in a smile that was half pleasure, half anguish. "Do you know, I just cannot think whom he reminds me of. Must be someone I knew rather well . . ." The sadness left her eyes. "Of course he's the image of Jamie."

Julia wondered how they imagined they could see, in those crumpled features a resemblance to anyone who ever lived. But they both saw with the eyes of longing. All that was left of Jamie lived in the child. That was what they saw.

Julia opened her eyes wide. The light was still bright at the windows. "What time is it?"

"A little after two o'clock. Janet has just given the doctor a good lunch."

"So early still?—it seemed a long time."

"Dr. MacGregor said it was remarkably quick for the first child."

Reluctantly Julia relinquished the baby into Lady Jean's arms, to see him laid in the old-fashioned rocking cradle which had been used by Jamie, and, before him, his brother Callum.

She felt herself sliding towards sleep, the memory of pain already being erased. "You do know, don't you? I was—no, I think he was—determined that he would be born at Sinclair."

6

A FEW days after the child was born—he was already being called Alasdair after Lady Jean's father—Julia was determined there would be only one Jamie in her life, and Lady Jean was equally determined that he would not be called Callum—she walked down to the housekeeper's room. Janet held the baby, and Julia held tightly onto the banister of the suddenly frighteningly steep and long flight of steps. Only Dr. MacGregor encouraged her in this. Lady Jean and Janet would have kept her in the confines of the Red Tower Room, and the longest journey would have been to the awkward bathroom. "Ah, nonsense—all for the better, so long as she doesn't overdo it."

So she sat and nursed Alasdair on the sofa, and complained to Janet that the fire was too hot. "It's almost July. We don't need a fire in here in the middle of the day."

"Ah, well, just to be safe."

Julia read over the messages that had come from the family. Lady Jean had telephoned and cabled the news of the baby's birth. On the first Sunday she was downstairs, Julia talked to her father and Luisa on the telephone. She re-read Connie's excited letter, and Alex's cable. *Delighted you and the baby are both well.* She re-read Jamie's letters. She carried the baby out onto the old seat in the overgrown walled garden. Beyond the high hedge, was the vegetable garden, which the Kerrs tended. There was not enough help available to have the old flower and rose garden ploughed under for vegetables. The Kerrs were barely able to keep the vegetable garden itself in good heart. So Julia sat among the ruin of the formal garden, saw sadly how the weeds and briars had taken over in many places, and how even the rose garden, which Lady Jean desperately attempted to keep in order, was drifting into decay. It had been October of 1941 since she and Jamie had strolled through here, and it was now July, 1943. In the months since Jamie's death she had taken little notice of what was happening to the world outside her own grief. Her only experience was grief, and the determination to carry the baby to full term. May, when she had been careless of any thing but those two facts, had seen the surrender of the Germans and Italians in Tunisia. The Desert War, in which Jamie had died, was over.

Sir Niall came to her there in the old garden, on his first visit since the baby had been born. "Well," he said gruffly, "I suppose all babies look alike, except to their mothers. He seems a bonny little lad to me." The baby waved its tiny fists. "Going to be a fighter, are you?" He turned fully to Julia, and asked, "Do you regret coming up here? It would probably have been a lot more comfortable to have stayed where you were. What do you think you'll do now?"

"Draw breath, for one thing," she almost snapped at him. "Why?—has Lady Jean sent you to tell me I must vacate the place as soon as we can travel?"

"What utter rubbish! She wants no such thing. Now she has her only grandchild, she wants him under her eye. I was thinking about you, my dear. What sort of future do you have—*here.* This is a lonely, rather desolate place—particularly in winter, and most particularly in war time. We have so few young people left here now. I'm sure they told you Lady Macpherson has died. Kirsty joined the WAAF more than a year ago. She's somewhere in Lincolnshire, I believe. Did they tell you her brother, Harry, went down when the *Prince of Wales* was sunk?—before Singapore fell? I have as much as I can do to keep my farm running. I'm desperate for help. The Land Army girls come and go. I'm damned grateful for them, but sometimes they're here just for a harvest, and then the Ministry moves them on. It's the same all over the region. I suppose it's the same in Kent, but you have better weather there—and a longer growing season, so the Ministry sets higher quotas for you. Your father seems very busy. I read he's got another film coming up. Something very patriotic, I don't doubt, and meant to send us out of the cinemas singing *There'll always be an England.* Well, someone has to do it. Everyone does what they do best. That's why I asked you what you're going to do now. You've had your baby. You've quietened some of the grief in Jean's heart—perhaps a little in your own. It was a mad, quixotic, romantic gesture to come here at all. But I don't see your life here. You belong to a different world. I think you'll miss it very much."

"Alasdair's life is here. That makes a difference."

"You can't give your whole life to a child."

"Many women do."

Janet was coming towards them down the weed-choked path, carrying a tray. "I thought a nice cup of tea wouldn't go amiss." The three dogs, Rory, Angus and Duuf were at her heels. They thrust their noses towards Alasdair, already, in these few days having realized that something pink and warm, smelling of talcum powder, lived beneath the shawl and cap. He put out his fist towards them, not yet aware that they were something different from those other beings which peopled his new world. Janet set down the tray on the seat between Julia and Sir Niall.

"No doubt when he's aware that there are animals in the world, he'll be just like his father with them. Jamie always had a wonderful hand with animals." Sir Niall took up one of the hot buttered scones and divided it between the dogs. They ate eagerly, and looked for more.

"Sir Niall!—do you think I do my baking for dogs? I brought this out for you and Mrs. Sinclair. And it's almost time, Mrs. Sinclair, that you came in. It's growing a mite chilly out here, even with the sun. I'll leave the tray for you to bring in, Sir Niall." The dogs stayed, hoping for more, and got it.

"Well, Julia?—what is it going to be? Do you think you'll stay here?"

"When Alasdair is weaned, I'll think about what I'll do."

"By then it will be winter. If you can survive a winter in the Highlands, I suppose you can do anything. But don't waste yourself in the mistaken belief that you must do everything for your child, now you have him."

"I'll just wait a while, and see what happens."

The high walls began to cut off the sun. Sir Niall gathered up the tea things, and they walked slowly back to the castle, going, as usual to the kitchen door. Hens and roosters scattered before them. Lady Jean had just finished putting out their feed.

"Come in, Niall—come in." She relieved him of the tea tray, and put it down on the kitchen table, where Janet was peeling potatoes. "Sit down with me for a few minutes." She went before them into the housekeeper's room. "There was a news bulletin about ten minutes ago. An Allied invasion of Sicily has begun. No details yet. So I suppose we're going into Europe by the back door."

She was pouring small glasses of malt whisky for them all. "Yes, you too, Julia. A little can't hurt. I feel it's something we must toast. Perhaps a real turning point." She shook her head rapidly, as if to blink away tears. "Jamie would have been there . . . Ah, what's the use. He went when he had to."

Julia found herself echoing Alex's words. "How I hate heroes!" And was aware of the look of unutterable shock on the face of Lady Jean. It would be a long time before she would be forgiven those words. In her arms, Alasdair began to whimper. "He's hungry."

Sir Niall tossed back his drink, and left them. Julia fed Alasdair before the fire, aware of the stare of outrage and hostility on Lady Jean's face. While she had been carrying Jamie's child, much, if not everything, had been forgiven her. If she stayed until winter, if she stayed through the winter, it would be a time of unease. Weariness overcame her. She had lived for Jamie, and afterwards, for his child. Suddenly she had no more strength. She was only twenty-two. How would she fill the future, when she could barely contemplate getting through the next hour?

But the days and weeks seemed to fill themselves.

Alasdair took a great deal of her time, the rest she filled by helping Janet in the kitchen. Her strength came back rapidly. Her body began to resume the shape it had once had. "You must do all the exercises the doctor told you about, Mrs. Sinclair," Janet urged her, while at the same time admonishing her to "take things easy, now". They had a cot which was rolled between the housekeeper's room and the kitchen, so the baby was always with them. It was too much trouble to carry him all the way back to the Red Tower Room, and once there, he could not be left alone. So he learned to sleep passively amidst the noise of the pans being washed, the fire being stoked. The dogs, particularly Rory, became his companions and guardians. He regarded them as part of his world. At least twice a day, when the weather permitted it, Julia carried him around the kitchen yard and to the stable yard. He was a regular visitor to Mrs. Kerr's kitchen. Julia held him upright so that he could try to focus on Catriona's head as it emerged from the stable door, looking for a carrot or an apple, or the lumps of sugar which Julia, without guilt, stole from the supply which came from Alex and Luisa. On the calm days she carried him across the bridge to the beginning of the long road which ran through the forest. Lady Jean had produced the ancient, high-wheeled baby carriage which had served Callum and Jamie, but Julia preferred still to carry Alasdair. "That thing gets caught in all the ruts, and anyway, all Alasdair sees is the sky. I want him to see *things*." She answered Janet's question lightly. "In fact I *do* do the exercises—faithfully. But why does it matter to you so much?"

Janet looked at her with mild astonishment. "Why,

surely you'll be making another picture soon? You can't just . . ." She looked around the big old kitchen, flagstoned, with its ancient oak dresser holding dishes, the Aga stove that had seen better days and needed cosseting. "You can't just *stay* here. You're a film star, Mrs. Sinclair. They'll be asking you to make more pictures. A waste if you stayed here . . . although it's home to me, how can it be for one such as you?"

Even Janet's evident friendliness did not mask the fact that she was a stranger in their midst. They didn't expect her to stay, no matter what she said about Alasdair growing up there. "Well, in summer," Janet once said, "we'd hope to see you. Wee Alasdair has to know where he belongs. But you, Mrs. Sinclair, are different." She didn't mean it unkindly. It was simply a fact they all recognized.

In late September Connie had a week's leave, and came to Sinclair. Julia realized the degree of sacrifice in this; Connie could have been available to see Ken Warren each evening, but instead had chosen the long, uncomfortable journey North. "I felt I had to come," Connie said, as Julia drove her from Inverness to Sinclair. "None of us have seen him. Father's only grandchild—a nephew for Alex and me. Naturally you can't get down to Anscombe while he's so young . . . So I came."

She was nervously dismayed by Castle Sinclair. "God, Julia, how can you *live* here. All these stairs and stone passages. It would need an army of servants to make it reasonably comfortable. To heat it . . ." She shook her head.

"We manage . . ."

"*We*. You mean you're one of them now."

"No, but my son is. I have to remember that. He will never know his father. His father's heritage is all he will have to cling onto to give him some identity as he grows up."

"Father and Luisa were rather hoping—"

"Hoping that I'd come to Anscombe to live?" Julia finished for her. "Is this what the visit is for, Connie? They know you too well, darling sister. They know you couldn't tell a lie. Obviously they both mean the message to be that I should come back to Anscombe. As Luisa so kindly put it, Johnny and my baby could grow up together. All very suitable and nice, and a damn sight more comfortable than living here." Together they stood over Alasdair's cradle in the Red Tower Room. She would take him down soon to feed him in the housekeeper's room. "But don't you see, Connie, that that would be their life. Not mine. It's Luisa's house now. I would be a permanent guest, however welcome. It's not a large house. It has no place for another woman and her child. Even if it were bigger, do you think I want my child to grow up always slightly inferior to Luisa's? They might appear to be equals, but they wouldn't be."

"And here he will be king in his own castle, is that it?" Connie retorted, with uncharacteristic acerbity.

"I think he has more chance of being an equal of the children of the farm workers here than he ever would at Anscombe. The future laird of Sinclair he might be, but there's no one in this country who's prepared to doff a cap or bend a knee to anyone whom they don't think deserves it. So . . . what if it is cold in winter? What if he doesn't grow up with all the little luxuries he might have at Anscombe? He will grow up independent. I can't give him anything more than that. He could be in real danger of growing up to be Johnny's whipping boy—or else his manipulator, if Johnny turns out to be the weaker character. I can risk neither."

"But what will *you* do."

"The best I can. Why is everyone so anxious that I make great decisions so soon? There's time. He's so young . . ." She bent over the cradle, and knew her tone conveyed the sense of yearning and loss that was forever with her. "And it's such a little time since Jamie went. I haven't got used to it . . . trying to plan for a future when there seems to be none. Life would be a great deal less complicated if there had been no child. But now I have him, I can't imagine life without him."

Connie touched her shoulder. "Julia, I'm sorry. I've blundered unpardonably. They didn't really send me with any message. It was my idea to come. I wanted so desperately to see you both. Now I've seen him—well, I know you can do nothing else. If he were mine . . ."

"You'll have children of your own."

"Someday, I hope. When the war is over . . ."

"Ken still won't consider marriage until then?"

Connie shook her head. "Never. He has to be totally responsible for his wife and children. Life is too uncertain, he says. He could be killed. I could be killed. Children shouldn't grow up without parents. He's eager—he wants marriage. But this terrible sense of responsibility gets in the way. I'd marry him tomorrow, if only he'd agree."

"Has Ken ever thought he could fall under a bus —even when the war's over?"

"The chances of surviving to old age are greater in

peace than in war. And you'll see—he'll have taken out very prudent insurance policies."

"Connie, how can you stand it? This need to be so careful about everything. How can you and Ken be so *sure?*"

"Because I grew up being so unsure. Father's and Mother's lives didn't make for certainty in anything. I know I'm a hopeless coward, but I need someone like Ken. I need to be sure of a few things in life."

"To live is to take chances."

"I know—I *know!* But I keep telling myself it will work out. I will sink back into domestic tranquillity, and have my children, I will have a loving and devoted husband, who wouldn't know how to be unfaithful if he tried. He will not neglect his children. And do you know something else, Julia?—I really don't care if I never attend another play, or go to another concert in my life. I want to forget the drama and excitement just as much as I want to forget the racked nerves, the screaming matches. I don't want the heights and the depths. I want a long wide smooth valley, which gets a lot of sun."

"Connie—you're so beautiful. You could . . ."

"People keep telling me that until I'm sick of it. I've got the wrong spirit for the body and face I was given. I should look like the dull little mouse I am. I can't help that." She dismissed the matter. "Now can we wake the young laird, and may I carry him downstairs?"

"Just as soon as we've changed him. You'll have to get used to such things."

"Believe me, I am. Luisa lets me do anything with Johnny—under Brenda's eye, of course. Johnny's inclined to be fractious. And of course he's spoiled rotten, even at his age. Luisa can't help it. But when he's with me, he just seems all smiles, bubbling with good humour."

Julia gently lifted up the sleeping child and handed him to her sister. "I hope you'll be godmother to him, and endow him with all the gifts a good fairy should have at her disposal. He couldn't have better than you, Connie."

For the brief days she was there, Connie slipped with perfect ease into life at Castle Sinclair. "What a good-hearted, sweet soul she is," Janet declared. "For all those good looks, she's so unspoiled. If I dare say it, Mrs. Sinclair, your sister has the face of an angel."

"And the nature of one, Janet. You're not the first one to find that out."

Lady Jean warmed to her. Julia detected something close to wistfulness in her mother-in-law. It was almost palpably plain what her thinking was; if Jamie had not married the girl his mother would have most liked, why could he not have chosen this girl, instead of her sister? Julia was amused and interested to see that on her morning round of the fowls and the stable-yard, her daily conference with William Kerr, Lady Jean actively invited Connie's presence. "She's so interested in everything. One thinks of these smart London girls . . ."

"Connie was never exactly a 'smart' London girl. She knows the farm at home pretty well, too. And she's been serving in the WAAF since before war was declared."

"Well, she has a good head on her shoulders." Lady Jean asked William Kerr if he would take Connie on his daily round of the farm. "I think she would be interested. It would be good for some of the people to get to know one of Mrs. Sinclair's family." There was no doubt Lady Jean had picked Connie as the most respectable, least remarkable, except for her looks, of all of Julia's family they were ever likely to meet.

"Oh, I've had so many cups of tea, and scones loaded with butter . . ." Connie complained. "This must be real Highland hospitality. Half the time I couldn't understand more than half of what they were saying. But they were all so welcoming. I always imagined the Highlanders were a stiff lot with people they didn't know."

"I'm very jealous," Julia said. "You've met more of them than I have. And they obviously love you."

"Well . . . don't forget I'm not Mrs. Sinclair. They're not going to live with me forever. But what a heavenly place it is here, Julia. No wonder Jamie loved it so . . . I begin to understand why you want to stay."

"*No!* I don't want to stay. I have to stay for Alasdair. Where else is there? Father's given up the flat in London—and in any case, who would bring a baby to London at this time? The filth and inconveniences and short rations. I can't do that. This is, for the time being, all I have."

Connie smiled gently. "Now that I'm used to it—great gloomy castle and all, I can think of worse places."

Julia returned her smile. "I think you're about the only person who's not hell-bent on getting me out of here to keep up with my so-called career. Even Sir Niall—whom I think is very fond of me. He's coming for dinner tonight. Just him— *en famille*. He doesn't expect a banquet in the dining-hall, like the one Lady Jean put on when I first came. The war has changed too much, even up here. You'll love him . . ."

"I do love him. I met him at your wedding, remember? Well, perhaps you don't. Who remembers much about their wedding day?"

"I thought I had every second of it locked in my mind."

"You do. Everything that matters."

While Connie was at Sinclair a letter came from Alex. Julia read it swiftly, and kept it out of Connie's sight. When the morning chores were done, and the baby had fallen asleep in his cot in the kitchen, under Janet's eye, Julia said, "It's such a beautiful morning. Connie's leaving tomorrow, and we hardly seem to have talked—I'd like a little walk . . ."

"Certainly, Mrs. Sinclair. The young man's fed and asleep. He'll be no trouble. You and Miss Seymour are owed some time to yourselves."

They walked across the drawbridge and the bridge, Rory, Angus and Duuf eagerly following. On the other end, at the entrance to the forest, Connie turned back to look at the castle. "It really is out of a story book, isn't it? All the romantic things one has ever thought that a real castle should have. It really only needs Rapunzel to let down her golden hair."

"And it has a history as bloodthirsty as any in the land," Julia answered. "Sometimes I almost hear the cries at night. But it has served its purpose. It has given shelter and protection to the clan in times of trouble—and there have been plenty of them. There must have been happy people here over the centuries.

It's only the tales of blood and horror that are remembered."

They walked along the road, crowded by the forest on both sides. The first frosts had already touched the leaves of the oaks and beech, and turned them to colours of red and gold and soft brown. With each slight stirring of the wind, leaves softly drifted down, making no sound as they touched the forest floor. "It's as different from Kent as one can imagine," Connie said. She pointed to the ledges and ridges of rock which showed through the trees. "Tough and hard—and beautiful. You're right. Your son will have to grow up knowing his land—his country. It will be good for Johnny to come here sometimes. To learn it's not all sweet and green and pleasant. And there's not always enough hot water to go around."

They had reached the McBain cottage. "I've noticed it as we've driven past and wondered . . ." Connie said. "No one lives here. Yet it's near the castle, and close enough to the main road."

"A lot of people don't fancy living in the middle of a forest. They'd rather have open spaces—a view. I suppose if Mr. Kerr could get as much help as he'd like, it would be occupied. As it is, he had trouble enough keeping the roof in order." Julia walked towards it, and lifted the latch on the door. "They used it as a shelter when they were felling, or dragging out windfalls. The forest isn't as well managed as it should be—but then, what is, at Sinclair? Not enough money—not enough workers."

She went in and felt for the little niche above the brick oven where matches were always kept. The dry kindling laid in the fireplace caught at once, and soon she was able to lay a larger log on the fire. "Jamie and I came here—I'll come back here tomorrow, and see that there's kindling left, and dry wood. It's like a mountain refuge. One always leaves it ready for the next person. But what we could really use is a dram of malt whisky." She dragged over the pile of old rush mats and sat down. The dogs squatted beside them, crowding the hearth. Then Julia took the letter from her coat pocket and handed it to Connie. "I wanted us to be alone when you read it. Sit down . . ."

Connie unfolded the closely written pages, and Julia leaned close to her to read them again.

> This comes to you by favour of someone I know in the military who is flying to London tonight, and will post it to you. There wasn't any point in sending a cable, since the worst was all over so long ago, and I know how you must feel about cables. I will write to Father and the same person will post that letter also. The sad, terrible, to me almost unbelievable fact is that Greg is dead. I heard today from the Red Cross that his name is on a list they have got from the Japanese. Greg died in Changi. They don't say how or why, or even when. I suppose it doesn't matter to them. He could have died of starvation, or beri-beri, or malaria or cholera, or any of the other plagues that infest those hateful places. My poor, sad, cheated Greg. He has been cheated of so many years of life he might have lived, of the things he might have written. I hate to think of him living and dying, being buried in one of their stinking prisons. But, dear little sister, I have to tell you that that is about all I feel, apart from a strange numbness. I had already lost the

Greg that used to be, and I feel almost certain he knew it. The few letters I had, especially in this last year, could have been written to a distant cousin. I tried so hard not to let him know that I had fallen in love with another man. But I'm not very good at lying, particularly in writing. I think most of all he must have missed my talking and planning for the future, as most other wives would have. I wasn't able to carry the deception that far. His death makes my sense of guilt so much worse. I wish I had been able to write the sort of letters which gave him the will to live. Perhaps I took away his future. Men without hope sometimes do lie down and die. But Greg was always such a fighter. I just pray that he didn't show such defiance that he was tortured. That would be the other side of him. When it's all over I know I will have to find the truth—find someone who was close to him there, who will tell me what really happened. It will not ease my guilt, but I have to know. It never occurred to me that I could love a man, and then not love him because he wasn't at my side. Am I really as shallow as that? Or has the world of power and influence which Elliot inhabits seduced me? It's equally bad to think I can be swayed by things like that. Can I say I simply fell in love? Elliot is fourteen years older than I—as Greg was older, and so much more mature. Have I always been seeking a father-figure? As I grew up, our own father seemed barely there. He seemed to flit in and out of our lives. As Mother did. There was always something they were doing that was more important—or so it seemed to me. The most stable figure I knew was Grandfather Guy—as different as any man could be from Igor Maslov. Why am I writing all this? It doesn't ease my heart or my guilt, but simply lays a burden on you—you, dear Julia, who so much loved the husband who died. I suppose Elliot and I will be married soon. No one here in Washington will be surprised. It has become a matter of "when" not "if"—the only "if" being how long Elliot's patience would stand a situation which was not to the liking of either of us. The waiting is perhaps proof of his love. I have to believe that. Life will change very much for me. To be a wife again—instead of a mistress. I want to go on working. Elliot doesn't discourage the thought. I love what I do. I particularly like to think that I, in small ways, help people who are Allies on both sides of the Atlantic understand each other a little better. I may have been a poor wife to Greg—he deserved better, but I have not been a bad journalist. In that, at very least, I have tried to measure up to his standards.

Connie looked at Julia with stricken eyes. "I didn't imagine . . . no one ever said anything. She never hinted in her letters . . ."

"Not to you, Connie. You have such a powerful aura of innocence which I think even Alex hesitated to shatter. But she's written very frankly to me about it. And I think Father suspected. Possibly he even knew for sure. Through Woolfie. It was Woolfie who gave Alex her introduction to Elliot Forster. Anyone who heard the Washington gossip, as Woolfie was bound to, must have known about it. But it wasn't just an affair. He always meant to marry her. Even if he had to wait until the war was over to do it. I don't think this is a slight, or selfish relationship."

"I hope she's happy," Connie said lamely. "I suppose it means she's going to be pretty important in Washington— being married to Elliot Forster. It frightens me a little. There's so much fame and money around. We've experienced fame before, with Mother and Father. But now with Luisa and Elliot Forster there's so much money—and he has all the power that goes with being a newspaper proprietor."

Julia smiled wryly. "I don't think at this stage Alex is likely to be corrupted by money. And as for Father —well, Luisa has liberated him from any pressure of money. For the first time in his life he's able to turn down a part if he doesn't think it's right for him, because he hasn't got to consider the money side of it. And Luisa encourages this. No—I don't think Alex will be corrupted by money." Julia glanced around the tiny room, the small windows which the filtered light of the forest shadowed. "Money isn't always corrupting, Connie. It can be used well."

"I don't suppose I'll ever know. Ken's unlikely ever to be earning a huge salary." She read through the letter again. "I wish I'd known Greg a bit better. But he was a . . . a remote figure to me. Rather frighteningly intelligent. But in such a different way to Ken, whom I know is brilliant, but sort of keeps it to himself. Greg must have thought me very stupid, because I don't remember having much to say when he was around. It can't matter now, though. But what a rotten way to die—what a terrible place to die . . ." Her hand stole over and linked into Julia's, both giving and seeking comfort.

They remained there, saying nothing more, until

the flames had begun to die. Then Julia pulled the rush mats back, away from even a dying spark. The dogs were up and waiting to go. She pulled the door closed behind her, and together, in silence now, they walked through the enchanted forest to the fairy-tale castle.

Julia took Connie to the Inverness station very early the next morning. The light wind had strengthened, and now held the chill of the winter to come. "When will I tell them you'll be . . . be coming down," Connie asked. Julia realized she had nearly said "home".

"I don't know. When the baby's older. When there's some reason to come."

The guard blew his whistle, and Connie scrambled into the carriage. "I wish you weren't so . . . so terribly far away."

Julia realized there were tears in her eyes as she returned the waves of the figure who leaned from the carriage window. She was terribly far away; she had voyaged, for love of Jamie, to a remote and nearly alien land. She didn't know how to live here, nor how to go back to her former world, now that love no longer sustained her.

The baby was christened Alasdair Michael James; Sir Niall was a godfather, and Lady Jean's brother, the Earl, had travelled, rather unwillingly, Julia guessed, from Ayrshire, to stand as another godparent. He and his sister did not seem to be on very good terms. But he was there at the ceremony at the kirk in Langwell, and at the small party given later at Sinclair. He stayed the night, and left very early the next morning.

Connie and Alex were named as godmothers, and Julia insisted that Janet should be a godmother as well. "She helped bring him into the world. She will help shape his values," Julia argued. It was Janet who held him during the ceremony. That caused surprise among the small number who gathered to witness the occasion. The young laird of Sinclair could have had others who were not servants as his godmother. Even Janet had been dismayed at Julia's insistence. "It's not done, Mrs. Sinclair. Lady Jean's only grandchild . . . and I'm but the cook and skivvy here."

"I am his mother," Julia said. "His only parent. I have explained my reasons to Lady Jean. She accepts them."

"Aye—and hard to swallow they'll be," Janet said grimly.

At the small christening party, Sir Niall offered the toast to the now sleeping child. "At his mother's wish, he was born here. He will grow up knowing his people and his country. He will never be a stranger in this land."

Christening presents were offered. A silver clan badge from the Earl; from Sir Niall a silver cup at least two hundred years old, bearing the Henderson clan badge and motto. "My boys and Jamie grew up together," he said. "I look upon him as if he were my own grandchild." There were humble gifts of knitted clothing which came from unexpected sources among the tenants of Sinclair, and touched Julia deeply. And from Luisa and Michael, along with a gift of shares in an American oil company which could only have come from Luisa's portfolio, there was a diamond ring which might have weighed, Julia guessed, about fifteen carats. A note from her father accompanied it.

I know it seems an extraordinary gift to give to a young baby but Luisa has made up her mind, and it's impossible to change in this matter.

From Luisa another note.

Please do not refuse, my dear. It was my first engagement ring—from André. The second engagement ring from Henry I have put aside for whomever Johnny should marry. I can sell neither of them—nor can I ever wear them again. But I would like them to stay in the family.

Julia knew that Luisa proudly wore a much less significant stone given to her by Michael before their marriage. Julia regarded the ring with some awe, and again wondered at the unexpected generosity of this woman she had once not been prepared to trust. *We wish*, Luisa added, *we could be with you for the great occasion, but travel is just too difficult*. It made Julia feel that she had moved to a realm beyond even her father's imagination. Was this the sentiment of the man who had played one of the greatest Macbeths of the modern English stage?

The strangest gift of all came from Elliot Forster.

I'm sure you're not aware of it, but my second name is Calder, my mother's maiden name, so through her, I suppose I may claim descent from the Campbells of Cawdor. Having studied the map of Scotland many times, and visited your region once, I know you are not very far from Cawdor, and very probably the present Thane is among your family's acquaintances. We are honoured that Alex is among the godparents. I will see that she takes her duties seriously. So that young Alasdair may have some interest in distant American connections, I am sending him a small number of shares in Forster Newspapers. In time they may have some value to him—or if I make a botch of steering this group, they may be worthless. So I don't know what kind of fairy I am sending to attend your son's christening. A fairy of good fortune, I hope. Call on me if there is ever anything I can do for you or your son. Alex and I will be married very soon. I wish you could be with us. Alex cares deeply about you, Julia. She describes your Jamie as the "beau ideal" of romantic love, and a hero. She grieves for the man who was lost to her, but she knows he was lost long before he died. It is now my right, my privilege, to take her as my wife.

She read the letter several times, thinking what a strange man it was who had written this. It seemed to bear little stamp of the press baron, the man of influence and power who did not, at times, hesitate to use that power, even when it hurt. She knew his reputation as a tough, and sometimes ruthless boss, who refused to hand over the running of his empire to other men. He controlled each day's events, took responsibility for hard decisions, and did not shirk from the unpleasantness of firing those he thought had not performed as they should. He was both liked and loathed; but he was respected. All of that had little to do with money, and it was not for money or power he would marry Alex.

Quietly Julia showed these two strange christening gifts to Lady Jean. The value of the stock, neither of them knew; Julia was only aware that Forster Newspapers was not a public company, and it was very closely held. There was no way to value it. But the ring caused Lady Jean to tighten her lips. "Ridiculous!—to give this to a child! There is no telling what it is worth, but it could be a great deal."

"Luisa means well. She said she wanted it kept in the family."

"In the family . . ." Lady Jean's tone suggested that she wanted no truck with those of foreign origin who could fling gifts like this at infants, and therefore buy themselves a place within this particular family. She seemed to indicate that gifts of this value were to be mistrusted. The stock, both in the oil company, and in Forster Newspapers, was more acceptable, more understandable.

The ring and the stock were deposited with the bank in Inverness where the family had always done its business, and, for Lady Jean, virtually forgotten. Sir Niall's christening cup was locked up in the almost unused butler's pantry with the rest of the Sinclair silver. The small spark of pleasure and excitement the christening had lighted died away. A feeling near to panic possessed Julia, the same as had engulfed her when she had waved good-bye to Connie. Why had she come here in the first place?—and what would she do now?

The winter had already closed in, when news of Alex's marriage reached her. It came in a telephone call from her father. "Alex was married today. She asked me to telephone you. She thinks you must be rather sensitive to cables."

"May she be happy," Julia breathed. "You've

known for some time about Elliot Forster, haven't you?"

"Yes, Pet. These things do get about. I can only wish her happiness. She's going to have a full life, keeping up with her writing and broadcasting, as well as being a wife and hostess. She's going to have a pretty rough row to hoe. There's a certain stigma attached to the fact of becoming someone's mistress when one's husband is in a prison camp. And then, she's made such a success of her job. The knives will be out the moment she makes any slips—and Washington is a very gossipy town. She *is* a foreigner . . ."

"So long as Elliot loves her, making slips won't matter. She knows the ropes pretty well now."

"She still will be seen as a woman who took another woman's husband—and deserted her own. Pretty hard stuff to live down. Unfortunate that it happened this way. People will tend to think that she was out for money and position. We know differently, but who else?"

"I wouldn't worry." She was remembering Elliot Forster's letter. There was a strength of devotion in it which would ride over any difficulties. He was not a man to admit they even existed.

For a few minutes over the crackling line she talked with Luisa. They exchanged notes about each baby's progress. "I wish you would . . ." Luisa bit off the rest of what she might have said, the renewal of the invitation to come to Anscombe to live. She satisfied herself by saying, instead, "Don't forget, when you want to come to London, the house is always available. Michael is longing to see his grandson. What is the weather doing that far north?"

"Snowing," Julia answered briefly.

That was the fact of their lives now. Snow had engulfed them early, and there had been no thaw. The harvest was long ago taken, and the cattle stored in byres. The sheep foraged on the hills for as long as they could. They had been brought down to lower pastures, and ate what was left over by the cattle, or the hay spread for them. "I feel sorry for the poor beasts—having to bear their lambs each year in snow and cold," Janet said.

"They are bred for it," Lady Jean said, "and nature sees that they don't lamb until spring is well on its way. Better pity the men who have to drag them out of the drifts."

William Kerr had ploughed through the forest to the main road by tractor. Every day, Rachel and Colin Kerr walked the two miles to the road to meet the bus, and each time there was a fresh fall of snow, Kerr determinedly ploughed the road again, making it possible, but difficult, to get a car through. Not that many journeys were made. A careful shopping list was made for Inverness once a month; beyond that, they hardly ventured out. No one came to call. Life seemed to stand still for the long months of short days, and bitterly cold nights. Julia marvelled that the postman struggled through each day, unless the weather made it impossible. Those were the days that even the Kerr children stayed at home. "It's dangerous," Lady Jean said. "When a little snow becomes a blizzard, they could so easily wander off the road, get too cold. Every mother in the Highlands learns to be a teacher of sorts. Mrs. Kerr is very good. They keep up with their books. They have their tasks and their hobbies. The girl is already very good at needlework, and the boy has taken to woodcarving.

We learn to have our own resources . . ." Julia felt rebuked because she had none beyond reading. Slowly, by observing, she was learning some of Janet's skills of cooking, and she admitted that she enjoyed the warmth of the big Aga stove, as difficult and temperamental as it was. "We will just hope," Janet said, "that it holds out until after the war. There's not a chance of a new one, and I doubt even a second-hand one now. Even if there was the money . . ."

For the sake of warmth and economy, Julia and Lady Jean had moved down to the little cluster of what had once been servant rooms off the passage to the kitchen. They all shared the bathroom with Janet. Despite advertising they had never been able to replace Morag, who had gone to a munitions factory on Clydeside. "Ah," Janet sighed, "who would want to come here, when there's work elsewhere—or the forces to join?" The three of them fought a losing battle to keep the large rooms in an acceptable state. It was easier to forget that the dust gathered in the dining-room and Great Hall, that the library smelled of mould, that the upholstery in the drawing-room was damp to the touch.

Julia had become aware of how long Lady Jean stayed closeted in the small office, crammed with old ledgers and piles of papers tied in untidy bundles, which was almost opposite the housekeeper's room, but which had its own entrance from the stable yard. It contained the only telephone, apart from one in the library, which no one used. William Kerr reported to Lady Jean there regularly. Julia was not invited to join those sessions. "Ah, she doesn't want you knowing too much. As if there is much to know,"

Janet sniffed. "The farming barely keeps things going. The Sinclairs lost too much of their good land. Way back at the time of Culloden was the worst—so the history goes. Backed the wrong side, as usual. But then an awful lot of Scots did. But the rest has been going these past hundred years, I'd say. A bit here, a bit there. Bad investment, bad management. Master Jamie's grandfather nearly brought the whole thing to ruin—living the high life in London, as well as his crazy investments. He had a woman or two on the side, so it's said. He didn't seem to notice what provided the money was slipping away. Better send Master Alasdair to some agricultural place than Oxford. We don't need more Latin around here—but a good eye for a bull or a ram. In the meantime, we get on with it—and wait until the war is over for things to pick up. By then, the whole country will be so in debt to pay for the war that Lady Jean will be hard put to it to borrow more." Janet banged the pan on the stove with unnecessary ferocity. "And the best men we had have been taken . . . when they're needed at home. 'Tis a shocking waste. I wonder how we'll ever recover."

So while the drifting snow piled against the castle walls, and sometimes the loch couldn't be seen for the driving snow, Julia had plenty of time to reflect what a marriage to Kirsty Macpherson might have done for the Sinclair fortunes. Doubts grew within her as the cold, bitter weeks of winter slowly dragged past. If Jamie had had to die, how much better that his widow be Kirsty Macpherson of Darnaway, who had the money to raise Sinclair from its depressed state, who, after the war, would have applied it, and her energy and skill to its revival. Once she voiced this thought aloud to Janet.

"Ah, put it out of your mind, Mrs. Sinclair. Kirsty Macpherson is not the piece of perfection Lady Jean seems to think her. A mite flighty, and an eye for the main chance. If they had married, and Master Jamie killed, it's my opinion she would have walked away from the whole thing, and felt she owed it nothing. There's nothing about her to tell me she would have given her heart to Sinclair. That's what it needs—heart, and a wee bit of money would be handy."

Christmas passed, with a modest celebration at which Sir Niall joined them. They entered what Julia realized was the true depth of winter. The only thing which lightened those months for her was the joy of her child, and the slow, gradual, but seemingly inevitable turn in the tide of war. The Allied raids on Germany were making their impact, the Russians were recovering the territory taken from them at the cost of millions of lives, Allied forces were painfully pushing their way up through Italy, and the world was stunned by the bombing and final destruction of the Benedictine monastry of Monte Cassino, which was the key to a vital pass. American pressure was felt at the furthest advance of the Japanese in the Pacific; island by island the Americans continued until hundreds of thousands of Japanese were surrounded and immobilized. Janet and Julia continued to study maps on the kitchen table. "I never thought I'd learn names like these. Why, they're turning them around, aren't they? It didn't seem possible—the way they raced through those islands—how long ago was that? I can't remember . . ." The newspapers always came by the postman, who gratefully drank the hot sweet tea Janet made him, and ate her scones.

"The RAF dropped three thousand bombs on Hamburg last night," he announced cheerfully one day in March. "That should keep the place warm for a bit." Julia envisaged the destruction; what she had seen in London would be little compared to this. Roosevelt's declaration of "unconditional surrender" meant the Germans would fight on, and so must the Allies until that day of surrender came. She looked at her rapidly growing child, and wondered how long before that day came. Jamie had been dead for less than a year. If only he could have stayed at Hawkinge there would have been a chance, a good chance, that he might have survived to the final day.

There were other matters beside grief and loneliness brought about by Jamie's death. One day Lady Jean invited Julia into the little office. A small fire burned in the grate, and she added a little precious coal before she turned and poured tea for them both. "I haven't wanted to trouble you with these matters. You've had enough to bear. But finally the tax people have been in touch. They have been conferring with our accountants in Inverness. They have taken their time, and are willing to be patient—which shows a degree of sensitivity one doesn't associate with tax people. But inevitably they have their way. You might say the mills of the taxman grind exceedingly slow . . ."

"Tax . . ." Julia had barely had to think of it before. She had been aware that her salary had been subject to income tax when she had been performing on stage; there were still discussions going on with D.D.'s accountants and the tax people over precisely how much she owed them of the monies which came in from her share of *Return at Dawn*, but D.D.'s accountants had been very cautious, and had placed in a separate bank account what they considered would be ample to meet any demand. What other tax could threaten her? She watched Lady Jean's face closely as the other woman bent towards the fire, the dancing light of the flames revealing lines more deeply etched than Julia had ever noticed before.

"Well . . ." Lady Jean's shoulders seemed to contract with cold. How much she had lost, Julia thought—her husband, both sons, and still struggling to hold onto this piece of earth that seemed so precious to her.

"You must remember that Jamie remade his will very shortly after you were married. Until then, I was next of kin. Then you became that. So his estate, which was left to him by his father, and which I held in trust until he was twenty-one, became yours. And now, of course, they want death duties. It seems to me we have only just managed to pay the death duties after his father's death. If Jamie had lived to . . ." She reached for her cup, and swallowed tea hastily. "If he had lived to a normal age, he would have had a chance to recoup a little. To gather up some capital again. Jamie was not a foolish or flighty young man. I *know*, given time, he would have made something better of the place. But he wasn't given time . . . And now the taxman is beginning to make his discreet enquiries. How much is the land worth . . . how much a year do we make from farming. Even, dear Lord, how much is the forest worth? Oak is worth money. Never mind that to fell the oaks would destroy a beautiful forest. That would break my heart

. . . There isn't a picture in the house that's worth anything artistically. Just ancestors in their plaids done by very indifferent artists. There was a good one —a Canaletto bought, or won in a gamble, by Jamie's grandfather. But that had to go when my husband died. It would have fetched a great deal more money now. We have so little good land left. We'll be reduced to hill farming . . ."

"The ring . . . Alasdair's ring," Julia said immediately. "The oil shares. The Forster stock . . ."

"We can't sell what belongs to Alasdair." Julia thought it was the first time Lady Jean had ever used "we" to include her.

"If we don't, then anything that's worthwhile for him to inherit here will be lost. You can't support a cottage roof, never mind a castle, on nothing—which is all hill farming brings. Just enough to pay the wages of the men and keep their families. How much do they want—the tax people. . . ?"

Lady Jean's mouth twisted. "Oh, they haven't come to that yet. They have to make an evaluation of the farm, the stock, the condition of the castle, how much it's worth. As if anyone would buy it in these times! Oh, they have plenty of time. They're in no great hurry. We have no great fortune to skip off with."

"Well," Julia said, putting her cup back on the tray. "That decides one thing, at least. If they give you time . . . I can make my contribution. And I don't rule out selling that diamond, nor getting Elliot Forster to redeem his stock. It's not on the stock exchange, so it would be up to him to decide its value." She raised her hand to stop the protest she saw coming. "I have a little money coming from my share of the film. Something I hadn't really thought about. But I have two film scripts which have been sent to me. One D.D. recommends to me, and another from Rank Films. I don't care much for either of them. But they're there. I have work if I accept it. No guarantee of a fortune, but something . . ."

"Work. . . ?" Lady Jean seemed almost puzzled. "The picture people want you to act again?"

"It usually follows, if one has a success. They've left me alone—because of Jamie and Alasdair. But I have that little Oscar for *Return at Dawn*. People will forget it if I don't appear in something soon."

"I see. You would leave here . . . What about my grandson?"

"It wouldn't be immediately. Film people always have difficulty in getting money together. They can line up the cast, even have a good script, but getting the backers takes time and persuasion. Myself, I'd be inclined to go for the Rank film. D.D. is thought of as being a theatrical producer, rather than a film man. The money from Rank would be there sooner, but the script isn't as good."

"So . . ." Again she said, "I see," and there was some bitterness in her tone. "You will leave the baby here? It wouldn't be possible for you to take care of him, and go to . . . go to work every day."

"I think that might be better, if you'd take care of him."

"Take care of him! Of course we will. This is his home."

Alasdair's home, Julia thought, but not really mine. She would never belong wholly in this place.

Before the snows of the Highlands had begun to melt,

Julia was back in London, living in Luisa's house. She had made her decision on the Rank Film because D.D. had not yet managed to put his production together. "Not to worry, darling," he said. "By the time you have finished the little Rank effort, I will have everything in hand, and you can just go from one to another."

Her father's naval film had won acclaim, and was doing well in the States. "Now I want him back on the stage," D.D. said. "That's where his heart is. He refreshes himself by these long, exhausting stage jobs, when he could be earning far more money, and be seen by millions of people, instead of mere thousands. Another producer is tempting him with something. And Luisa . . . she will allow him to accept nothing but the best."

"Good for her," Julia said promptly.

She went down to Anscombe, mostly to see Luisa and Johnny, since her father was often in London, conferring with his agent and D.D. She exclaimed over Johnny's growth. "He will be tall—like Father. And so good-looking." She tried to thrust aside her heartache over the absence of her own child, only a few months younger than this one. He had reached the stage where he was pulling himself up on any piece of furniture within reach, and taking a few wobbling steps before falling on his backside. He usually laughed at this, more pleased with what he had accomplished than frightened by the fall. "He has so much of Michael in him," Luisa said. "He is not solemn—like my family. He laughs so much."

"He looks very much like my father," Julia said, "and as far as I can see, there's quite a resemblance to my father in Alasdair, although I think he will remain fair like Jamie. Though I don't say anything about the resemblance at Sinclair, because they all declare him the spitting image of Jamie."

"It's a pity . . . well, I shouldn't say it again, but I must say it. I wish you would bring Alasdair here, Julia. He could grow up with Johnny, more matched in age than any brothers. What is Johnny—your father's son, and Alasdair your father's grandson. Does that make Johnny Alasdair's uncle?"

They both broke into laughter. "Absurd, isn't it? I think I must leave Alasdair where he is for a while, Luisa. I never thought I could feel so much about her—but I think it would break Lady Jean's heart if I took him away. She's lost so much. And there are so many worries. Sometimes I see her looking at the baby when she thinks no one notices. She doesn't cuddle him the way most grandmothers would. She sits with him in her lap and talks to him—never baby talk. There's such hunger in her, as if she's starved for love, and the chance to give it. But she doesn't show it, except in bits and pieces. She's holding back. It's as if she's afraid to love him too much, in case he's taken away too."

"You said 'other worries'. What worries?"

"Little that money wouldn't solve. We have none, you see . . ." Almost against her will the whole story of the state of the farm, the impending death duties, tumbled out. "Forgive me, Luisa, but I even told her we'd sell your beautiful ring before we sold any more land. That was terrible of me—but I meant it. It seems such a rotten shame that someone who died fighting for his country should have his little estate taxed so heavily. He died too young. If he had been able to *give* it away to his son years before he died, it would have been untaxed. We have lost a generation, Luisa. This poor little estate may never recover."

"You must not sell the ring," Luisa answered. "I will speak to my advisers. We will find a way to help you. You cannot be put in this position. Alasdair must not lose his inheritance. I understand these things—my family was not rich, but we loved our land. We would have done almost anything to keep it, poor as it was. It was a stroke of luck that I and my sisters made good marriages. I do understand . . ."

Julia said tentatively, "I'd borrow on the Forster shares, even the shares you gave Alasdair before I'd let you get into this, Luisa. It isn't fair. It would take so long to repay you."

"I *know* Elliot Forster," Luisa flared. "He would be mortally insulted if you borrowed on those shares without going to him first. Then he would simply buy them back at some highly inflated price. Do you want to begin your relationship with Alex's husband on those terms?"

Julia sighed. "Well, you know far more about money than I suspect I ever will. There's no haste at the moment. As Lady Jean said, 'The mills of the taxman grind exceedingly slow . . .'" She saw the frown of puzzlement on Luisa's brow. "It simply means we have time. They haven't made any demands yet. All in good time. Their time."

She went to work on the Rank film, a script for which she had only slight regard. This time, on the strength of her Academy Award, she had the leading female role. And opposite her, on loan from the US Army and MGM, was William Fredricks, a veteran of many "B" pictures from Hollywood, but someone who would guarantee the film's circulation in the

United States. She was cast as the young wife of a Canadian killed overseas, left struggling to run a small farm on partly cleared land, partly in native woods, on the edge of a lake near the US border. A German-American, detailed by his masters to undertake an espionage mission, was trying to cross the border. The Mounties and the US Immigration Service were already seeking him when he took over the farmhouse at gun-point. It was a claustrophobic film, and meant to be tense, as outsiders came and went, and she was forced to hide the fugitive. It was mostly filmed at Elstree, because costs were low by comparison to the US. But to Julia's disgust, the whole cast was transported north to the west of Scotland to do the outdoor shooting. "Why in God's name didn't someone tell me?" she stormed at the director. "We could have done it on my back doorstep—the lake, snow and all."

Whereas with *Return at Dawn* she had been frightened by the director, and his almost overwhelming presence, with this one she felt impatience. He crowded her and Bill Fredricks, nearly destroying whatever rapport they were trying to achieve. She knew the American had hardened himself against the jokes flying around the set about Errol Flynn winning the war in Burma single-handed. Her leading man was seen in the same light, since he had yet to see any action except on the back-lot of a studio. She hated the director's interference in what was supposed to indicate the growing intimacy between her, a lonely, shaken young woman, and the nervous and increasingly doubtful older man who rated his chances of success in his mission very small once he had managed to cross the border. She was intended to grow to care about him, to worry what would happen to him. Out of increasing despair and loneliness, they became, briefly, lovers. The director had other ideas about how the role was shaped, so that it would seem that she had been taken by force; he almost destroyed what she and Bill Fredricks were able to achieve together. At last the German was shot in the back as he finally made his bid to cross the border. She saw his hands go up in surrender on the long snow-covered space between the farmhouse and the beckoning woods. But the shot which killed him was fired after that moment. They photographed her in close-up at that moment, and the tears on her cheeks were real.

"OK. Wrap it," the director said.

And they did wrap it. At a hotel in Oban, the gateway to the Western Isles, they had the traditional "wrap" party. There was plenty of whisky, and the talk and the laughter was loud, but there was no feeling that they had made a great film, or even a good film. The best of the cameramen, who had always been assigned to take the close-ups of Julia said, "You Scots—you really know how to pour it on." Julia didn't remind him that she had only been briefly married to a Scot. "I hope I'll work with you again," he added, not yet quite drunk. "You've got a wonderful face to photograph."

Bill Fredricks, in one of the quieter moments of the party, gave her a handmade woolly black lamb with a rather absurd bonnet in the Royal Stuart tartan which he had found in one of the few Oban shops with anything to sell. "For your kid," he said. "It was all I could find." Then he produced a standard studio photograph of himself; he had bribed the only carpenter on the set to make a frame for it. It was signed: *To Julia—here's looking at you kid! Bill Fredricks*. She thanked him, and realized that she would cherish both gifts. "I'll be talking about you back in Hollywood," he added. "I'll even be boasting about playing opposite the great Michael Seymour's daughter, and telling everyone she's on her way to following in her Dad's footsteps. Pity that God-awful director got in the way. We could have made a better picture—you and I." He kissed her gently on the lips, and they turned back to join the party.

The next morning she travelled by train with them all to Glasgow; there they were all changing for a train to London, and she, across country to Edinburgh, and on up to Inverness. Many hands waved to her as she stood on the platform watching the train pull out; she waved back with the woolly black lamb. She held it in her lap all the way back to Edinburgh, and even during the wait for the Inverness train. She nursed it during the drive back to Sinclair.

William Kerr had come to meet her in the old station wagon. "My wife sends her regards, Mrs. Sinclair, and hopes everything went well. We've missed having you about the place . . ." She realized he had had to express that emotion in his wife's name. He drove her round to the kitchen yard. "Janet will have something good and hot waiting . . . Goodnight, Mrs. Sinclair."

Janet received her with a beaming face. "I've kept him out here. I knew you'd want to see him the first instant—but he's asleep."

She looked down at the sleeping face of her son, and the tears started in her eyes. She laid the woolly black lamb in the cot beside him. His baby's face had altered slightly since she had seen him. She had missed part of his growing; it would never come back.

She hungrily ate soup and stew, often casting glances at Alasdair's cot. "Ah, he's still there, Mrs. Sinclair," Janet said. "And haven't we all missed you . . ."

Lady Jean did not concur with this sentiment, but she had greeted Julia with a dram of malt whisky, and insisted she take a Drambuie with her coffee. "It will help you sleep. You look exhausted."

Mostly for Janet's benefit, she related stories of what had happened on the set, most particularly the parts they had shot on location near Oban. "I told them they could have done it here—and we could have made some money from it."

As she talked, she kept looking into Lady Jean's face, when the other woman wasn't aware of her gaze. Like her baby's face, something had happened to alter it since she had left. It wore lines of strain she had never seen before; perhaps she had never taken time to notice, she chided herself.

When she had finished eating, since she had no little presents to give them, she brought out Bill Fredericks's photo, knowing it would please Janet. Janet examined it eagerly. "I've always enjoyed his pictures, Mrs. Sinclair. Just imagine . . . you making a picture with him."

In her turn, Lady Jean took the framed photo in her hands, and read the inscription.

"How extremely vulgar," she said.

A laggardly spring had at last come to the Highlands. The lambs born in late March and April were gaining some independence from their mothers, and eating the new green grass. The forest had burst from bud into leaf. Julia slept heavily in the new silence of the world about her. She had lost weight during the filming, and Janet thrust food upon her. She played with Alasdair, and pushed his pram along the rutted road through the forest. They were often at the main road when Rachel and Colin Kerr got off the bus on their return from school in Langwell. For them she saved the wrapped sweets that came in the unceasing flow of parcels from Alex. They chatted easily now to her and Alasdair, having lost their shyness. Julia always gave a secret little nod and smile to the McBain cottage as they passed it. It was all growing into a blessedly familiar routine.

By now she had travelled with William Kerr on his rounds of the farm, so the tenants all knew her. She always carried Alasdair with her on these journeys, and the women were always eager to have a sight of him. In the farmhouses where there were children, and that was most of them, she shared the contents of Alex's sweet boxes. Alasdair now had a full head of fair hair, much the colour of Jamie's, and his vivid blue eyes. "Ah," one of the older women, taking care of her grandchild in a remote farm cottage on the far side of the loch, from which the castle truly looked as if it had sprung from a fairy-tale, "I remember them so well." She examined the baby's features, which now truly were beginning to form a shape which resembled Jamie's. "Your husband was the younger—the fair one. A very bonny boy—a real Gael. Such a handsome young man. But the older—he was dark. Took more after Lady Jean. They tell me Lady Jean's ailing. . . ?"

Julia denied the fact, not wanting to believe it

herself. "Oh no—nothing to be worried about. She's just tired. As most people are these days. The winters at the castle are difficult. No fuel to heat it. Hot water is a luxury, and we only have Janet to help us. Mrs. Kerr has enough to do to mind her own children. But Lady Jean will be better as the summer goes on. And of course now that we can begin to believe there really will be an end to the war . . ."

"Aye, that's the truth. We live on hope. We may have our men back again. But I wonder if Lady Jean has the heart for the struggle any longer."

Julia found the words tantalizingly enigmatic. What did this woman, living so far from the castle, who must only rarely have caught a glimpse of Lady Jean —perhaps at a Sunday attendance at the kirk in Langwell—know what she, Julia, did not? She allowed for the chain of gossip that must radiate about all that went on at the castle, but had she been so blinded by her weariness after filming, by her absorption in her baby, that she had not noticed what she should have?

That evening she took particular notice of Lady Jean's appearance. It was true; she looked more worn and thinner than when Julia had left for filming. She was tired of the burden she carried; the hope she had cherished of Jamie returning to take it from her had been cruelly destroyed. But she had carried on, and continued to do so, taking her share of the household tasks, going over the books with William Kerr as carefully as always, no doubt in growing fear of what the tax people would demand of their meagre possessions, and only grudgingly allowing Julia some knowledge of their financial affairs.

"We manage. We survive. If it weren't for the tax

vultures hovering . . ." They sat together before the fire with a last cup of cocoa. Janet had long ago gone to bed. Alasdair lay sleeping in his cot. "As soon as the snows were gone they were all over the estate, examining buildings, fields, the stock. They went all through the wood, with experts, no doubt, who could estimate how much each oak would be worth to the timber merchant. I'm sure they counted the spring lambs. Naturally, they have been to examine the books—a number of times." She added with bitterness, "All on the taxpayer's money, of course. I suppose we will know their demands in time. They have plenty of time . . ."

She rose to collect the cups to put them on a tray, and Julia thought she saw a spasm of pain cross Lady Jean's face. Or could it merely have been the flickering of the fire playing on the lines of that delicate skin which seemed to grow deeper each week. "Is there . . . are you not well, Lady Jean."

"Well? Well enough. Tired, like all of us. One worries . . . naturally one worries. But we'll find some way around this tax business. They are infinitely patient, these people. But we have to recognize that in the end they get their pound of flesh, no matter what." She gave a slight laugh, which ended in a cough. "What a pity they didn't call them all up. We would have had them off our backs for the duration. But they're all old and grey—I think they were born grey—they with their neat shiny grey suits. If I offer them even a cup of tea when they come, they look at me as if I were trying to bribe them. But they do take it, and Janet's scones. But I make the tea weak, and just scrape the butter on the scones in case they report us to the Ministry of Agriculture for holding back food . . ." She bent over Alasdair's cot, and looked at the sleeping child. "We'll have to fight them as hard as we can, won't we, Baby? We mustn't let them take away all that's yours—your father didn't die for that!"

The day came, early in June when Julia came into the kitchen with Alasdair in her arms. Dawn had long ago reached them in these northern latitudes, and she had listened to the cries of the birds in the forest, and the ones who nested in the craggy battlements of the castle. Janet was there before her, and the radio was on. She turned an excited face to Julia. "They've landed! Our troops have landed. Normandy, I think they said." She was studying the worn, smoke-grimed map which had been tacked to the kitchen wall since war had come. "That looks a longish distance—not the shortest way across the channel, but perhaps the shortest way was where the Germans were expecting them. No real news yet—just that they've landed."

They had been expecting it for some time. The concentration of troops along the southern and eastern shores had turned all that area of England into one huge armed camp. A camp which no one could leave. Weeks ago her father had moved Luisa and Johnny and Brenda Turnbull to London, which was now virtually free of air raids. He was starring in *Arms and the Man*, and he would no longer move readily back and forth to Anscombe.

One letter had reached Julia from Luisa, posted in London.

Poor Harry Whitehand can hardly turn around but there isn't a tank or a lorry full of soldiers in the road. A great many Americans . . . all looking lean and fit, and oh, dear Julia, so young . . . so young. When I think of what they face . . . This is exactly what I am not supposed to write, but everyone knows they are there. Hundreds of thousands of them. The joke goes around that if it were not for the barrage balloons, England would sink beneath the weight of all the men and the weapons. God help them, everything will be needed. Stella and Cook decided to stay . . . I suppose they are safe enough. There's little chance now the Germans could possibly launch retaliation attacks. But they said they weren't going to abandon Anscombe to these young lads running all over the fields, pitching their tents wherever there's room. Truth to tell—I think they want to be part of it all. They take a delight in passing out tea and biscuits. Thank heaven for Alex's parcels, and those my loyal friends still send. We can afford to be generous. Do you hear anything up there of this rumour that the invasion might be through Norway? Surely that would be the hardest way of all. Reports are coming from D.D. that the word is that you have done very well in this William Fredricks's film. A pity it was not with a better actor, but at least he's well known. Please come when you can, and bring Alasdair. We are longing for a sight of him. Connie is so enraptured with him that I am quite jealous that he has stolen her heart from Johnny. She is very—what do you English say—moony?—about the two babies. It amazes me that Ken Warren hasn't long ago married her for fear someone else will snatch her away, and give her the babies she wants. Her fidelity to him is quite touching and quite incredible. They will probably marry the second the war is over—only the good Lord knows when that will be—and they will be one of the few couples who live happily ever after. But it stretches my poor imagination to see Ken Warren as the dashing prince. But he seems to be the rock Connie has found to which she can cling. I wonder if she truly knows how beautiful she is, and what kind of marriage she might have made. Perhaps she does, and is wiser than all of us in choosing the way she wants to set her life. I hear from a friend in Whitehall that Ken Warren is highly regarded in the job he is doing—whatever that is. No doubt he sits there costing out how much the bombs cost, and how much the planes, and how much we will owe when the war is over. But who will care?—so long as the war is finally over. We'll face the bill then. You write nothing, Julia, about how you are facing the tax bill up there. Have the sharks presented it yet? I wish you would come down so we could talk further about this matter. And I don't care if the formidable Lady Jean thinks it is none of my business. All that concerns you is my business. You father is well, and seems happy with his work. How magnificent he is! Surely the world's greatest actor . . . and equally surely the world's fondest and most foolish father to his young son. I swear I see some of your father's gestures in the way Johnny waves his arms when he and his father are having a conversation. I mean, your father speaks words and Johnny makes noises, but to them it is a most marvellous dialogue. I have even heard Michael reciting pieces of Richard III to Johnny, and he answering back. To me, it is all sweet music. Come soon, Julia . . . Love, Luisa.

But through the days of heady delight in the knowledge of the slow advance of the Allied troops through Normandy, and the equal despair in the realization that the slowness of that advance must mean heavy casualties, Julia remained at Sinclair. Each day the women studied the map on the kitchen wall, not quite sure that what the newspapers told them was true, but wanting to believe it. Softly, alone except for Alasdair, in the walled garden, Julia sighed for Jamie. If he had had to die, how much easier it would have been to bear the news at this time when they knew that victory was a matter of time, not of chance. He had died at the moment of the turn of the tide, but had he known that? He should have gone with a song of triumph in his heart. Perhaps he had felt only doubt. *Tread softly, for you tread on my dreams*, he had written to her.

His dreams had been entwined with Sinclair, and now she knew that soon she would be making the major decisions about its future. There was no longer even the faintest chance of denying Lady Jean's illness.

One bright afternoon she had set off much earlier than usual on the road through the forest, determined to make the four miles to Langwell where the children attended school, and Dr. MacGregor practised. She tried her best to stop the dogs following her, but they refused, thinking it was the usual afternoon walk. So they trudged, Julia pushing the baby carriage, and the dogs increasingly heavy-footed, until they reached the village. She had to wait until almost the end of afternoon surgery before Dr. MacGregor could see her. The dogs and the carriage crowded the small waiting-room, but the other patients didn't seem to mind. In their immemorial fashion the women clucked over Alasdair, and the dogs lay quietly, grateful for the rest, at her feet. Everyone seemed to know who she was, and addressed her by name. Finally it was her turn, and as she was called, she started to push the carriage forward, and the three dogs rose to follow her. "Ah, Mrs. Sinclair, you've no need of that crowd in there," one woman said. "I'll keep an eye on the wee bairn, and so long as he's here, the dogs will be content."

Dr. MacGregor removed his glasses and rubbed tired eyes. "I've been wondering when you would come. I know it's not for yourself. You're looking bonny, lass, though I might add, a mite thin—though I suppose that's fashionable for actresses. And there's nothing wrong with the wee lad. . . ?"

"It's Lady Jean."

"Ah, yes . . . well, Lady Jean. Well, she'll not thank me for breaking her confidence. We doctors are not supposed to. But you have seen it for yourself, and I know that stubborn old body does not take kindly to questioning. Even when I sent her to Inverness for a specialist examination, and a week in hospital while you were away on that picture business, she made me promise that you would not be told. Only Janet knew, and she had to make the same promise. The Kerrs thought she had gone to meet the family solicitors in Edinburgh—that she was meeting her brother, the Earl, there. Well, they did a wee exploratory operation—and there was no point in going further. She made visits several times a week into Inverness for radium treatment, but it was only a last desperate chance. No one expected it to have worked. I'm amazed she managed to keep it from you for so long as this. Seeing the tax people in Inverness, she always said—or the accountant. Oh, I expect the Kerrs had their suspicions, but how were they to be sure? She always went alone by bus, took her treatment, which is not easy, and managed to get back to Sinclair by evening. No doubt feeling terribly sick and tired. She would only let Kerr meet her at the bus. Of course, the doctors kept me informed. There was nothing I could do but respect her wish that it should not be widely known."

"Cancer . . ." The word had a dull and hollow sound. It was not a question.

"Aye—and it won't be long before everyone knows, no matter what Lady Jean wishes. It is in the stomach, and the pancreas, and it has spread. Metastasized. She has pain-killers prescribed, but it'll not be long, I'm thinking, before you'll be calling me to the castle for morphine shots. But she's stood up to it better and longer than I expected. Tough body, she is. Comes of a good, strong line. But with cancer . . ." He shrugged. "We doctors have done what we could, but our knowledge is pitifully inadequate. Hit and miss."

"If I persuaded her to go to London. . . ?"

He shook his head. "I managed to get the best cancer man in Edinburgh to look at the results. He even travelled up to see her when she was in Inverness. They don't know anything medically in London that they don't know in Edinburgh. Finest medical school in the world, in my opinion—and many others. Accept it, lass. If she sees it through to the end of

the year, it will be a miracle—though we all kno
cases of remission. But you must understand we'
tried all we know—there's nothing more we can
except try to ease the pain."

Numbly Julia waited outside the school for t
Kerr children, Rachel and Colin, to come rushing o
with all the others. They were surprised to see he
but she invented an errand she had had to do in t
village, and they accepted it unquestiongly, with the
usual politeness. "Are we to walk, then?" Rach
asked.

"No, it's too far for you to walk. I'll just see yo
onto the bus, and take my own time going back wi
the dogs. It's such a lovely evening . . . Tell Jan
I'll not be long."

But when the bus came, the driver, who by no
knew her and the baby carriage and the dogs we
from the many days she had waited where the fore
road joined the main road, insisted she ride wi
them. "Ah, 'tis a long way to be pushing the bairn
He left his seat and between them they lifted the b
carriage into the bus, the three dogs scrambling
behind them. The other occupants made room, ar
no one complained. The remoteness of their situatio
and the war itself had bred a high degree of awarene
that many times they depended on each other. A fe
shy smiles and greetings came to her. Perhaps, s
thought, it pleased them to see that the laird's wif
and someone they thought of as a "film star" wou
share the humble necessities of war. No one we
hungry on the farms of the region, but petrol was
precious commodity. A few hands waved to her
the carriage was unloaded again, and she started, wi

the children and the dogs on the road through the forest.

The castle, in all its ancient, forbidding splendour, was bathed in the warm afternoon light. No wind stirred, and the loch mirrored the furthest of the sheer walls, but not its decrepitude. Just at the edge of the forest they had startled a doe, which had fled, with its light, graceful leaps, and a flick of a white tail. Far above, coming from the mountains, they saw the soaring glide of what might be a peregrine falcon, or even a golden eagle. It was a scene of magical beauty; and within the castle Julia knew that only pain and approaching death awaited.

Through the summer they charted the Allies' slow and bitter progress through occupied France. But in mid-June there appeared a weapon whose existence had only been rumoured or whispered before. It was something Hitler had believed all through the years of the war would be the final subjugation of his enemies, which would, in the end, make Britain sue for peace. The "V" weapon, quickly christened the "buzz-bomb" appeared, and fell on London, and any other place that their launching pad at the Pas de Calais enabled them to reach. There was an unearthly menace in their hellish rattle, and everyone heard it, held their breath while it passed over them and then wondered what happened to those under it when its motor cut out, and it fell. A pilotless weapon, carrying far more power of destruction than any single bomb they had known before. The area along the South-east coast became swiftly known as "Bomb Alley". London was shaken as it had not been, even

at the height of the Blitz. A brief note came fro
Luisa.

> Michael has insisted that Stella and Cook lea
> Anscombe. The houses are being so shattered an
> blasted here, and of course, since one does n
> know until that deadly silence falls, that the bom
> is coming down, there is no use to take shelte
> Over my protest, Michael has arranged that we
> —the women and Johnny, that is—go to a cotta
> in Wales which some friends are lending to u
> How I hate to leave him in London alone, but
> have now Johnny to consider. Michael has ve
> skilfully played on my fear for the safety of t
> baby. Oh, such joy and relief at the news of t
> invasion of Europe at last, and now we must
> banished by this new terror. Will it never end?
> has been so long . . .

Connie wrote,

> The little house Ken's mother and father have be
> sharing with his sister ever since their house
> Hampstead was bombed has been so badly shake
> they have had to move out. They are in "tempora
> accommodation", and I'm sure it's as grim as
> sounds. Plaster-board pre-fabs, at the very bes
> Ken thinks that his father's worry about h
> mother's health has made him slightly derange
> He always did consider that he married abo
> himself, and he feels ashamed that she had
> endure these years of living and sharing a hou
> that belongs to another woman. On Sundays, wh
> it is fine, he takes Ken's mother back to the bom

site in Hampstead, and promises her that very soon she will have a rebuilt house in the place where she was born. However much money his father has been clever enough to make during these years, by sheer hard work, it's difficult to see how he'll ever be able to keep his promise. Even when peace comes, as it must soon, getting materials and labour to build houses is going to be difficult . . .

There could have been, Julia thought, few Sundays that summer when it was fine enough to go for expeditions from South London to Hampstead. It was universally damp and wet, with leaden skies. As the Allies slowly advanced into France, Hitler's determination seemed not to flag. The "V" rockets were mounted on planes and released so that they travelled as far north as Yorkshire, and as far west as Manchester. It seemed an almost unbelievable irony to Julia that the Allied forces could be within striking distance of victory, and yet the British population suffered killing and maiming and homelessness as never before. There was, she sensed, no longer the spirit of "Britain can take it". It had been a long, cruel and infinitely tiring war. Even the courage of the bravest souls wore thin in this last, seemingly interminable wait.

The person whose courage did not seem to falter was Lady Jean. Sensing what Julia knew, she admitted the illness. "Mind—there is to be no talk of it. I will not accept pity." She was more than the "tough body" Dr. MacGregor had described. She possessed, Julia thought, a stoic soul, which would wage its hopeless battle with death, until death could no longer be denied. She had given up attending kirk on Sundays so that the congregation would not see her deteriorating appearance, and so enquire about her health. Daily she seemed more worn, and she grew desperately thin. But she carried on her daily routine, helping Janet in any way she could. Her only concession was that she stayed a little longer in bed in the mornings, but refused Janet's offer of breakfast there. She would take a cup of tea, and nod her head in thanks, and then later appear in the kitchen where she took a piece of toast, ignoring Janet's entreaties to have a little bacon, an egg, perhaps a kipper. She did not go early to bed, and Julia could not bring herself to leave her alone on the sofa before the fire in the housekeeper's room. Alasdair slept peacefully in the cot beside them, and they sometimes talked, or read, or just gazed into the fire, always remaining until the last news bulletins from the BBC had been broadcast.

"I'm glad," Lady Jean once said, "that Alasdair seems to have inherited his father's temperament. Jamie was always a stable, self-controlled child. I don't remember temper-tantrums. I feared he might have taken more of the 'artistic' temperament—from your family. Volatile—highly strung." She seemed suddenly to realize that her words might have given offence. "Oh, of course, I didn't mean that I wished he would not be so highly gifted. But his job in life will be here. For that he must have the temperament of an ox pulling a yoke, capable of the long, slow haul. The one thing that disturbs me, angers me, is that I shall not be here to help him."

Julia bit back the retort she felt like making. A woman bearing pain, and facing a death inevitably soon, with such calmness, was not one to be quarrelled with. She simply gathered up her sleeping child, and prepared to take him to bed. "I'm glad he has inherited the Sinclair temperament too. He will need it."

Julia had that summer made her own personal sacrifice. D.D. had finally put together his package for the film he had planned for her. He had telephoned excitedly from London. Shouting over the crackling line. "Darling, *The Border* has turned out much better than anyone expected. Or else that stupid director suddenly developed genius in the cutting room. It has been taken by all the usual circuits who always take Bill Fredricks's pictures, but it's going to get extra promotion—something he could use, and certainly will help you. Now Worldwide say that they will come in on my production, and will use Rod McCallum to play opposite the part I had marked for you." When she did not immediately reply, he shouted more loudly, "Did you hear, darling? *Rod McCallum!* Of course the script is his usual thing of taking on all the Japs single-handed—I *had* to agree to script changes for that—and winning the war. But he's become a star doing that. Yours is only a small role—the girl left behind. I suppose rather like *Return at Dawn*, but this time the hero has to live. Wounded—heroic—but alive. Rod McCallum can't die, or the war effort might collapse. But, you see, darling, you are the *only* girl in the film—the one whose photo he carries, and talks to, in flashbacks, when he's not leading heroic charges. I don't have to tell you any more—you know the plot. But, naturally, you would have to go to Hollywood. They are talking of location shots in Hawaii. A long journey, darling, but not nearly so dangerous crossing the Atlantic

these days. You might even fly, if we could get yo
onto military transport. And I think, for Worldwide
and Rod McCallum, the US Air Force would b
prepared to do that. After all—he's won a few Pacifi
islands for them. On film. The chance of a lifetime
It will *make* you!"

She had taken the call in the little office, and Lad
Jean had discreetly withdrawn to the kitchen. Sh
could hear the murmur of the two women's voices.

"I can't, D.D. It's wonderful of you to have pu
all this together for me. It's wonderful that they wan
me. But I can't leave here."

"What!" Even on the crackling line, the tone o
sheer incredulity was evident.

"I can't explain now. I'll write to you." Julia wa
aware of the local operator whom, she didn't doubt
would be avidly listening to this conversation. "I *can'*
explain it now, D.D. But you'll understand when yo
get my letter."

"Darling, I have wrung my heart out to get thi
role for you. Not a little British film this time, bu
one with a role opposite one of Hollywood's mos
popular actors. All right—he's not a genius. Who is?
—with the exception of your father. But he is big *box
office*. And you can ride all the way with him. Al
you need is your name coupled with his on the
credits. You are made! Your qualities as an actress
far outweigh his as an actor, but what does tha
matter?—for the moment. You need the audience.
Soon you will be able to pick and choose."

"D.D., stop it! It's breaking my heart, but I can't.
I'll explain it all in my letter." She hung up, to stop
the further explosion she knew was coming.

He tried further persuasion by letter after he had

received hers. She had impressed upon him that he must not again telephone Sinclair.

So, the old harridan is dying. Why must you sacrifice this magnificent chance—which, I must stress, may never come again—for an old, dying woman who has always disliked you, if not hated you? Oh, I do have eyes in my head. I spoke with her briefly at your wedding reception. You were as welcome as her daughter-in-law as a nest of vipers. Not good enough for her son. You, the daughter of Michael Seymour and the divine Maslova! What madness is this? What can you do to help her? She will die, no matter what you do, and you will have thrown away the chance of a lifetime. I am now reliably informed that Rod MacCallum has seen both your pictures, even though *The Border* has not yet been released, and he is personally keen to have you in this role. To have the co-operation of such a star any girl would give her eye teeth. But the option does not remain open forever. You must telephone, or telegraph me by return. Worldwide and Rod McCallum do not wait forever. There are dozens standing in line for this part.

From her father, by the same post came a short letter.

Darling Pet,
What a terrible, or courageous decision to make. I understand your feelings—or at least I try to understand them, and wonder how someone of your age can have such maturity. The actor part of me is amazed that you can turn down this offer—we actors are a selfish lot, as your wonderful mother

learned, I'm sure often with heartbreak. But w
must all live by our decisions, and I love an
respect you even more . . . You face a gruellin
time . . . telephone us, write to us if you need help
Always, your loving Fathe

It isn't just Lady Jean, she wrote to D.D.

As you said, she will die, no matter what I do. Bu
how can I leave her here to die alone? With onl
Janet and the Kerrs, for as much as she will permi
them into her life? How can I bear to go to Holly
wood, and think of her and my baby here withou
me? How can I leave my baby alone after she dies
It is too much responsibility to place on Janet'
shoulders. Shall I go away and not care? Don't yo
think that every strain that crystal-clear girl Ro
MacCallum is supposed to love won't show in m
face, no matter how they light and photograph me

Her father wrote back, having read the letter to D.D

It is just this feeling, which will show in your fac
forever, which will make you, someday, a grea
star.

From D.D. there was only an angry, bewildere
silence.

So she settled down for the long vigil with Lad
Jean and Janet, well aware that many others knev
that Lady Jean was ill, but only in Sir Niall had sh
confided the precise details. Occasionally Lady Jea
would take the bus into Inverness, and request onl
that she be met on her return at the junction wit

the forest road. She guarded her little vial of tablets, supplied by her doctor in Inverness, jealously, still, perhaps believing them to be secret. That July saw the original launching pad of the "V" rockets overrun by Montgomery's troops at Caen, and then in August, Paris was liberated. But still the "V" rockets continued to come from bases in Holland, until in early September the first of the greater menace arrived. The almighty blast and explosion it made on impact in a London suburb was described on the BBC as the explosion of a "gas tank". Soon they came so regularly, four to six a day, that they were known, with bitter humour, as "flying gas mains". It wasn't until November that the Government admitted the existence of what everyone knew, the "V2" rocket, the ultimate weapon which thundered on Britain even while the Allied troops struggled to reach the bases from which they were launched.

The snows arrived in the Highlands before the Allies crossed the German border. Lady Jean held stubbornly to life. Dr. MacGregor had told them that there could be such cases of remission, the reason for which none of the medical profession understood. "Though in my opinion it has much to do with the spirit of the person who struggles."

Once, while they waited for the last BBC bulletins of the day, Lady Jean confessed to Julia, "I couldn't bear to go before I knew that what my son was part of, in this sacrifice, had been accomplished. I only pray that Alasdair will never have to know such a time."

One of Alex's letters referred to the arrival of winter in the Highlands.

Elliot has given me a small present—one of tl
many presents he gives me, but this, I think, ha
most meaning for us both. It is a paperweight l
found while he was browsing in an antique shc
one day. I never imagined he found time for suc
things, but he takes it as a break from his desk
instead of going for lunch. I think it was made i
Germany—possibly Bavaria—about a century ag
It is the smallest image of a baronial castle, standir
with its tall towers, and its drawbridge, and its flag
flying. When I shake it, and the snow flies, I ca
imagine you in your Highland fastness. I share you
vigil. I envy your courage. If only I once had stoc
so fast, I feel that Greg might still be alive.

They celebrated Christmas quietly, with only Sir Nia
as a guest. Toys had arrived from all the family fc
Alasdair, in a bewildering variety, but not unde
standing what the fuss was about, he clung to the tc
he seemed to like best—the little black woolly lam
given by Bill Fredricks. By now its tartan bonnet ha
mostly been chewed off, and it had the look of som
thing well loved and worn. Janet laid a crisp whi
cloth for the dinner, and polished some of the Sincla
silver. "Ah—why not?" she replied, when Jul
protested at the extra work it made for her. "Won
it be the last Christmas the poor woman will kno
on this earth? I've been saving all the ingredients you
sister, Miss Alex, sent, and those from Lad
Seymour. As you know, Mrs. Sinclair, Christmas
not our great celebration here. It's New Year-
Hogmanay we call it—we toast. But it will be a mi
quiet this year, and I doubt Lady Jean will stay u
to see it in."

But she did stay up, listening to clocks chime the hour. There was a mild sense of celebration on the radio stations. Early in December the Home Guard had been stood down. "And about time, too," Sir Niall growled. "Bloody useless we would have been if there had been an invasion—falling over each other's broomsticks. Those of us who had guns would probably have blown each other's heads off in the confusion."

There had been no fresh snow for days, so he had made his way over frozen icy ruts in an increasingly battered vehicle to see in the New Year with them, stopping at the Kerrs' cottage with a bottle of whisky, and what he called "sweeties" for the children. For them he brought whatever Inverness could offer, modest gifts of toiletries, for which he must have expended soap coupons. For Alasdair there was a white lamb, "For when he decides not to be a black sheep." To be shared with them all, particularly as the hour of midnight struck, was a bottle of twenty-five-year-old malt whisky. "Well, we have an interest in the distillery, and I gave up a few shares in order to collar this lot for my cellar. This is a special year dawning, for surely this is the year of victory."

He never referred to Lady Jean's illness, or remarked on her appearance. He never asked how she felt. There was an unspoken agreement between two friends not to speak of an impending event.

The snows were deeply around them in February when they learned that Dresden had been consumed in one enormous fire-storm. The full news of the bombing only drifted through during the next few days. "The price of victory, I suppose," Lady Jean said. "But I wonder if we needed to go to these lengths . . ." And then, with a thickening of he weakening voice she added, "But they would not hav hesitated to do the same to us if it had been possible."

She lived to hear the news of the Allies takin Cologne, to them encircling the Ruhr. She staye later in bed these days, and retired there after lunc for several hours. Her eyes were now far sunken int her face, but she wore an almost ethereal air of on who has looked at the worst, and was not afraid. Juli believed that she was seeing before her own eyes role so magnificently acted that it dwarfed any stag acting she had ever witnessed. Lady Jean wrestle with a devil that was grim and real, and she knev which would win. But she continued the struggle.

In April the snows dwindled into what for th Highlanders were showers. They heard of what th Americans found when they took the camps of Belse and Buchenwald. The Russians occupied Vienna "God help whomever is there," Lady Jea murmured, as she held her grandson on her lap When the news came that Hitler had committe suicide in his bunker in Berlin, she just nodde weakly. "A cowardly end—the only one possible fo him."

She had delayed as long as possible the momen when she was forced to take permanently to her bed and to summon Dr. MacGregor for the stronger drug she now needed. But now she returned to the towe room she had once occupied. "It is only fitting," Janet said. "You cannot really expect her to spenc her last days down here next to the kitchen."

The April days had lengthened to the long norther twilights, and she kept the curtains drawn back fron her western-facing windows for as long as light lastec in the sky. Sir Niall shared their vigil. He came every evening, bringing bottles of his precious old malt whisky, waiting for Dr. MacGregor's second visit of the day, when the injection which might give Lady Jean a few hours of sleep was administered. The gaunt figure sat upright in bed, wearing a faded bed-jacket, and agreeing to take a single dram of whisky which Dr. MacGregor said could only do her good. During the day, when Julia or Janet sat with her, she liked to have Alasdair's crib brought into her room, and she watched him seated on a blanket, playing with his toys, and chattering his unknown language. The last of the "V" bombs had fallen in Kent in March. There was now, over the whole country, a quiet air of expectancy. They almost held their breaths. Early in May came the news that Berlin had been occupied by the Russians.

"A big mistake," Sir Niall observed to Dr. MacGregor, when they shared their nightly dram with Lady Jean. "We should have raced to get there at least at the same time. Stalin is going to demand a king's ransom just to let us get our noses in there. Doesn't look good for the future." They always carried on a normal conversation, as if Lady Jean could participate if she wished. But her strength now would not permit her to sit up, and she whispered only a few words. Alasdair no longer played in her room. "Let her have whatever rest she is able to get," Dr. MacGregor said. Julia was aware that the doses of morphine must have been gradually increased, for Lady Jean seemed to spend most of her days in semi-sleep. In the last weeks Julia had brought, over Lady Jean's protests, a nurse from Inverness. "Can't pay," she said hoarsely. "The taxes . . ."

"The taxes be damned!" Julia had replied. "I have money from *Return at Dawn*, and I'll soon be getting some extra from *The Border*. There's quite enough to pay for what will make you comfortable." She sought for something to comfort the dying woman. "Did I tell you Alasdair has just received quite a handsome dividend cheque from his Forster Newspaper shares, and the American Oil Company . . ."

The other woman's hand gripped hers with surprising strength. "Not to be spent. Even for taxes! His education . . . He must go to his father's school. To Oxford . . . If he is to labour here for the rest of his life, he must understand it's . . ." Julia had to bend close to her to hear the words she struggled to say. ". . . must understand it is worth it."

Daily Sir Niall brought the spring flowers from his garden, and they helped to dispel the smell of illness and impending death in the room. They were placed in many vases and pots, so that wherever Lady Jean could look, she saw them. Julia was strongly reminded of the rose bush dug up and sent to Anscombe, on Jamie's insistence, for Ginette Maslova's garden. She remembered the rose bush from Sir Niall she had carried back from her first visit here. According to her father's letters, they both thrived, and flourished.

Sir Niall and Dr. MacGregor were both in Lady Jean's room on this, Dr. MacGregor's last visit on his rounds for the day, sharing their slowly sipped whisky, when Julia entered to give them the news. The nurse hovered in the doorway, understanding that Lady Jean loved these few minutes when the men talked together as if the dying woman were perfectly able to join in their talk. "It's just come on the news,"

Julia said, "Churchill and Truman have declared that tomorrow is officially Victory in Europe Day. I think I'll just have a dram with you to mark the occasion."

Lady Jean's head stirred, and half turned, painfully, on the pillow. "I think I'll have a sip . . ." The long rays of the western sun mercilessly revealed the ravages of her face. She allowed Julia to raise her momentarily to take a small sip of the fine malt. "So glad . . ." she murmured. "So glad . . ." Instinctively the two men drew close to the bed. "So glad I lived for it . . . lived to know Jamie died for . . . for the ultimate victory." Slowly Julia lowered Lady Jean's head to the pillow again.

". . . another pillow please . . . I want to be able to see . . . to see the last of the light." Propped up, she stared into the spectacular sunset over the loch.

"Well now," Dr. MacGregor said, coming to feel his patient's wrist, then to put a blood pressure cuff around her skeletal arm. "If you'll all leave us, I'll just give Lady Jean her little medication, and hope she will have some sleep tonight. All right, Nurse . . . all right! No need to stay." He was holding up a syringe, and preparing it with liquid. "Lady Jean prefers it comes from me—with no offence meant to your good self. I'll leave a wee vial if she should wake during the night."

She did not wake.

Other titles in the
Charnwood Library Series:

THE ADVENTURERS
by Vivian Stuart

The fifth in 'The Australians' series, opens in 1815 when two of its principal characters take part in the Battle of Waterloo.

THE COLONISTS
by Vivian Stuart

Sixth in 'The Australians' series, this novel opens in 1812 and covers the administration of General Sir Thomas Brisbane and General Ralph Darling.

THE EXPLORERS
by Vivian Stuart

The fourth novel in 'The Australians' series which continues the story of Australia from 1809 to 1813.

FIREFOX DOWN
by Craig Thomas

The stolen Firefox—Russia's most advanced and deadly aircraft is crippled, but Gant is determined not to abandon it.

SEA LEOPARD
by Craig Thomas

HMS 'Proteus', the latest British nuclear submarine, is lured to a sinister rendezvous in the Barents Sea.

THE DREAM TRADERS
by E. V. Thompson

This saga, is set against the background of intrigue, greed and misery surrounding the Chinese opium trade in the late 1830s.

THE RESTLESS SEA
by E. V. Thompson

A tale of love and adventure set against a panorama of Cornwall in the early 1800's.

SINGING SPEARS
by E. V. Thompson

Daniel Retallick, son of Josh and Miriam (from CHASE THE WIND) was growing up to manhood. This novel portrays his prime in Central Africa.

PAY ANY PRICE
by Ted Allbeury

After the Kennedy killings the heat was on—on the Mafia, the KGB, the Cubans, and the FBI. . .

MY SWEET AUDRINA
by Virginia Andrews

She wanted to be loved as much as the first Audrina, the sister who was perfect and beautiful—and dead.

PRIDE AND PREJUDICE
by Jane Austen

Mr. Bennet's five eligible daughters will never inherit their father's money. The family fortunes are destined to pass to a cousin. Should one of the daughters marry him?

CHINESE ALICE
by Pat Barr

The story of Alice Greenwood gives a complete picture of late 19th century China.

UNCUT JADE
by Pat Barr

In this sequel to CHINESE ALICE, Alice Greenwood finds herself widowed and alone in a turbulent China.

THE GRAND BABYLON HOTEL
by Arnold Bennett
A romantic thriller set in an exclusive London Hotel at the turn of the century.

A HERITAGE OF SHADOWS
by Madeleine Brent
This romantic novel, set in the 1890's, follows the fortunes of eighteen-year-old Hannah McLeod.

BARRINGTON'S WOMEN
by Steven Cade
In order to prevent Norway's gold reserves falling into German hands in 1940, Charles Barrington was forced to hide them in Borgas, a remote mountain village.

THE PLAGUE
by Albert Camus
The plague in question afflicted Oran in the 1940's.

THE RIDDLE OF THE SANDS
by Erskine Childers
First published in 1903 this thriller, deals with the discovery of a threatened invasion of England by a Continental power.

WHERE ARE THE CHILDREN?
by Mary Higgins Clark
A novel of suspense set in peaceful Cape Cod.

KING RAT
by James Clavell
Set in Changi, the most notorious Japanese POW camp in Asia.

THE BLACK VELVET GOWN
by Catherine Cookson
There would be times when Riah Millican would regret that her late miner husband had learned to read and then shared his knowledge with his family.

THE WHIP
by Catherine Cookson
Emma Molinero's dying father, a circus performer, sends her to live with an unknown English grandmother on a farm in Victorian Durham and to a life of misery.

SHANNON'S WAY
by A. J. Cronin
Robert Shannon, a devoted scientist had no time for anything outside his laboratory. But Jean Law had other plans for him.

THE JADE ALLIANCE
by Elizabeth Darrell

The story opens in 1905 in St. Petersburg with the Brusilov family swept up in the chaos of revolution.

BERLIN GAME
by Len Deighton

Bernard Samson had been behind a desk in Whitehall for five years when his bosses decided that he was the right man to slip into East Berlin.

HARD TIMES
by Charles Dickens

Conveys with realism the repulsive aspect of a Lancashire manufacturing town during the 1850s.

THE RICE DRAGON
by Emma Drummond

The story of Rupert Torrington and his bride Harriet, against a background of Hong Kong and Canton during the 1850s.

THE GLASS BLOWERS
by Daphne Du Maurier

A novel about the author's forebears, the Bussons, which gives an unusual glimpse of the events that led up to the French Revolution, and of the Revolution itself.

THE DOGS OF WAR
by Frederic Forsyth

The discovery of the existence of a mountain of platinum in a remote African republic causes Sir James Manson to hire an army of trained mercenaries to topple the government of Zangaro.

THE DAYS OF WINTER
by Cynthia Freeman

The story of a family caught between two world wars—a saga of pride and regret, of tears and joy.

REGENESIS
by Alexander Fullerton

It's 1990. The crew of the US submarine ARKANSAS appear to be the only survivors of a nuclear holocaust.

THE TORCHBEARERS
by Alexander Fullerton

1942: Captain Nicholas Everard has to escort a big, slow convoy . . . a sacrificial convoy. . .

DAUGHTER OF THE HOUSE
by Catherine Gaskin

An account of the destroying impact of love which is set among the tidal creeks and scattered cottages of the Essex Marshes.

FAMILY AFFAIRS
by Catherine Gaskin

Born in Ireland in the Great Depression, the illegitimate daughter of a servant, Kelly Anderson's birthright was poverty and shame.

THE SUMMER OF THE SPANISH WOMAN
by Catherine Gaskin

Clonmara—the wild, beautiful Irish estate in County Wicklow is a fitting home for the handsome, reckless Blodmore family.

THE TILSIT INHERITANCE
by Catherine Gaskin

Ginny Tilsit had been raised on an island paradise in the Caribbean. She knew nothing of her family's bitter inheritance half the world away.

THE FINAL DIAGNOSIS
by Arthur Hailey

Set in a busy American hospital, the story of a young pathologist and his efforts to restore the standards of a hospital controlled by an ageing, once brilliant doctor.

IN HIGH PLACES
by Arthur Hailey

The theme of this novel is a projected Act of Union between Canada and the United States in order that both should survive the effect of a possible nuclear war.

RED DRAGON
by Thomas Harris

A ritual murderer is on the loose. Only one man can get inside that twisted mind—forensic expert, Will Graham.

CATCH–22
by Joseph Heller

Anti-war novels are legion; this is a war novel that is anti-death, a comic savage tribute to those who aren't interested in dying.

THE SURVIVOR
by James Herbert

David is the only survivor from an accident whose aftermath leaves a lingering sense of evil and menace in the quiet countryside.

LOST HORIZON
by James Hilton

A small plane carrying four passengers crash-lands in the unexplored Tibetan wilderness.

THE TIME OF THE HUNTER'S MOON
by Victoria Holt

When Cordelia Grant accepts an appointment to a girls' school in Devon, she does not anticipate anyone from her past re-emerging in her new life.

THE FOUNDER OF THE HOUSE
by Naomi Jacob

The first volume of a family saga which begins in Vienna, and introduces Emmanuel Gollantz.

"THAT WILD LIE . . ."
by Naomi Jacob

The second volume in the Gollantz saga begun with THE FOUNDER OF THE HOUSE.

IN A FAR COUNTRY
by Adam Kennedy

Christine Wheatley knows she is going to marry Fred Deets, that is until she meets Roy Lavidge.

AUTUMN ALLEY
by Lena Kennedy

Against the background of London's East End from the turn of the Century to the 1830's a saga of three generations of ordinary, yet extraordinary people.

LADY PENELOPE
by Lena Kennedy

Lady Penelope Devereux, forced to make a marriage of convenience, pours all the affection of her generous nature into her children . . . and her lovers.

LIZZIE
by Lena Kennedy

Tiny, warm-hearted but cruelly scarred for life, Lizzie seems to live only for, and through, her burly, wayward husband Bobby.

ACT OF DARKNESS
by Francis King

What happens inside a family when an act of brutal violence suddenly erupts without warning or explanation?

THE LITTLE DRUMMER GIRL
by John Le Carré

The secret pursuit by Israeli intelligence agents of a lethally dangerous and elusive Palestinian terrorist leader.

THE SHAPIRO DIAMOND
by Michael Legat

Set in the late 19th century, the story of a man struggling against fate to prove himself worthy of his family's name.

THE SILVER FOUNTAIN
by Michael Legat

Jean-Paul Fontaine came to London in 1870 with a burning ambition to be the proprietor of an exclusive restaurant.

THE CRUEL SEA
by Nicholas Monsarrat

A classic record of the heroic struggle to keep the Atlantic sea lanes open against the German U-boat menace.

BETWEEN TWO WORLDS
by Maisie Mosco

Alison Plantaine was born to the theatre. As a child she knew only the backstage world of provincial theatres. Then as a young girl she discovers with the shock of the unexpected, her Jewish heritage.

ANIMAL FARM
by George Orwell

The world famous satire upon dictatorship. The history of a revolution that went wrong.

THE FAMILY OF WOMEN
by Richard Peck

A panoramic story of women whose indomitable spirit brings them through the turbulent, events of the 1850's Gold Rush to the Europe of 1939.

SNAP SHOT
by A.J. Quinnell

On Sunday, 7th June 1981 an Israeli F.16 jet aircraft bombed and destroyed the Iraqi nuclear installation at Tammuz. This is the subject of this thriller.

THE BETSY
by Harold Robbins

Loren Hardeman rose to become the driving force behind Bethlehem Motors. At 91, still dynamic but confined to a wheelchair, he makes a last desperate gamble to head the entire industry.

SPELLBINDER
by Harold Robbins

Takes the reader into the world of the newest and most disturbing phenomenon in contemporary American life—the rise of religious leaders.

THE SEA CAVE
by Alan Scholefield

The naked body of a woman is found washed up on a wild stretch of African coastline. A young immigrant is drawn inexorably into the resulting murder enquiry.

HARRY'S GAME
by Gerald Seymour

The Prime Minister himself was ordering a special agent to be sent into the dangerous world of the I.R.A. gunman. And Harry was the choice.

IN HONOUR BOUND
by Gerald Seymour

A thriller about the forgotten war of the 1980s in Afghanistan.

RED FOX
by Gerald Seymour

Two unconnected events make headlines. A British businessman is kidnapped and Italy's most wanted woman terrorist is captured.

ACCEPTABLE LOSSES
by Irwin Shaw

A strange voice in the dead of night full of menace and loathing shatters the confidence of Roger Damon, a respected literary agent.